D0389407

Also by John Ehrlichman: THE COMPANY

by John Ehrlichman

THE WHOLE TRUTH

SIMON AND SCHUSTER / NEW YORK

Copyright © 1979 by John Ehrlichman

All rights reserved
including the right of reproduction
in whole or in part in any form

Published by Simon and Schuster
A Division of Golf & Western Corporation
Simon & Schuster Building
Rockefeller Center
1230 Avenue of the Americas
New York, New York 10020

Designed by Irving Perkins
Manufactured in the United States of America

2 3 4 5 6 7 8 9 10

Library of Congress Cataloging in Publication Data

Ehrlichman, John.
   The whole truth.

   I. Title.
PZ4.E335Wh   [PS3555.H74]   813'.5'4   79–1377
ISBN 0–671–24358–6

FOR CHRISTY

Part I

THE QUESTION

CHAPTER **1**   It was June twenty-first, the longest day of the year. The formal, crystal-chandeliered East Room of the White House, the scene of countless Presidential receptions, galas and historic moments, was on this day being prepared for a media event. The President of the United States would have his monthly televised press conference here in one hour and twenty-two minutes—precisely at noon Eastern Daylight Time.

President Hugh Frankling was not among those who looked forward to this press conference; he had very reluctantly agreed not to cancel it. The Uruguayan mess had jarred highly cultivated political instincts which told him to take shelter and let the storm blow itself out. It was against his better judgment to expose himself to questions now, but his press secretary and chief of staff had persuasively argued that the Uruguayan problem was really only beginning. It might be with them a long time; if he canceled this regularly scheduled press conference his troubles might only be aggravated in the days to come. He realized he had been foolish to promise he'd have a press conference every month. That campaign rhetoric had won a few complimentary editorials but had immediately become hard to bear after the election. Now he was in a risky situation. The staff always wanted him to preempt prime television time in the evening for these things. Instead he would do it at noon when no one was watching.

The long portraits of Martha and George Washington, the heavy gold drapes and gleaming expanse of white wall between them were being concealed behind a sky-blue cloth backdrop hung on a framework of two-inch water pipe. As usual, President Frankling would be provided with the best television picture the experts could devise. A lighting consultant from New York worked with a crew of union stagehands to erect tall poles of spotlights. Three workmen were moving a heavy rostrum into place at the center of the riser as the White House maintenance crew placed rows of chairs from north to south across the room. The heavy camera platforms were assembled against the west wall; there network crews performed final tests on their cameras.

The White House has only two rooms of any size, so the East Room has become the President's ballroom, assembly hall and theater. On Monday it might be used for some ceremony imbued with traditional pomp and dignity. On Tuesday, it would be prepared for another kind of show, a jazz group or opera singer or cellist performing after a dinner in the State Dining Room. On Wednesday, perhaps a charity party or lunch for the aging, even a press conference. And with each new use would come the technicians, the lighting men, cameras, sound experts—the Presidency had become, in the truest sense, show business. The theater people were increasingly indispensable to a Presidency and its productions.

The National Press Building, some seven or eight blocks east of the White House, is a drab stack of nondescript offices, topped by a shoddy set of clubrooms and a dining room, all venerated by the otherwise tradition-starved journalists of Washington. A few of their number, having seen better clubs elsewhere, occasionally tried to fan interest in a new Press Club, but the annuated and superannuated journalists in the club membership invariably squelched such radicalism in favor of the familiar surroundings.

Morey Masters had just eaten a late breakfast in the nearly empty dining room. He rode the scarred elevator down to his two-room office on the sixth floor to collect his notebook. The glass door of his suite read

SEATTLE HERALD-AMERICAN
WASHINGTON BUREAU
M. L. MASTERS
BUREAU CHIEF

The legend always amused him. He was manager, bureau chief, general-assignment reporter, society columnist, and White House correspondent. That's the way it had been for seventeen years, and it looked as if he would be the *Herald-American*'s one-man bureau until he dropped dead in his tracks; then, when they had to replace him, they'd find out that it was too much for one man. They'd probably hire three to take his place when that time came, and even three wouldn't be able to cover the territory.

He checked his coat pocket for the big plastic White House identification plaque, grabbed a handful of pencils and pulled the door closed behind him.

"We're a little early, Morey." Carl Sandifer was pressing the sixth-floor elevator button, his press pass hanging around his neck on one of those little chains still found occasionally on bathtub plugs.

"I like to have enough time," Masters said as he stuffed the pencils into his jacket. "One time I was late for one of LBJ's and they wouldn't let me in. I caught hell from the office for a month after that."

It was a gray, hot and sticky summer day, typical for Washington but unseasonably early. Usually it didn't get so unpleasant until July. It took them a few minutes to hail a cab. As they rode out F Street toward Treasury, Morey Masters flipped open his notebook, wet a finger and turned to the last page.

"What's this—prepared questions?" Sandifer chuckled. "Since when does Masters come to one of these things with prepared questions? You trying a new method?"

"Yeah, something like that. But I've got about one chance in a million of getting called on, I figure. Frankling only calls on his friends."

"Friends and the wires and networks. Only the people who'll do him some good. But what's different about that? That's what they've all done. Ever notice who Carter called on? Nobody from west of the Mississippi, for damn sure."

But today it mattered. Morey Masters had something with which to really bang the son of a bitch out of the park for a change, if he only could ask his question. He knew the question by heart but, just in case he clutched at the crucial moment, he had it all written out word for word in the back of his pad. He tested his memory as the cab lurched into Pennsylvania Avenue at the front of the Treasury Building.

At the White House, Masters and Sandifer split the fare, checked in at the northwest police gate and walked to the Press Room door in the portico, about halfway between the residence and the West Wing. This space had once housed the White House stables, and later the Roosevelt swimming pool. Nixon had converted it into plush quarters for the press because he wanted them out of the space they occupied closer to him in the West Wing. The inappropriately fancy furniture Nixon had provided was now worn and seedy, the carpet in need of replacement.

A young woman of the White House press staff was posting the seat assignments as Masters walked in. He ran his finger down the list, found his name and jotted his seat number in his book.

"I'm out in Siberia again," he muttered to Sandifer.

"Who the hell do you think you are, Barbara Walters?"

"Just this once I'd like to be down front where he couldn't pass me over. Just this once."

"If you're going to get up and give a speech over there this morning you'd better comb your hair, Masters. You look like an unmade bed."

Next to the Oval Office is a small room used at different times by Presidents as a study, a bedroom, or to dress after a swim in the Ford swimming pool. Hugh Frankling disliked swimming as he disliked all forms of physical effort, and he used the small, quiet room only as a den in which to read and to nap after lunch. The room was ideal for the kind of cramming that a press conference required—so small that there was space only for him, without the constant noise from the hallway and adjoining office that made the Oval Office impractical for serious work. He needed to study alone and in absolute quiet.

The small desk was covered with notebooks. The three black ones were labeled "The Economy," "Domestic," and "National Security." The blue book contained the press secretary's briefing—it told which correspondents were currently working on which special subjects, of any recent troubles at daily press briefings, the identity of particularly hostile press people, and it furnished pages of biographical data on the White House press, complete with their pictures and a chart showing where each would be sitting at the press conference.

Last night he had worked through all four of the books from beginning to end, but now he felt the urgent need to flip the pages one more time. This was a press conference about which he was deeply uncomfortable. He felt as though little of the briefing material was sticking to his memory.

Last evening's run-through had not gone well. After a half hour with the "Domestic" book his brain was virtually numb. He had been working on the "National Security" book all that afternoon, saturating himself in subtleties, memorizing the key phrases. Much of the foreign stuff was easier for him, since he'd been on the Senate Foreign Relations Committee for years. He was no expert on foreign affairs, but he knew the phrases and the danger areas. The domestic subjects were a different matter: they were strange to him and dull. Very dull, but also very tricky. He could be in deep trouble in two seconds if the wrong words were used. The special-interest groups always watched and listened for the phrases that are signals, ready to pounce on any mistake. The pro-abortion people were sent into a frenzy by the words "right to life"; the National Rifle Association would not stand for any gun control talk unless it included the qualifying and limiting phrase "Saturday Night Specials"; farmer organizations wanted exact and particular words used if there was any talk about changes in price parity.

And there were so many dangerous subjects for which his administration simply had no position. On those he was expected to walk the tightrope—with no net—leaving all the options open until something could be worked out.

He opened at random to a page in the "Domestic" book.

```
Subject:   Wheat

           Wheat drought
           Wheat prices
           Sale of wheat to Russians
           Farm politics
           Crop price supports/subsidies

Question:  Mr. President, there is a serious drought
           that will cut next year's wheat harvest by
           40 or 50 percent. What will be done to
           prevent an increase in bread prices? Will
           foreign exports be curtailed?
```

Suggested Answer:
   "We are watching the drought situation very close-ly. I am not sure it will be as bad as you say, but we are not underestimating its potential seriousness. We have two principal concerns:
   (1) That the consumer will be able to buy a loaf of bread at a reasonable price.
   (2) That the wheat farming families receive a helping hand to enable them to stay in business, because the family farm is vital to this nation.
   "As to foreign exports, we have certain export com-

mitments, undertaken by the previous administration and ratified by the Congress.

"As far as I am concerned, the American Consumer and the American Farmer must come first. Therefore I have directed the Secretary of State and the Secretary of Agriculture to examine our foreign commitments and make recommendations for best protecting the interests of our own citizens."

Dangers:

(1) Foreign Policy: You must not say that the U.S. will—or even might—cut our wheat exports. The export agreements are firm. There is no escape hatch on account of U.S. crop failure. The Secretary of State strongly warns against your using any words that might be taken as an abrogation of the Wheat Agreements. He fears retaliation in current negotiations (copyright, minerals, SALT VIII) with the U.S.S.R., and softening of our treaty partners' support at the UN regarding mineral and oil extraction in the pending Deep Oceans Agreement.

(2) Domestic Politics: The wheat farmers are your strong supporters. They want two things: (1) continued wheat exports at the high export price and (2) drought relief for those whose crops have failed.

(3) Budget: The Council of Economic Advisors, the Secretary of the Treasury and the Economic Policy Council warn not to commit to drought relief at this time. If there is a 60 percent wheat crop loss (as Dept. of Agriculture reports predict) the relief subsidy could approach $1.8 billion. There is no budget slack for an outlay of that magnitude. There will be heavy Congressional pressure for such relief. Anti-military Congressmen will propose it be paid for with balancing cuts in the Defense budget. You must guard your options until the Congressional picture clarifies.

Related question: Mr. President, apparently there will be a wheat shortage. How can you justify sending wheat to the U.S.S.R.—a potential enemy—when there is not enough for Americans and their friends?

The briefing book's Probable Questions and Danger Areas and Special Phrases and Suggested Lines swirled and became muddled. He had not had cramming fever for years—certainly not during the Senate years. But now it was back, along with the headaches, and it was a little frightening to him.

He never displayed his fear, of course.

Somehow, whenever he walked up to a podium, he was able to look confident; and he still had a way of sorting out issues pretty well. The spoken words came as easily as ever, and he recalled most of the important stuff in the briefing books. Once in a while he forgot to include the jokes they wrote in for him. And names of people came hard. But so far, knock wood, he could recall most of the main points; he had always avoided the big dangers they had marked out in red for him. And, after all, wasn't that all an incumbent had to do to stay alive? Just avoid the dangers?

An aide tapped lightly on the door, opened it and looked in.

"Yes?"

"Mr. President, it's time to dress. You have thirty-nine minutes to air time."

"OK, I'll shower. Is Valencio here with my suit?"

"Yes, sir. He'll be here when you come out."

The President closed the black notebook with finality and let the young man open the door for him. Across the narrow hall was a bathroom, complete with an elaborate tiled shower. Above the built-in soap dish someone had inlaid the Presidential seal in multicolored ceramic during the Lyndon Johnson era.

As Frankling began to undress, a black-suited Filipino eased into the room and received the President's clothes as he took them off. The valet turned the knob to start the shower as Frankling sat pulling off his stockings, then carried off the clothing as the Presidential ablutions began.

As the deputy press secretary led the straggling crowd of reporters into the East Room, Morey Masters experienced the same quick twinge of excitement he always felt when he came into this room for a press conference. The rows of gilt chairs began to fill up with the familiar Washington press people and also the television "news personalities" who now had begun to come down regularly from New York to occupy the prominent front seats for these events. Behind them the great television cameras and smaller film units were mounted on tripods on the three-tiered platforms, tended by their cameramen and other technicians. One riser was set aside for still photographers who held long-lensed automatic cameras. At the front of the camera platforms crouched the sound men, already twisting dials on their boxes to set voice levels as a man in the center aisle tested the two long-wand microphones held by Army Signal Corps men. There was an excitement and anticipation that was tangible.

"Jesus, look where they have us today," muttered Masters as he sidled into row eleven. "If they'd had a pillar I'm sure I'd have ended up behind it."

With a long, flat clatter, the bright lights in the East Room went on at 11:54 A.M. The steady sound of voices abruptly stilled. The few White House staff members and their guests, standing along the side walls, looked expectantly toward the hall doorway behind the camera platforms. Most of the press sat looking toward the empty rostrum. It would have been bush-league and unprofessional for a Washington journalist to turn around to watch the President enter.

"Ladies and gentlemen, the President of the United States," boomed the loudspeaker. Everyone stood up.

Hugh Frankling, following his press secretary, moved briskly down the center aisle as the reporters manifested feigned disinterest. The press secretary moved off camera to the left. He stood at the edge of the backdrop and faced the crowd. The reporters seated themselves noisily; President Frankling coughed into his fist.

"Good day, ladies and gentlemen," Frankling said quietly. "I have no statement or announcement today, so let's go directly to your questions." He nodded toward a short man in the front row. This was the Associated Press White House correspondent, who would traditionally put the first question and later end the session with "Thank you, Mr. President" when the press secretary gave him a signal to do so.

"Yes, Mr. Tornley?"

"Mr. President," the AP man said, "the government of Uruguay charged today that the unsuccessful coup in that country was only partly financed by multinational business interests, as originally suggested. They now charge that the principal sponsor of the coup was the CIA, and that our intelligence people covertly organized an assassination of their Chief of State and an overthrow of their government. Is there any truth to those claims?"

The President took a quarter-step toward the rostrum and gripped it. "Mr. Tornley, as you know, we are now investigating the Uruguayan charges. I can't yet reply to them without running the risk of being very unfair to various individuals. I need more facts. I am determined to have them very soon—probably within hours. Then I intend to tell . . . to have a press conference or—at least—you will all know; there will be a full statement—possibly a briefing—at that time."

Forty reporters jumped to their feet crying, "Mr. President!"

Frankling pointed to a woman on his right, Sandra Martin of the *St. Louis Post-Dispatch.*

"Mr. President, assuming that the CIA is involved, isn't that involvement a violation of our foreign policy?"

"That question calls for an assumption that I'm not willing to make, Miss—uh—Miss Martin. This country does not interfere in the internal affairs of our Latin-American neighbors—that's our policy. The United States doesn't plot overthrows, assassinate leaders or manipulate elections. That all stopped years ago. I'm not willing to assume that anyone has violated that policy."

The President nodded to a familiar face directly in front of him. "Mr. Carmody?"

Thirty standing reporters slowly sat down.

"Mr. President, if it develops that the CIA really was involved in Uruguay, what will you do?"

"Oh, Mr. Carmody, that's really too speculative for me to try to answer today. I prefer to wait for the facts."

The spindly gold chairs creaked all over the room as three dozen journalists jumped up, shouting, "Mr. President!" Frankling raised his hand and pointed to a fat man in a white suit about ten rows back on his right. He had no idea who the man was.

"Mr. President, how could the CIA be involved in the coup in Uruguay without White House approval? What are your safeguards against something like that happening without your authorization?"

"As I said, we are still attempting to gather all the facts in that matter. You know, uh, Mr. uh, uh—you know that in most cases the CIA Director reports to me, through my National Security Adviser. I don't see everything, of course. Time just does not permit it. That's why I have a staff. But I issued standing orders, when I first took office eighteen months ago, that I wanted to consider the major questions personally. I don't know if that order was violated in this case or not, but I intend to find out."

As the large reporter sat down, his chair emitted a loud splintering noise which was lost in the clamor of the other reporters seeking to be recognized. The President pointed to the Cleveland *Plain Dealer*'s man.

"Mr. Ackeroyd."

"Mr. President, industrial production for the first quarter shows a weakening which was reflected in the stock market this week . . ."

"Shit, he *does* pull to his right," Morey Masters muttered to Rolf Allen. "He's taken all of them from that side, and here we are on his left."

"Come on, Masters, relax. He's not going to call on you. He's working the Ohio home-town press and the big boys, as usual. He looks kind of puffy and pasty today, don't you think?"

"Mr. President!" Masters jumped to his feet, his chin and right arm thrust forward, pencil semaphoring side to side. "Mr. President!" he shouted again, after the others had stopped.

The President looked at him quickly, then pointed to a woman in the front row.

"The son of a bitch," Masters said under his breath. His heart

21

was pounding as he sat down on the frail chair. He had been to a hundred of these shows and ordinarily they didn't excite him. Many times he just watched the others ask questions and took a few notes. But he had a chance today to really nail the man, and it made the old juices stir.

"Mr. President!" he screamed. A man in the third row on the other side of the room got the nod.

There were only about eleven minutes left in the half hour. With a hot issue like Uruguay, Frankling was not likely to let it run overtime; he'd get off as quickly as he could. Now Frankling was up there making some long-winded answer about Veterans Administration Hospitals, for God's sake! Ten minutes.

As the President's voice began to drop, Morey Masters' legs tensed. He moved his small pad from left hand to right and raised his right arm. On the last word of the answer he was on his feet, bellowing, "Mr. President!" The pad moved back and forward over his head. "Mr. President!"

Hugh Frankling's eyes met Morey Masters' for just an instant, but it was long enough. The rumpled little man held him, and in spite of himself the President nodded and pointed. "Mr. President," Morey began. "Another question about Uruguay. . . ."

It's odd how these things work, Frankling thought to himself. *Sort of Russian roulette. I figured that little fellow in the back— what's his name?—would have some parochial, regional question. A safe one; flood control, maybe. But he's got another Uruguay question, goddamn him. I've got to get all that sorted out again. Be careful. I may have gone too far already.* They had put all the dangerous Uruguay stuff right in the front of the briefing book.

Danger: <u>Do not deviate</u> from our announced policy (of February last year): The U.S. repudiates any interference in the internal affairs of any nation of the Americas. The U.S. <u>repudiates</u> <u>covert intelligence</u> operations against established governments in this hemisphere.

Suggested line for answers:
(1) The Uruguayan charges are being investigated. It

is too early to comment on them.
(2) Any coup attempt is <u>deplored.</u>
(3) Any U.S. citizens (if any) who may be involved <u>violated</u> U.S. policy.
(4) <u>We value the friendship of the Uruguayan people.</u>

Morey Masters' voice was cracking with nervousness. "Mr. President, it is true, is it not, that you personally authorized the CIA to kill the Uruguayan chief of state and overthrow their government? That a phone call from you, made from your yacht, began that operation?"

A flat, humorless smile flickered across Hugh Frankling's face and was gone. "No sir, that's not correct." He looked grim and surprised at the same time.

The press secretary held up his hand. "No more," he mouthed to the wire service man. Morey Masters gingerly sat back on his chair and stared at his blank notebook. He wrote in a shaky hand: *"That is not correct."*

The wire service man jumped to his feet and shouted, "Thank you, Mr. President."

As the press secretary led the President back up the aisle and out the door, Morey Masters looked at Rolf Allen and muttered, "Well, what do you think?"

Allen's eyebrows arched. "As usual, no hits, no runs, no errors. Everybody loses."

Masters shook his head. "I'm not so sure. Not so sure this time."

CHAPTER **2**   There is no more remarkable grandeur in Washington than the offices of the members of the President's Cabinet.

The Attorney General's office is perhaps the most baronial of all, designed, some say, "by King Arthur's own architect." Its richly paneled central room is eighty feet long, the windows eighteen feet high, the fireplace huge. At its far end a door leads to a small, low-ceilinged room some twelve feet square. Recoiling from their first impression of the huge official office, many Attorneys General have made this modest side room their working office; some have refused to ever use the large room for any purpose.

When Carleton Smythe was in private practice in Massachusetts his law office had been one of the finest in Boston, as befitted his professional status. It compared favorably with such offices in other parts of the country. The tinted family photograph, the stuffed fish and the expensive antique clock to be found in most senior partners' offices were prominent in his. One or two celebrity photographs are optional; Smythe elected to hang in his office the inscribed face of his friend Senator Hugh Frankling of Ohio, and that of a famous aging motion picture comedian whose longevity entitled him to elder-statesman status.

When Carleton Smythe first visited the offices of the Attorney General to call upon his retiring predecessor for a symbolic transition, he saw his office for the first time and marveled at the architectural glory which had befallen him. He was a man with an appetite for the perquisites that were about to be bestowed upon him.

In the following days he received the good things of his office and station in life; he took them without a qualm of rectitude. Nor did he pause to wonder at the motives of the assistants and aides and administrators who, like so many British tailors, measured him for a new limousine, a new desk, a new attaché case, found him an apartment, taught him the operation of the private elevator, assigned him a team of FBI agents. He was assured that the FBI men could be used twenty-four hours a day, to guard his body, run his errands, chauffeur his wife, walk his dog, or do anything else the General needed—he could be certain that FBI men were very discreet. There was the guest house at the FBI

Academy at Quantico, complete with fishing ponds (all equipment furnished), horses, a golf course on the base, and skeet and trap shooting. And Camp Hoover, and Camp David, and the lodge on a lake in the Tetons. Or a cabin on the Atlantic, by arrangement with the Department of Defense.

Yet the first time he rode to the White House, in his predecessor's long black Cadillac, in spite of himself he felt a pervasive sense of sham and unreality. His role in the play was to portray the Attorney General of the United States. People called him "General," and their roles required them to say and do deferential, respectful things. He was required to act superior. Also omniscient.

Carleton Smythe admitted to himself that he was typecast; ideal for the part. He photographed quite well. He was dignified, even somber, and his old friends were telling interviewers that beneath all of that exterior crust there was a slow and gentle wit—not a bad combination. He was a past president of the American Bar Association, and on the face of it, if one didn't know too much about how a lawyer became president of the ABA, that certainly had to count for something.

He had no qualms about accepting the emoluments of office: Attorneys General and their wives had used limousines for shopping and runs to Williamsburg since McGrath and before. Katzenbach, even Clark, had probably used the vacation places frequently, and Robert Kennedy logged thousands of miles on the airplanes. So had his kids. And his dogs. And his lady.

Carleton Smythe used the drab little back room as his office; as a result he was credited with modesty, simplicity and discretion. That was just as President-elect Hugh Frankling had told him it would be. Frankling had plainly ordered him to use the small office. They were sitting around the lodge at Camp Hoover late in November, a few weeks after Frankling's election. There were a big fireplace fire, strong martinis, and a background of good music. And the Attorney General designate was regaling his friend Hugh with his expansive impressions of his new Justice Department kingdom.

25

"By God, Hugh—Mr. President—have you seen it? It's ten times as big as this room!"

"I know, Carl. I've been there for meetings. Your stupid predecessor had a huge desk right in front of that walk-in fireplace, like he was some goddamned emperor or something. Bad taste and bad politics."

"Ah. How so, bad politics, Mr. President?"

"Jesus, Carl. Think about it. You and whoever becomes Secretary of HEW are going to have to hold off all the civil-rights nuts and the professional welfare people in the poverty lobby. You can't come on to them like the Czar of all the Russias, for God's sake. If you do you're going to be up to your ass in protests and sit-ins and violence all the time you're there. And I don't need that."

"Ah," Smythe replied, crestfallen.

"No. Stay the hell out of that big room. There's a little office over there. Use that..And keep it simple. Not all the fancy crap you had in your Boston office. Forget the ABA plaques and the stuffed fish. Just a picture of your wife—OK?"

"OK."

"By the way, how is Jane—better?"

"I think so. The therapy and isolation seemed to help; it quieted her down. She seems to realize that if there is any more of that shit she'll go back to the sanitarium. And she's scared to death of that. She hates the place. She's apparently under control."

"That's good to hear. You know what a problem that could be for all of us, if she started drinking and acting up again, Carl."

"Yes, sir. As I told you, I had some doubts about taking the job for just that reason. When I was gone so much I put her in that place for treatment to be sure nothing would happen during the campaign. It apparently has cured her. And terrified her some. She's dried out, and she's much better emotionally. Otherwise I wouldn't take it on. And I understand about the little office. That's fine with me."

"General, your wife is on the way in." The Attorney General's secretary sounded defeated over the telephone.

26

"Goddammit, I have people here, Mary. Can't you keep her there?"

"Sorry, Mr. Smythe. She insisted, and there wasn't anything I could do. She's coming through the reception hall now. She says you're running late."

As the Attorney General lowered the telephone to its cradle the south door from the large room opened slowly.

"Gennelmen," said Jane Smythe from the doorway.

The two Assistant Attorneys General who had occupied chairs in front of Carleton Smythe's plain desk stood quickly as Smythe looked toward his wife.

"For Christ's sake, Jane, we aren't finished. Didn't Mary tell you that? You know Austin McCready and Jerry Levine, don't you?"

"I surely do, Carl, dear. And it's time they were goin'. Don't they understand that the Attorney General of the United States has a very important social engagement with the President of the United States in a few minutes, an' his wife is here in all her finery to be taken to the White House?"

"Jane—"

"Now, you gennelmen jus' come on back tomorrow when the General here has more time, won't you? We are goin' over to see the President to tell him what a wonderful job he did in his press conference today."

Carleton Smythe grinned grimly, shook his head in helplessness, shrugged his right shoulder. "I hope you'll excuse me, men. I'm outnumbered."

"Good night, Carl, Mrs. Smythe," said Jerry Levine. The two men moved into the long room and the door closed.

"What's the big hurry, Jane? It's only a little after seven. When are we due there?"

"Listen, Mr. Highandmighty Attorney General," his wife began, "I am sick to death of that snotty secretary of yours. She practically tried to throw me out just now. Who the hell does she think she is?"

Because it had turned hot and humid Jane Smythe chose to wear the only short-sleeved gown in her closet. It was an old floral silk print she had owned for years. She'd been very fond of it before her arms had gone fat. Now it exposed her abdomen and arms; she shouldn't have worn it but, instead of changing into one of the newer dresses which camouflaged better, she'd had a couple of drinks at home and worn a fur cape over it. No one could expect her to look her best in such hot weather, she was sure. She was not comfortable in the dress and it made her irritable.

Jane Smythe was nearly as tall as her husband. He had been blond and fair; now what little hair he had fringing his pate was gray. She was determined never to show a gray hair, but she could not find a hairdresser in all of Washington able to color it to her satisfaction. She was wearing a jet-black wig, square cut, shoulder long, and it too was hot and uncomfortable. Her eyebrows were darkened to match; her lids heavily blued; lip rouge thickly caked her full mouth, around which tiny beads of perspiration would gather all evening. As the young Secretary of Commerce would comment to his wife later in the evening, Jane Smythe looked like a road-show Aïda.

"I've told you before: when I come here, which is not often, God knows, I expect to be treated like the Attorney General's wife, not some goddamned tourist from Tennessee. Have you told that bitch that I'm to be treated like the Attorney General's wife?"

Carleton Smythe lit a cigar in slow puffs as he scrutinized his pacing wife. "She's all right, Jane. She does a good job. And she really respects you, you know. She's a good executive secretary; I couldn't get along without her. How much time do I have to get ready?"

"You don't seem to care. She was goin' to have me thrown out and you don't do anythin' about it! That's the way it always is with you—everythin' someone else does is great, especially another woman. But everythin' I do is wrong. You and that bitch are makin' love up there, aren't you? That's why she feels she can push me around!" She pointed to the ceiling.

"Don't talk that way, Jane. That's just foolish. Who, besides you, would want anything to do with a bald old fellow like me?"

Jane Smythe turned and flounced across the room, opened a door opposite the desk, crossed a narrow vestibule and quickly climbed a dark flight of stairs, followed by her muttering husband. At the head of the second tier she opened the door to the small apartment which for years had been a seldom-discussed perquisite of the office of Attorney General. The bedroom and bath were originally designed to provide overnight facilities when unavoidable duties kept an Attorney General at his desk. Rumor had it that the double bed was the historic scene of demanding if unofficial activities of Smythe's predecessors, their high-ranking brothers and sundry surrogates. Jane Smythe had heard these stories and believed every one of them. Moreover, she believed her husband himself made full use of the apartment to conduct countless romances behind her back.

He was her third husband but her first politician. One of his connubial predecessors had been a junior-high-school physical-education teacher. The other was a regional sales manager for Firestone Tire and Rubber. Both had been sensual, physical men and, admittedly, she had been much younger. But from the beginning Carleton Smythe had been an indifferent partner. Jane had always plumbed a deep well of natural suspicion about all her husbands, fed by an ample flow of insecurity and self-doubt. She knew with total assurance that all men had strong sex drives, whatever their ages, and therefore Smythe's physical needs were being met by others. There could be no other explanation for his lack of carnal interest in her. But she acknowledged that he had always been clever about it; there was never any evidence.

As Smythe shaved she searched the bedroom, opened a drawer, lifted a pillow, peered behind a drape for the telltale signs of his infidelity which must be there.

"If you don't hurry we are going to be late," she said loudly. "Do you think this dress is all right?"

"You look fine," he said with lather-stiff lips. "The car is waiting; it's not far to go; we have plenty of time."

29

The Cadillac idled in front of the Tenth Street entrance to the Justice Department, the air conditioning cooling its lone black occupant. The Attorney General's private elevator descended to that seldom-used door; it was there that the young black FBI agent in chauffeur's gray had delivered Jane Smythe an hour before. When the Attorney General, his ample lady and two FBI bodyguards in tuxedos came down the steps toward the car the chauffeur emerged from the front right, opened the back door and removed his uniform cap.

"Thank you, Charles," Jane said. "We're goin' to the White House," she added loudly. The three FBI agents crowded into the front seat. Jane Smythe pressed a silver switch on the armrest, raising a thick glass to divide her compartment from theirs.

"It's the King of Norway tonight," she said.

"I know," her husband replied. "There's something I need to read here in the *Star* about Hugh's press conference. They really got to him, I guess. Do you want the society section?"

"See, that's what I mean," she began, her voice rising. "Why wouldn't you offer me the front page? Am I too dumb? That's it, isn't it? You really have no respec' for me as a woman, do you?"

Smythe forced a thin smile. "Are we going to argue tonight, Jane?"

"Goddamn right we're going to argue, Mr. Patient, Long-Suffering Attorney General. I intend to have a good time tonight, and I intend for you to stay close an' act like an attentive, lovin' husband. Or I'm jus' liable to pour champagne all over your distinguished bald head."

"I'll try to remember," Smythe said wryly.

The Attorney General's limousine rolled smoothly through the southwest gate to the White House grounds and stopped at the green café awning sheltering the Diplomatic Entrance. A military social aide in formal blue uniform, tiny medals, epaulettes and white gloves briskly stepped forward to open the right rear door. Jane Smythe bent forward to alight. It was still sultry in spite of a light breeze from the river.

The Diplomatic Reception Room is a perfect ellipse, decorated with painted French-wallpaper-scenes of Colonial battles. Its doors open to the Map Room on the left, to the Vermeil Room on the right, and to a side of the wide, red-carpeted hallway straight ahead. A few spindly antiques and a small horsehair couch border the carpet.

Three social aides stood at the social equivalent of parade rest just inside the hallway door, watching the guests enter. All three were Army captains in their late twenties, bachelors and friends of the young major whose job it was to recruit and train fifteen neat, presentable, well-behaved and socially acceptable officers for this extra duty. They would not receive medals or hazard pay but it was a place to meet the attractive daughters of the nation's elite and to escort their famous, notorious and remarkable elders. They lit guests' cigarettes, smiled more than was necessary, arranged the receiving line, furnished directions to the well-hidden public toilet facilities, and offered slightly inaccurate historical information. At the end of the evening they would dance with the women guests whose husbands would or could not, and, hopefully, with their young, wealthy and beautiful daughters.

"Mrs. Smythe, good evening," the blond captain murmured, extending his arm, elbow high.

"Why, good evenin', Captain," Jane Smythe replied. She was being too loud, and she knew it. The drinks she had had before she picked up her husband, more than an hour ago, shouldn't have put her out of control. They weren't that strong. The captain was shorter than she was and very slim. Everything seemed to be conspiring to make her look huge tonight. They walked into the hall with Carleton Smythe trailing, as social custom required. At the foot of the stairway a butler presided over a table covered with small stiff white envelopes. He held hers out to the social aide, then handed Smythe another. Her name was calligraphed on the outside; Smythe's said "The Attorney General."

As they slowly climbed the stairs Jane Smythe was annoyed by the small clatter of two aides rapidly descending the steps on the other side of the brass midrail, their heels striking the bare marble steps. The butler behind her was chatting with the next guests. A

Marine Corps string orchestra had begun to play somewhere upstairs. The captain was saying something. Carl was climbing the hard steps behind her. And her upper arms were loosely swaying, counter to the motion of her body, fat and ugly; in a moment she would be on show in a dress she hated before a roomful of people and they would all be talking about her.

"Oh yes, Captain. I am lookin' forward to meeting the King. I understand he is the most lovely man. My, aren't they beautiful tonight?" She nodded toward the string ensemble, arranged in the small foyer called the Great Hall, archaically attired in the scarlet tunics and black trousers of the Marine Band.

The Smythes were turned left by their escort into the carpeted hall which ran the length of the main floor between the East Room and the State Dining Room. At the door to the East Room the captain nodded to a major holding a small silver microphone. "The Attorney General and Mrs. Carleton Smythe," said the captain. The major lifted the microphone. "The Attorney General of the United States and Mrs. Smythe," a hidden loudspeaker boomed in the East Room.

Four steps into the room the captain bade Jane Smythe farewell as he gave her hand to her husband. A grizzled black butler simultaneously materialized with a tray of assorted drinks.

Smythe maneuvered his wife across the room, his hand on her elbow. There were people whom they should avoid—for example, Mr. Justice R. B. Morely and his pinch-faced wife. With Jane as close to being drunk as she was, and as drunk as she was certain to get, he had to keep her away from Morely's wife. Or risk a real cat fight. The Bensonhursts would be safe, Smythe thought quickly; Lydia Bensonhurst seemed to like Jane and tolerate her excesses. And they were alone in the corner by the Green Room door. Smythe turned his wife to the right and propelled her to Lydia Bensonhurst's side. "Evening, Lydia; Benny," he said.

"Hello, Carl. Jane, dear." The ladies touched right cheeks.

"My," said Jane Smythe too loudly, "my husband was just drawn right to you like a magnet, Lydia. You should be very flattered. I couldn't even tarry for a drink. He wanted to get right over here to your side an' couldn't wait for anythin'."

"It's wonderful to see you tonight, Jane," Congressman Bensonhurst said. "That's a lovely dress."

"Oh, goodness. Thank you, Benny. You're the first one to notice. It's new. I wish my husband was so attentive and gallant, Lydia. But the General is so preoccupied these days, aren't you, CeeCee? It's just the President and that old job that has all his attention, and there's just no time for the rest of us." She took a Scotch from a passing tray.

"Well, that's Washington, Jane," said Lydia Bensonhurst. "Welcome to the widowhood."

"Oh, my, Lydia! I think tha's jus' terrible. What you said is terrible! I'd rather have my CeeCee alive, even busy and indifferent and distracted, than dead. Oh, I'd just hate to be a widow! There is something so dried up an' useless about being a widow." She drank deeply and handed the empty glass to a waiter.

Bensonhurst had begun to talk quietly to Carleton Smythe about a letter he had received that day from the chief executive officer of Pinemount Foods about an antitrust problem that firm was having with the Justice Department. Jane Smythe reached in front of her husband to take Bensonhurst's right forearm in her left hand. As she interrupted him she pulled on his arm.

"Did you hear what I said, Benny? There is nothing more desolate than widowhood, hear? You men! Don't you dare treat us like widows! We must be loved and cherished, and you had better treat us like you are thoroughly alive husbands! Or else! If all you Republicans insist on treating us like widows we are not goin' to stand for it! Do you hear me?"

Smythe was lighting a cigar, hiding behind the starting smoke, an amused look on his face.

" 'Cause if we're neglected," she went on, pulling on the Congressman's arm to punctuate her words, "we will tell the women of this nation and the world what kind of men you all are. I will tell them. I don't mind tellin' the press. So you jus' better start

33

lookin' after your wives, all you mighty and powerful men, if you want to get yoursel's elected again." She dropped the arm she had been holding and took her husband by his right hand. "If you want all these lovely parties and big cars and fancy offices you jus' better remember." As she finished her drink Lydia Bensonhurst moved to her husband's side. They smiled and turned away from the Smythes in the practiced Congressional choreography of escape.

"Watch the booze, Jane," Smythe said quietly. "It's getting to you."

"Let me tell you what's getting to me, Mr. Attorney General Smythe. It's not that little drink." Her voice became higher and louder. "Your dear friend, the President, serves very weak drinks, in case you din't know it. What burns my ass is the way you are chasing after every skirt in this town. That is what is getting to me. Even my friend Lydia Bensonhurst, for God's sake—"

"Jane," Smythe said in a low tone, "shut up. You are talking too loud. People are looking at you."

"They are looking at me because ah am speakin' my mind. Tha's the only reason. The other women in this place are jus' afraid to do that. I know."

When a majority of guests were checked off the arrival list, the social aides began to ease around the room suggesting that the receiving line be formed. Each aide carried the protocol list prescribing the order in which the guests would be received by the President, beginning with several Norwegian officials traveling with the King, followed by the Secretary of State. He and his wife were gently parted from their conversation group and herded to the wall to the right of the entrance. The next couple on the list, the Secretary of Defense *et ux,* were moved behind them. Then the others were made to form a ragged arrangement around the walls, the unranked out-of-town people standing in alphabetical order, last of all.

"Ladies and gentlemen, the President of the United States, His Majesty King Harald, Her Majesty Queen Sarah, and Mrs. Frankling," the loudspeakers boomed. From the hallway the Marine band sounded "Hail to the Chief."

Several guests were caught with drinks in their hands. Experienced State Dinner attendees had handed their glasses to the butlers and the social aides minutes before; now the minions had vanished. There was nothing except a pecan-wood grand piano upon which to set a drink; the room was bare. As the President and his party came to the entrance to take the guests' applause, several men bent to stash glasses and napkins along the baseboard of the wall, then arose, flushed, to join the applause.

The King introduced his colleagues to the President. A military aide took the Secretary of State's arm and gently drew him toward the President to begin the receiving line. "The Secretary of State," said the major to a captain standing at the President's left, close by his ear. "The Secretary of State," said the captain to the President.

"Sam, how are you tonight?" said the President with good humor. "It's been twenty or thirty minutes since I've seen you."

As each guest reached the major he elicited a name or title to give the captain, and then made certain that the male member of the next couple preceded his consort in the reception sequence.

The President repeated the guests' names to the King. The King presented his Queen. Mrs. Frankling was on her own, since the Queen spoke little English and hated reception lines. So the President's wife greeted strangers with "I'm Gloria Frankling" and a strong handshake born of countless campaigns across Ohio. Then she skillfully moved them along toward the door to the Green Room, where a social aide pointed the way toward dinner.

"Mr. President, the Attorney General," said the social aide.

"Good evening, Carl," said President Hugh Frankling. The President was freshly scrubbed and massaged, barbered and dressed. His dinner jacket was flawlessly tailored to broaden his shoulders and drop straight in spite of his rounding girth and heavy hips. Beneath the starched shirt was a pale and flabby middle-aged man, once a lawyer from Ohio, now and for many years a politician of the city of Washington, whose ties to the state of Ohio now were perfunctory and waning.

"Your Majesty," said the President to the King, "may I present the Attorney General? He is my most trusted confidant."

"Ah, Mr. Attorney General! It is a great pleasure to meet you. May I present my Queen?"

"Your Majesty. I am honored."

The dark-eyed Queen smiled at Smythe, shook his hand lightly and half turned to the President's wife to pass him along.

"Hello, Carl. How are you tonight?" Gloria Frankling's voice was high and sharp, the accent as angular as her wiry, spare frame. She wore her blond and graying hair short, in tight ringlets, hardening the gauntness of her face, exaggerating her aquiline nose and high cheekbones.

"Good evening, Gloria," said Smythe, a glance to his right betraying his concern. His wife was still talking to the President and the King, holding the long receiving line at a standstill. Frankling was always uncomfortable with Jane Smythe; it was evident that he wanted her to move along now, but she was intentionally oblivious to his discomfort, determined to hold the place which was, at that moment, the ultimate center stage. The Attorney General's face composed itself into a mixture of quizzical and tolerant amusement as he stood three paces beyond Gloria Frankling, looking back.

"That's the Attorney General's wife talking to the King," the First Lady said to the Norwegian Queen.

"Ah," the Queen murmured as she stared fixedly at Jane Smythe.

With a patient smile Carleton Smythe took a step back toward his wife. She sensed his approach and tossed her head.

"That big man is comin' to take me away from you, Your Majesty. I think he's jes' horrible, don' you?"

The King smiled thinly.

"We're so glad yoah here, with our dear President. I hope you jes' have a lovely time!" Her head danced coquettishly.

"Thank you, madame, most sincerely," the King said evenly. Then he turned, with obvious dismissal, to greet the Secretary of Commerce, who stood waiting next in line.

Carleton Smythe moved to take his wife's elbow in his hand.

Jane Smythe had not moved from the Queen; she felt her husband's hand tighten.

"Ah'd love to visit with you, Your Majesty," she said, "but this big husban' of mine is goin' to hurry me right on by. It's jes' so lovely to meet you."

"Good evening, Jane," the President's wife said coolly.

"Evenin'," Jane replied as she walked by without extending her hand.

As the Smythes moved to the Green Room doorway it was obvious that she was giving him hell, although both held fixed smiles as they passed the social aide at the doorway.

"The idea of you tellin' me when to move and when to chat jus' makes me sick, Mr. General. Ah am the President's guest here, jus' like you, an' it was plain that he and the King *wanted* to talk to me. Ah'm sure you can't unnerstan' that, since *you* never want to talk to me, but it happens to be true. Otha men do happen to fine me interestin'." She grazed against the doorjamb at the entrance to the Blue Room and lurched against her husband.

"Take your goddamn hand off me, CeeCee, so ah can get through these narra places. You don' need to push me aroun'."

"Jane, either get a grip on yourself or we're going home. You are making a perfect fool of yourself." Smythe looked benign and relaxed, but his words lashed her. "If you can't handle a social evening any better than this then perhaps we'd better get you some help, again."

She stopped and turned to him. "Tha's not funny. Ah won't have that. Tha's one thing you mustn't joke about, CeeCee. Ah can't go back to that place again. Ah can't. Ah can't!" Her face slumped, the pale eyes darting to the corners of the ornate room. She could feel how it would be back in the sanitarium, the patient in Room 212. She could taste the rubber tube they put in her nose, feel the soreness in her stomach muscles from retching. No band music, no White House, no limousines. Only the dull, mustardy headache and the pain in her gut.

"D'you think if I sat here a while you could fine me some nice strong coffee? Ah want to please you, Carley, ah really do. Ah can't go back there to that place. You know that, don' you?" She sat heavily on a Victorian chair inside the door to the Red Room and looked up at her husband. Her face and shoulders sagged.

Carleton Smythe smiled sympathetically. He put a hand on her shoulder, the fingers patting gently. "I'll get your coffee, dear. You just sit here until you're feeling better."

Jane Smythe was one of the last to find her seat in the State Dining Room. Gloria Frankling and her social secretary had decided on round tables for this evening rather than the stiff and crowded E-shaped pattern of the usual state dinner table. It took a little longer for people to find their places at the rounds, and they could not seat as many, but the informality often made for a better evening. By the time the Attorney General delivered his wife to table nine and found his seat at table three over in the corner, the waiters had begun to serve the consommé escargot.

Except for the large Lincoln portrait over the fake fireplace, the State Dining Room was unremarkable. It was rectangular, plastered white, embellished only with wall sconces and a crystal chandelier, a colorless and difficult room to use for formal dinners. The small family dining room which adjoined became a serving pantry. The food was hoisted from the kitchens two floors below; cold dishes often arrived warm, hot food cooled, waiters collided in the narrow passages and the small elevator failed at crucial times. All this inconvenience was borne in the name of the historic preservation of a relic of a house that really was not a relic at all since it had been entirely rebuilt during Harry Truman's term.

The centerpieces on the round tables were wicker baskets of spring flowers and white candles. At each place there was a handwritten place card in the center of the formal setting plate. To the left, on the napkin, was a calligraphed menu. Each was embossed with the Presidential seal. In the left margin of the menu, opposite each course, one found the name and vintage of the wine which would be poured by the waiters.

The seating arrangement was, as always, a mixture of protocol, prudence and politics. Known enemies were separated, possible contributors were favored, and one or two members of the White House staff were paired with the wives of needed Congressional votes.

At table fourteen the young wife of the Governor of Arizona found herself seated between Tony Yarmouth, the famous old portrait painter, and Robin Warren, a young Special Counsel to the President.

During the dessert the music began. The corner door to the Red Room opened and a file of soldiers in epauletted blue uniforms appeared, playing violins, violas and violoncellos. They flowed to all parts of the room among the tables, playing "Lara's Theme" from *Doctor Zhivago,* then bridged easily to other favorites. As the music faded and the last musician disappeared, the doors were simultaneously closed by the waiters and the President arose from his chair in front of the Adams fireplace, clearing his throat.

Hugh Frankling shrugged his waistline into a comfortable latitude and beamed too broadly at the Queen of Norway, seated on his left. As he began to deliver the little speech the State Department and his speech writers had put together, his eyes darted from table to table. At some level of his mind he reflected on the faces he encountered, some famous and others unknown to him, some his colleagues, a few his adversaries, one or two his unavoidable enemies.

Just at the moment when he called upon his guests to rise and toast the King, some movement of those between them opened the President's view of Robin Warren. Frankling noted that his young aide was seated beside a young and beautiful woman in a bright-blue dress. The sight of Warren caused Hugh Frankling's mind to jump from its track for a moment. He called for a toast to "His Honor," quickly corrected it to "His Majesty," and turned from Robin Warren to the table where the King sat next to Gloria Frankling. The President held his glass high for a picture by the two press pool photographers who stood by the hall door, then drank a sip of the champagne.

As the King haltingly read his return toast the President

39

motioned his military aide to his side and muttered into his bent neck. The young Navy captain straightened, looked about the room, then fixed on Attorney General Smythe at the far corner.

Hugh Frankling backed his chair gently until he could see Robin Warren again between the intervening diners. Warren looked very young; younger than the President remembered him; perhaps it was just his coloring. Those strawberry blonds always looked younger than they really were. His hair was cut modishly, the light eyebrows bushy over ice-blue eyes. Warren had a firm chin, a straight, wide mouth and a rather long upper lip. Regular features. Almost handsome. Perhaps Scandinavian or German. He was, undoubtedly, attractive. But his magnetism was less in how he looked than in how he moved.

There are those men, envied by their friends, who manifest an inherent grace—a confidence of motion, an expression of style that is beyond athletics, different from mere physical coordination. It is a unity of physique and the motor centers. A knowing possessor is often able to translate that appearance of sureness into a presumption of intellectual command. Robin Warren had some of that— not all of it, but more than most men. He had enough to make some awkward men jealous, to make female conquests easier, and to give him a professional edge over most of his intellectual equals in the office or at meetings. Warren knew some of what he possessed and he used it.

The diners rose and applauded the King's toast. As their clapping subsided the President rose and said loudly, "If you'll all come into the East Room after your coffee we have a fine motion picture that none of you have seen. Then there'll be dancing afterward for all you young people." He took the Queen's arm and led the way to the double doors.

The naval aide circled behind the congestion at the door and tapped Carleton Smythe lightly on the arm. "May I give you a message, General?"

"Yes, Captain."

"Sir, the President asks that you come to the Lincoln Sitting

Room in the family quarters during the motion picture. Please come up as soon as it begins."

"Very well. Thank you."

The aide then moved to the young chief of staff, David Hale, with the same instructions. Hale nodded curtly and turned back to the brunette by his side to make his apologies.

One floor below, the wide, vaulted, red-carpeted hallway was crowded with women in long dresses and men in tuxedos. They were predominantly young, white, thin and noisily talkative. Most of the men were upper-middle-level Presidential appointees in some government agency or department, and most of the women were their wives. Three women had been invited in their own right. These young people were the "after-dinner invitees"; they had been given a glass of rather inferior champagne while they waited, and most were genuinely thrilled to be at the White House at all. A majority of the wives had written or called home to their parents when the President's engraved invitation had come in the mail. Many had bought a new long dress especially for the evening.

These second-class invitees were soon permitted to file slowly up the marble stairs into the Great Hall as the dinner guests followed the President, the King and their wives into the East Room. That room had been quickly transformed from a reception hall to a theater as dinner was being served. Several ushers and six General Services Administration men had moved hand trucks with the spindly wooden chairs from a subbasement, arranging the chairs in rows facing a large movie screen mounted against the south wall. Four overstuffed chairs were placed in the front row, side by side, for the chiefs of state and their ladies. Now, as they were seated, the social aides motioned the other guests into the rows behind. On a signal from his naval aide that everyone was in place, the President stood and turned to face the audience, his hands clasped behind him.

"Ladies and gentlemen, sometimes we have singers, pianists or other musicians for our after-dinner entertainment. But I've had this nation's vast intelligence network busy learning all it could about our distinguished guests' preferences. I didn't find out much about the King, but I can report that the lovely Queen is a Kurt Kirboe fan, and so we have arranged to show tonight the very latest Kirboe film, *A Romance*. And by the way, when the Queen and the King get to California later this week, she is going to have lunch with Kurt Kirboe at Superior Studios. I understand this film is very sad at the end; the social aides will have extra handkerchiefs for any of you who need them." He sat down amidst light laughter and applause, leaned to place his hand on the King's arm and explained in low tones that he was required to leave for a few minutes to see to a bit of urgent business. The King nodded his sympathy and understanding.

As the film set its scene with wide and colorful shots of the Riviera, Hugh Frankling ducked low and moved along the front row to the Green Room door, followed by the naval aide and a Secret Service agent. He walked quickly to the waiting elevator near the State Dining Room and rose slowly, alone, to the floor above. There he walked the length of the wide hall into the chamber once used by Abraham Lincoln as his Cabinet Room. He passed slowly along the end of the old, leather-topped Lincoln Cabinet table, trailing the fingers of his right hand across the tooled pattern.

CHAPTER **3**   David Hale rose from the horsehair couch to a near stand-at-attention when President Hugh Frankling came into the doorway. The young chief of staff had been waiting in the Lincoln Sitting Room for nearly five minutes, at first daydreaming about Abraham Lincoln, then, with a characteristic turn of mind, thinking ironically about the blatant fiction of the place. The room was a total reconstruction—all new materials, air conditioning, everything. It was true that most of the furniture was authentic, some of it from the Lincoln period, but only one or two pieces were actually from the original room. The antiqued wood floor, the wainscoting, fixtures and wallpaper were like a pure Disneyland reproduction. The cube of space that had been the actual sitting room in Lincoln's time coincided with the same space in this Frankling White House, hung up here halfway between the roof and the basement on the south wall. But it was only Lincoln's space; it was not Lincoln's room.

Frankling unbuttoned his dinner jacket and waistcoat as he came through the door. He dropped into his old brown lounge chair and looked up at Hale. "Where's Smythe? Is he coming?"

"Yes, sir; I'm sure he's on the way." It was always "sir" or "Mr. President"; it had been that formal between them since election night twenty months before, without Hugh Frankling even raising the subject of how he was to be addressed by the staff. Hale had thought it through, briefly, and found it impossible to think of calling this man anything else, even in their most private conversations.

David Hale knew a great deal about Frankling's predecessors. He had read everything he could find about them and their Presidencies. His research had begun as a matter of necessity as Frankling became a serious candidate for President, but in the process David Hale had become more idealistic than he realized, more than he would have believed possible had he considered it. When he had been appointed chief of staff there had been a lot of newspaper copy about his quick mind and mild manner. Some of the writers had called him pragmatic. He liked that description; that's the way he thought and talked about himself.

Other stories described his role as Hugh Frankling's alter ego. But none of them described how that always tightening alter-ego relationship had changed Hale. He barely realized it himself, but from the beginning he had begun to accept Hugh Frankling's opinions and attitudes, yielding his own. Frankling's preconceptions had eventually become David Hale's own beliefs, and now he fought for them without admitting to himself the transference which had taken place.

When Frankling was elected President, he had gained in Hale's mind a strong presumption of infallibility; it was not the result of Hale's objective analysis of Frankling the person, or even of the man-in-the-office. If asked, Hale probably would have said that Hugh-Frankling-the-man was just as capable of mistakes as any other human being. But to David Hale all Presidents, impersonally and generically, were presumptively infallible because they had become President. He did not admit this subjective anomaly in himself. More, he did not consciously notice, or recognize, or concede it.

Had he encountered such romantic political notions in any young member of his staff he would have dissected the unfortunate fellow with incisive irony. He demanded absolute objectivity in the work of the eight junior executives who managed White House operations at his direction. From the first days of the new administration they were so eager and singularly dedicated to him that they had been called the Beaver Patrol. The Patrol was aggressive in their devotion to David Hale and his President; there was staff-dining-room talk that the government would soon list the beaver as a dangerous predator.

"Why is Robin Warren here tonight, David?" the President asked, loosening his tie.

"No special reason, sir. His name was on the list, and it was just easier to leave it there than to take him off. Why? What did he say to you?"

"Nothing. I don't think he came through the line. I was just surprised to see him at dinner. It seems to me we ought to use these dinner invitations to reward our friends."

"Yes, sir."

Carleton Smythe tapped his knuckles on the open door and came in.

"I'm sorry to be so long, Mr. President. I couldn't get Jane to go home, so I had to get an FBI agent to come in and look after her during the movie."

"Is she all right, Carl?"

"Most of the time. But there are episodes of craziness that I just can't handle. It's usually when she's got at the sauce. That was the problem in the receiving line tonight."

"Too bad, too bad. Sit there by David, Carl. We need to talk about Robin Warren and Uruguay. That goddamned place! That's all anyone can talk about today."

"Right. I was surprised to see Robin Warren here tonight." Smythe lit a cigar with deep, slow draws that curved his cheeks. "What's wrong, David—can't you find enough friendly people to fill the chairs at these things?"

Hale shifted on the horsehair plush settee and smiled thinly. "We were just talking about that when you came in, General," he said quietly. He suspected Smythe had overheard the President's criticism from the adjoining room and was taking a free ride on the Presidential coattails. Pompous bastard.

The President waved a hand to stop the potential bickering. "Carl, as you know, I was bombarded with Uruguay questions at the press conference today. I held to the temporary position we agreed upon, but we can't stay there much longer."

"I understand. David asked me to talk to Jepson Valle about Warren, and I finally found him this afternoon."

"Will he get Robin Warren into line?"

"He promised he'd try, Mr. President, but you know Jep Valle. Everything is a horse trade with that slippery gentleman and it's going to cost you."

"I realize that, Carl. That's all right, as long as Jep Valle can be trusted. Can we be sure he'll keep quiet about this? How much did you have to tell him?"

"Not very much. Valle knows that his former employee has apparently made a serious mistake. And that young Mr. Warren is not willing to step forward and admit it. I told him that David fears that Robin Warren may try to save his skin by blaming others—

even the President—for the Uruguayan situation. Valle realizes that could only result in everyone being badly hurt, so he promised to try to get his protégé to do the right thing. He asked no questions."

David Hale leaned forward. "That sounds good in theory, General, but what are the chances that Valle will try, and if he does, what are the odds that he'll succeed?"

"About one in ten, I'd guess," intervened the President. "Right? Carl?"

"It depends on his leverage, Mr. President. Maybe he has some hold on the young man that we don't know about. That could help the odds greatly."

"Well, David, you ought to know about that—you had Warren checked out thoroughly before we hired him, didn't you?"

"Yes, sir. He was clean, as far as the FBI could learn. But Valle will know more about him than anyone else. He had nearly two years with Valle; before that he practiced law in San Francisco with a good firm. He's divorced from a society girl there. He plays around a little, but he's pretty discreet, I guess."

"Well, gentlemen, it's up to you." The President stood. "Either he admits that he authorized the Uruguayan thing by himself or his credibility must be totally destroyed. One or the other. I'd prefer that he step forward, of course. We could help him after that, couldn't we, David? Someone could fix him up with a good job somewhere abroad, right?"

David Hale smiled thinly. "I'm sure we could arrange it, if he's willing. Can Jep Valle suggest that to him, General?"

Smythe tapped the ash off his cigar and nodded. "Yes, but don't get your hopes up. I personally doubt that young Mr. Warren will budge; he's been looking forward to a magnificent career after he leaves here. You're asking him to cut his own throat; that's an unnatural act for a bright, ambitious young man."

"All right," said Hugh Frankling with finality. "You two stay here and figure out what you're going to do. Warren's got to be handled one way or the other. The nation has a great stake in the proper outcome of this Uruguayan problem. I'm sure you realize that. It couldn't have come at a worse time in the United Nations. And it could be awkward for us up in the Congress if the Democrats handle it adroitly." Frankling half closed his eyes and folded his hands in front of his chest. "However, we are not without resources there, eh, Carl?"

Smythe had expected the soliloquy to continue much longer so he had permitted his mind to drift. In response to the unheard question he drew deep on his cigar, blew a great cloud of smoke and chuckled. As usual, that was a sufficiently Delphic answer to meet the need of the moment. The President paused briefly, then went on: "It must appear to the people of this town that Warren is a slick opportunist who would say anything to save his own ass. If he blames us for Uruguay it's got to fall on deaf ears. I have confidence that you two can produce that result. That shouldn't be too hard. He's single, attractive, and we know he's had something to do with that actress. Right? By the way, she's in that picture we're showing downstairs. You can get a look at her before it ends. What's her name?"

"Lani Romera," said Hale.

"That's not her real name, but that's the one. Doesn't she have a Jewish name?"

"Goldberg. She used to be married to a producer named Goldberg."

"Anyway, you two will have to figure it out. I have an early breakfast meeting tomorrow; I'm going to have to give our guests a send-off, then I'm going to turn in. Good night, gentlemen."

"Good night, sir."

"Good night."

The President walked to the hall door, took the doorknob and turned. "May I suggest that time is very short? I'd like to know what Valle has done, and what our plan is for neutralizing Robin Warren, by no later than noon tomorrow." He closed the door behind him.

The Attorney General rose from the horsehair couch, walked to the President's chair and settled into it. "David, really now, how clean is your Mr. Warren?"

"I'm not sure. He's been here since the beginning. I think we should focus on the period of time he's been in the White House, not the prior years. I suspect it has been a time of great temptation for him. He's well-built, good-looking and all that. And he doesn't have much money. I know there have been women around. One of them is Jep Valle's daughter. Can the Bureau look into what he's been doing this last year?"

"Oh, I'm sure it can. Where does he live?"

"Georgetown."

"Since Uruguay and the United Nations are involved, I see no reason why we shouldn't put a national-security tap on his phone. That's the fastest way to know whom he talks to."

"I think you ought to go ahead with that, General, even before we hear from Jepson Valle." Hale shook his head and leaned forward. "I don't have much confidence in the wily Senator Valle. He's too smooth. I don't think he's going to produce for us."

"All right. Do you think we might find enough this way to persuade Warren to assume full responsibility, David? It would have to be some very strong stuff."

Hale grimaced. "I don't know, but it's worth a try. Maybe there's a woman. Maybe there's money—in his job he's certainly in a good position to do some moonlighting. I think there's at least a chance of hitting something. And if there isn't—we'll just have to dream something up."

"I guess there always must be a first time," the Attorney General of the United States said, with a smile.

Part II

THE TRANSITION

CHAPTER **4**   "Robin Warren is young, bright, attractive, ambitious and knows his way around this town, gentlemen." Bert Fallon held the thin file folder in his left hand, a cigarette in his right. Always a cigarette. Balding and slight, quick as a small bird, Bert Fallon was one of the hardy perennials of Washington politics. Whether his party was in or out, he survived. It was better, of course, when the Republicans were in the White House. Then he was always called on to help, and his help was well rewarded at important times. But, at all times, there would be survival. Bert Fallon was a survivor.

He had spent his early Washington years under the wing of a powerful committee chairman at the Senate; it had been a time for learning tribal rites and developing a tolerance of sloth. In the Eisenhower years he had found a nice niche on the White House staff. He had come back in for a few months during Nixon, but his feral instinct had told him the storm was coming long before it struck, and he'd found safe shelter with Coreolis Technology Corporation, quietly looking after its Washington interests. Then Senator Frankling was elected President.

Bert Fallon had known Hugh Frankling on the Hill for years; from time to time Senator Frankling had come to him for advice or help. Coreolis Technology was an Ohio company, from Hugh Frankling's state; what helped Frankling helped Coreolis. It was natural that Bert Fallon had been asked to come in after the election. But after two months on the transition staff Fallon had decided not to take a permanent job with Frankling.

He could sense trouble the first day he'd met with the top Frankling people. All but a few were from Ohio and were provincially hostile and lacking in Washington experience. David Hale, Frankling's top staff man, was bright and able, but he was an outsider. Hale was a successful Ohio businessman with some campaign experience, but he was a stranger to Washington ways. Frankling reposed full confidence in Hale, feeling that Frankling's Washington know-how and Hale's organizational talents would be a good combination.

But now Hale was necessarily involved in political decisions for which he was poorly equipped. It bothered Fallon that Frankling's transition office was in Cleveland and that most of his staff insisted on being there, close to the President-elect. David Hale came to the Washington office only two days a week at most, too few hours for Bert Fallon to explain the real problems and to begin David Hale's Washington education.

The top floor of the "new" Executive Office Building, a block from the White House on Seventeenth Street N.W., had been designated for Frankling's use. A Presidential commission and part of a bureau were hurriedly shuffled to the old Pension Building in the high-crime area so that the GSA could redecorate the transition suite. But Hugh Frankling had no intention of using this transition office; he had decided to wait in Ohio until the day of inauguration, leaving the Washington details to his new and growing staff.

When he was in Washington David Hale would slouch behind the huge GSA desk in the President-elect's office, flanked by the Presidential ensign, the flag of the state of Ohio and Old Glory, a Styrofoam cup of instant coffee making heat rings in the wood of the desk's pull-out tray.

Bert Fallon was supposed to be recruiting people for the White House staff, but Hale and his Ohio mafia had been hiring people, too, often for the same jobs. Hale was hiring professors, Ohio newsmen and whiz kids with no Washington know-how or connections, while Fallon had files of deserving applicants with good Washington experience and strong Congressional backing. There would be quick and lasting trouble if they didn't begin hiring some Congressmens' favorites. The Frankling staff badly needed a meeting to iron out the conflicts and to make some decisions on some of the key jobs. Inauguration was only five weeks away; time was short.

"You're going to need a fellow like Robin Warren, Dave, believe me," Fallon said to Hale. "Someone will have to spend his time with the special-interest groups, whether you like the idea or not. Either you furnish the interests with a convenient White House ear or they'll kill you on the Hill and within their memberships. You can't freeze them out of the White House. You'd better realize that now."

"All right, Bert. Don't beat it to death; I understand." Hale grinned slowly. "But why this particular young man? His résumé doesn't show me much."

"Well, for one thing, I know him and I've watched him work. He's been in Washington a couple of years, working for Jepson Valle, and he's well thought of. He's good."

"Isn't his connection with Jepson Valle a drawback for us? Is Robin Warren a wheeler-dealer like Valle?" Hale stirred his coffee with a pencil.

"Robin Warren is very self-collected and careful, Dave. He's not a flashy operator. Actually, there isn't all that much razzle-dazzle to the real Jepson Valle either. I know his television and platform style give that impression, but he's a cold and calculating

53

riverboat gambler. He's only about ten percent Senator Claghorn. I think he puts on that Old Senator show to throw us all a little off balance so he can pick our pockets easier. Jep is a very, very deep pool."

"I'm just going on reputation. It was one thing to have Valle's help during the campaign. But whether he should have his hand in the Frankling administration is another question. From what I've heard, Jepson Valle is someone we ought to steer clear of now."

"I think that's just dead wrong, David. If you cut Hugh—the President—off from Senator Jep Valle you'll be doing your administration an injustice. Valle works for his clients, it's true, but he knows more about what is going on in this town than anyone else I can think of. You need him; if he's willing to help you from time to time, you're lucky." Fallon waved his cigarette-yellowed fingers. "His reputation can't hurt you! Most of the gossip about Jep comes from old enemies in California, and most of it is jealousy anyway—he's just a better politician and lobbyist and a better lawyer than the people who whisper about him behind his back."

"Let's get Broderick in here," Hale said. "I know he had some doubts about this Warren, too."

In quick response to Hale's summons, Elwood Broderick, Counsel to the President-elect, shuffled into the ornate office as if he were wearing bedroom slippers. "Good afternoon, gentlemen. Are you getting all the kinks out of the personnel process?" He was sixty, with gray locks framing a face of circles, large soft brown eyes, round cheeks and chin. He was tall and gave the impression of obesity; he favored carefully tailored suits which, within hours, rumpled and sagged to his bodily contours. Now he wore shirtsleeves and a bright-blue bow tie. "How can I help?" He looked slowly at Hale, then at Bert Fallon, as he settled into a large leather chair like a deflating balloon.

"We're talking about Robin Warren, Woody. Bert thinks we should take him as liaison to special-interest groups."

Bert Fallon nodded once. "I've been telling David, I don't think you have anything to fear from his connection with Jep Valle. I think Valle is going to be a great deal of help to your administration."

"What if Valle is put in the Cabinet, Bert? Should we still take Warren?" Broderick asked slowly. "My esteemed ex-partner, your President-elect, is toying with the notion of making Valle the Secretary of Defense, or Treasury, or something."

Fallon looked surprised.

Hale shook his head slowly. "I can't imagine sending Valle's name to the Senate for confirmation. The Democrats still hate him for changing parties seventeen years ago, and a lot of Republicans do, too."

Bert Fallon held up his hand. "Not so fast—that's what Jep had to do to be elected Senator from California. The California Democrats wouldn't endorse him because he'd been Secretary of the Army in a Republican administration. So he changed his registration. It was exactly the right thing for him to do at the time. He has some enemies, it's true, but I think he could be confirmed. It depends on what department he's up for—what Senate committee would have jurisdiction. Most of his clients would break their necks to help him. That would make a lot of difference."

"Then what about Warren?" Hale pressed. "Would you take both of them?"

"That would probably be too rich for most folks," Fallon conceded. "It should be one or the other, but not both."

"Then I guess we'd better wait to see if the President decides to take Valle. If he doesn't, Warren is all right with me," Hale said.

Bert Fallon leaned forward intently, lighting a cigarette. "Look, Jep Valle is a friend of mine. But I think Valle in the Cabinet could be a huge problem for you all. He still wants to be President more than anything else, and you would have to live with that every day he was with you."

"Hell," said Elwood Broderick, "he can't be President! He lobbies for the Arabs, and Texas oil, and defense contractors, and polluters, and railroads, and he sleeps with a different woman every night. What party is going to nominate Jepson Valle?"

Fallon nodded. "I know that, and you know that, but Jep Valle

55

either doesn't know it or knows it and won't believe it. He probably doesn't admit even to himself that he made his choice six years ago and can never go back. He still thinks that every American boy can be President, no matter whom he sleeps with. More than that, if he saw the chance he'd run against Hugh—the President—next time. He'd be absolutely cold-blooded about it. On the outside, as a lobbyist, he's a dependent and he'll perform for you. Count on it. Don't forget, you fellows will have everything we tattered supplicants of the lobby want and need. Just holler 'jump' and watch us leap." Fallon smiled.

"We're going to get a lot of outside pressure to appoint Jepson Valle to the Cabinet. I'm already hearing from some of our fatcats. How do we head that off, Bert?" asked Broderick.

"Well, here's one way." Fallon held up the personnel file labeled "Robin Warren." "Give this kid the public-contact job now. That would be the new President's signal to the country that Valle is not under serious consideration for the Cabinet."

"Estoppel," grunted Broderick.

"Whatever," said Hale. "I'm going back to Ohio tonight, and I'll suggest that to the President-elect first thing in the morning."

At dusk David Hale's GSA Chevrolet emerged from the underground garage into Seventeenth Street, en route to Andrews Air Force Base. Less than a half block away a sunset ritual was being performed in the corner office of Jepson Valle, Gerber and Rogers, Attorneys and Counselors at Law.

A fire burned quietly in the fawn marble fireplace. Recessed lights had been dimmed. Street noises and the advancing winter rainstorm were muted by curtains drawn across the full-length windows.

The upholstery, the carpeting and the walls were all in muted shades of beige and tan. The desk and other tables were dark woods, accented with brass fixtures and ashtrays. One wall held a Peter Hurd landscape. A Fechin oil from his California period brightened the panel above the fireplace.

The low brass-trimmed birch coffee table held a tray of cheeses, fruits and crackers. A slim young woman in a pale aubergine slack suit fixed drinks at the built-in bar near the door.

Jepson Valle was in a pose of complete relaxation, gray-maned head back, legs crossed, lounging in a deep leather chair and holding a thick tumbler in his left hand. Opposite, on the long divan, Robin Warren leaned forward to put some very ripe Brie on a strip of toast.

Valle spoke to the blond girl. Even if Robin Warren had been a stranger to their relationship, he could have guessed from Valle's tone that he and his secretary had been lovers.

"Marya, I have to have a serious talk with this young man about his future. He needs a strong drink, then we want to be uninterrupted. You and I are through for the day, aren't we?"

"You promised Atlas that you would talk to Senator Hubert today, for sure." Her manner was more distant than his. Warren noticed the difference.

"Why don't you get Hubert for me? I'll talk whenever you reach him. Otherwise, no other calls, eh?"

"All right. Here's your drink, Robin."

"Thanks, Marya. Good night."

When they were alone Robin Warren leaned toward Valle, elbows on his knees. "I don't like to be thinking about leaving here. It's a great place to work."

"I understand; but is there any real question? If you have—"

The telephone emitted a single low chime. Valle bent out of the deep chair and walked to his desk to pick up the tan receiver. "Yes, thanks. Senator? You're kind to take my call. Oh, no. It's still working hours around here. I'm calling to ask a favor. Jerry Nicholson, the chairman of the Atlas–North Slope Oil Consortium, will be in Washington next Monday and Tuesday. I'd like to bring him by to say hello, if you can see us. It would be very good for him to get to know you. No, nothing special, just a get-acquainted. About three on Monday? Perfect. Room 102E on the Senate side? We'll be there; I'll look forward to it. Goodbye."

Valle pressed a button.

"Marya, tell Atlas: Nicholson and I will see Hubert at three P.M. Monday, Room 102E in the Capitol. He's not expecting to do any business this visit. All right. Good night. See you tomorrow." He walked to the bar, freshened his drink and went back to his chair.

"Help yourself if that gets weak, Robin. Now, what's the question? You are one in ten million; you've been asked to go to work for the new President, you have good health, reasonable intelligence and all that. I don't see the problem!"

"It's not quite that cut and dried, Jep. I've been approached, but so far I don't have a firm offer from the White House. God knows, I want to be asked. And yet I'm really ambivalent. That's why I asked to talk to you. I think I need to know more about it—mostly more about Hugh Frankling, I guess. The job would be the same special-interests job that Johnny Johnson has had. It's not so different from what I've been doing here for you the last couple of years. I think I could do it."

"I'm sure you could, Robin. You would do it very well. But I can understand your doubts. It's not surprising that you're ambivalent about Hugh Frankling and the White House, as you say. It's not an unmixed blessing."

"Hugh Frankling doesn't excite me much, Jep. I was for Bob Burley in the primaries, as I told you. Frankling seems so goddamn stolid and uninspiring, I'm not sure how it would be working for him. I'm anything but turned on by the man. I know him a little. I've had to call on him a few times when he was in the Senate—and he was courteous and all that. But he's like most of those guys up there—nothing is for real. When I went up to see him he acted like he was on stage. It was all a stuffy act. There was no sincerity."

"Well, Hugh is what he is—he's one of the hybrids we breed and mutate in this town. He's a single-purpose being with all the unimportant, human characteristics clipped off and discarded so that the political organs will grow big and strong. I'd say that's one thing we learned from Nixon and forgot when we elected his successors, including Frankling: the damn selection system elects hybrids, but the Presidency requires more than that once the successful candidate gets in the chair." Valle spoke to himself aloud, as if he were alone in the room. "I'm not sure Frankling has enough of the other qualities to make a great President. That's about par for the course."

"That sounds like trouble. Is he another Nixon?"

"No. Not really. But he has things in common with all of them—any of them who have succeeded in the television era. He's had to subordinate—even hide—much of what he really thinks, in fact much of what he really *is*. A lot of the real stuff, like family and friends, gets tossed over the side. Sooner or later, such a man comes to see his family as a bunch of enemies with adverse interests, pulling and hauling on him for attention. Frankling has a brother who could be a real disaster for Hugh—he's a high roller with no sense. He'll be influence-peddling before they know it, and he'll get Hugh's ass in a sling. Hugh will have to fight him to avoid that. His own brother! That's what happens. We force our Presidents to do unnatural things."

"Is Frankling someone I could work for? I just can't read him."

"I'm not sure, Robin. I have a hunch he'd be all right; not great, but good enough. One thing for sure is that you'd be good for him. He lacks staff people who know this town, even though he's been here himself more than twenty years. The staff they're putting together looks awfully green to me. A lot of Ohio professors and junior executives, plus a few old hacks from the National Committee. Hugh dumped most of his Senate staff after the primaries, but that was no real loss. They were terrible. He's not a man who has attracted a good staff over the years. For some reason he kept Jimmy McLeavin for speech writing, and that's hard to understand; he was the worst of the bunch. McLeavin drinks too much and is mean as hell; I can't imagine how he's going to get along with all the new whiz kids. If you go over there you'll stand out like a gold tooth; you'll be the only one who knows how to get to Du Pont Circle without a street map. I think Frankling would give you a lot of responsibility."

"Even though I've been around a while, I know damn little about how things will work over there. Will I have a chance to run my own shop, do you think?"

"No. That's the price for all the glamour and glory, Robin. One man runs *everything* over there—regardless of who is President. Everything you do, you do for *him*. It's a true monolith; all the orders come from on high. And you either conform or leave. They damn well may prescribe your haircuts, how you dress, who you do or do not sleep with, and for sure they'll prescribe what you will and will not say in public. There never is room for 'healthy dissent' over there. There never has been, and Hugh Frankling isn't any different."

"Sounds a bit confining," Warren said with a wry smile.

"You'd better believe it will be. Frankling isn't noted for being 'one of the boys' either. There won't be many intimate, shirtsleeve sessions, just you and the President and one or two others. He's pretty stiff and humorless. But he's bright and an activist; he'll keep things hopping. And you'll see a lot of action, even if you are only twenty-two."

Warren grinned. "Thirty-six, thanks."

"Well, you still look like you're twenty-two. I think you could really help Frankling. He's pretty bottled up within himself. He was a pretty cold fish as a Senator, and he'll be unwilling to spend time with the interest groups and people from the outside. Maybe you can put some humanity and sensitivity into that operation, and perhaps even save him a lot of trouble. Speaking of which, Tom Foreman at Air World Transport has asked me to help on their Atlantic route expansion. I suspect we'll do better with the outgoing White House people than with the new crowd—what do you think? It'll take Frankling's new Counsel three months just to find the men's room, won't it?"

"True. It's Elwood Broderick now, and no one knows what his views are on air routes. At least old Charley Noss is a known quantity."

The door opened, stabbing bright light into the room. A young woman leaned into the room, one hand on the doorknob, the other pressed against the doorjamb. The backlight silhouetted her yellow slicker and rain hat.

"Jesus, men, are you going to sit here drinking the night away? Who's going to take me to dinner?"

"Maggie!" Jepson Valle smiled broadly. "You're making a puddle on my very expensive carpet. Take off all that wet gear!"

"Hi, beautiful New Yorker," said Warren. "Did you bring us all this bad weather for the weekend?"

"It starts at Philadelphia. We had a fairly sunny day up in New York for a change." Maggie Valle unsnapped her coat clasps and backed out of the room. She reappeared in brown slacks, green sweater and a man's white shirt, open at the collar, her dark hair tousled and damp. She buried her fingers in it and shook it lightly, head cocked to the side, as she walked to her father's chair. She bent low and kissed Jepson Valle's forehead, then joined Robin Warren on the couch, taking his left hand in her right. He kissed her hand lightly.

"We're nearly finished," Robin said. "I'll feed you shortly; where shall we go?"

"Some place close. It's pouring! Sans Souci?"

"Maybe. I'm getting some good advice about the White House job. Want to listen?"

"No. I'll go out and upchuck in a wastebasket while you're talking about that. I couldn't sit here and be quiet. Jep, are you encouraging him to quit you and go to work for that fat idiot? I can't believe it!"

"Thank you for that well-reasoned contribution to our search for truth," Jep Valle said ironically. "How about a drink to calm your prejudiced thought and jangled nerves? Doubtless this has been a hard day at the book factory."

"Scotch rocks, please. I've been reading a famous author's hopeless manuscript on the train. Maybe that's my problem. No, wait a minute; goddammit, Hugh Frankling is my problem, as usual! That doesn't change. He was a tired and useless Senator, and he will be a tired and even more useless President, and the idea of you going over there with him"—she jabbed a finger in Robin Warren's side—"gripes my ass."

Warren turned quickly and grabbed her finger in self-defense. Jep Valle's back was to them as he poured her drink. Maggie and Robin were close on the couch, and their face-to-face look became a firm, deep kiss. There was an easy, demanding attraction between them that had been a part of their relationship from the very beginning.

Jep Valle turned, took a step toward his daughter and stopped, smiling. "Scotch, anyone?"

Maggie pulled away from Robin Warren and reached for the tumbler her father offered. "I need that. It's warm, tiresome work saving the bright young men from their lust for power and fame."

"So I notice," Jep Valle said.

CHAPTER **5**   Maggie Valle first met Robin Warren at a wedding reception in the coastal foothills of California. She had been on a short vacation between New York jobs, soaking up sunshine by her father's Portola Valley swimming pool. At breakfast on Sunday morning he had suggested she go with him to a wedding.

"Do I know the couple?" she asked.

"I'm sure you don't. The young man is the son of a client," Jep Valle replied. "But it might be amusing to go to the reception; it's at Rossotti's."

"The beer place?"

"The bride and groom both went to Stanford and that's where they first met."

"Love at first sight over a stein of Tecate? Who said the youth of today isn't sentimental? Actually, I thought I'd just stretch out by the pool and finish that awful book I've been reading."

"We haven't done much together since you came here, my dear," Valle said. "I wish you'd come. We can go to dinner after." She looked up at her father quizzically. "Since when do you . . . ? Well, OK. Sure; that would be nice."

Heads turned as she moved easily among the tables under the oaks at Rossotti's. Her youth and tan were shown to advantage in a sleeveless white linen dress. She had no interest in the men at the party who were looking at her—Dan Cooper was already one man too many.

Maggie had come to California to get away from Dan Cooper, but had, in fact, spent most of the days sitting by the pool trying to figure out what to do about him. She couldn't tolerate indefinite relationships. Dan had begun as a support and a lover. Although he was still her lover he was now also her chronic, emotional dependent. And he was married—eternally married, to a graying stout woman about his own age. He was a pessimistic and self-pitying man who took constant reassurance as the desert takes rain. Recently, when Maggie did not placate his insecurities, Cooper became bitter and unpleasant. Her refusal to renounce whatever she held important became a symbol to him that she didn't love him. One of the reasons she had left her job at Geowagen and Company was to escape Cooper, who was one of their novelists. There was no future with him, she now knew.

Jep Valle brought her a stein of beer and nodded toward a tall man at a far table.

"Will you be OK for a while?" he asked. "That's a fellow I've been trying to reach for a week."

"Sure. Go get him. I'll just do fine." She leaned back against a redwood fence and drank. She felt comfortably detached from the people around her; as the hops effectively reached the top of her head, lifting weight lightly from her eyes and ears, she closed her eyelids to savor the sun's warmth. In a moment some movement of

63

shadow made her open her eyes. A young man was standing very close to her, so close their noses nearly touched. He had reddish-blond hair and bright blue-green eyes. His features and body made her think of the Swedish skiers she had known. But this one was warm behind the eyes.

Now, she thought to herself, *he* is a beautiful animal. At once she realized she had spoken some of her thought: "Beautiful."

"Just what I was thinking," he said. He was dressed in a morning coat, ascot and wing collar. "My name is Robin and you are Miss Valle," he said.

"Pretty good research," she murmured.

"Would you rather have champagne?"

"As a matter of fact, I would." She smiled.

"Let's go inside. It can be arranged."

She felt his hand, light on her back. She led him into the crowded tavern and stopped, unable to see in the dimness.

"There's a table over here in the corner." He took her hand. "Sit and I'll go get the wine."

He returned with an open, wet bottle and two glasses. "You are Margaret?"

"Maggie."

"Live around here?"

"No. New York. I'm an editor for a publishing house."

"I'm a lawyer, in San Francisco."

"Are you in the wedding?" She nodded at his outfit.

"My wife is. No one seemed to be sure what I should wear, so they rented me this. It's truly hot."

"You look nice. Are you a skier?" she asked. She realized that the question went a little beyond innocuous small talk; it displayed her more than slight interest in him. She didn't care. The sun and the beer and the elegantly dressed people in that raunchy setting all relieved her of responsibility. It was total unreality. She wasn't flirting with another married man. They were only trouble and dead ends. This gorgeous young man was a sort of a daydream, a lovely, amusing Sunday imagination.

"Football."

"What?"

"I played football. The coach wouldn't let us ski."

"Stanford?"

He nodded. "How long are you going to be here?"

"Three more days." She held up her glass for more champagne.

"What are you doing tomorrow?" he asked.

"Tomorrow I've got to do some shopping."

"Will you come up to the City? I'd like to meet you for a drink."

"What about . . . ?"

"The matron of honor? We're sort of legally unseparated at the moment. She could care less." He looked at Maggie intently. "Please come."

Tomorrow. A real place, a real time. That kind of detail could turn him into a real man, married, and a thing of trouble. She smiled; it was all without meaning. She would never go. But it was amusing to think about a new romance. And he was so damned attractive. Maybe. All unreal, but just maybe. She would be on the Coast only another three days. Why not? Just for the fun and to feel that new beginning sensation again, after so long, instead of the deadly attrition of the end game she was playing with Dan. "Maybe," she said.

Next day she dressed and went from Jep Valle's home to San Francisco on the train as though she were merely going shopping. There was no anguish of pro and con. She simply went.

Robin and Maggie had a drink at the Fairmont, then a good lamb dinner at the Bistro with much talk about his hollow marriage and her ruined affair. He had kissed her lightly in the cab en route to dinner, and they kissed each other more than lightly in a parking garage, and again on Skyline Drive and finally in Jep Valle's driveway. She didn't see him again before she left for New York, but they talked on the phone six times.

She was improvidently infatuated, she told herself as she flew east. She had no need for Robin Warren. He had been beautiful and great fun and a magnificent necker, but now there had to be a return to reality and New York and Daniel Baresch Cooper with his marriage and all his doubts and troubles, and her new job. No time for California musical comedy; it was a time for sanity, celibacy and cool reason.

She tried to discourage Robin Warren on the telephone the next day when he called from San Francisco. The same day she resolved to stop seeing Dan Cooper. Then, two weeks later, Robin's firm sent him to New York on business and he unexpectedly knocked on her apartment door on a cold Tuesday evening around seven.

She was lonely, he was charming, and she knew she had continued to want him in a physical way since San Francisco. Now she wanted him in other ways, too, that she didn't have the time or the courage to explain to herself.

Dan Cooper had refused to make it easy—she had told him she wanted to break it off and, in his usual style, he had nodded sadly. But he contrived to hold her emotionally entwined; he called often, wrote notes, knocked on her door late at night, waited for her outside her building after work to coerce impromptu dinner dates. Maggie Valle did not flatly and finally turn him away; she would not be cruel yet but, intellectually, she knew it must quickly end.

Suddenly there was Robin Warren at the door of her apartment and, at once, Dan Cooper was gone. She felt in all her parts the warmth of the California sun from that strange wedding Sunday.

That night she took Robin Warren to bed. She had begun to suspect that she was somehow stronger than Robin but she did not want to know that. She rejected the thought that he might become another dependent married man. He was a patient and giving lover; the contours of his body excited her in new ways as she touched him. No one had ever kissed her as he did. She wanted him for what happened between them physically. The sensation of his upper arms against hers and the smell of him and the feel of his body were sufficient unto the moment.

Within a month Robin Warren had taken a job with Jepson Valle's law firm. Valle favorably remembered him from their brief introduction at that nuptial beer bust at Rossotti's, and that had helped a little. If Jepson Valle was also aware of Robin's interest in his daughter he didn't hint it. Robin Warren's professional credentials were good, his reasons for leaving the Butler firm in San Francisco were plausible and Jep Valle liked him.

Robin called from California one night after Maggie had gone to bed.

"You woke me up," she complained.

"I don't think you'll mind."

"Wrong. I mind a lot. I have an early day tomorrow. What time is it, for Christ's sake?"

"It's nine here—twelve there. I have some news."

"Oh? Are you coming to New York?"

"No, Washington."

"Can you come up to New York while you're back?"

"Sure."

"When are you coming? God, I'm still asleep!"

"I should be there in two weeks. Assuming I can get everything settled with Sandy by then."

"What settled?"

"Property, house, cars, that sort of thing."

"What's all that? Divorce?"

"Right. I told Sandy tonight. I have a new job too. In D.C."

"How did she take it? Are you going with the government? Shit! I'm wide awake now! How did all this happen at once?"

"I've been waiting until I knew about the job. Sandy took it OK. She knew it was coming, I'm sure. Some tears, but I think it was wounded pride rather than sorrow. She hates to admit we've got a busted marriage. In our neighborhood it still isn't respectable."

"So you're moving to Washington! Damn; why not New York?" She sat up.

"I got a job with a very good firm in Washington that I couldn't pass up. Maybe you've heard of it."

"What do I know about law firms in Washington? Even when I'm awake I don't know any."

"This one is Jepson Valle, Gerber and Rogers."

"Jep's firm? You're going to work for Jep? What the hell? Oh, Robin, my love, I don't think I like that at all! That's a horrible business he's in; corrupt and corrupting! You're too good for that!"

"Look, Maggie, don't say anything more now. The phone is a bad thing for serious talk. I think your dad is good. And the work is what I want, where the action is. Please keep an open mind."

"OK," she said. She sank back into the pillows, relaxing. "Who am I to criticize, anyway? It's your life, not mine. But I would have guessed you were cut out to do more worthwhile things. You're so goddamned able; you could do anything."

"I want you to approve, Maggie. It's important. I really trust your judgment. Wait until I get there and we'll talk about it."

"Sure, Bird. Sure."

But they didn't speak of her misgivings when they were together again. Two weeks after Robin Warren arrived in Washington Maggie's persistent and melancholy lover, Dan Cooper, stepped in front of a New York taxicab and was killed.

The police found Maggie's name on a morose note he had written her and she was invited to come talk to a detective. When she arrived at the precinct station she found herself in the middle of a confused and angry scene with Cooper's wife. Maggie was, at once, shocked, repelled and guilty. She rushed from the police station, crying bitterly, flagged a cab and went straight to Pennsylvania Station. She needed to be in Washington. Jep and Robin were in Washington.

Three hours later she sat in a phone booth in Union Station in the capital, red-eyed, waiting for a secretary to find Robin. At last he came on the phone.

"Bird? Maggie."

"Hi, babe," he said. "What's the matter? Are you sick? You sound terrible."

"I've been crying. Dan Cooper was killed by a cab this morning." She began to weep again. "I'm here."

"Where?"

"Washington. I want to hide out at Jep's for a while."

68

"He's gone to Texas and California. For a week. Do you have a key?"

"I can get in, but I need to see you. Can you come over?"

"In an hour. OK?"

"Make it soon, Robin. I'm in tough shape. I'll be in Jep's part of the apartment. You know?"

"I'll be there, babe. Take it easy."

Jep Valle's apartment was on the top floor of the old Mayflower Hotel; it was two suites, joined and decorated to his specifications nearly two years before. He used it as living quarters, but a part of it also served as a Washington *pied-à-terre* for clients, friends, stewardesses and his daughters and son-in-law. It seemed that everyone had keys to the three rooms which served as Valle's guest quarters.

As it was designed, Valle's private apartment was not affected by the constant flow of out-of-town users through the adjoining rooms.

Robin arrived at the Valle apartment about 5 P.M. Maggie had not been able to eat the soup and sandwich she'd ordered. But the spasmodic crying had stopped; it was followed by a feeling which she imagined to be the emotional reaction of sole survivors of airplane crashes and other disasters in which friends had been killed. Loss, relief, guilt, uncertainty, trauma and secret, undeserved pride at having escaped the same fate, all combined. The resulting, vectored emotional force was inexplicable, but easily identified: she was horny. She wanted Robin in the most elemental of ways, strongly and urgently. She couldn't wait. She wanted him naked and hot and with that odor which was uniquely Robin at stud.

Maggie realized that Robin expected to find a bereft mourner, not a nymphomaniac. As she walked toward the door to let him in she wondered if other disaster survivors had passionate reactions. There might be a book idea in that. The eternal editor!

"Hi."

"Are you all right?"

"Sure. But I really need to be with you just now. I want to tell you about it."

"Was it an accident?"

"Pure accident. But his wife was at the police station and she wanted them to hot-brand a scarlet 'A' on my forehead. There was a lot of screaming and swearing. I just had to run away from New York."

He put his arm over her shoulder and drew her to him. "You seem pretty calm now."

"My terror has been replaced by the most extraordinary need to be had by you, very long and very hard and very, very soon. Is that like necrophilia or some other grisly and macabre practice? I can't help it."

"No, that seems to me to be merely an absolutely irresistible invitation."

They had not been together for weeks. Their coupling this time was urgent and almost entirely physical, without the gentle preparation Robin had offered her before. She demanded that he take her at once, urged his vigor and welcomed the immediacy of the pain he gave her. Then suddenly she thought of Dan—some movement of Robin's shoulder was Dan's—and at once her passion collapsed like a matchstick castle and she began to sob uncontrollably. He withdrew from her, turned her on her side and held her tightly to him, her forehead in the hollow of his neck. His left hand caressed her upper arm in a gentle rhythm.

"Look, it's all right. Just relax. We're together and it's warm and safe and quiet and you're just fine."

"Dan's note said that he sensed that I loved someone else. It was almost like a suicide note. But the police said the taxi ran the light. So he didn't kill himself on account of me. I know that. So why do I feel so goddamned guilty? Why can't I stop all this crying?"

"No reason. You have nothing to feel guilty about."

"Do you feel guilty, Robin? About leaving your wife?" She moved her head back to look at his face.

"I suppose in one way I do. But that's my upbringing, I guess."

70

Maggie wiped her eyes on the end of one of the pillowcases and moved back against Robin's body. "I've got to get over this. I cried all the way down here on the train like an idiot. I don't do that kind of thing. I haven't cried like that since the Olympic trials."

"It's all right. It doesn't matter. Everyone cries. It's good to know you're not as tough as you act."

"Far from it. If I had been tough I'd have cut the cord to Dan long ago. But I couldn't; he seemed so damn helpless. I guess I always felt that I was to blame for his anguish. He managed to unload all that guilt on me, and I couldn't do anything but carry it around. Robin, what makes human beings such tyrants?"

"Our own inadequacies. You asked if I feel guilty about leaving Sandy. I do. She has a lot of needs. For all the social standing and dough and beauty, she is a very insecure young lady, and I know my leaving has aggravated her problems. I feel badly about that. But I finally saw that I had lived for years without a serious thought of what was best for me—it's selfish and violates the Boy Scout oath to leave her, but I can't help it. It's what I have to do. For me, for a change."

"You're assuming the ultimate in responsibilities, Warren. You're going to run your own life. What are you going to do with it? Be a lobbyist and earn a lot of money and fuck stewardesses like your new leader, my father?"

"Speaking of tyrants, how come *you* always know just what I should and shouldn't do?"

"I don't . . ."

"Shut up, then. I probably won't do it all very well, Maggie. I don't start out with a very well articulated set of values, you know. I never needed values—people were always nice enough to impose theirs on me. So I'll be feeling my way along." He rolled over on top of her. "You feel good. Do you want to make love, eat, talk or none of the above?"

"God, you know what? I'm starving! Let's go over to Duke's and then come back here. I want a dill pickle! And no cracks."

He rolled off her and stood beside the bed. "Come on,

beautiful. I won't worry about the pickles unless you order them à la mode."

The high-ceilinged dining room, decorated with pictures of athletes in action, bright mural montage and photographs of the famous and forgotten, was serviced by ancient waiters each of whom moved about with the confidence of an owner's brother-in-law. The genial host found a sheltered corner table for Maggie and Robin, handed them oversize menus and flagged a short Popeye in a black jacket and long white wraparound apron. As they ordered drinks Robin looked about the room. Four Catholic priests boisterously occupied a center table in the crowded main dining room, closely attended by Duke, the portly owner.

"What are you thinking?" Maggie asked.

"Goddamn it, Maggie. That's what I was talking about," said Robin levelly.

"I don't understand."

" 'Penny for your thoughts' is the way Sandy says it, but it amounts to the same thing. It's a part of what we were talking about before, Maggie, my friend, and I'm probably too touchy about it. But that question about a person's thoughts seems to me to be a gross trespass, and I can't handle it. I'm sorry—"

"No, you're right. It is. I'm the one who should be sorry. I'll try not to do that again. I was trying to get into the subject of your job with Jep, and I blew it. Can we talk about that?"

"Sure. But what's to say? You think it's a parasitic social role and you wish I'd go to work for Common Cause or the Red Cross, I guess. I don't feel that way. Does that cover it?"

"How do you feel? Why do you want to be a lobbyist?"

"Well, first of all, I'm a lawyer. 'Lobbyist' is some kind of pejorative with you and it'll just get in our way if you keep calling me that. I represent clients. But that's beside the point. Look, I was fine at the Butler firm in the city. In ten years I'd have been a full junior partner the way things were going. But I wasn't in the parade. You know? It was as if I was on the sidewalk watching all the time. People like your dad were in the action, going somewhere, while I just stood there. For the last couple of years I've felt that way—left out and shut in; some of the others were out there doing things, and I wasn't. Finally I've stepped off the curb and joined them."

"A limelight junky, eh?"

"No, it isn't the publicity I need, really. It's the action."

"There's plenty of action in the public-interest groups too. Why hook up with the likes of Jep Valle?"

"Partly because he's related to you, obviously. But also because my sympathies lie in that direction. Let's face it: I'm a child of the establishment. I'm not sure I could keep a straight face working with the PIGS."

She leaned forward intently. "Robin, I don't know everything that Jep is involved in; maybe some of it is worthwhile—but it just seems to me that most of it borders on the crooked. It's influence-peddling, using massive money and power to influence the legislative process, and I don't like it."

Robin shook his head. "I've only been there a couple of weeks, but I haven't been asked to do anything even remotely unethical. The clients we have need help—in fact, everyone with federal problems needs help these days. Things in this town are just too complex for the average citizen or company to find their way anymore. Who should help them?"

"OK, someone has to help them. Some lawyer has to defend ax murderers, too. But why you and Jep? Why not someone I don't like?"

"Look—do you want me to quit Jep? Is that what this is all about?"

"I can't answer that, Bird. There is no yes or no to that. Talk about tyranny! You can't live with *any* answer I might give to that question and neither can I. What if I said yes? Or no? Take it back, darling!"

"All right, I never asked it."

The old waiter bustled around their table moving off some of the plates, then glanced at Maggie's somber face and scuttled away. She put her hand on top of Robin's.

"Robin, let me say my fears. This isn't meant to even hint that I want you to do any certain thing. But I'm afraid and I have to tell you."

"Maggie—"

"Please. I have to. Then you can get up and walk away if you want to. But I have to, because I care about you."

"OK."

"You shouldn't sell liquor to an Indian, you know, because they are supposedly more susceptible to it than most people. There are some types of Americans who have the same problem with this town—it's an intoxicant that they just can't resist, and once they're here they can't handle it. They go out of control."

"That's me, eh?"

"I'm afraid for you, Bird. All that talk about the passing parade scares me. You are just coming out of your nice, sheltered San Francisco cocoon into the big, fast, exciting world of Jep Valle and the shakers and movers, and I'm scared for what may happen to you."

"Don't be afraid, Mag. I'm a big boy and fairly bright."

"OK. You're all grown up? Then why don't you have the guts to get into something that will challenge you? You can do Jep's work with one hand tied behind you and in your sleep—you're charming and ten times smarter than your victims in the Congress. But the stuff he'll have you doing won't require you to use your soul and your moral being and your sensibilities. How are those muscles going to develop?"

"The Boy Scouts took care of my character, Margaret. Please, for God's sake, stop trying to save my soul."

"OK, Robin Bird. That's the end of the sermon; I'm through with your soul for tonight." She turned his hand over and lightly raked its palm with her nails. "Let's eat fast and go back to the hotel. I'm *not* through with your body."

CHAPTER **6**   "Senator, it's very good of you to see me,"
Robin Warren said.

The inner office to which he'd been taken by the Senator's
administrative assistant was cluttered with old leather furniture,
little tables, a floor lamp, a worn Oriental rug over the government
carpet; there was even an atmosphere of seedy decline about the
large wooden desk. A little American flag stood at one corner,
faded nearly white. Some of the piled papers obviously had not
been moved for months, perhaps years.

Behind Senator Harley Oates was a tall bookcase. Most
Senators preferred to place their desks in front of the single
window these Senate offices provided, especially if there was a
view of the Capitol dome. But Harley Oates's desk was in front of
rows and rows of books about the United States Constitution.
They made a superb backdrop for photographs, and they enhanced his reputation as a legal scholar and a Constitutional
expert. And they were sometimes useful to the men on Harley
Oates's staff whose responsibility it was to write his speeches and
prepare his learned remarks upon the subject of the greatest
governmental charter in the history of the world. Thirty years
earlier, as a circuit judge in Arkansas, Harley Oates had some
nodding acquaintance with the Constitution, so the phrases "due
process of law," "search and seizure" and "full faith and credit"
were not foreign to him. But years in the Senate had dulled his
curiosity and atrophied his powers of analysis. He had become
wholly dependent upon others to provide the grist for his mill.
Harley Oates was still deemed to be the undisputed Constitutional

authority in the Senate. The fact was, however, that his staff was quite efficient and the competition was almost negligible.

"Bill says you want to educate me about log exports, Mr. Warren," Oates said.

Robin Warren was listening closely to the Senator's accent. Jep Valle said that Oates's deep Southern drawl was more for homespun publicity and television display than a matter of philological necessity. It was not much in evidence this December day, he noted.

"Senator, you have S. 1034 coming up for markup in the Import-Export Subcommittee tomorrow."

Oates nodded. "Who you representin', Mr. Warren?"

"I work for Senator Valle, as you know. Georgia-Pacific and Weyerhaeuser are clients of his. They would like to have your help on two things, Senator, which do affect jobs in Arkansas."

"We're all interested in that, of course, eh, Bill?" Oates winked at his assistant.

"We sure are, Mr. Chairman."

"S. 1034 would restrict any export of Arkansas pine logs beyond the quantity shipped in the base year—1979. That was a low-volume year, as you'll recall, Mr. Chairman."

"You people prefer a different year?"

"Yes sir: 1978. It's a difference of 138 percent."

"That much," Oates said. "What else?"

"The bill permits Treasury to change the allowable export volumes without prior notice. Our cutting is based largely on advance sales contracts. We could be blocked after we'd cut and moved the logs dockside."

"How much advance warnin' do you think you're entitled to?"

"One hundred and eighty days minimum."

Oates folded his hands on the desk in front of him, his lips quivering slightly. "I'm delighted that your clients are concerned about Arkansas jobs, Mr. Warren. Delighted. Because your Georgia-Pacific client closed its mill at Daltonville last year and put a great many of my constituents out of work." He picked up a slip of paper and glanced at it. "Four hundred and nineteen out of work, to be exact. That was a very unfortunate thing for G-P to do. It made difficulties for all of us."

Robin Warren nodded. "The price of pine just went to hell, as you know, Mr. Chairman."

Oates's voice rose perceptibly. "Well, how's the price of pine now, Mr. Warren? It's up, isn't it?"

"Yes, sir."

"Yes, it is. About seventeen percent. Is that mill going to open soon?"

"It can be arranged."

"Then I think it should be. I'd like to announce it from here. When can we do that?"

"I'll work out a date with your staff, Mr. Chairman."

Oates nodded once. "You do that, Mr. Warren."

"Can my clients count on your help in the markup, Mr. Chairman? On those two points?"

"That mill at Daltonville means a lot to my state, Mr. Warren. We'll just work a swap; how's that?"

Warren stood. "That's agreed, Mr. Chairman. I'll see you at the markup tomorrow."

"Fine. Fine. You do that. Bill will show you the way out. Good day."

Warren briefly considered making one more call, looked at his watch and decided against it. He'd have to ask Jep Valle to work out this Daltonville mill swap with the client as soon as possible. He hailed a cab at the foot of the House Office Building steps and returned to the office.

CHAPTER **7**   Other than the rare assassination, virtually no news, good or bad, falls upon the city of Washington with unexpected suddenness. Rather, it approaches gradually in the manner of a distant summer storm, preceded by barely perceptible changes in temperature and humidity, then faint and distant rumbles and an alteration of light. Finally the first sprinkles begin, and all at once it is there.

Robin Warren knew the White House job was his when Jep Valle came into his office, smiling in faint amusement.

"I just had a call from Melissa Mordant at the *Star-Post*," Valle said. "She wanted to know all about you. She evidently thinks you're about to become newsworthy."

"It's a good sign when they call like that, right?"

"I'd say so. What will you say when the press starts to call you here?"

"I don't know. What should I say?"

"Well, you could tell the truth: you are consumed with ambition and want the job so bad you can taste it."

"Oh, sure. Thanks for the great advice. How about just saying I know I'm being considered but any word would have to come from the White House?"

"Not very original."

"No, but it's safe. I don't want to blow my chances now."

"Have you heard from Hale or anyone?"

"No."

"Are you prepared to demand the perks?"

"Which ones?"

"The staff you want? Which office. A car and mess privileges on the A list, not the B list. And, most important, access to Frankling?"

"How much bargaining strength do you think I have?"

"Some, but not as much as you'd like, I'm sure. You'll probably have to trade off some of those things. But access is the one to hold out for. That is the coin of the realm over there, under any President."

The telephone rang as they talked. Warren listened, grimaced and put his hand over the mouthpiece. "The White House switchboard. David Hale." He grinned.

"Yes, Mr. Hale. Sure. No, I haven't. Really? That's truly good news. Yes, I certainly could. Three? I'll be there. Where do I . . . ? OK. The top floor. Fine. No, I'm just a block away. Fine. See you at three. Goodbye." He looked up at Valle. "I guess I'm hired. Hale wants to see me at three. Hot damn!"

Valle extended his hand. "Congratulations, Robin. I'm very happy for you."

"I know I have you to thank for this, Jep. I'm really grateful. I think I'd like to call Maggie and tell her."

"Sure. Drop by after you've seen Hale. I'd like to hear how it went."

Robin Warren was a few minutes early at the Frankling transition office. A federal policeman found his name on an appointments list and made a telephone call. Almost immediately a stout young woman appeared to escort him, and as they walked along a bare corridor she advised him loftily that she was Mr. Hale's personal secretary. Robin surmised that she was from Ohio and efficient.

He had expected to find frantic bustle and confusion in these precincts; there were only thirty-odd days left to complete the transition. But instead of panic there was the calm usually associated with the offices of prosperous investment counselors.

"Where are all the people?" he asked the secretary as she officiously led the way down the hallway.

"Most of them are in Cleveland. That's where the President-elect and Mr. Hale spend most of their time. That's where our main office is. The President-elect actually won't come here until January—next month—for the inauguration."

She brought him to a carpeted secretarial area bounded by the pale movable metal walls favored by efficiency experts of the GSA. A photograph of Hugh Frankling seated by an American flag was the only decoration. Hale's secretary knocked once and opened a door at one side. "Come in, Mr. Warren," she said, leading him into the President-elect's large office. Robin guessed she disapproved of him for some reason.

David Hale was standing by the window, looking down on the White House; he was in shirtsleeves, alone in the room. He looked at Robin Warren and gestured. "Welcome, Robin Warren. Come over here and look at this view. Did you know that in Abraham Lincoln's day there wasn't a fence there? People could just walk right up to the front door. Old Abe strolled around that area"—he pointed—"as free as you please, even with the Civil War on. He had an office in the building that used to be next door. The original War Department has been torn down and replaced. But Lincoln walked back and forth from the house to the office every day, and mingled with the job seekers and ordinary people over there as he went. We've really lost all that over the years, haven't we?"

It was an odd, stilted speech, Robin thought, and it rankled him to be lectured to. He was tempted to reply with sarcasm, but he knew it was time to just play it cool. "Yes, I guess we have lost all that," he said.

"So that's where you come in, isn't it? We need someone who's in touch with the folks, to be the President's eyes and ears on the outside, right?"

"And to be a lightning rod if there's trouble, so I get blasted and the President doesn't. That's the job, too, as I understand it." Robin smiled.

"Well, not entirely," Hale said, gesturing toward a leather chair as he settled behind the massive desk. "We also need a man explaining the President's positions to interest groups and community leaders. Think you can do that?"

"Sure. I'm sure I can."

"Why do you want to work for the President-elect?" Hale asked laconically.

This whole thing, Robin realized, must be Hale's standard, prepared-in-advance little interview with new staff people. It's probably all written out in a staff briefing paper for him.

"Oh, a great many reasons, I guess," Robin replied. It was like the first day of school. "For one thing, I'm a Republican and always have been. And I'm drawn by the challenge of working for a President. It's the fastest track there is, I'm sure."

"Well, Robin, that's not really what I asked you, is it? You haven't mentioned Hugh Frankling. I asked you why you wanted to work for *him?*"

"Mr. Hale—"

"Call me David."

"Sure, David. I can't say that I've been a big Frankling loyalist, but he's the President and I do respect and admire what I've seen of him. I called on him several times when he was in the Senate. I think I know him, a little. I'll have no trouble giving him personal loyalty, I assure you, if that's what you're getting at."

"That's precisely it. You'll have a close personal relationship to him in this job. That's why your loyalty must be absolute."

"Understood."

"All right. Then let's talk details. First, money. Forty-seven thousand."

"That's really less important than some of the other things."

"Such as what?"

"Such as access."

"Access is through me."

Robin shook his head. "In order to do you and the President any good with people outside, like Perkovich at the AFL-CIO for example, they have to know that I have real access to the President. If I don't they'll know it, and they'll gravitate to someone who does."

"Robin, I'm sure every new President operates differently and every new White House staff reflects the personal characteristics of the man it's working for. Hugh Frankling wants to deal with the staff through me on routine matters. That's just the way he is. When you need to see him I'll arrange it for you, I assure you. You'll get in."

"Well . . ."

"Don't confuse actuality with appearance. Just like Nixon and Ford and Carter, we'll be telling all the world that the President has an open-door policy for the Cabinet and staff—people coming and going all the time. The hub of the wheel. But you and I know that the place just can't work like that. Some one person has to guarantee him free time to read and think and nap and eat without a lot of well-meaning Tom, Dick and Harrys running in and out whenever they think they have a problem. So I'll be the traffic cop; access is through me."

"Not to be unreasonably withheld, as the lawyers say?"

"Of course. If there are any rumors to the effect that you aren't in close to the President, we can stage some reassuring events. You can be the one at Camp David with him, or on the boat, like Nixon used to do, to bolster your image."

"How about staff? I'll need quite a bit of help to cover all the bases."

"Well, here again, everyone always campaigns on the promise that he'll cut the White House staff, and we promised all that, too, as you know. How many did Johnny Johnson have for that office in the last administration?" Hale flipped open a red notebook and turned to the third tab.

"Was it eleven staff and fifteen clerical?" Robin asked.

"Eleven and fourteen," Hale replied. "Can you get along with ten and thirteen?"

"I doubt it."

"Well, you'd better begin at that level, anyway. We'll be putting out a lot of press releases about the great economies, staff reductions and reforms we're making, right at the beginning. So you'll have to be lean for a while. I'm sure we can expand it after the PR effort has had its effect. Let's figure on ten and thirteen. You pick them, subject to the President's final OK."

82

"How about car and mess arrangements?"

"Oh, shit, Warren. I was hoping you were different."

"Afraid not." Robin grinned.

Hale flipped in his notebook to the back tab. "I have you on the B list; that's full car privileges during—"

"I know what it is," Robin said. "You'll never convince the city of Washington that I'm the man they should talk to if I'm on the B list. I've been one of them here, and I know. There's no sense in my taking the job and going through the motions if there's no chance for results. I'm sorry."

"You mean unless I send a car for you every morning you won't take the job, right?" Hale was exasperated.

"I mean this town deals in symbols. The A and B lists are largely symbolic. They tell the tribe who the chiefs are and who the Indians are. If I'm only an Indian I won't be able to do the job, so I shouldn't take it. Beyond that, my deputy has to have A mess privileges so he can entertain at lunch. It's just essential."

Hale rose and walked to the window. "I just don't believe what I'm hearing, Robin. Oh, it's not just you; I've had this same routine from others. Look at my problem. We have a very small dining room, a limited number of cars and a lot of press focus on who gets what. I just can't make it all stretch. I suppose you have to have your office in the West Wing, too?"

"David, I realize all of your problems. But there are only a few of us who are going to be dealing with the Washington establishment here—mostly the Congressional liaison people and the staff in my office. We've got to be credible. When I say, 'The President wants . . . ,' either it will be believed or it won't. That will depend almost entirely on external appearances. You'll have to trust me on this; I know."

"And us hicks from Ohio—we don't know, right?"

"This is a strange town, David, full of folklore and arcane customs. Don't take my word for it; ask some of the real old hands here."

"I have. They are worse than you are. OK, how about this: you and your staff will be in the Old Executive Office Building over there." He hooked his thumb. "You will be on the A list for car and mess. Your deputy will be on the A mess list, but he'll be a B for all other purposes. That's the best I can do."

By the time they'd achieved an accord and satisfaction, and Warren had handed Hale a short typewritten staff recruiting list he'd prepared, a tentative but mutual liking had developed between the two young men. Robin Warren saw in Hale a person with enviable self-control. He obviously fired his shots only for effect, without wasted words or motion, and with a clear idea of his objectives. Hale was a trifle stiff and unreal; but they could get along. It would be all right. Hale found Robin much more mature and self-confident than he had expected. His résumé had been good, but it had not depicted his self-assurance. Nor his physical attractiveness.

Hale had a weakness, one he recognized in himself at times—a proclivity to give more than a little weight to the physical aspects of a person in making a decision. He would sooner buy from a good-looking salesperson than from an ugly one. He found Robin acceptable, even likable, in large part because of his appearance and obvious style. The portly young secretary outside his door had not been his choice; she was the efficient sister of a friend of the President-elect. David Hale found it most difficult to work with her. He refused to dwell on the reason, but he knew that it was because of her ugly face and body. Irrational. Unfair. But in January, when he moved over into the West Wing of the White House, she would be replaced. He was not looking forward to telling her. He had already picked her successor, an attractive ash-blond widow who had been secretary to one of the senior staff in the outgoing administration. The new woman knew her way around over there, and she would be easier to work with. And she looked better.

Robin Warren and Maggie Valle celebrated his new job at La Niçoise. After the French proprietor had greeted Maggie with the ritual kiss, he turned his attention to the new White House man with unashamed passion. It was evident that Robin's potential for power had been instantly known to this social arbiter; the table he had reserved for them was the best in the room.

After dinner, Robin returned Maggie to her father's Mayflower apartment. But something was wrong with their lovemaking that evening. He had been aggressive and intense, and she had intended that it be celebratory and fun. But as he lay, spent, a leg across her body, she heard herself say, "Feeling better?"

"You feel good—what do you mean?"

"Is your male ego all back in shape?"

"Jesus, Mag, let's not have that now."

She propped up on one elbow and looked at his face. "You know your problem, Robin?"

"No, but I'm sure you'll tell me."

"Well, if I didn't, who would?"

"God, wouldn't that be terrible, if no one told me what's wrong with me tonight?"

"Yes it would. You know why? Because you need deflating, about every hour on the hour. Otherwise your head would get bigger and bigger until it exploded. You are the best man I know, darling, and I wouldn't like that to happen to you. You are damn good: you're smart and you have a gorgeous animal face. Erik the Red probably looked a lot like you. You have elegant arms, you know, and I like your prick more than is decent. You are so damn alive! But you are so vulnerable that at times I weep in fear for you." She came off her elbow to rest her cheek on his chest, her arm around his neck. He adjusted to fit their bodies. "Sweetheart," she continued, her voice lower and less urgent, "I'm afraid for you because I can see that you are about to like and believe all the sycophantic bullshit that this town is going to dish up for you. You are going to think that those headwaiters and lobbyists love you because you're a great man. You're a wonderful person, I know that, but you won't be if you believe them. That's paradoxical, isn't it?"

"Hmmm?"

She raised her head to look in his face. "You son of a bitch, you aren't even listening to me, are you?"

"Sure."

"What did I say?"

"You said you liked my prick."

"Yeah, but I didn't like the way you ate up all that flattery that fellow Clark gave you in the restaurant. Why didn't you tell him to get lost?"

"He's one of my new customers, Maggie. He represents a big association."

"What a jerk—all belly and toothy smiles. He made your dinner get cold."

"The rigors of the job, you know. Hey, I forgot to tell you. We get all kinds of inaugural tickets; the fancy balls and all that. You'd better get a fancy dress." He stroked her back lazily.

"Crap. Take someone else, Bird. I've been to one of those, and you couldn't pay me to go through all of that again."

"Really? The fancy balls and parade and everything? It should be pretty unique and exciting. I even get a military aide to look after us. He whistles for our car and holds your coat and wipes off your chair at the parade."

"I know. Jep had all that when he was in the Senate. But as much as you try to glamorize it, it's still horrible, sweaty and boring. Don't count on me, baby. I'm going to wash my hair and go to bed with a bad book that night."

"I hope you'll change your mind."

"I won't. I had a *déjà vu* when that clod Clark came over to the table tonight. When Jep was in the Senate that happened to us all the time. Did you notice how he reacted to me, darling?"

"No, did he breathe down your cleavage?"

"God, no. Just the opposite. You're the one to be seduced now, not me. I have a theory about that. I think a lot of political marriages break up just because of the way that slob treated us. You were the bitch in heat and I was invisible. The press does it, too. They come up to a political couple and make love to the man and act like the wife is not even there. A lot of women can't take that. It's not easy to be a graceful nonentity." Suddenly she asked,

"Who do you intend to hire to work with women's-rights groups? You're not going to have a woman for that job, right?"

"I don't know."

"I thought so."

"Look, Maggie, that's going to be up to Frankling. That comes under the heading of political policy."

"And what about your role? Are you going over there to make the country better, or just to be his errand boy?"

"Oh, hey—" He shook his head helplessly.

"No, seriously, Bird. Look. There are two ways of thinking about a White House job like yours. One is that you are just a mechanic, doing whatever Frankling and Hale tell you to do. If you do as you're told and never say no to anything they come up with, then at the end of the term you can join the board of the Kennedy Center or win the Medal of Freedom."

"And the other way is to be a freethinker and raise hell, right?"

"The other way is to *really* serve the country and, incidentally, the President, by speaking out on the important issues, hiring and protecting bright, effective and controversial people for your staff, and always doing what you believe is right, regardless."

"And get fired after two weeks."

"That's not such a bad thing if it happens for the right reasons."

"But I'm not the President. Hugh Frankling was elected, not me. He's the one who is going to set the policy and make the decisions. You can't have a White House staff with ten guys, each making up his own mind how things ought to be. It's a one-man outfit. There is no room for a freethinker over at 1600."

"Well, there should be," she said. She had moved away from him, bristling. "Maybe that's what's wrong with the damn country. And maybe that's also what's wrong with Hugh Frankling. If he were the kind of man that you should work for, he would want you to tell him when he's wrong. He'd want fresh viewpoints and dissent and ferment. But he's not. He wants you to be an errand boy, and I hate him for that."

"Isn't all this intensity just a little premature?" he said sharply.

87

"You don't know that's the way he will be. He isn't even sworn in yet, for God's sake. I haven't told you he's like that—I don't know that he is. I only said that what I do on women's rights will be up to him. And it will. It would be with any President!"

"You're losing your cool, Mr. Special Counsel. The neighbors will be talking."

"Well, you are so compulsively judgmental, it gripes my ass. Why do you have to condemn everyone in advance?"

She looked at him intensely. "I'm bad for you, aren't I? I've ruined your big evening."

"You are a strong, beautiful, opinionated and ornery bitch. And I have this irresistible urge to keep your naked body against mine." He reached for her arm to draw her back to him.

"Promise me something, seriously, Bird," she said quietly.

"What?"

"That you won't let those people use you."

"They won't use me. Don't worry."

"One other thing."

"What?"

"That every day you will spend some time on the things that are truly important to you."

"Sure." He brought her hard against him. "You are."

"I mean you'll constantly try to keep some perspective. To keep from believing what all your admirers are going to be telling you about yourself."

"Sure." His right hand slipped down across her belly.

"Robin?"

"Hmmm?"

"Be safe. I love you. I don't know why, but I do. And I'm really afraid for you."

"Don't worry, baby. Have I ever told you how much I like this little place, right here?"

CHAPTER **8**   After his first meeting with David Hale, Robin Warren had flown to Cleveland overnight for a ceremonial meeting with the President-elect and a brief press conference, then hurried back to Washington to assemble his staff and begin to work.

His impression of Hugh Frankling was one of remoteness. Robin's new leader appeared not to be in touch with Washington, nor was he trying to be. Evidently he cared, almost excessively, about being elected President. He had obviously campaigned hard for two years, but now that he had been narrowly elected he didn't seem to care much about the details of the conduct of the Presidency. In fact, Robin had the feeling during their conversation that there had been a four-inch pane of glass between the new President and himself as they talked. There was no passion or enthusiasm. No vitality. No vibrations.

Maybe the man was just tired from the campaign. Sitting there in a hotel in Cleveland, it would be hard to adjust to the Washington tempo. Perhaps twenty-three years in the Senate had made him blasé. He'd seen all the country's problems come and go. He'd been to five or six inaugurals. There would be very little fresh and exciting after all of that.

Or, perhaps, he was the wrong man to be President.

My God, if she could read that thought, wouldn't Maggie give him hell! No, it's unfair to judge a man on the basis of one five-minute conversation. Frankling obviously must have what it takes to lead the country. How could someone be elected—endure all the trauma of a campaign—if he didn't have the drive and ability to do the job? He couldn't. Doubtless Warren had seen him at a bad time.

Robin Warren's predecessor in the outgoing administration, Johnny Johnson, moved out of the office, Suite 149, EOB, the day before the inauguration of Hugh Frankling as President of the United States. That night a GSA crew on special overtime repainted the walls, refinished the doors, washed the windows and the carpet, and removed Johnson's nameplate from the small chrome frame to the right of the outer door.

Johnson was friendly and forthright. He had arranged for the GSA man assigned to the White House to come by and talk about Robin's "special needs." Did he want new furniture, or new coverings on the old? Would he be moving the desk, and should the telephone be relocated? Robin noticed the ugly ropelike cable to the call-director telephone on Johnny Johnson's desk, and made a mental note to ask for a better-looking telephone installation.

A large color television set mounted on a rolling stand could be moved to a different place if he wished. The White House Communications Unit, the Army, would see to it.

Robin began to feel uneasy; it was too much, too urgently pressed upon him. He'd have Miss O'Reilly contact the GSA man with instructions. He thought to himself that the little fellow seemed genuinely disappointed not to be told forthwith to tear down all the walls, change all the furnishings and relocate every wire.

Kathy O'Reilly had been a government secretary for ten years and was efficiency itself. She typed without flaw at an amazing speed, knew the name of every maître d' in town, and was on a first-name basis with most of the secretaries of important men in and out of government. She knew what was going on, what was about to happen, and how to get things done quickly; she was well worth the $24,000 a year she would be paid.

As soon as Robin told her that he liked the office as it was, she went to work on a young Hale staff man to finalize the assignment.

She badgered the poor Ohioan so persistently that within seventy-two hours she delivered Hale's memorandum to Robin with a look of satisfied vindication.

OFFICE OF THE PRESIDENT-ELECT

From: David Hale
To: Robin Warren
      You have been assigned office space as follows:
      EOB suite 149 (146, 147, 148, 149)
Your   other assignments are:
White House Mess:
   List A. Executive Dining Room
   Dining room and in-office steward service.
   Your secretary has tray privileges.
   Please deposit $150 with the Mess at once.
White House Garage: List A. Service in connection with
   duties, 24 hours, as required.
Health and recreation: List A. Membership and full
   access to the EOB.
   Health Unit for massage and exercise.
   Please deposit $50 with the Health Unit manager.
Telephone: Attached is your telephone credit card for
   business use, chargeable to your office telephone.
   Both Admin and Signal lines will be installed in
   your home.

The inaugural balls had lasted very late, and Maggie's prediction was accurate: they were terrible. They were physically difficult to move in and out of, even with the help of Robin's Army major, his driver and an olive-drab staff car. Maggie refused to come to the inauguration or any of the parties, so Robin Warren went alone to four of the seven balls, fought his way through the steaming crush to say hello to a dozen of his "clients" and to pay his respects to the new Cabinet people, then accepted an invitation to a private party in a Senator's *pied-à-terre* penthouse at the Watergate. Although Robin didn't get to bed until four, the morning after the inauguration he was in his new office by nine, impatient to sit at the slim new table he'd ordered, in the antique-style judge's chair

91

he and Kathy O'Reilly had selected from a GSA furniture catalogue.

The first two months in that office were euphoric for Robin Warren and his colleagues. They were each spotlighted in the news, and their pictures and biographies ran with such frequency that Robin's clipping file bulged.

Frankling was congratulated by editorial writers for bringing a steady and experienced hand to the tiller of state. He and his wife were photographed raiding the White House icebox in their pajamas and bathrobes. Their Scotty dog, nieces and nephews, backgammon games and favorite soup were ecstatically reported to a waiting nation by hard-bitten White House reporters, presumably smitten by the new President's winning personality and charm. He rose steadily in the popularity polls.

But on the fifty-eighth day of this mass adulation the press turned on Frankling like a rabid dog and sank its fangs deep. An aged and very liberal Supreme Court justice resigned amid anonymous rumors that the new Attorney General, Carleton Smythe, had called upon the elderly jurist and coerced his departure. The press rallied around the departed justice in full cry, accusing Frankling and his administration of everything from court-packing to blackmail. There were no more cozy pictures of the Franklings popping popcorn at Camp David; instead, cruel and crude Herblock cartoons appeared in the *Star-Post,* Frankling's hands dripping with the jurist's blood, Carleton Smythe holding a severed head, and Frankling and Smythe carrying a frail old body in black robes into a field for burial.

The President huddled with Carleton Smythe, David Hale and the press secretary, Les Carew. Robin Warren and the rest of the staff read the papers and gossiped with one another in low tones in the White House mess. A couple of the speech-writing staff wrote Hale memoranda suggesting historic precedents and diversionary ploys. The President's political confidants began suggesting to columnists, off the record, that Mr. Justice Malloy was prone to the use of narcotic stimulants.

During the first two honeymoon months Robin Warren saw the new President in person only four times. In the second week there had been a mass meeting of the White House staff, six hundred and fifty strong, in the State Department auditorium. Robin saw him at much closer range in a meeting Frankling scheduled in the Oval Office with the four emperors of organized labor that same week. Then, for some unexplained reason, Warren was also invited to audit the second Cabinet meeting, which turned out to be a perfunctory affair at which economists pointed to charts and predicted more inflation. The President largely ignored the speakers while he read a memorandum on how the various ethnic voter blocs had voted the previous November.

Just before six o'clock in the afternoon on the forty-sixth day David Hale had called Robin to the President's hideaway office in the EOB. Robin arrived a little breathless. He had stopped by the men's room to comb his hair on the way. Other than a Secret Service agent at the receptionist's desk in the narrow, hall-like anteroom, there was no one to receive him when he got there.

The agent disinterestedly waved him in. Robin knocked on the tall heavy door.

"Go on in," said the agent with impatient amusement.

Robin opened the door and looked in cautiously; he certainly didn't want to interrupt anything of importance. The room was empty. It was large, handsomely appointed and possessed an air of pristine disuse, like a shelf of books which had never been read. The walls were covered with framed political cartoons about Hugh Frankling. An ornate crystal chandelier dominated the center of the room, overhanging a small conference table and chairs.

Robin looked about in doubt. Voices could be heard beyond a door in the far wall. One voice sounded enough like David Hale's that Warren moved to the door and knocked lightly. In a moment Hale, in shirtsleeves, opened the door wide.

"Come in, Robin," Hale said. "Mr. President, you remember Robin Warren?"

"Of course," said Frankling. He was seated in a deep armchair

93

in the far-left corner of the room, a pile of papers on his lap, his feet on a hassock. He too was in shirtsleeves, but there was no air of informality about him.

"Of course." He looked over the top of his glasses at Warren. "Come in, Rob, come in. I won't keep you long. Come in."

The office was larger than the anteroom, dominated by a huge mahogany desk along the left side in front of the tall French windows. Drapes of magenta and white stripes ran from floor to ceiling all along that wall. Opposite was a long, bare wall and an oversized couch covered in off-white silk. Three easy chairs were grouped around a butler's table between the couch and the desk.

Robin noticed the absence of papers. There were none on the desk or the table; the only papers were on Frankling's lap and he rummaged through them as he talked.

"I wanted to see you for a minute about this memorandum you sent me the other day. It's here . . ."

"The one about women, Robin," said Hale. He was sitting on a straight wooden chair against the end wall. A wooden table and a lamp separated him from the President. Neither had invited Robin to sit; he assumed that one stood in The Presence unless there was a dispensation, so he waited, saying nothing.

"I don't want us to get into the fight over the proposed Women's Civil Rights Act, Rob," said Frankling. "I wish I could find the damn paper; I made some notes on it, but . . ."

"It's in a blue folder," Hale said.

"Ah, here. Yes." He looked at Warren. "You note here that there are more women than men, and that's true. But how many of them vote? Of those who vote, how many can *we* get? And how many really care about this women's movement?"

"Well, sir . . ." Robin began.

"The question is, are we better off to get into the fight or stay out of it?"

"I understand," said Robin.

"Four years from now when I go back to the people will it be a plus or a minus? That's the question. Right?"

"Yes, sir, I guess it is, but there's also the basic issue. The Equal

Rights Amendment has never been implemented by a comprehensive statute, and without it what does ERA mean? It's just a statement, without machinery. You yourself supported ERA, I believe."

"In a manner of speaking, I did. And that's just my point. I already have a record on ERA. Isn't that enough for the militants? Do we need to aggravate their opponents by bringing in this activist woman you want? Does she have to be on our staff?"

"Barbara Rorrick?"

"Whatever her name is." Frankling removed his glasses and looked at Robin Warren. "I would not be in favor of bringing her onto my staff, Rob. I think it's asking for trouble we don't need."

"Mr. President, I've already hired her. She's here; she's right down the hall at this moment."

Frankling dropped his heavy eyeglasses onto the pile of papers and shrugged his shoulders helplessly. "Can you control her?" he asked mildly. "Will she insist on speaking out for this Civil Rights bill?"

"I'll do my best, sir. I'll tell her your decision and she can take it or leave. Would you consider talking with her? She's very much on your side; she has your interests at heart. I think a short meeting could be very helpful."

"Look, Rob," the President said abruptly, "I don't even want her here. I certainly don't want to meet her. She'll go out and tell the press I'm a chauvinist pig and she's resigning. Then I'll be even worse off. I'll tell you where I made my mistake. I never should have supported ERA in the first place. The women who are for that are not the women who vote for me. It's a loser. No, you'll either have to control her or get rid of her. I'm sorry. It was a mistake to let her in here in the first place. David—" he looked sharply at Hale—"we've got to get the rest of this paperwork done so that I can see those people."

I guess I'm not here anymore, thought Robin. I've just disappeared. "Good night, sir," he said.

Frankling looked up with surprise. "Good night, Rob," he said abruptly.

CHAPTER 9

To: R.W.
From: K.O'R.
Re: Your trip to the Business Council meeting April
      22–23, at the Hot Springs Hotel, Spring Valley,
      Virginia.

David Hale called to say the President and the
Secretary of the Treasury think it is a good idea for
you to attend the spring meeting of the Business
Council.

The Secretary's office sent over the attached memorandum describing the agenda. Briefly, you are only
expected to mingle and get acquainted. You are not
required to give a speech.

Others from the administration who will attend are:

Harold Sample,	Secretary of the Treasury
Murray Tillerman,	Assistant to the President for Domestic Policy
Hill Gossett,	Assistant to the President for Economic Policy
George Gollub,	Special Trade Representative
Larry Andrino,	Office of Management and Budget
Charles Montgomery,	Undersecretary of Commerce (The Secretary will be in Europe April 15–25.)

The Chairman of the Federal Reserve and the Assistant Secretary of Treasury for Monetary Policy will fly
in from a Tokyo meeting the second day.

The Business Council

Three hundred executives of business, finance, communications, manufacture and service industries con-

stitute the Council. It is self—perpetuating and considered very prestigious. A paid staff of five runs their office in Washington and plans the two meetings held each year:

Spring Meeting: Always at Hot Springs Hotel; it features lectures on domestic and international economic subjects for which leading fiscal and monetary experts are paid substantial stipends. Government figures are often included as speakers or guests. Seminars on similar subjects. All sessions are off the record.

Fall Meeting: Always in Washington, and features government, especially Congressional, speakers. (Congressmen are paid very substantial retainers, one way or the other, to be speakers.)

Both the meetings are heavily covered by the business—oriented press and the contents of meetings seldom remain secret for long.

Among the Council officers for this year are:

Elwood Martin, CEO, United Ore and Steel

Patrick Allway, Chairman, ABC (Television, Radio, etc.)

Minerva Stein, Vice—President, Technical Bank & Trust

Arrangements:

1. Travel: A car will pick you up at 7:00 a.m. at home, Thursday, April 22. You will fly in the Secretary's Convair (Tail #0710—a prop plane for energy PR purposes to contrast with all of the private executive jets, and because the Spring Valley airport is small and marginally dangerous) leaving from Andrews A.F.B. promptly at 8:00 A.M.

Secretary Sample requests all his passengers to be on time.

Return arrangements the same.

2. Attire:

On the airplane: business suits.

Take: sports wear, tuxedo, sport jackets and slacks, swim suit.

3. Accommodations: You have a single room. All meals, etc., may be signed for and will be comp'd by the Business Council.

97

4. Sports, etc.: See brochure attached. Take your tennis racket. I gather no one works very hard down there.

People:

Attached is a list and brief biographies of Business Council members you have had some contact with this year. I have marked Jep Valle's clients with a red star.

Warning: Larry Collingwood of Triad Computer Systems is sure to be there. We have not yet been able to get him an appointment with the President (you recall, he wants to talk about Japanese competitive dumping). You should try to get him to talk to Gollub, Special Trade Representative, while you are there.

Also attached is a list of media people accredited to cover the Council meetings. Carew suggests that you particularly watch for Dale Edwards of the Star-Post and try to get acquainted. He once worked with John Solomon at the Enquirer and is thought to be friendly to the President.

Have fun!

The wide lobby area of the old Hot Springs Hotel was clotted with small circles of people, some greeting one another, some being gently seduced by the financial and political reporters, making dates with each other for golf or tennis, and, in the case of a few, attempting to mask the fact that they didn't quite know what to do next.

Robin Warren registered, then leaned back against the front desk to look around. The couples were all just beyond middle age except for one tall, thin grayhead and his silver-gray wife; the other men were all beefy. A small roll of fat between their ears along the backs of their necks seemed to be a Business Council hallmark, shared by all of the members in the lobby at that moment. The wives were groomed, bangled, chained, pinned and accessoried; every woman in the lobby wore her wealth like a Ubangi. Warren looked in vain for an exception; he distrusted such easy, characteristic generalities. He wanted very much to see another man who was skinny, a woman unadorned.

They were made to appear the more affluent by the journalists who had been assigned by their bureaus to lurk outside the closed meetings and write impressions of what probably took place. The reporters were obvious contrasts. Two hadn't yet changed; they were still wearing their J. C. Penney three-piece suits. The other two had switched to slacks, turtlenecks and sweaters, but the cut and quality of their clothing, shoes and haircuts gave them away.

The lobby itself was indefinably disquieting to Warren. Some public rooms enfold one at once; this room was inharmonious and, in an odd way, forbidding. The old wood had been varnished too brightly. The carpet stopped two feet from the wall and gave the impression of being worn and frayed when it was not. The wood window trim, the carpet and so much of the wall as was painted had been given that austere lifeless green so often found in government and military offices.

"Mr. Warner?" A lanky man in a red bellman's suit slowly muttered the name.

"Me? No. It's Robin Warren. Warren."

The liveried man leaned over the counter and clicked the hotel key at the pudgy clerk.

"Hey! Hey! This man say he ain't Warner for 227. He is some other name." The accent was as rural as smoked ham.

The clerk bustled into their view. "No, that's right. He's the one for 227."

"What name you have?"

"Warner. Robert Warner," said the clerk.

"No. It's Robin. R-O-B-I-N. It's Warren, W-A-R-R-E-N, not Warner. OK?" Robin smiled in spite of himself.

"Certainly. Marcus will take you up, Mr. Warren."

They walked up a flight of oak-railed stairs that creaked comfortably. The second-floor hall was painted the same GI green. The lock on the old wood door was not elaborate, nor was the small room itself. It had been years since Robin had seen a hotel room containing one twin bed. A vintage shaded floor lamp offered the only alternative to the three bare bulbs in the ceiling fixture. An old telephone without a dial sat beside a Bible on the bedside table. Marcus found a suitcase stand in the closet and opened it under the window. He took Warren's five dollars with undue gratitude and closed the door firmly. Robin looked around the small room. As far as the Hot Springs was concerned he was not their most important guest, obviously. He wouldn't be doing much entertaining in this room.

Within an hour Robin began to form a better impression of the place. A different bellman arrived with a basket of fruit, a fifth of Scotch and a spring bouquet, courtesy of the management. Fortified by a nip of Scotch and an apple, he changed to slacks and a jacket and began to explore the old building. His wandering took him along a covered walk behind the lobby to a large old hexagonal building remodeled into a pavilion, where, obviously, the beautiful people were lunching. Bright banks of potted summer flowers, and the artful use of light pastels, white awnings and wall panels combined to give the room a spontaneous and sophisticated gaiety. The diners overlooked a dozen superb outdoor tennis courts on which a few players in warm-up suits defied the chill. The first tee of one of the golf courses could be seen out the opposite windows. Three chefs in tall white hats at the far end of the room were presiding over an extravagant luncheon buffet. Warren looked around the room from his vantage point just inside the door. A rich and much-spoken-of U.S. Senator sat at a near table with two women, all in tennis clothes. Robin recognized several businessmen whom he had met at White House parties. A former astronaut, now an airline president, was lunching with the Secretary of the Treasury and a beautiful woman.

Scattered about among the hundred guests were six or seven— six to be precise—young women who could pass Warren's preliminary visual screening. Six percent. Not too bad. One, especially, reclaimed his glance, as much because of her resemblance to Maggie Valle as for her other physical virtues. She was lunching with a tall man about forty, dressed in golf clothes.

The junior member of the Council of Economic Advisers, Eric Schlossberg, caught Robin's eye and waved him over to a table of five younger men. After introductions and drinks Robin moved with them to the buffet for lunch. He found himself chatting in the line with a dark slight man named Meyer "Mike" Meyerson who had worked in the Carter White House and was now personal assistant to the well-known Auguste Capron, chief executive officer of the conglomerated business known as United International Companies. Warren and Meyerson displayed for each other that fraternal affinity that nearly all White House staff people feel for one another, regardless of which Presidents they may have served, and of which political party. As they stood in line they compared notes. Meyerson's desk had been the one Nick Gurley now operated just outside the President's office. A few of the same secretaries were still around. The mess menu was the same. But few of the publicized Carter austerities had survived. The limousines, television sets and other superficial perquisites were restored to the President's staff once the public-relations gods had been propitiated.

The luncheon conversation among the young men was witty and helpful. Warren began to get a feel for the tempo of the week and how it would go. He relaxed.

That afternoon he attended the first of the assemblies at which the members of the Business Council heard the experts and gave their own opinions. Of the three hundred members, about twenty were given to making strong speeches from the floor at these sessions, most of them surprisingly undoctrinaire, a few even radical considering the identity of the speakers.

The opening banquet that first night was formal and dull. Two prominent economists offered inconsistent observations and diametrically opposite forecasts, and the new Council president was installed.

Warren went to his room after dinner, shut off his telephone and slept very soundly until a waiter brought his breakfast in the morning.

By the second seminar of the next morning's session he was convinced that he was useless and out of place. The high-level executives who were the self-perpetuating members of the Council were all at least twenty years older than he. They were polite in the encounters he had with them, but not forthcoming. The few contacts he was making were at the junior level—the Mike

Meyersons; useful perhaps, but more useful for those he was meeting than for the White House.

At times he felt the invisibility which invests the stranger at a convention. He walked into a seminar room late and most heads turned to see who had opened the noisy door. But no one really saw him; as far as the turning heads were concerned, no one had entered the room. Some combination of Puritan ethic and inertia kept him from walking out of the seminar on "The Federal Reserve; M-1, M-2 and You." He drifted with the crowd from there to lunch.

The luncheon was held in the large convention room off the lobby. The table to which he was assigned was down close to the head table, off to the right. A large spring bouquet centered a round table which was already occupied by four men he did not know. He found his place card, then went around the table introducing himself to a railroad tycoon, two textile magnates and a reporter from *Barrons*. The chair to Robin's right remained vacant until the shrimp cocktail was being served.

As he began to eat, Robin was aware that the four men at his table were standing, shaking hands with a blond man of medium height dressed in pale-yellow golf slacks, a white cotton polo shirt and dark-brown cashmere sweater, pushed up on his wide forearms; a pair of dark glasses rode on his tanned forehead. He looked as if he'd dropped in between his approach shot and his first putt. His thick yellow hair was trimmed longer than the consensus style of his fellow Council members around the room, and Robin immediately categorized him: movie director type, beautiful teeth, $3,000 wristwatch, $200 loafers, pilots his own jet, scratch golfer, maintains a harem, no roll of fat on the back of his neck.

"Mr. Warren? I am Auguste Capron. Mike Meyerson has told me a great deal about you. I am very happy to have this opportunity to become acquainted with you."

Robin had recently read a long profile of Capron in *Business Week,* but neither the reporter's description nor the photograph had done the subject justice. Like so many of the truly successful people Robin had come to know in Washington, this man defied accurate printed description. He exuded a physical magnetism. He obviously knew it, and he enhanced it by what he wore and the way he was groomed. The reporter had simply missed the essence of the man. The facts about him which had been reported were remarkable enough to be newsworthy, however. He had built the United International Companies from one modest electronics company into one of the strongest multinational conglomerates in the world.

"You once worked for us," Capron said. "I think you helped United Bauxite with a quota problem."

"Well, Jep—Senator Valle did most of the work on that."

"It was a good job. Did you do legislative work before you came to Washington?"

"No. I practiced with a large firm in San Francisco."

"Oh?"

"Butler, Pilbane and Monroe."

"I know Hew Butler."

"Sure. A fine man."

About fifty-five years old now, Capron had come to the United States from Eastern Europe as a boy. He had been a U.S. Marine at sixteen, had seen combat in World War II, and in the mid-1940s "transferred" from the military to Wall Street. In the process he had petitioned a New Jersey court to change his name from Abraham Krapowicz to Auguste Capron, in realistic recognition of the prevailing employment practices in the American financial community.

As Auguste Capron he quickly had found a job as a messenger boy for the venerable investment firm of Coleman, Sture and Company. For twelve years he worked there, studying accounting at night, advancing from job to job, learning, investing and waiting. In the thirteenth year he began his moves. For the next ten years he invested in, acquired, merged into or took over the fourteen corporations his patient study and analysis had identified as his targets.

At Coleman, Sture and Company he had forced himself to become a student, and demanded of himself the most careful preparation possible; now his thousands of employees were held to the same standard. Embedded in the surface of the sleek, uncluttered desks in his New York, Los Angeles and Zurich offices were small gold plates placed where one could not fail to read the one engraved word: *"Prepare."*

Auguste Capron knew as much about Robin Warren as his careful staff preparation could provide. He was genuinely interested in what the dossier showed; there was something untypical about this bright young man.

"Why did you leave the Butler firm?" Capron asked.

"I guess I just craved more action. I'd once met Jep Valle, so I asked him for a job."

Capron waited for more. He half expected a short speech about Serving the Nation or Going to Washington to Make My Voice Heard. Robin, instead, ate his lunch. This may be a young mercenary, Capron thought. There were a number of young people on Hugh Frankling's staff whom the press releases called highly motivated and public-spirited. But if Capron was any judge of young men, Robin Warren was talented, ambitious, and for sale to the highest bidder.

"You're getting plenty of action now, I'm sure," Capron said.

"Plenty."

"I used to know a great many people there in the Carter days." Capron shook his head slowly. "So much promise. Such a fine beginning. Then, with all the changes, suddenly I no longer knew anyone. So we hired Jep Valle and others to help us in Washington. I know President Frankling very slightly; we once had meetings about bauxite tariffs, when he was a Senator. Although I am no Republican, I think well of him."

Robin nodded. Capron's syntax was oddly stilted at times.

The *Business Week* article said Capron was now in his third phase, consolidating his ownership, refinancing, improving profits and going to the public for capital investment. From the beginning he had been the principal shareholder and chief executive officer of the United International Companies. The conglomerate was symbolized in its advertising by a three-link chain in which molecular symbols were enclosed. He had joined together electronics firms with companies which owned and mined bauxite, reduced aluminum, owned and distributed natural gas, imported and distributed liquor, built ships and bridges, and controlled a chain of retail stores. His particular headache was United International Services, a company which owned and operated the telephone and telegraph systems in eleven foreign countries, five of them in South America; his favorite acquisition was Hollywood's Superior Studios, a leading producer of feature films and the increasingly dominant studio in the creation of successful television and home cassette programs.

In the past ten years Capron had become an extremely wealthy man; with the ancillary benefits provided for in his employment contract, his annual pretax income had risen close to $700,000 a year—his United International stock alone was worth about $150 million. Reporters called him the self-made man personified. He liked that. He worked hard. He earned his money every day; he was a voracious reader and an early riser.

"He is tough, I think," Capron continued. "Your President laid down the law to Brazil in that offshore-minerals dispute, and that is good. This country has been too soft with the Latins in matters of that kind. I am waiting to see what he will do in an expropriation case. That will be a real test. I hope he is equally resolute."

"Is there something particular that's been expropriated?"

"No, nothing specific; I mean in general. Especially in South America. The Latins have it in mind that American assets in their countries can be taken away from American companies with impunity. And they now have reason to believe they can pay any little price they wish for the stolen goods. I hope your President will someday show them that this country is not helpless."

Capron spoke quietly but with total involvement and passion. Robin Warren realized that he was in the process of again changing his preconceptions about Auguste Capron, replacing both his first impressions and whatever ideas he had held as a result of reading the magazine profile. The *Business Week* reporter should be excused for missing him by a mile. This complex man was not to be easily defined.

"Will you go back to Jep Valle when your tenure is expired at the White House?" Capron toyed with the food on his plate.

"I don't know, Mr. Capron."

"Auguste."

"Sure. Auguste."

"No, I suppose it is too early to think about such things, Robin. But it will be an important decision when the time comes. Either you will stay in Washington—be a Washington lawyer, with all that implies—or go to one of the other action centers. New York is the important one, of course. Perhaps Los Angeles or Houston or Chicago. You will be sought after by law firms; you will have had unique experience."

"What do you think I should do?"

"Come to New York, I believe. It is the very center of the world now. You would have an important contribution to make. We in business must be expert in the nuances of Washington, but we do not yet master the art. We have *not* mastered it. This government in Washington and the metaphysics of its relationships to finance, business, trade unions and all that are not well understood in New York. What is being written about it in magazines and books is very poor. One cannot merely read about it to learn. You will be most valuable when you come."

The lunch program was about to begin. As the chairman tapped his glass with a fork, Capron put his hand lightly on Robin's arm. "I am not going to stay for the speech, Robin. Please excuse me. I enjoyed it. We will meet again."

They shook hands briefly and Capron was gone, striding erectly among the tables to the door.

The place where Capron had sat showed little sign that he had been there. He had restored the napkin to its original folds. The shrimp cocktail and salad were untouched. A knife and fork rested on the plate; he had cut only one narrow slice from the steak. None of the vegetables had been eaten. Obviously, thought Robin, he didn't come in here today because he was hungry.

CHAPTER **10**   Less than a week after they had first met at the Hot Springs, Robin Warren heard again from Auguste Capron. Or, more precisely, Kathy O'Reilly heard from Meyer Meyerson. One afternoon his secretary came into Robin Warren's office with a short typed memorandum in her hand.

"Do you know the great Capron?" Kathy O'Reilly asked quizzically. "I'd suppose you do, but I want to make sure."

"I met him at Hot Springs."

"Well, his assistant called me this morning to invite you to a formal dinner party Capron's giving at his apartment in New York. Movie after."

She reread a part of the note and scratched her head. "It's a little odd; you're not the guest of honor, but he said if the date's not convenient they'll change the whole thing to a night you can come. Maybe you're the duck at the dinner. I refused to talk dates with him until I'd checked with you. It's a small dinner at home."

"When is it? Am I free?"

"April thirtieth. You have the French Embassy that night."

"I'd like to do Capron's instead; can I get out of the French thing?"

"Sure. Do you want to take Maggie Valle?"

"Oh, hell, I've got to invite someone? I guess." He sounded reluctant. "It's in New York? I'd better call her, hadn't I? She doesn't like it when you call." He reached for his telephone and dialed her direct office number.

"Margaret Valle," she answered.

"Hello, Margaret."

"Well, hi. I heard you were dead."

"No, alive and well, and in the large intestine of the anatomy of government."

"I couldn't have phrased it better myself. How are you?"

"Fine. I wish to lure you. We are invited to a small party Auguste Capron's giving on April thirtieth. In New York. A Friday night."

"What kind of party?"

He looked at his secretary with raised eyebrows. Kathy O'Reilly turned and left his office, closing his door behind her.

"Formal, at his apartment, movie after. He says he wants to have it at a time when I can make it, for sure. Can you imagine that?"

"Sure, Bird, I can imagine it. Can't you?" Maggie Valle's question was sarcastic. "It might just have something to do with where you work, don't you think?"

"Sure, beautiful. Sure. I'll let you know what time I'll pick you up. That's April thirtieth. OK?"

"Fine, Bird. I'll look forward to it. I may go shopping for some new brass knuckles just for you. 'Bye."

He hung up with an air of resignation, pushed a call-director button and waited for his secretary to come in. "That is one ornery lady," he said to Kathy O'Reilly. "I don't know why I put up with all that crap."

"Oh? Maybe on sober reflection some explanation will occur to you."

"Another smart-assed woman? My life is replete with them. Maggie consents to accompany me to the party."

"All right. I'll confirm for April thirtieth, you and Maggie Valle, right? Do you want a plane?"

"Might as well. I can work a little longer if I don't have to take the shuttle."

Two days later Kathy O'Reilly received a letter from Mike Meyerson on stiff linen notepaper, folded at the center, a small "c" embossed at the top.

Dear Miss O'Reilly,

Mr. and Mrs. Capron are delighted that Miss Valle and Mr. Warren will be with them at 8 P.M. on April thirtieth.

Mr. Capron's car will meet Mr. Warren at the Marine Air Terminal at La Guardia at 6:45 P.M. that day. His airplane will be Able Able Charlie 947, I understand.

I have taken the liberty of arranging a suite at the Carlyle for Mr. Warren. The car will take him there to change, then on to pick up Miss Valle at 155 East 83rd St.

Enclosed is the guest list for the dinner party, as you requested. I do not yet have the final seating, but I'll let you know Mr. Warren's dinner partners as soon as I know the arrangement.

Thank you for your efficient help.

Sincerely,
Meyer Meyerson

Miss Kathy O'Reilly
Secretary to Mr. Robin Warren
The White House
Washington

Meyerson's detail work was flawless. Capron's big car was waiting when the small twin-propeller Air Force plane landed; Robin Warren was preregistered at the Carlyle, and there were flowers and a note from Capron in the suite. The car waited while he dressed, then whisked him to Maggie Valle's apartment exactly on time.

She opened her door to him, a drink in her hand, an off-the-shoulder dress of light-blue silk revealing her tanned arms and shoulders, outlining her breasts, then dropping in loose folds to her sandals. "Miss Valle, you look absolutely the best yet. That is some outfit!"

"Just a little something Bergdorf's and I whipped up for the occasion. I'm glad you like it. This drink is for you if we have time."

They had one drink, sitting close on the couch. The evening news was on the small television perched precariously on an old coach trunk in the corner of her living room. They were stiff with

109

each other; if asked they might have blamed it on the formal attire. In fact they silently shared the renewed realization that with every hour they had spent together since Robin began at the White House, their affinity for each other had deteriorated. It was no longer exciting; it was merely awkward.

"Before you got here they reported that Frankling is going to be at the UN tomorrow. Are you going?"

"Nope. It's nothing to do with me. He's making a speech about the Deep-Sea Treaty. That's getting to be a preoccupation with Durrien and the President these days. They think there's a chance of getting a very favorable result by aligning with the landlocked countries and some of the Third World against Russia."

"What's that all about?"

"We want a treaty that will allow our deep-ocean companies to take oil and minerals from the floor of any ocean. Anywhere outside the forty-mile continental shelves. But we're so far ahead in the technology of deep-water extraction that Russia's trying to limit us to our halves of the Atlantic and Pacific."

"Big bucks involved, no doubt?"

"Untold big bucks. We'd have to pay a royalty into a trust for the poorer countries, but if we can go into the Indian Ocean, and along the African and South American coasts, we can well afford a payoff. The big battle is over the limits on where Americans can dig."

"Why would the Third World line up with us?"

"They want those royalties in that trust fund in a hurry. We've offered a lot of front money, and they know that our people will go in and extract right away. If we're kept out of some of the seabeds, it may be years before the nearby countries can exploit the resources."

"Sounds like 'exploit' is the right word."

"Let's go to the party," Robin said with a smile. "I will not rise to the bait."

"What bait? Jesus, a girl really has to watch her tongue around you big Republican government men. Here, give me your glass."

He handed her the glass and moved to get their coats.

110

"Tonight," he said, "you are sitting with Perry Germane, the economist, and some motion picture producer, Mags. Germane is one of Capron's consultants."

"Who are you with?"

"Their dates. Mrs. Germane on one side and Lani Romera, the actress, on the other."

"Hoo, hoo! Lani Romera! Won't that be nice?"

"Should be interesting. I've never met her."

"Well, let's not keep the love goddess waiting, Bird. I'll just put that old Republican cloth coat over my shoulders."

The limousine pulled up at the door on the Park Avenue side of one of the fine old cooperative apartment houses in the low Sixties. Mike Meyerson was waiting in the doorway; he hurried across the sidewalk, opened the car door and introduced himself to Maggie Valle. Briskly he helped her out, greeted Robin, ushered them past the doorman to the elevator, and nodded a signal to the young lift operator. Without a word they were elevated to the ninth floor, where the sliding doors opened into the entry area of the Caprons' apartment. The Caprons evidently occupied the entire ninth floor. A maid in a formal black uniform took their coats. The butler took their names, nodded, opened a double door and led them into the living room where Auguste Capron and his blond wife stood near a grand piano in front of the Park Avenue windows.

Robin's first impression of the room was: wood. The floors, walls and ceiling were of rare woods; the moldings in the corners of the ceiling had been embellished in hand carvings of leaves, vines and fruit. Much of the furniture was of various fruitwoods; the piano was in exquisite pearwood. The window blinds were delicately slatted wooden shades. The drapes carried a subtle leaf figure in warm tones. A cordial, welcoming room, like the friendly couple who greeted them, Robin felt.

Maggie Valle first noticed Auguste Capron's wife, Julie. Her long quilted dress was extremely simple; the only jewelry she wore was one gold bracelet, set with ten of the biggest diamonds Maggie had ever seen. Julie Capron was a native Californian, with a lithe

111

sportswoman's body, a thin, regular and sensible face, and the fresh and friendly manner of one who knows who she is and is comfortable with her identity. Maggie quickly concluded that Mr. Capron had married well and was protecting his investment with care.

Both Capron and his wife lavished attention on Maggie and Robin. Julie Capron was evidently fond of Jep Valle and made a special point of telling Maggie why she was, as she introduced her to the guests who had already arrived. As they were moving around the long room, Julie Capron excused herself briefly to go to the door to greet Senator Sim Coggins, the young junior Senator from New York. A dashing bachelor, Coggins won far more than his one percent share of the media's allotment of attention to the United States Senate. He had been there one full term plus a few months, and was already being openly discussed as Presidential timber.

Coggins was a favorite of the gossip columnists and did his best to earn their suspicions that he slept with a different girl every night. Within a few moments he was confessing to Maggie Valle that he too was trying to write a novel, with poor result; before long she found herself sympathetically offering him editorial suggestion.

Julie Capron was a skilled hostess; when the last guest had his first drink in hand, she subtly began to move the men about the room to join their dinner partners. Meanwhile her husband was having a few words with each guest with unobtrusive but systematic precision. When the dinner partners had been paired off, Julie Capron quietly suggested to a few men that they begin to move to the tables, one in the dining room, the other set temporarily in a large study which opened through double doors to the living room.

Julie Capron led Robin to the far corner of the living room where Lani Romera stood talking with two men. She wore a calf-length dress which appeared to be blue bandannas sewn together. Her waist was gathered with a loose silver concha belt set with turquoise; coral and turquoise necklaces accented her wide, intense pale-green eyes. Robin knew her face; he had seen some of her motion pictures. She was the magazine photographers' current favorite; her picture was unavoidable. But he was not prepared for the impact of her coloring in person.

Some great artists depict shape, motion and design less with line than by their adroit manipulation and arrangement of hue. Lani Romera owed her beauty less to the shape of her features than to her natural color—the flush of her cheeks, her tan, those remarkable green eyes, red-blond hair and brows. No camera had ever truly captured those natural tones. Her mouth was wide and full, her front teeth large. She looked like a Celtic peasant. Her nostrils flared an otherwise straight and lovely nose. Her eyes were almost too big for her oval face, her brows too heavy.

The publicity department at Superior Studios said Lani Romera was twenty-eight years old. Robin would have guessed she was twenty-four. She moved with the grace of a younger athlete; her legs were slim and strong, her wrists wide and freckled. At close range he found her beauty stunning.

"Lani, may I present Mr. Robin Warren? He is your dinner partner, you know. He is our White House representative tonight." Julie Capron beamed.

"Hello, Robin," Lani said. Her voice was low and vibrant. It threw him completely off stride.

"Hello."

"Will you two excuse me, please?" the hostess said. "I will get us moving toward dinner in a moment, if you two gentlemen will come with me." Julie Capron moved away, a man on each hand, leaving Robin alone with Lani Romera. She was under contract to Auguste Capron's Superior Studios and sometimes made command appearances at his parties; when she did she was in effect a second hostess, and she played the role well, notwithstanding some resentment she felt at the economic realities which dictated that casting.

She was showing no resentment as she smiled broadly at Robin. "You're not at all what I expected."

"Oh, what did you think you were stuck with?"

"A big tummy and a big cigar. What kind of a politician are you?" She looked him up and down with amusement.

"Oh, the new breed, lady, the new breed; we're smart and tough and do six hundred sit-ups every morning."

"No wonder there's no big tummy. Six hundred?"

"Well, maybe sixty."

"What do you do at the White House?"

"I'm the contact man for outside groups—citizens who have something to communicate to the President."

"You mean unions and old people and the Screen Actors Guild—things like that?"

"And environment groups, and the PTA, and the grocers. Right."

Her emerald eyes darted around the room. "Which lady did you bring tonight?"

He nodded across at Maggie Valle. "The tall brunette. The shoulders, in blue."

"Very nice. Are you living together?"

"She is a book editor in New York. There's a feeling on the part of some of the participants that our relationship isn't all it once was, but there are several views on that. The jury is still out."

"Hmmm," she mused, as she looped her arm in his and they strolled slowly into the dining room. The room was not large; the table seated twelve. It was dominated by a ceramic Flemish chandelier holding twenty-four candles. The flames were reflected in the gold and brown of the central orb, giving the small room warmth. Lani Romera was assigned to preside over the table from a seat halfway along on one side. Robin Warren was on her left. To her right was Senator Sim Coggins. When Coggins had seated his elderly dinner partner he turned to Lani with a subdued and familiar grin. "Good evening, Miss Douglas," he said. "How enchanting to see you again."

"Senator." She nodded curtly.

They were obviously not strangers. Robin quickly sensed that

114

she constantly turned to him as much to snub Coggins as for any other reason. But Robin didn't care what the reason was. As Capron's servants served the excellent bisque and warm toast, Robin basked in Lani Romera's continual attention. It took only a few minutes for her to dispel the matinee-love-goddess aura and make Robin realize she had a strong individuality apart from her film persona.

"What's the Miss Douglas?" he asked, nodding toward Senator Coggins. "Is that your married name?"

"Douglas is my unmarried, real-life Corvallis, Oregon, name. Lenore Douglas, the best little cheerleader Willamette Union High School ever had. My married name was Goldberg. Accent on the 'was.' I'm just a poor single girl once again, trying to get along."

"How did you get from Corvallis to Hollywood?"

"Pretty much the usual." She grimaced. "I came here to New York to model. Did pretty well, too. But the money in pictures is better."

"Ever go back to Corvallis?"

"Sure. All the time. My folks are still there. My dad is a high-school principal. And I love that country. Have you been there?"

"Once. Driving through. But I've spent more time over on the Oregon coast; around Yachats and in there."

"Isn't that beautiful? I adore it."

She did something with her mouth when she talked about things that pleased her: a sensual working of her lips that was a giveaway.

Senator Coggins turned from the banker's wife and tried to join the conversation, but Lani pointedly ignored him. For a little while Robin talked across her to the Senator to disassociate himself from her deliberate rudeness, then looked at her once more.

"Which fellow did you come to the party with?"

"A studio man. Auguste is showing a new Superior Studios film tonight, so this was supposed to be ninety-five percent goodwill-ambassador work, five percent pleasure. The studio handled the

115

details, including the escort." She turned to look toward the den. "I'm a little concerned about him, too. He said he wasn't feeling well."

"Who was Goldberg? He must have lacked good sense."

"Thank you; that's nice. He's an aging boy-wonder producer at Superior. He works for Auguste. I guess you'd say Bob Goldberg discovered me. He put me in my first picture. Haven't you ever heard of him?"

"I don't think so."

"My God, that's remarkable. In Hollywood he's a very big deal. And you've never even heard of him! I suppose there are big political powers in Washington I've never heard of, too."

"You're divorced from Goldberg?"

"Umm. Bitterly, absolutely, and with great hurt. It was not a marriage, as we are raised in Corvallis to think about marriage. I'm not sure any marriage in real life is. But it will be an unshirted miracle if any man is ever able to talk me into trying it again."

"Children?"

"No."

"So you're going to live alone in a tiny white cottage with eighteen cats and grow old alone, gracefully. Right?"

"Wrong. I live in the most beautiful yellow beach house at Malibu, no cats, and I have fun. Don't feel sorry for me, kid. I'm well rid of Goldberg. I'm well rid of all male entanglements."

"If I get to California again next month would you have an unentangled dinner with me?"

"You come up to the beach, Robin, and I'll cook you a dinner. I'd like that."

"So would I. But also, I've always wanted to go to Chasen's. Will you show me Chasen's?"

"Using me already, and we've just met. You don't need me. You can get a good table there on your own." She grinned.

"What's your favorite place to eat?"

"At home; really. I'd rather cook our dinner than go any-where."

"That really sounds good."

116

"You've never married?"

"I was married; divorced about three years ago. We lived near San Francisco. It wasn't such a bad marriage, as long as I obeyed all the prescribed rules and regulations, but when I started having independent thoughts it all fell apart." He swiftly changed the subject. "What are we seeing tonight? Is it any good?"

"Not bad. There are some good location shots even if you don't like the acting. Some of it was shot in Jasper up in Canada. Fabulous country. Do you ever get out in the fresh air?"

"Not much right now. I used to spend a lot of time in the back country of the Sierras, until I moved east."

"Have you ever fished the Rogue in southern Oregon? That's really my country."

"No, but I've always wanted to. That's the one the Indian boats go up, isn't it?"

"Right. It's much tamer now. When I was a kid they had little one-lung engines and propellers on long shafts that they lifted up in the shallow rapids. Now they have these water-jet boats that can go anywhere. But it's still one of the few wild rivers—the Corps of Engineers hasn't wrecked it yet, thank God."

"Where do you fish it—way up?"

"No, you don't have to go that far. The boat will drop you off anywhere, but it's hard to move up and down along the bank, so you have to go where you can get to several riffles easily."

"Riffles?"

"That's what the people there call the rapids. You fish the tail of the riffle. Or the big pools, or where the creeks come in. I could show you one place—"

"Sounds great. When?"

"If you're serious, we'll do it. Can you go fishing with a scarlet woman? How about your Republican reputation? How about the lady with the shoulders?"

"Fishing is as American as apple pie, Miss Douglas. The President is in favor of large families, homemade bread and fishing. Maggie does not check me in and out. I think it could be arranged."

He was, at one level, already hopelessly infatuated with the girl he identified as the movie star—an erotically desirable female whose mobile mouth he wanted to feel. He was intellectually intrigued with the contrast between that glamorous person he linked with the motion pictures and news photographs and the real woman he now encountered beside him, Lani Douglas of Corvallis and the Rogue River. Right then, during the salad course, he wanted to touch her, as if to reassure himself of her tangible reality. If he touched her and she welcomed his touch they would touch again, and it would be easier the second time. But he feared that if he only sat and talked, and did not reach out, then in the coming nights when his thought rested on her she would become disembodied for him, too unreal.

"You asked about children," she was saying. "Do you have any?"

"No."

"My sister has two. I'm an aunt and I love it. I spoil my nephews."

"You want a child, don't you?" he asked. She put her hand on top of his on the table, impulsively, as if to stop the question. But it was asked. So she answered it.

"I still want a baby. More than anything else in my life." Her mouth worked. "Goldberg wanted nothing to interfere with the shooting schedules. He was too old for it, anyway. He'd have been a lousy father."

She had touched him. Now with certainty he knew, intuitively, that they would touch again. He would know that mouth.

"What is your White House office like?" she asked.

"Very old-fashioned. It's not really in the White House; it's next door. Do you know the EOB—the old gray building west of the White House, with all the porches and chimneys?"

"No. I don't remember it."

"Well, that's where I am. The ceilings are sixteen feet high; the door handles have the symbols of the departments that were housed there in the old days. Once the State Department, the War

Department and one other were all in there at the same time. My handles have the War Department eagle on them."

"Mr. Warren, excuse me," said the lady on his left. "I want to tell Miss Romera how much I liked her latest picture."

Robin leaned back so the two women could converse over his plate. He resented the interruption. He was consciously flattered that Lani Romera wanted to know about his work, and he didn't want her to stop asking questions. The dinner would end soon and there would be no more opportunity to talk with her this way. Time was precious; he was not interested in spending it on Mrs. Perry Germane's opinions.

With their company divided in the two rooms, the Caprons proposed no toasts after dinner. Champagne was served with the fruit, then Julie Capron appeared at the double doors to invite everyone to find chairs in the living room for coffee.

The room was rapidly filling with guests; the servants moved among them with trays of small coffees. Julie Capron appeared at Robin's side. "Would you mind sitting on cushions, Mr. Warren? I'm a little short of comfortable chairs, but those big pillows should be nice. OK?"

"OK, provided you call me Robin."

"Sure, Robin. Don't you like Lani? She is one of my favorites."

"Yes, I'm truly grateful to you for the seating arrangement." He was looking around the room. Julie Capron anticipated his question.

"Lani is in our bedroom," she said. "Her escort became ill during dinner and went in to lie down. She's looking after him."

"Our film tonight," Auguste Capron began to announce, "is so new I haven't seen it myself. But Larry Zionnet swears it is the most beautiful thing Superior Studios has done in years. It's rather long, so we should begin it now, I think. Is everyone comfortable?"

As Robin settled into a pile of very large harem cushions he heard a buzzing above and behind him. A six-foot section of the paneling was sliding to the side to expose four projection windows.

Down at the other end of the living room a large screen was appearing in the same way, all by remote control. The lights dimmed; Robin had room beside him on the pillows and watched for Lani to appear in the hall doorway, as the film credits began, but she did not come.

The picture was beautiful enough, but Sim Coggins' constant whispering to Maggie and Lani's disappearance put Robin out of the mood for the Canadian Rockies. Sometime during the first reel Julie Capron joined him on the big cushions to watch the picture with more intentness than it deserved. Perhaps that's what the Caprons talked about in the eighteenth year of their marriage, Robin thought. She led the occasional laughter, a bit too soon, a bit too long. Warren looked at her in the dancing light reflected from the screen; perhaps she was a bright and attractive woman with some problems in her life that came out only in the dark.

The projectionist raised the room lights gradually during the last fifteen seconds of the film. Robin helped Julie Capron to her feet.

"Did you like it?" she asked.

"Very much. Wonderful scenery."

Auguste Capron came to them from the front hallway.

"Lani had to leave; her escort was ill," Capron said. "She was sorry not to be able to say goodbye. She asked me to give you this note. I think you impressed her very much."

"Thanks. I found her very different than I thought I would. Very genuine."

"That's what makes her a star. That genuine quality comes through on the screen. I am very proud of her."

"I've enjoyed myself this evening, Auguste. You were very kind to think of me."

"I've been thinking of you a great deal lately, Robin. I want us to have a serious conversation very soon when I come to Washington. Perhaps a lunch or dinner?"

"I'd like that." As Capron placed a hand on his upper arm, then moved away, Robin felt a surge, a foretaste of his future. All the disparate and uncertain elements of his life were beginning to

120

converge. This is where it all really happens; in a rich room like this. This is where directions are determined, the courses and distances that the nation would travel, in quiet dinner talk and small conversations over coffee. And he was obviously going to be a part of it. He moved to one side of the room and opened the heavy envelope. Lani's handwriting was large and plain.

"Good night, Robin," it said. "John is ill and I'll take him home. I wanted to talk to you more, but we'll save it for next time. I'll be in D.C. in a few days. Let's have a date. I'll call you. Love, L."

"What's that, Bird? Mash notes?" Maggie Valle had moved beside him as he read.

He folded the note too quickly. "My dinner partner had to leave during the movie. She left a note saying good night."

"The lovely Lani? Sim Coggins says you two really hit it off. She hardly said two words to him all night."

"Well, you made up for that, I noticed. I think she and Coggins have a past together. She really cut him dead."

"He filled my ear about her. I gather that she collects lumberjacks—and politicians."

"What are you collecting, Mag? Trouble? That Coggins is the Senate's biggest chaser, you know."

"Don't worry your little head about your Aunt Maggie, son. She can handle it. How do we get home?"

"That car will take us. What's the hurry? You got a late date?"

She shot him a revealing look. Either she had a date or wished she had. "No. I'm tired. Can we go? That damn movie bored me stiff."

The Caprons had stationed themselves near the door to the entry area and were saying farewells. Julie Capron embraced Maggie while Auguste quietly renewed his suggestion to Robin that they lunch in the next few days.

Mike Meyerson was downstairs to show them to the limousine and bid Robin an effusive farewell. He quickly reviewed the next morning's schedule, promised the car for ten at the Carlyle, and

121

double-checked the location of the White House airplane. He would be prepared. Above all else Mr. Capron's people were prepared.

As the chauffeur wheeled around the corner and headed east, Maggie and Robin said nothing. At Third Avenue Robin found the silence too awkward. "What's behind Julie Capron's interest in your father?" he asked.

"I don't know. She was certainly open about it, wasn't she? Sim says she's very loyal to her husband."

"Coggins should know; he probably has a form book in which the entire female population of the Eastern Seaboard is rated on things like loyalty-to-husband, favorite position and glove size. That is one miserable shit, if you'll pardon my saying so."

"I don't know. I thought he was very attentive and quite attractive."

"Dumb as dirt. When he asks questions in committee hearings you know what the old hands do? They know that all his questions are canned for him by his staff in advance. So a witness who wants to duck one of his questions just asks him to please explain the question. That ends it."

"That's not my impression. He seemed very quick to me."

"Fast, maybe. Not quick."

"Listen, I am really tired, Bird. My shoulder hurts. I think I'll just say good night and go to sleep, if you don't mind." Remote. Businesslike. Get rid of the stiff.

"Sure. I'll just ride up with you to be sure you aren't mugged in the elevator."

"As you wish."

At her door they kissed. She held him at the back of his neck with her hand, drew him to her and they kissed again, tongues deep.

At last she drew back and looked down at their feet.

"God, you are hard on me, Mags," he said. "When are you going to let up a little?"

She frowned. "I told you this once before, Robin, and I really feel it: I have some kind of a predestination where you're concerned. I can't leave you alone. And I can't let you be less than all you are. I know you hate it, but I can't help it. Is that love?"

"If it is"—he took her arm and moved her toward the door—"it's not the kind I have in mind for tonight. No predestiny tonight, OK?"

"OK. The only other thing I have to give you tonight is a very tense shoulder muscle. Very tight. How's chances for a little massage?"

"That same one? Sure. You'll be all relaxed before you know it."

Maggie's apartment was cold. She was taut and tired, and it all went badly.

Maggie excused herself and went into her bedroom as soon as she put her coat in the small entry closet. Robin didn't feel like having another drink. He looked out the window. The apartments in the building opposite were either dark or shaded. He walked into the bedroom. Maggie was hastily remaking her large bed. A pile of sheets and pillowcases was on the floor by her feet.

"What the hell are you doing, Mags?"

"Freshening the bed. It was awful."

"You don't need to do that." He took off his jacket and hung it on the doorknob to the closet.

"I wanted to." She brushed a strand of hair off her forehead.

"Not necessary. Want a drink?"

"I don't know." She straightened up, then bent to pick up the linen. She tried to move by him with the bundle, but he reached for it and took it from her.

"Look, Mags, you get into a good, hot bath. I'll make you a drink. You'll feel a lot better."

"I hate baths. But a shower sounds like too much work. OK. I'll run a bath. I'd like a whiskey, rocks."

By the time he'd blasted ice cubes from her old refrigerator and made their drinks she was stretched out in the big tub, steaming water still pouring in around her. He handed her an old-fashioned glass, put his on the sink and pulled off his necktie.

"Close the door, Bird. It's cold."

"Sure. You're beautiful." He put the palm of his hand on her cheek. She was very warm. He pulled a short stool beside the tub, rolled up his shirtsleeves and took her shoulder muscle between the fingers of his right hand. It was hard. He noticed little goosebumps race down her arms in response to his touch. Her nipples rose and hardened. She stirred the water with her hands.

"Turn it off, will you, Bird? That's enough. When I fill it too much it leaks on the people downstairs."

"OK. You relax. You're tight as a bowstring."

"I know. I can't help it. Listen, I won't be very good company tonight, even if you get me drunk." She took a big drink and handed him the glass. "I'm very tired and very tense. I think I just want to be all by myself."

"I owe you a massage."

"Not tonight, OK? I'm just not very good company. As you know."

"Sure, Mag."

"Good night, Robin. I love you. I guess that's the problem."

"Goodbye, Mag. I'll call you."

Back at the Carlyle, Robin Warren removed his jacket, tie and shoes, poured a light drink and polished an apple on his pant leg. He picked up the telephone on the desk in the very yellow-and-green living room of his suite and gave the White House number to the operator.

"White House," said the clipped, overworked voice.

"This is Robin Warren. I'm in New York for the night at the Carlyle."

"One minute, Mr. Warren. Yes, sir, Miss O'Reilly gave us your itinerary. You'll be back here tomorrow at eleven-thirty?"

"Right.. While I have you, could you do me a favor? I want to reach a Miss Lani Romera. She lives in California, but she's in New York tonight. Mike Meyerson would know how to reach her."

"I think we still have a number for Mr. Meyerson," the operator said. "One minute."

The apple was soft and pulpy. He threw it into the tin

124

wastebasket and drank a little Scotch to erase the mossy taste. The operator was back in four minutes.

"Mr. Warren? Miss Romera is at the Plaza. Shall I ring there for you?"

"If it's no trouble, please."

New York to D.C. and back to New York. One time when in Dallas he had gone through the White House board to call a General Motors executive in Detroit, and the GM switchboard had, in turn, connected him to a telephone in Florida. He was getting accustomed to this kind of magic. Mike Meyerson would know why the White House operator wanted to reach Lani. So Capron would know. But what difference did it make?

"Mr. Warren, Miss Romera has retired and left word she would take no calls. Shall I have the Plaza operator ring through anyway?"

"No, that's all right. Thanks for your trouble. Good night."

"Good night, Mr. Warren."

He clicked the cradle button and gave the Carlyle operator Maggie Valle's number. She answered sleepily on the third ring.

"Hi. I just wanted to say good night," he said lamely. He had not expected her to answer.

"That's bullshit too, Bird. I don't need your goddamn telephone bed check tonight. I'm not your property. You make me fucking furious. Now I'm wide awake and mad and I won't sleep for hours. You goddamn infant!" She hung up. It was just as well. He didn't know what he had intended to say to her. Perhaps nothing.

CHAPTER **11**   The three-block walk to the Metropolitan Club was unpleasant. The May heat was gray and lay upon the noon-hour crowds of Washington like a warm, damp cloth.

Robin Warren left a moist handprint where he pushed the glass door to enter the vestibule of the old yellow-brick men's club; he was a few minutes late. A small L-shaped area between the door and a large display board was the territory of a wispy black man whose sole function was to recognize the members of the Metropolitan Club and place a sort of cribbage peg in a little hole next to the member's name on the display board. He was also supposed to require guests to register in a ledger on the narrow table in front of the board, but sometimes he forgot. Robin had invaded these hallowed precincts on several other occasions, with club members at his elbow, and had watched with amusement and curiosity as the little majordomo was greeted by name—he was Henry to the members—and he, in turn, mumbled the member's name in response, diffidently tapped the guest book with a long finger, then fumbled in a little cardboard box for a wooden peg.

"I'm to meet Mr. Capron," Robin said to Henry.

"Miz Capronee," Henry mumbled. He shuffled to the board and ran his finger down the pegs from the top of the first column. "Miz Capronee." Robin saw a peg next to Capron's printed name. Henry ran past it, then returned, tapped the peg twice with the tip of his finger and nodded. "He here."

"Do you want my name?"

Henry blinked his rheumy eyes twice. "No, suh. Miz Capronee have sign you up, suh. Coatroom on yo' lef'."

There was no need for a coatroom attendant that steamy spring day. Robin turned into the lobby, where a knot of men stood in front of a narrow elevator door. Others were sunk in deep leather chairs reading the *Wall Street Journal* or the *Star-Post,* then glancing at the doorway as they waited for hosts or guests. The door to the men's room swung to and fro at one side. Robin didn't see Capron in the lobby, so he decided to wash his face.

The washroom was less elegant than those of the Bohemian Club and the Pacific Union League, both of which Warren had visited in San Francisco. The Metropolitan Club's old marble had been retained on the walls, but new fixtures rather cheapened the effect. One could tell a good deal about a men's club by its

126

washroom. Those that still put out hairbrushes, toothpicks, cuticle sticks and linen were the holdouts for Something Still Worthwhile, but all of those costly extras were breasting an economic tide. The Metropolitan Club still offered good cloth towels, but the other amenities had vanished when the House Committee decided it could no longer afford a full-time washroom attendant. Even the little bars of Ivory Soap wrapped in monogrammed paper had given way to the liquid soap dispensers. Robin washed away the street grime and emerged as Auguste Capron came from the bar across the lobby. The industrialist smiled broadly and extended his hand. He wore a gray worsted suit of rather narrow cut, a vest, and soft dark tie with tiny figures in light blue. And as always, loafers polished to a diamond gleam, Robin noted.

"Robin, so good of you to come," he said. "Isn't it an awful day?"

"I made the mistake of walking." Robin laughed. "It was a real workout. As bad as summer."

"Well, it will be cool upstairs. We can have a drink up there. Shall we?"

They crowded into the little elevator with three other men. All three greeted Capron deferentially. He nodded in return. On the third floor Capron led Warren to the door of the large dining room where he was greeted warmly by the maiître d' and ushered to a table by the window. The room lacked some of the aura of wealth and elegance one associates with men's-club dining rooms. The wooden furniture was of medium weight, the drapes nondescript, the silver dining service a little battered and passé. The waiters and busboys all seemed harried and overworked.

As Robin and his host walked to their table, heads turned just as if Capron had been a beautiful redhead in a bathing suit. At the west end of the room at his regular table, Poolie Smith, the syndicated columnist, stopped buttering his toast to watch Auguste Capron lead his young White House guest to his table.

Poolie was having lunch with an Assistant Secretary of Energy in an effort to flatter from him some hint of whether the Frankling people would relax restrictions against superports along the

Atlantic Coast. He was not having much luck. Now it appeared that the arrival of Capron with that young what's-his-name from the White House just might make a better story anyway. He would stop by their table on the way out and see what kind of sparks he might strike.

Poolie Smith always sat at the west end of the room on the right, where he could see everything and everyone. No one else had the same table every day and it cost him a considerable sum at Christmas to make certain of it. A few of the members had informally complained to the chairman of the Dining Room Committee that such a regular arrangement was deplorable, but the Club Board had tacitly countenanced it for years. Poolie Smith was a special case; he was the club's only working journalist. In fact, Poolie's father had belonged to Metropolitan for many years before he died, and he had put up Poolie's name for membership while the boy was still at Yale. Everyone thought the boy would follow his father into the bank, and when he came down from Yale Poolie had tried it, but it hadn't worked out. No one remembered quite why anymore. The war came along and when Poolie came back from the Navy he'd gone to work for a New York paper for a while. Then he and a *Business Week* reporter, Bill Kapotnik, got the idea for their Washington column. During all these years away Poolie had paid his club dues on time.

It was virtually impossible for an active newsperson to be admitted to membership in the Metropolitan Club. They had their own club of sorts in one of the hotels. Nor were actors encouraged. The only black members were government officials of high rank. Three. Since 1965 a number of Jews had been accepted. But no women.

Most of the membership was Permanent Washington, not the governmental transients who came and went with the election tides. Good solid bankers, lawyers and businessmen, a few established lobbyists—including Jep Valle—and about fifty New York members, of whom Auguste Capron was one.

As he and Robin began to order lunch the "drop-bys" began. Robin did not try to keep a count, but during their lunch several

128

prosperous members came by Capron's table to say a few words of greeting to Capron and be acknowledged. Capron bore the visits with good-humored *noblesse oblige*. The mighty of the Washington establishment lined up to pledge him fealty, curry his favor, gain his custom unashamedly, and he accepted their groveling as his due, nothing more, without relish or evident satisfaction. During gaps in this ritual visitation Capron and his young guest ordered salads and observed the conversational amenities.

"I bring you greetings from my wife, Robin. As I left this morning she especially asked to be remembered to you."

"That's very nice. She is a lovely lady. And what a hostess! She ran that party of yours with a deft touch."

"She's a remarkable girl. You made a very favorable impression on her—and on our guests who met you. Jamey Jamieson at the bank mentioned you when I saw him this week at our directors' meeting."

Warren didn't know how to respond to this very obtrusive flattery. He found something to do with his water glass until Capron began again:

"Robin, you recall I mentioned the expropriation of American properties when we first met?"

"Yes, I do."

"This country is now faced with a serious situation. Have you heard anyone discussing the problem our telephone and telegraph company is having in Uruguay?"

"No, I don't believe so."

"As you know, the military government there is a Russian satellite, thanks to Castro and thanks to Carter's naïveté. Atfirst we were able to do business with the Marxist Junta. They needed our technical know-how. But they insisted that we train Uruguayans to operate the telephone and telegraph system, and over a period of two years they have gradually forced out our people by revoking their work permits, one by one."

"Aren't they nationalizing what industry they have now?" Robin asked.

"Yes, they've gone slowly since the takeover, but this year they

129

have begun to nationalize everything owned by foreigners. We are certain that our communications company will go very soon."

"Will they compensate you?"

"Only a token payment, if they treat us as they have the others."

"What can you do?"

"Nothing, unless the President is willing to help us. I very much need to speak with President Frankling about the general problem of expropriation. The difficulty is not limited to Uruguay, you see. There are steps that can be taken in Uruguay, however, that other countries will recognize as a signal that the United States does not intend to permit that kind of abuse of its citizens. I really must see him. Can you arrange it for me?"

"I'm not sure, Auguste. But I will certainly be happy to try. Have you tried to see General Durrien? He might help."

"My vice-president for international operations has talked to him. But your General suggests a study, and the creation of a compensatory fund, and an examination of the options, and a referral to the State Department. While all that is creaking along, the Junta will have seized the prize, and our opportunity will be lost. If the President is to act effectively he must do so at once."

"Will you be in Washington long?"

"I will stay as long as is necessary. I will be at my Georgetown house until I hear from you—"

"Ah, Mr. Capron," interrupted a nasal rasp. "I'm Poolie Smith. We met at Ambassador Rashid's this winter."

Capron looked up at the intruder blankly. "Yes?" he replied.

Smith wore a high-neck gray sweater under his tweed jacket. Ivy League even on the hottest day, Robin thought.

"You are Robert Warren, aren't you?" Smith asked.

"Robin Warren," he said.

"I didn't know you knew one another," the columnist gambited.

"Yes," said Capron tersely.

"I guess the President's Open Door is open to the titans these days, eh?" Smith pressed.

"We're open to everyone," Robin replied. It was up to Capron to brush this fellow off; it was his club.

"I'd like to come talk to you some day soon, Warren. Any objections?"

"Fine. Call my office."

"I'll do that. Nice seeing you again, Mr. Capron." Poolie Smith slouched away, tapping a roll of paper against the back of his left hand.

"Sorry for the interruption," Capron said. "I really do not care for that man; for some reason he is invited to most of the dinner parties I go to in this town. I see him everywhere. I don't understand why hostesses here include the press. Is it that they want to see their names in the paper?"

"Some do. Others like to think they are maintaining a salon of sorts, I guess," Robin replied.

"What are my chances of seeing President Frankling tomorrow or the next day, Robin?" Capron was returning to the interrupted subject of their luncheon.

"I'll talk to David Hale this afternoon. He has total control of the President's schedule. And before I see him I'll have to prepare a memo proposing your appointment; so I should ask a few questions."

"Surely."

"About how long do you think you'd need?"

"No more than twenty minutes. I'll be prepared to be brief."

"Should General Durrien or some other expert sit in with you and the President?"

"I would prefer no one else. We know more about the situation there than anyone in government, actually."

"What would be the result of the meeting—that is, what—"

"I understand," Capron interrupted. "What the President decides to do is up to him; I don't know his policy in such a case. I wish only to present the facts. I will abide any result."

"And you're available the rest of the week?"

"If need be. But time is of the essence. Uruguay is vulnerable just now, as I will explain to President Frankling. Next week, less so. Next month, probably not at all."

"Good. I think that's all I need to ask."

"Someday, Robin, we must discuss your future in detail. The President is very fortunate to have you now, but he cannot expect to keep you too long. There are opportunities and challenges even beyond those you are experiencing now. We must talk about them."

"I really can't do that until I decide to leave, Auguste. I don't want to develop divided loyalties."

"Of course. That's very wise of you. But remember what I've said when the time comes."

As he walked back to the White House, Robin rehearsed what he would say to David Hale about Capron's appointment. If a passerby had stopped him on the sidewalk and asked if he had been seduced by Auguste Capron's suggestion of future employment, Robin would have stoutly assured him that he had avoided even the appearance of such influence with an immediate rebuff. But he could not help but entertain the notion of a high-paying and challenging position in United International's tall, thin headquarters building on Fifth Avenue. He might take an apartment at the Dakota, and it would be exciting living in New York, moving in that social set which Capron described; he would move about the cities of the world, working in the interest of United International; all intriguing possibilities to be overtly denied while being savored *sub rosa*. On returning to his office he sent a red-tagged priority schedule request to David Hale, recommending that the President see Capron at once.

David Hale responded to Robin Warren's memorandum within two hours. Hale's secretary called Kathy O'Reilly to summon Robin to meet with Hale at 7 P.M. Hale was eating his dinner from a tray at the end of his conference table when Robin was admitted.

"Want to talk to you about Capron," Hale said, cutting a chop and larding it with thick mint jelly.

"Sure." Robin pulled back one of the shiny leather armchairs

132

which were shoved under the table, sat down and at once slid forward to its edge in spite of himself.

"The President's not opposed to seeing him. But Capron's been a heavy contributor to Democrats for years. What brings him to us all of a sudden?"

Robin briefly recounted his Business Council encounter with Capron and described in detail Capron's favorable comments about the President. "I think he really is ideologically close to the President," Robin concluded.

"If that is so," Hale said, "will he be willing to support the President?" He wiped his mouth with a large red linen napkin and threw it over the tray. "Can we expect him to show his approval of the President in some very tangible way?"

"You mean a contribution?"

"Sure. Oh, not a declared contribution; that might embarrass him with his Democrat friends. Just something quiet. Something large." Hale grinned, quick and flat.

"I really don't know," Warren replied. "I didn't discuss anything like that with him. I couldn't guess."

"OK. I'll take it from here. He's waiting to hear from one of us, right? I'll call him tonight. I'll let you know how it goes."

"Wait a minute, David. Capron is mine. I see no need for you to get in between us."

"Actually, I won't. Do you know Archie Goheen?"

"He was the President's partner in Ohio."

"Right. He handles contacts of this kind. He's known to be close, but he's way off there in Cleveland. A *very* discreet gentleman."

"So he'll lift Capron's wallet?"

"No one will feel a thing. And no one in the White House is involved. It's better that way."

"Okay. But I'd like it understood that I'm Capron's contact here. Not you or Smythe or anyone else. I think with the right kind of cultivation we can win him. He could be of great help in the long run."

"He may have some antitrust problems," Hale said casually.

"You might chat with Smythe about them someday. Capron's like everyone else: he's got his troubles."

"Yeah. I'll do that."

Warren gathered himself and moved out the door into Hale's tiny waiting room. Hale's secretary was talking to one of her children on the telephone about fixing dinner. The hallway beyond was vacant. Warren walked a few steps to the stairway, stepped unevenly to the basement level, and went out into West Executive Avenue in the canyon between the West Wing and the Executive Office Building. The dusk was warm and heavy; the light breeze pushed heat against his face. He didn't want to go back to his office; there was nothing there he wanted to work on. He turned back into the basement hallway and went to the policeman's desk. In addition to the large black telephone console a single instrument had been installed at the far end, to be used for non-police calls. He picked it up and punched his office number.

"Mr. Warren's office; Miss O'Reilly."

"Kathy, Robin. I'm going to find a long, cool drink. How about joining me?"

Her pause was a half beat too long. "Oh, gosh, thanks, Boss. But I have a date, with that Marine I was telling you about. Would you like to join us?"

"No, thanks. We'll do it another time. Have fun."

Capron never mentioned his $250,000 "contribution." The invisible Mr. Goheen had handled it all. A late-afternoon appointment with the President was arranged for the next day and Robin was designated to sit in on the meeting as note-taker. It was customary for the President to include a third person from his staff in a meeting like this, as some insurance against misquotation and to handle any follow-up details that might arise during the conversation. Robin seldom was assigned the job unless the President was seeing one of the outside pressure groups that Robin serviced.

Robin arranged with the receptionist to be notified when Capron arrived in the lobby of the West Wing, and again five minutes before the President would see him. When he received the five-minute warning Robin had Kathy O'Reilly arrange for Capron to be moved to the Cabinet Room; then he walked slowly from the EOB across the street, along the basement hallway, past the barbershop, the Secret Service control room, and up the back stairs to the hallway outside the Cabinet Room.

"Auguste, welcome," he said as he swung open the heavy door.

Capron rose and shook his hand. "I'm really very grateful, Robin. This is vital to me."

"I'm glad it worked out. I am going to be in there with you, in case there's some follow-up."

"Of course. Of course."

Young Nick Gurley opened the door at the end of the room and leaned in. "Mr. Capron? The President will see you now." He held the door, then led the way across the small secretarial office to the President's curved door, preceded them through it, and moved to his right to hold the door behind him. "Mr. President," Gurley announced, "Mr. Auguste Capron."

"Yes," said Hugh Frankling. He looked up from the one-page memorandum he was reading, took his glasses into his left hand and stood. As always he was dressed in matching double-breasted coat and pants of dark blue, a red striped tie with a large knot, a white handkerchief in his breast pocket. Capron's plain madras sport coat and gray slacks were too casual by contrast, but it was the President who appeared uncomfortable. He pressed the greeting too hard.

"Over here, Mr. Capron, over here. Come sit by me. Rob, you take that chair and pull it up here to the desk. Fine." He shook Capron's hand across the corner of the massive desk and sat back heavily, waving his glasses at Capron. "I'm told you're concerned about expropriation." His jowls and chins quivered with intensity. "I want you to know, I'm concerned too. Very concerned. As Rob here knows, this is a subject that has come up often. And I can tell you, I am goddamned frustrated over it. There's just not a great deal I can do, beyond providing some compensation for our companies when it happens. Most of the countries that do it don't have a dime's worth of assets in this country, so we can't reciprocate. And we can hardly go to war over a sugar mill or a packing plant. Right? Can hardly go to war."

Robin was embarrassed. His leader was talking too much, pressing too hard. The memorandum which the President had been reading as they came in evidently was the briefing Robin had prepared for the meeting, and Frankling had just regurgitated it. It was a poor, transparent performance, apparently designed to give Capron his money's worth and yet make the meeting a short one. But it was transacted with no style. Robin wanted to interrupt and set a new tone, but he knew he would not. He was a spectator, not a participant in this meeting.

"Mr. President," Capron began quietly, "I am most grateful that you would take your valuable time to see me."

"Of course I'd see you. Of course."

"I would not come here were it not a matter of national concern. One of our companies is threatened by Uruguay, it is so, but what I wish to speak of is a larger issue. Actually, it is an opportunity, rather like the 'window' in a space shot. It will exist for a brief time, and then it will vanish forever. If the United States moves decisively within the next few days—no more than thirty—a Russian client in South America can be restored to the West. If that happens it well may reverse the entire leftward drift in that half of the hemisphere."

"Really? I didn't know. What opportunity?" The President folded his glasses, unfolded them, leaned forward toward Capron, then glanced to see if Warren was taking notes, as if to assure Capron that his words would not be lost.

"General Gómez, the head of their Junta in Uruguay—actually he is the dictator—is about to make his big move. Up until now he and the Junta had not dared to extinguish the political opposition completely. The Marxists narrowly came into power in the last election, as you know, but they have retained a semblance of parliamentary government. The other two parties have been allowed to speak up in opposition. A newspaper has been kept going, but in the past six months the military has clamped down on

136

the newspaper and television, bit by bit. Now it's almost totally in control."

"I often think how nice that would be." Frankling smiled. "Oh, not really; the press is the bulwark of freedom. But what a nuisance." He chuckled twice.

"Foreign companies like our telephone and telegraph company have been subject to more and more restriction since the FPR Junta has been in power. But until now the Marxists haven't felt strong enough to take us over. As you may know, General Gómez has been to Moscow and negotiated a new Russian loan and military aid, and he's feeling very confident. He just returned to Montevideo on Monday, and my people tell me that he plans to dissolve Parliament when it reconvenes June twentieth; then he will nationalize all foreign properties, confiscating any American-owned companies. It will be a total takeover."

"That's less than a month," the President exclaimed. He put on his glasses and fished the briefing paper from his out box. "I don't recall being briefed on that situation," he said.

"It may be, Mr. President, that my information has come in before yours. There are advantages to having the telephone system in a country."

"But the CIA must have fifty men down there. We must spend millions in that place. Why the hell don't we know about things like this in advance?" The President shook his head helplessly, his wattles vibrating lightly. He tossed the stiff memorandum into a wooden desk box, as if abandoning hope that the CIA might help him, then leaned forward, twined his fingers and looked at Capron. "Well, Mr. Capron, what is to be done?"

"I would not ask you to act upon my word alone. The first thing, I suggest, is for you to verify what I have told you. If you are satisfied that the Communists are about to move, then we can move first. How, when, are matters for the experts. The CIA and my people have collaborated before with some success. I will put my Uruguay people at your disposal, of course."

"Good. That's what we'll do." Frankling nodded at Robin. "I want the CIA told what Mr. Capron has told me. When it's verified I want a plan of action on my desk. If we wait until after the takeover it *will* be too late. We've done that too often. Cuba, then Peru and Bolivia. It's time we turned this around." His fist came gently to the desk top. "Rob, I want you to follow up on this; be sure the CIA contacts Mr. Capron's men. Keep them moving. I want a plan immediately. Is that clear?"

"Yes, sir."

"I'm glad you came in, Mr. Capron. It's seldom that I get an early warning of this kind. But when I do I intend to act, and act decisively."

"Mr. President, I am simply delighted at your decisiveness and strength. I congratulate you."

"Not at all, Mr. Capron. It goes with the job, as they say." Frankling stood. Capron and Robin stood.

It was stilted role-playing. Robin wondered if Frankling ever realized how false and pompous he sounded at times like this. Capron was too clever to be believing his own enthusiastic act; it had to be a put-on. But he was getting exactly what he wanted from Frankling, with surprising ease. Maybe it was the money that he had given Hale. Or perhaps there were other motivations. Frankling was a devious son of a bitch; often his reasons were obscure. But underneath he was clever and bright, and had to realize how insincere his orotund phrases sounded. And Capron was playing right along.

"Thank you, Mr. President, for your courtesy in hearing me." Capron extended his arm and shook the President's hand enthusiastically. Capron was more animated than Robin had ever seen him. "Thank you," he repeated. Frankling began to move him toward the hall door at the far end of the oval.

"I think we'll keep this project out of the normal bureaucratic swamp, eh, Rob?" The President looked at Warren and winked conspiratorially. "If we go through the regular routine we'll have the damn State Department sniping at us every minute. No, I'll handle it right from here. Right from the cockpit." Frankling put his hand on the doorknob. "Rob here will be your contact. Keep us informed of whatever you learn from down there, right?"

"Of course, Mr. President. We'll do that.

"Rob, stay with me, please. I want you to do something for me. Goodbye." The President opened the door for Capron, delivering him into the hallway, then let the door swing shut behind him.

"Rob," Frankling began as he walked slowly toward his desk, looking at the great Presidential seal embossed in relief in the plaster ceiling, "I don't want this Uruguay project talked about. Not even to Durrien. I'll brief him—and David Hale—but it must be kept absolutely graveyard if it's to succeed. So you're not to talk to anyone about it except the CIA, and there only at the highest levels. Understood?"

"Yes, sir."

Frankling patrolled the edge of the carpet in front of the French windows, looking at the floor.

"I want you to call Cooper Dewey at the CIA. He's the head of their clandestine operations. Tell him to come see you. Get everything they know about that Junta. Check Capron's facts with Dewey. No one else. And have him tell us how to move. I want to move quickly."

"Yes, sir."

"It's right to do, you know. And there are other considerations, far beyond Uruguay. If we tip over that little tinhorn Communist dictator right now, it will send a shudder all through the seacoast nations that are lining up with Russia. By God, there can be real dividends in this for us."

"Mr. President . . ." Robin began. He was in General Durrien's territory and it made him uncomfortable.

"I want you to follow through on this, Rob. Drop anything else. This is top-drawer; vitally important." As if he were alone, Frankling added, "And it is right to do. It's right to do." He looked up and brightened. "This should be a welcome diversion for you after sitting there listening to those dreary special-interest groups day after day." He chuckled. "I'm glad it's you who has to listen to them and not me."

"Oh . . ." Robin began to say something appropriately, inanely reassuring.

139

"Well, have fun with the CIA for a while! And remember: not a word to a soul. I'll tell Hale you're to see me whenever you need to, but I may not tell him why quite yet. Don't you tell him. I'll let him know when it's appropriate. Understood?" The President leaned forward across his desk, both hands flat on the shining wood top.

"Yes, sir. You're telling me to tell no one here. Not even the General?"

"Not even Durrien."

"I'll go call Mr. Dewey right now."

"Good. Let's get started." Frankling sat erect in his big leather chair. "It is the right thing to do," he breathed. "It really is."

CHAPTER **12** Warren returned to his office enveloped in euphoria. He had just been invested with a significant and exclusive responsibility by President Hugh Frankling—a delegation of personal, Presidential and Constitutional prerogatives, no small thing for a man of thirty-seven. He had received the demonstrated confidence of his President, and in addition the gratitude of Auguste Capron, explicitly expressed by the industrialist during their farewells at the door of the West Wing. He felt elated and fulfilled. The job was, after all, in the biggest league, and he was doing it well.

He breezed through the reception area of his office, taking seven call slips from Mary Marlbone's outstretched hand as he passed her desk. "No calls, Mary, for the rest of the day, OK?"

"Yes, sir. That one from the League of Women Voters is urgent, the lady said. Kathy has some others."

"They'll have to be returned later."

Kathy O'Reilly followed him into his office with her pad. He dropped his notebook on the desk, shed his jacket, loosened his tie and sat down.

"I've got something I must do right now, Kathy. What is it?"

"Barney Mulloy at the Associated General Contractors says that their convention program is going to press tonight, and he must know today whether the President is coming to their convention, and which day."

"OK. Tell Nick Gurley to call him."

"The Attorney General's wife called."

"What does she want?"

"You. She wouldn't tell me what it was about. Is she all right?"

"I don't know. Why?"

"She called just after you left and she sounded pie-eyed."

"That's the rumor. I don't know her at all, but there are a lot of stories around about her. Why the hell is she calling me?"

"I wish I knew. But she made it plain that I'm only the hired help."

"Amazing. What else can happen today?"

"Well, for openers, you are due at the German Embassy at eight, your dress clothes are in the closet, and your massage appointment is in forty minutes."

"Thanks. Now beat it, will you?"

"Sure. Don't forget Mrs. Smythe."

"Impossible to forget her. Out! Out!"

The brunette laughed, pretended to run a few steps, and closed the door firmly behind her. He reached for his telephone as he flipped open the black notebook and told the White House telephone operator he needed to speak to a Mr. Cooper Dewey, one of the assistant directors at the CIA. She left the line briefly, then came back on. "Mr. Dewey," she announced.

"Mr. Dewey, my name is Robin Warren. I've been asked by the President to have a talk with you about Uruguay."

"Certainly, Mr. Warren." The voice was spare and reedy. "When would you like to come over?"

"I think, under the circumstances, it would be better if we met here. How about nine in the morning?"

"We'd better say ten. Give the Virginia traffic a chance to clear. Let me have my staff meeting. Uruguay, you say?"

"That's right."

"Where do I find you?"

"I'm in the EOB, first floor, west."

"I'll be there at ten, Mr. Warren." He was obviously reluctant to travel, but everyone knew that the CIA people had their Langley headquarters wired; if the Senate Intelligence Committee hearings had accomplished nothing else, they had resulted in seventy-five percent fewer meetings being held where the CIA could tape them.

After calling the League of Women Voters and the White House staff man who was liaison to the House, Robin asked the operator for Mrs. Carleton Smythe.

He waited about a minute. At last the operator came on the line: "I'm sorry to keep you waiting, Mr. Warren. Mrs. Smythe is there, her maid says, but she has not yet come to the telephone; I—"

The intervening voice was heavy but smooth. The ends of certain words lilted upward, the accents heavy on interior syllables, in the Southern fashion.

"Mister Warren? I'm so appreciative of your calling. [Ahm so *pre*ciative uv yo' *call*in'.] We met at the White House, do you recall?"

"Of course, Mrs. Smythe. How can I help you?"

"That is so kind of you—being so forthcoming with your helpfulness [hepfuhnesh]. I do need help, badly. Badly."

"What's the trouble?"

"The trouble, Mr. Warren, is not a what, it is a who, named Mrs. Gloria President Frankling, that's what the trouble is. That's *who* the trouble is."

"The First Lady?"

"I call her the so-called First Lady, is what I call her. I hope you have some guts, Mr. Warren. Because you have got to be

142

courageous; you must be a brave person to do something about the so-called First Lady. If you love the President of the United States, you've got to. Do you know why I'm calling you for my desperate help, Mr. Warren? Do you?"

"No, ma'am." This was one for kid gloves. The lady was obviously drunk.

"I'll tell you why. Because you, you love the President of the United States and you are a quarterback, that's why. You are cool under fire. You played rough, tough football, didn't you? Out there at—at—"

"Stanford."

"That's right. That's where you were the quarterback. [Tha's whea yo' wuh the quarrbeck.] That's why. You're cool and you're strong. That's the kind of man that I need for my desperate help."

"What can I do, Mrs. Smythe?"

"I'll tell you, Mr. Warren. I'll tell you." She paused. He could hear glass on glass. "Now. Do you know about my project? Do you?"

"No, ma'am. I don't."

"It's *my* project. The Cabinet wives. For the President of the United States. I'm doing it for him. I—he said I could. I told him. For the welfare mothers, you know. All the Cabinet wives."

"And?"

"I'm going to have this lovely meeting at Blair House for everyone and Secretary—uh—the wop at Welfare with the fat wife—"

"Secretary Amandola?"

"He's sending a Welfare man to talk to us. Blair House is going to fix up a lovely luncheon and I've looked after all of the arrangements, and the invitations have all gone out. It's going to be just beautiful."

"It sounds very nice."

"Oh, but the trouble! That so-called First Woman. What she is doing to the President of the United States! She refuses to come to my lovely luncheon. Now, she cannot do that to me, Mr. Warren! She cannot do that to our President. And you are the cool, strong quarterback who is going to throw the touchdown pass and save my lovely luncheon! That skinny bitch cannot do that after the President of the United States of America has told me that I could. She has *got* to come. That's all there is to be said, honey."

"Have you talked to Mrs. Frankling?"

"Have I tried a hundred times? She won't talk to me, honey. Refuses. Too goddamned busy, her secretary says. You know what that is. Am I the wife of the Attorney General of the United States? I wouldn't treat a dog the way she treats me. You have got to do something, Mr. Warren. And you have got to do it at once!"

"Well, Mrs. Smythe, my job over here has nothing at all to do with Mrs. Frank—"

"Are you wondering why I even want her at my lovely luncheon? Treating me as cruelly as she does, why would I favor her with one of my precious invitations? Is that it? I'll tell you why, Mr. Warren. Because if she doesn't appear the whole thing is *ruined*. You know? If the Cabinet wives hear she has declined my invitation, they may just not come, either. Some of them are very weak ladies. And she knows that, the dirty bitch. If she comes they have *got* to come. Understand how that works, honey?"

"I understand, but—"

"So it's trouble if she refuses. Wait a minute."

Glass on glass again. A drink-long pause.

"Will you call me back today, Mr. Warren? I'll wait right here by my telephone for you. Won't budge an inch. The President of the United States of America and I are counting on you!"

"This is something I know nothing at all about, Mrs. Smythe . . ."

The telephone went dead in his ear. She had hung up on him.

Warren pushed Kathy O'Reilly's button and picked up the phone.

"Who handles Mrs. Frankling's appointments?"

"Sandra Cappoletti. Why?"

"She's declined Mrs. Smythe's luncheon. Cabinet wives."

"Do you want to get into a mess like that?"

"No."

"Let me check on it."

"Thanks. Drunken Southern belles I don't need right now."

"I'll let you know."

Cooper Dewey looked like an elderly schoolteacher, sallowed by years in the classroom, his energies spent keeping order with a stern hand. He looked like an ascetic, unhappy—unwell—man in his sixties, who peered out at the world through thin wire glasses. He was propelled everywhere in a chrome wheelchair by a large black man.

He was not thrilled to be at the White House, that was clear. There were few greeting amenities as he was wheeled into Warren's office. Dewey dismissed his helper with a bony wave and blinked sourly at his host. Robin wondered when Dewey had last been pleased, if ever.

From his notes, Robin described Auguste Capron's meeting with the President, and the President's instructions for the CIA. Dewey took no notes. Occasionally he shifted painfully in the wheelchair, lifting his body with his thin arms.

"The President wants an intelligence estimate of the situation in Uruguay?" Dewey talked through his nose. The words turned on their sides to make it through, vibrating thinly.

"That's right, Mr. Dewey. He wants to know if you concur with Mr. Capron's estimate that the situation could be turned around in the next couple of weeks. And, if so, how."

"I can have something via the General in about ten days, I'd guess."

"No," Warren replied. "Not via General Durrien. This one comes through me. No one else here is to know about this. That's the way the President wants it." He pointed to the last lines of his notes for corroboration. "And we'll need your recommendations by next Monday at the latest. That's May thirty-first."

"I see." Dewey sniffed. He shifted his weight to his left hip.

"Capron's people will be available to you. Do you know them?"

145

"That will be no problem."

"Can we meet here next Monday morning about eleven? I'll ask questions and take your memorandum then. OK?"

"I guess it will have to be."

"Is there something wrong, Mr. Dewey?"

"The channel is very unusual. I customarily work with the President via General Durrien in matters of this kind. He provides the interface with State, Defense and the others. Are you prepared to do that?"

"Well—no. I can't do that. But President Frankling can. He is handling this himself."

"Very unusual. Very unorthodox. But, ours but to do and die, I guess."

He turned the wheelchair ninety degrees and looked toward the door. "I'll be here on Monday with whatever I can pull together."

"I'll see you then. Goodbye."

Warren walked to the door and opened it. Dewey rolled by him without a word. Robin felt totally inadequate; had he been stupid and inarticulate? He felt all shoulders and ass and big feet. He had intended to dominate the meeting; he was the President's delegate, after all. He was speaking for the President. But this skinny old spy on wheels had one-upped him. Interface!

Warren shuffled the stack of pink call slips desultorily. Before he reached for the telephone Kathy O'Reilly opened his door and looked in.

"Got a minute?"

"Come on in."

"Want to know about Mrs. Smythe?"

"Yeah. What the hell was that all about, anyway?"

"Mrs. Frankling's secretary says for you to stay all the way out of this one. It's a real beaut."

"Believe me, I'd love to stay out. Is the First Lady going to Jane Smythe's luncheon?"

"Nope. Not this or any other week. The East Wing is finished with Mrs. Smythe. Forevermore."

"What happened?"

"A couple of things. Jane Smythe has told all the gossip reporters that the First Lady is coming to this luncheon because, she says, the President has specifically instructed Gloria Frankling to be there. She's told all the Cabinet wives that Mrs. Frankling is coming, so they'd better be there. And at the last luncheon she put on for the Cabinet wives, Jane Smythe showed up drunk and insisted on being the center of attention every minute. So Mrs. Frankling is through."

"I don't blame her. So I guess I get to give Jane Smythe the happy news, eh?"

"She already knows it. Sandy Cappoletti has written her Mrs. Frankling's regrets, and Mrs. Smythe has had it by now. That's probably why she called you. Could I suggest something?"

"Please."

"Pass this one to David Hale. You really don't belong in it."

"OK. Let's try that." He picked up the call-director and asked for Hale. He explained to Hale's secretary that the call concerned Mrs. Smythe. Hale quickly came on the line.

"Robin? Do *you* have a Jane Smythe story, too?"

"She called me a while ago and I made the mistake of calling her back."

"What was it, her complaint about the President's box at the Kennedy Center?"

"No. Mrs. Frankling won't come to her Cabinet wives' luncheon. Something about welfare mothers."

"Was she smashed?"

"Well on the way, and still working on it. I'm supposed to report back. What shall I do?"

"Mrs. Frankling absolutely refuses to go, of course. It has the potential of a very bad one-day story, since Jane loves to see her name in the paper. But the choices are all bad. If you don't call her back she'll hound you at all hours through the switchboard until she gets you. So you might as well call her back. I'll cover you with the Attorney General. I have to talk to him tonight about something else, anyway. Be prepared. She will tear your ear off. And you'll read about yourself tomorrow. You will join me as one of those disloyal varlets in the White House who are disserving the President of the United States by isolating him from his real friends and supporters. Can you handle that?"

"Sure. Why not?"

"I'll put you in for the Blue Ear Medal."

"Blue Ear?"

"You'll see. Good listening."

Robin tapped the telephone hook, then impatiently pushed a different button to the switchboard. "Mrs. Carleton Smythe, please." He looked at Kathy O'Reilly and pointed to a chair. "I'm supposed to call her back. Stay here in case I need first aid."

"'Lo."

"Mrs. Smythe? Robin Warren."

Silence.

"At the White House," he supplied. "We talked yesterday, remember? Would it be better if I called back tomorrow?"

"Why?"

"I wanted to tell you about your luncheon invitation to Mrs. Frankling."

"Whaboutit?"

"You asked me to look into it."

"The mizzablebitch."

"She can't come, Mrs. Smythe."

"Bullshit, honey."

"It just won't work out, they tell me."

"Who's they?"

"Mrs. Frankling's appointments people." He rolled his eyes at Kathy O'Reilly and pointed to the second telephone on the end table by the couch. She moved there and quietly picked it up, listening with her hand over the mouthpiece, smiling.

"'Pointments people tell the President of the 'nited States of 'merica what to do, do they?"

"No, but they know what else Mrs. Frankling must do that day and it just can't be done."

"That's bullshit, honey." The words were precise and clear-cut, sharp-edged. "I am just a nigger to that stuck-up bitch an' I knowit." The careful diction slurred and collapsed. "Jus 'cause ah cum fum a lil' bitty place noan 'ver heard uhv en ah nehr wunt twan em uppity guhl's skewls, them cunts wunt hev nuthin tew dew wif me, ah know."

"The schedule—"

"Fuck the schedule, sonny. You're like that shitfaced Hale and the others—too good to help me. Well, I have one friend over there, you miserable son of a bitch, and that's the President of the United States of America and he's going to read about you motherfuckers and how you are sabotaging him."

The phone went dead in his ear.

CHAPTER **13** "Mr. Dewey is here, Mr. Warren," Kathy O'Reilly announced.

Cooper Dewey rolled into the room under his own power. He appeared less fragile than he had at their first meeting, but he strained to push the wheels forward. There was new color across the bones of his cheeks and in his narrow lips. He wore a dark-blue suit and bright striped tie. A going-to-church outfit. Robin wondered if Cooper Dewey ever went to church.

"Good morning, Mr. Warren," Dewey said through his nose. "Shall we wait for Dooley?"

"No. If you don't mind, I have some questions before he comes. Did Capron's story—what he told the President—did that check out?"

"Recall, sir, I had that from you orally and secondhand. I took the liberty of also asking Mr. Dooley for his estimate after I talked with you. Dooley has been known to us for a long time, you see."

149

"Fine."

"His estimate coincided with ours almost precisely. We believe Gómez is ready to expropriate American holdings. He will act very soon, unless we do."

"Can Capron's people down there be of any help?"

"Oh, yes. Enormous help. As you will see, our recommendation involves the use of Uruguayan nationals to the largest extent. Not one hundred percent, but to the greatest possible extent. And United International has some excellent people to be employed. Excellent."

"The President wanted information on the Junta there. And the head man. Do you have that?"

"Oh, yes. Of course. All of that. Of course. That is pure exposition, however. I would hope that in this meeting . . ."

Robin's telephone buzzer sounded. They had been sitting in the corner farthest from the desk, Dewey in his wheelchair. Robin, on the couch, reached for the telephone on the end table, spoke briefly to his secretary and stood. The door opened and a tall athlete with snow-white hair strode toward him with outstretched hand.

"Don Dooley, Robin. How are you?"

"How do you do?"

"Chief, good morning."

"Hello, Don. We've just gotten started."

"Sorry I'm late. I had to go by our office here first, and I got held up by a phone call. Mr. Capron sends you his regards, Robin."

"Thank you."

"I was telling Mr. Warren here," Dewey began in his high, reedy voice, "that you and I have been talking about Uruguay, and have agreed on a recommendation for U.S. action. We hope we can see a green light this morning."

"That's right." Dooley had taken the armchair and was leaning forward, hands clasped, elbows on his knees.

He was about sixty; even as he sat at rest he dominated the room. The thick shock of white hair made him seem extraordinarily tall. Warren's eyes were drawn to his face, a face of promontories and plains: big long nose, jutting chin, deep creases, broad forehead. This was a man whose face, all by itself, qualified him for leadership as Auguste Capron's man in South America.

"We think immediate action not only is advisable but can be very, very profitable for the United States," Dooley said. "And at almost no risk."

"Oh, Don, let us be candid: there is some risk." Dewey shook his head. "There is always risk. But the risk has been weighed. In comparison to the gains to be made, I would say it is slight. Risk is there; we can see it, but it is slight." He shifted painfully from one bony hip to the other on the canvas sling seat in his wheelchair.

"Do you have a memorandum for the President?" Robin asked Dewey.

"Ah," Dewey's voice slid up, "a memorandum for the President? Was I to give you such a thing?"

"I asked you for a briefing memorandum on the Junta in Uruguay. Don't you recall?"

"Yes. I recall. It has been done."

"How so? Is it here?"

"Such general information was included in the President's morning briefing book. He received it this morning."

"So what have you brought me to take to the President?"

"The plan of operation, Mr. Warren. I have brought you *Methodist Missionary*. That is, *we* have brought you it. Both of us. Mr. Dooley's organization and connections are integral to the success of the operation. Integral."

"We have been in Uruguay a great many years," Dooley began, "and we have been bribing Uruguayans all that time." He smiled wryly. "We have a big investment in what passes for loyalty down there, I assure you. A lot of dollars in a lot of Swiss accounts. When the time comes we can call on a few folks. And I think they will respond."

"As is always the case," Cooper Dewey nasally intoned, "timing is everything. I gather from your words that you do not feel empowered to give us the green light this morning? Is that right?" He looked sharply at Robin Warren.

151

"No. I have to take your report and recommendations to the President."

"When can you do that?" Dooley asked.

"I'll try and see him this afternoon."

"But you're not sure," Dewey declared in a tone which was an accusation of incompetence. "Well, if you are not empowered, you are not. But you must hurry. If you delay, nothing can be done."

"How soon?" Robin asked.

"Within twenty-four hours. No more. One day. By noon tomorrow at the absolute latest."

"Suppose you get the go-ahead? What will happen?"

"I'm sure you don't want the responsibility of too many details, Mr. Warren," Dewey said. "Most of us in this type of work prefer not to know the names of the agents involved, for example. We would then hold their lives in our hands. It is enough to know that on Navy Day in Uruguay there will be a parade—a military review—and the recommissioning of a warship which Uruguay recently acquired from the Russians. The dictator, Gómez, and his fellow Junta members will all be together on those two public occasions. We propose that there be an uprising, that the organs of communication be inclined to the rebels, thanks to Mr. Dooley's friends, and that the Junta be deposed by dissidents in the Navy."

"Specifically, how will you do that?" Robin asked. "Can you capture them without things going wrong? People still remember what happened to Allende in Chile."

"Going wrong?" Cooper Dewey sniffed. He turned to Dooley. "You were in and out of Chile, Don; did things go wrong?"

Dooley smiled blandly and shook his head. "As a matter of fact, Mr. Warren, the Allende coup went very much according to the scenario. He was clearly marked for executive action."

"Executive action?" Robin repeated. "You mean he was supposed to be killed? Is that what it means? I thought some rebel soldier got carried away and disobeyed orders."

"As a matter of fact," Dewey said, "that is what was reported. But there was no hope of salvaging Allende. He was a dedicated

152

Stalinist, you know. He could not have been convicted in a Chilean court without some kind of propaganda trial, and no one wanted to go through that. Nor was the outcome of a trial entirely certain. The best possible course was the one followed; he had to go."

"Are you going to kill Gómez and the other four?"

"*We* aren't going to kill anyone, Mr. Warren. The Navy people, Uruguayans down there, will do whatever is done."

"But the program calls for them to be killed; right?"

"Many of the same considerations are present, Mr. Warren, as were in Chile," Dooley said earnestly. "Uruguay is a Russian satellite right now. Gómez and two of the others were extensively trained in Moscow. A couple of years in prison won't change Gómez' mind. He is going to cause trouble there so long as he is around. The same goes for the others."

"In the larger picture," Cooper Dewey added, "a great many thousands, even millions, of other lives are involved if Gómez is allowed to consolidate his position there now. Russia will indisputably dominate the southern Atlantic and eventually control the tremendous natural resources of the Southern Hemisphere. Uruguay is of far greater strategic importance than Chile or Cuba ever were."

In spite of himself, Robin Warren experienced a thrill. This is how it must have been done when Kennedy embargoed Cuba, and Nixon invaded Cambodia, and Ford rescued the *Mayaguez*. Those moments in recent history began with a few men in these very rooms, deciding life and death; now *he* was one of those men. It was not so much a feeling of pride; it was fulfillment. He was able, and intelligent, and capable of heavy responsibility. And it had come to him in this form. These older men had doubtless known such a feeling for years. He had now joined a very small circle of Americans: Kissinger, Bundy, Bob Durrien, Arthur Schlesinger, Helms, Brzezinski. He wondered if they always felt high when they dealt with these issues of life and death.

Death. Someone had to decide whether five men in Uruguay would die.

153

The President must decide. But no one must know it was his decision. There must be insulation and deniability in case something went wrong.

For a fleeting moment Warren wondered about the morality of taking the question of this killing to the President. The Allende murder in Chile was widely condemned. Was it immoral to bring such a question to the President? What if it were, and an aide refused to present such an option? This wispy old CIA man in the wheelchair would surely get it delivered to the President one way or the other. So would Dooley and Capron. General Bob Durrien would take it in for them in a minute.

As a practical matter there were plenty of conduits. These two men would know the other ways to get it to the President, too. Keeping their plan from the President was not an available option. But was he ready to take it in? Did he know all the questions and all the answers? That was the only problem he had now.

"What happens if the plan fails, Mr. Dewey?" Robin asked.

"Exactly what will happen if we do nothing: Gómez will move to lock Uruguay to the Soviets. American interests will be seized. Our embassy will be closed. And they'll start to build missile sites and submarine pens. Then, very soon, it will infect Paraguay, then Argentina, then run up both coasts. Repression will be stepped up. South American troops will appear in Africa and Asia. Remember the Cuban adventure in Africa a few years ago? We'll relive the Cuban experience all over again."

Dooley leaned on one elbow and gestured widely with his free arm. "You see, Mr. Warren, there is no other way to insure a return to a republican form of government there. Those Army men can be expected to rule by fear. Their secret military police will have their hands on the throats of the people; they won't give up and go away peacefully. It's like a boa constrictor—you must crush its head. Then its coils will relax."

"Just so I understand—you are going to kill others besides the Junta?"

"We seldom operate first-party, Mr. Warren." Dewey spoke

154

like a lecturer. At Stanford Robin had taken a sophomore economics course from a professor in a wheelchair. He was experiencing flashes of recollection of that elderly and bitter professor as he listened to Dewey. "The *President* is well aware of that. Most of this operation will be conducted by the most reliable Uruguayan nationals one can identify. The Navy down there is most *malcontent*"—Dewey gave the word a French accent—"and offers us discreet and most disciplined people. They don't want widespread bloodshed."

"Then how do you make sure there will be no expropriation?"

"I think that will follow, as the night the day," Dewey said with exaggerated patience. "Liberty will follow tyranny."

Dooley rode in on Dewey's last words: "I have been in and out of Uruguay for twenty years, Mr. Warren. I know those people— it's a small country; it's not hard to get to know everyone of any importance. The seeds of freedom are well planted, I can assure you. There are tens of thousands who want to throw off the Junta's yoke. They hate it. Once they are liberated there will be a republic in full flower within hours—within a day. I can pretty well tell you who the new President will be and who will sit in his Cabinet. Some of them are just waiting in nearby countries, in exile. They will hurry home when the strike is made, believe me."

"But it must be on Navy Day, you understand," Dewey said. "That is when they will all be together. All five must go at once or it is no good. So I must hear from you very quickly."

"Yes, I understand. I'll do my best on that. What are the chances that this plan will fail?" Robin returned to failure because he guessed the President would ask about it.

Dewey and Dooley looked at each other with ill-concealed amusement.

"It is a carefully conceived operation, Mr. Warren, in a small country. Our man in charge is excellent. Mr. Dooley's people are the best. There is ample money, and such logistics as might be required are, ah, not difficult to arrange for. Of course, there are always possible lapses. The dictator might be ill that day. He might not appear. We can't guarantee against acts of God. But it is an operational plan of simplicity and much merit. I believe it will succeed."

"Can I give the President an estimate—your estimate—in percentages?" For the first time in the conversation Robin Warren felt he had the initiative. He was the President's man in this, after all. It was a heavy foreign operation and he had been entrusted with it; this damned Dewey was only one of the governmental instruments by which it would be effected. If the President approved it, of course. It was his place to speak to them with the President's voice, if he could. So far these two had talked down to him, but now it was turning his way. "What is your estimate of the percentage of success?"

"Assume the Junta appears at the Navy review, and assume they go to the shipboard ceremony," Dewey lectured. "Assume further there is no cloudburst, earthquake or other divine intervention. With those assumptions I would put the chances of success at well over fifty percent. Eh, Dooley?"

Dooley nodded his large head. "Well over," he said.

"Let's look at it the other way," Robin pressed. "What can go wrong?"

"Mr. Warren," the man in the wheelchair said with exasperation, "I have been in government service nearly thirty years. In that time I have learned that *everything* can go wrong. Everything. Or any one thing. A flat tire. A missed train. One man delayed. An operation of this kind depends on four or five or six things happening in sequence. If one of them doesn't happen, then the people on the scene must improvise. Everything can go wrong. I know President Frankling knows that."

"Perhaps he does," Robin conceded. "Is this proposal in writing for him?"

Dewey shook his head slowly. "In writing?" His voice rose through the words.

"Yes: as you know, the President prefers to work from the written page."

Dewey shook his head widely, from side to side. "Not in these matters, Mr. Warren. Not in these matters, I assure you. Since that Nixon-papers case in the Supreme Court there have been no writings in these situations, you know. None whatever."

"Well, then . . ."

"As a matter of fact, Mr. Warren, it is for that reason that I would prefer to discuss this plan with the decision-maker directly, if you are not empowered to give us the go-ahead now. If at all possible, one or both of us, Mr. Dooley or I, should brief him directly. I urge that. I cannot insist upon it, of course, but I urge it."

"Well, I'll tell him that, Mr. Dewey. But it's up to him."

"Of course it is. Do you have other questions for us? If not, we'll be going."

"No. I guess not." Robin stood. "Thank you for coming. Mr. Dooley, good to meet you."

He ushered them to his door, closed it behind them and rang for his secretary.

"Kathy, I need to see the President. Tell Nick Gurley that it's about Cooper Dewey. I'll wait to hear back."

He cradled the phone and leaned back in his chair, bending a paper clip into a little crank which he twirled between his fingers. "Executive action." He was now a shaker and a mover, on a *very* broad playing field. Dewey was right. Nothing in writing. He ran over what he'd been told, organizing it to present in a conversation with the President.

He smiled. Trust an old bastard like Cooper Dewey to come up with a phrase like "executive action." It used to be something about extreme prejudice—or was that the Mafia? Even a code name—*Methodist Missionary*. All it lacked was the trench coat and the cyanide pill.

O'Reilly's phone buzzer sounded.

"Mr. Warren? The President has just left for Goddard Space Center. He'll be there all afternoon, watching the Space Shuttle return operation. He says you're to join him for dinner on the yacht. Leaving West Executive at six P.M. sharp. OK?"

"Sure. Can you cancel the other—Nebraska and the Red Cross?"

"I'll take care of it," she said. Even O'Reilly was impressed; he could sense it in her voice. Dinner on the Presidential yacht.

CHAPTER **14**   The shrill rise and fall of the bos'n whistle's arcane salute was muffled by the thick evening heat. Near the stern of the old white yacht, President Hugh Frankling shook hands with a tall Navy commander, then watched him greet Attorney General Smythe. Robin Warren got out of car three and walked slowly toward the gangway. He didn't want to blunder into some ceremony in which he didn't belong. Before he came close to the edge of the dock, the President and the Attorney General moved past the commander into the wooden cabin of the yacht. Warren then stepped onto the canvas-sided gangway.

"I am Commander Jepson, Mr. Warren. Welcome aboard the *Sea Island*."

"Thank you." They shook hands.

The commander's hand was damp. His white uniform was extraordinarily starched. A gold enamel Presidential seal on a blue background was pinned to his shirt pocket, rows of battle ribbons ranged above it, and he was sprinkled with gold: gold stripes, buttons, gold filigree on his hat.

The instant Robin's foot touched the polished wooden deck he heard the engines start somewhere below; two crewmen slid the gangway to the dock while others simultaneously closed the hinged railing, cast off lines, and bore the yacht away from the dock with boathooks. Neither the President nor Carleton Smythe acknowledged Robin's presence until their double martinis were in hand.

158

Then Smythe nodded a perfunctory greeting: "Evening, Robin."

"Tell them what you're drinking, son," the President said. "Then come on up and join us." The two stout men ungracefully climbed a wooden stairway into the ceiling of the rear lounge and disappeared. A mess steward came from the saloon to take Robin's order.

"What are they drinking?" Robin asked.

"Martinis." The steward smiled. "Double doubles."

"Not for me. Put some white wine in a Manhattan glass, will you?"

"Yes, sir. I'll bring it up."

He found Frankling and Smythe standing at the starboard rail on the top deck, staring up at the underside of Douglas Bridge as the outbound commuter traffic sped over their heads. Two Coast Guard speedboats with narrow prows and deep V hulls cruised beside the yacht at low throttle, one on each side. Robin recognized one of the Secret Service men from the White House detail aboard the starboard flanker.

Frankling, Smythe and Warren looked at a small sloop as it was overtaken. The family aboard recognized the President and the woman waved. She pointed to the President, then put her arm around a young girl in an orange life jacket. The girl waved bashfully. When neither Frankling nor Smythe made any gesture, Robin Warren felt obliged to return the wave. The man and woman on the sloop smiled and waved back. The family continued to wave at the President until they fell far behind the yacht and its escorts.

When the *Sea Island* was abeam old Fort McNair, near the confluence of the Anacostia and Potomac rivers, the President sat heavily into one of the molded-plastic chairs arranged in a half circle on one side of the deck. He gestured for Smythe and Warren to join him. Smythe sat in the chair on his left, Warren sat next to Smythe. The motion breeze was warm and humid. Robin felt perspiration move across his chest and down his side.

"By God, Carl, that Carter was crazy to sell that yacht. There's nothing like getting out on an evening like this."

"He was a submarine man, Mr. President. Maybe he didn't like boats that float." Smythe smiled. "I'll bet he didn't save twenty cents by selling that old boat."

"Of course he didn't. The Navy crew just went to other ships. No one got laid off; they didn't close the Navy Yard; it was just a sham. And the thing is so damn handy—get ten or twelve Congressmen on here, away from the phone, and you can sell them anything. Carter's people never understood things like that. Too bad. This boat here was some admiral's plaything, so we didn't lay out a dime to put things back the way they were. But try to convince the press of that! Either they are blind to the truth or they don't care if they write the truth!"

Two stewards brought fresh drinks and hors d'oeuvres, including a silver bowl of caviar and a tray of toast slices. The President began to shovel caviar enthusiastically. A screaming jet airplane passed low overhead, its wings lowering into National Airport across the Potomac River ahead of them.

Carleton Smythe crossed his legs. He was wearing white slacks, white shoes and a blue blazer. The President wore gray slacks and a blue windbreaker with a large cloth Presidential seal over his left breast. Robin wondered if the President had changed from his gray coat to the windbreaker in the car.

"You look warm, Rob," the President said. "Take off your jacket if you want. You too, Carl. Be comfortable. Another drink, Carl?"

Smythe quickly finished his martini and nodded. The President depressed a button on a panel on the table and a steward emerged from below with a tray of fresh drinks and a plate of hot canapés. The yacht turned gently into the Potomac from the Anacostia River, rocking slightly in the new current. Maryland was on their left, Virginia across the river. Warren took off his jacket and put it on a vacant chair.

"Carl," the President spoke to Smythe as if they were alone, "I've been looking at the South again. We didn't come close to our potential down there last time, did we? We should have had

Louisiana, Mississippi and Alabama along with the others we got. Am I right?" When he talked electoral politics Hugh Frankling became animated. His full cheeks flushed. He unzipped his jacket and leaned toward Smythe, displaying a roll of fat overlapping his belt.

"I think you're right about all but Alabama," Smythe began owlishly. He slowly reviewed Frankling's strengths and weaknesses in the Southern states, one by one, stabbing with his cigar for emphasis.

Robin Warren's mind wandered. He was once again thinking of Lani Romera until he realized a steward was demanding their attention.

"Dinner is served, Mr. President," the man said.

Frankling came out of his chair unevenly, lurching into Carleton Smythe. Smythe caught him by the arm.

"I'm OK. I'll get my sea legs in a minute," Frankling said. "Let's go down and try the roast beef. You like beef, Rob?"

"Yes, sir."

"Good. We have beef tonight, and a special dessert. Something the Gennal here likes." Frankling didn't quite manage the word "General." He moved to the stairway with elaborate care. Smythe stayed close to him, one hand extended.

When Robin descended the stairs and entered the darkly paneled saloon the President was already seated at the near end of a long dining table in the center of the narrow room, his back to the door. Smythe was in the process of sitting down to the President's left. The table was elaborate: crested china, a wicker basket of fresh flowers, candles and a forest of wineglasses. Always the same fresh flowers, Warren noticed, even here on the boat. In every senior staff man's office was a little wicker basket of the same assortment from the hothouse, replaced every two days: daisies, zinnias, asters, babies' breath. In the Oval Office, always two huge arrangements.

Robin Warren sat across from Smythe, facing Maryland. The wooden bulkheads on both sides of the saloon extended only waist high, with a solid line of windows running from end to end. A door on each side reached the narrow covered deck along both sides of the yacht.

The *Sea Island* was abeam the airport. Warren could not hear the President for a moment; a departing jet screeched over the yacht and roared away to the east.

". . . are Puget Sound crabs. One of the Senators from up there sends 'em over. You like 'em, Carl?"

"Delicious, sir. Simply delicious," Smythe replied.

"I've ordered red wine with our beef," Frankling said, his mouth full of crab. "But if you want white with your crab, they have it. Wha' say, Carl? White with your crab? Rob?" Frankling raised his hand to the steward who was standing just inside the galley door.

"Yes, please," Robin said. "If it's easy."

"Everything on this boat is easy." Frankling chuckled. "That's the whole idea." He finished his drink and handed the glass to the waiting steward. "We are going to have wine now," he loudly announced to the Filipino steward. "I will have red, the Burgundy I ordered. The young man wants white. You have a very good white?"

"Yes, Missa Pesdent."

"Fine, you bring him that. What for you, General? Red, white or blue?"

"I'll join you with the red, please," Smythe said.

"Two red, one white," Frankling said to the steward. "And I'll have another martini while I'm waiting. To keep me from getting blue." He chuckled, returned to the salad, spooned a pink cream dressing onto a pile of Dungeness crab legs. When the martini arrived he dispatched it in two breaths.

As the *Sea Island* came abeam Old Alexandria, Warren's attention was drawn to a fire on the Maryland side of the Potomac. There were tall silver vent stacks topped by flames like great candles in the late-afternoon light. The President and Smythe were inconsequentially arguing about the relative merits of the Eastern soft-shell crab versus the Pacific Dungeness crab. When the roast

162

beef arrived Frankling began to talk about that. Warren wondered if the President was avoiding the subject of Uruguay deliberately. Perhaps he and Smythe felt ill at ease with an outsider present. Or might their talks together always be limited to such trivia?

The drinks were obviously having their effect. For reasons he did not examine he felt a vicarious and irrational shame for the President and the Attorney General. They were drunk and he was embarrassed for them, and for himself. He was slightly ashamed to be a part of what was going on. Usually drunks, especially benign old drunks, didn't bother him. But Frankling was the President. That made it bothersome.

As the President avidly ate and drank, he appeared to Warren to fold inward somehow—to physically lose his aura. He seemed less commanding. His heavy cheeks and chins were increasingly florid. Once he dropped his fork on his plate with a clatter. His words of apology were slurred.

Carleton Smythe, on the other hand, became more precise in speech and movement the more he drank. He began referring to Robin as "Mr. Warren." The movement of his fork from plate to mouth was slower and more exact, an act of conscious will, perhaps the result of some remembered danger.

The two older men ate and drank without serious interruption, maintaining a paced duet through the courses, and finally laying down their utensils at virtually the same moment. Warren finished a slow third while both Frankling and Smythe drank more wine.

Dessert was a huge Baked Alaska, ice cream and meringue flambé, awash in extra brandy. As it was being served, the yacht passed under the Woodrow Wilson Bridge which carries eight lanes of the Capital Beltway high over the Potomac; its great concrete piers seemed to glide by the yacht's windows. The abutments had cut off the dying daylight as the steward entered with the flaming dessert dish. The effect was accidentally and unforgettably dramatic.

"Who does this 'ssert remind you of, Carl?" the President asked with a lopsided grin. "'S a riddle."

"I don't know," Smythe said slowly.

"Well, 's a Baked 'laska. Tha's a clue."

"I don't know. I know it's a Baked Alaska. I do not know the answer to the riddle."

"Give up?"

"Yes sir, I do," Smythe said deliberately. "I give up."

"Wally Hickel. That ol' sonuvabitch, Wally Hickel." Frankling giggled.

Smythe looked at Frankling. "Why?"

"He came from 'laska—right?"

"Right."

"And he wen' up in smoke when he got here." The President turned to Robin. "You get it?"

"I'd forgotten about him." Robin smiled.

"Interestin' man," Frankling said seriously. "Riddle: man like Hickel, hated to read, writes a big long letter 'bout V'etnam? 'Nother riddle. Riddle of history. If *he* didn't write it, who did? Got him fired—so they say. I always believed there was more to it than that, but so they say."

"I once had a client like that," Smythe began. He emptied his wineglass, then looked at it with mild disfavor. "That wine does not complement the dessert. I believe I'll have a brandy."

"Damn good idea." Frankling nodded. The steward, at his station by the galley door, turned and disappeared. In a moment he returned with three large snifters and two bottles on a tray.

The remaining dessert and cigars were accompanied with desultory conversation about brandy, cognac, Smythe's wartime experience with homemade fruit brandy, and the President's encounter with Calvados at an American Legion convention.

Robin had visited Fort Washington once while on a picnic in the Maryland countryside. He recognized the old battlements looming over the river from among the trees as the yacht began a slow turn to the west. At first he thought the boat was turning around for the trip back to Washington. He had not realized before that at the fort the Potomac made a curve west, then south again. The fort was evidently designed so that its cannon would command the short east–west leg of that jog from its eastern end.

Two stewards cleared the table of dishes, leaving only the large basket of flowers, the three brandy snifters and ashtrays.

"The Legion is washed up, you know," Frankling said. "No young men; all old farts. The Vietnam vets din't join."

"That's not quite true, Mr. President." Smythe jabbed with his cigar. "I beg to differ."

"Oh, you beg to differ, do you? What the hell do you know about it?"

"I happen to know quite a big lot abot—about it, since I am a member of Post 222 in Boston, Mass, and I get the Legion magazine and read it and know all about the dem—the damorg—the makeup of the membership. And you are in error, sir, and I say that with great respect."

"You beg to differ, do you? With great respect? I think you are full of shit. I don' think you know that much about the 'merion Legion. Not that much." Frankling held his thumb and finger an inch apart. "This boy here knows more about the 'merican Legion than you do. Don't you, boy? Steward? Where the hell is the steward?"

Unnoticed, the steward had quietly gone forward into the galley, then out onto the foredeck of the yacht with the rest of the crew. The yacht's engines slowed, then stopped. In the following quiet a bell tolled at precise intervals.

"Goddamn him, you need some more brandy, Carl. Where is that son of a bitch?" Frankling said loudly.

"We've stopped for something," Robin said. "I'll go see what's going on." He stood. "Excuse me, please."

"You do that. Find that steward. Carl needs more damn brandy. Bram dandy. Dan Bramidy. Do that."

Robin slid back the door in the starboard wall of the saloon and walked forward, one hand on the polished wooden railing. He heard a sharp command ahead of him. When he came to the wheelhouse he saw the yacht's crew in two lines facing the Virginia shore at rigid salute. From somewhere a bugle sounded "Taps"; then, at the last long note of the call, "The Star-Spangled Banner" was played. The recording of the anthem was tinny and distorted. Robin faced northwest along with the crew and put his hand over his heart. The waning sky was orange-brown, the river a deep ocher. His eye was drawn across the water to the crest of a wooded ridge, now nearly black-green in the dusk. Bathed in floodlights, Mount Vernon could be seen plainly, a white dollhouse at the back of a great swath of lawn.

The recorded music ended solemnly, but the commander kept the crew at the salute. In the quiet interval before "Order arms," Frankling and Smythe could be clearly heard in the saloon, loudly arguing the fate of the American Legion.

"No one'll join anymore, goddammit." The President's high-pitched voice carried in the evening stillness.

"No Sir, that's not so. They do—they did join after Vietnam. Lots of them joined up. Fine men. And women too."

"Betcha not more than five percent. Less'en that. Two percent. What'll you bet? Bet a hunnerd?"

"I'd hate to take your money."

"Don't worry."

"*Order* arms!" the commander said sharply. Right hands slapped on legs. "Formation dismissed."

Warren gestured to the black steward. "The President would like more brandy, please."

"Yes, sir. Right away. Had to pay our respects to Ol' George, you know, sir. Right away." He moved between Robin and the wheelhouse, ducked into the galley door and was followed by two crewmen in whites.

Warren could hear men talking in the wheelhouse. As he passed its door, following the crewmen along the narrow deck, he glanced in. Two men in white were talking.

"Hear that back there?"

"Couldn't help it."

"Sonsofbitches."

"They probably didn't know. He's got a lot on his mind."

"Bullshit."

The taller of the two turned and looked at Robin. He took a step into the doorway, gripping the doorjamb on either side like the uprights of a ladder.

"He's drunk, isn't he?" the lanky young officer said.

Robin was offended. A Navy man didn't impugn his Commander in Chief like that. Robin had never been in the Navy—or any other service branch—but he knew junior officers were supposed to watch what they said. The man wore a black plastic name tag over his pocket, as all the *Sea Island*'s crew did. Warren had to read it twice—it was one of those names that looked like another word when you glanced at it quickly. "Lt. M. Slinde," the tag said, white on black.

"We didn't know there was a ceremony going on," Robin replied stiffly.

Lieutenant Slinde nodded. "Someone should have told him."

Warren nodded, walked along the narrow deck, turned through the saloon's open door and back into his seat at the table.

"There you are. Wondered what had become of you, Mr. Warren," the Attorney General said. "The President said you are goin' to brief us on Uruguay. That right?"

"No 'merican Legion there, by God," the President exclaimed. "Anyone want to bet on that?"

"I'm prepared to brief you, General, whenever you and the President wish. But perhaps tomorrow would be better . . ."

"Where the hell are we goin'?" the President demanded. The engines had begun to throb, a faster cadence than before, a new tempo to compensate for the adverse current of the river on the return trip.

"I think we're headed back, Mr. President," he said.

"Well, then, le's get to all your important business. It can't wait till tomorrow. Big hurry. Tha's what they tell me."

"All the same, Mr. President, you are relaxed now and I hate to press you for a decision tonight."

"That's my fushion—my funk—my func-ti-un—and I'm here now and ready to hear all the facts on both sides, and weigh the ev'dence with great delib'ration, and render a decision that can be 'scribed in the great book of hissory." Frankling folded his hands over his belly and leaned back. "So let us proceed. Mr. Rob has the floor. Everyone else be silent."

"I'll be silent. You can count on that," Smythe said slowly. "I won't say a goddamn word."

Warren looked at them both, leaned both arms onto the table and clasped his hands. He paused, then nodded. The timing was terrible. He should have forced the subject earlier, perhaps on the upper deck before the drinking began. But tomorrow would be too late. And the President was insisting. He had no choice.

"You recall, Mr. President, that Auguste Capron came to see you to tell you that the Uruguayan government was about to move. He said the Junta there would take over American businesses and suppress any opposition. You asked that the CIA check that."

"An' the CIA says it's all true?"

"Yes, sir. It is."

"Goddamn red Communist bastards!"

"You asked for the CIA's recommendation for countermeasures."

"An' CIA says to shoot them all, right?"

"That's pretty close. They have designed an uprising that would restore a republican form of government. A coup. The Junta would be eliminated by Uruguayan Navy officers."

"Good idea, don't you think, Carl?"

"Not a goddamn word. You tol' me to be quiet. Not a word."

"Well, I think it's a 'streamly damn good idea," Frankling said. "Will it work?"

"No one can be positive, Mr. President. Cooper Dewey at the CIA thinks—"

"Now, there's a creepy son of a bitch!" Smythe exclaimed.

"Dewey says," Warren continued doggedly, "it has a better than fifty-fifty chance of success. The CIA says that if they *don't* try, the Russians will have their submarines in there in a month."

"It's like Cuba!" Frankling exclaimed. "We'd have another damn Cuba in the South 'lantic. That can't be! Fifty-fifty chance should be good 'nough, don't you think, Carl?"

"You know me, Mr. President. I'm a patriot through and through. Your decision, of course. But one Cuba is bad enough. Can't have two Cubas. Too bad we can't have a rev'lution in the first Cuba, I say. Stamp out the little bastards, clean 'em out."

"All right, what else?" Frankling asked Warren. "What else we got to do before I render a decision and recess this court and we have another drink?"

"I only need your decision on the CIA operation, Mr. President. Do you want more details?"

Frankling waved his large hand back and forth in front of his face. "No more. Heard 'nough. I rule in favor of the CIA. God damn!" His empty wineglass fell as his cuff brushed it. He picked it up carefully with thumb and forefinger and raised it high. "Steward! Please!" The steward, on station beyond the galley door, entered at once.

"Yes, sir?"

"Champagne for the trip home, eh, men?"

"Please," Smythe muttered.

"None for me, thank you," Warren said. "I'll have to call the CIA tonight to be sure this moves ahead on time."

"You do that, Rob. Right over there." Frankling hooked his thumb over his shoulder.

"Sir?"

"Use that phone right over there. The red one. Call 'em now."

"Yes, sir." Warren rose and walked slowly to the semicircular couch behind the President. Red and black telephones sat on a low end table beside a brass ship's lamp. Both phones had the White House Communications Agency logo in place of a dial. He sat down and picked up the red receiver and put it to his ear. There was no sound. He clicked the buttons on the cradle. Dead.

"Sir, this phone doesn't . . ."

"Hold down the bar."

Warren looked at the receiver. There was a long raised section under the handle. He pushed it in and heard crackling in the earpiece.

"Sir?" a male operator said.

"Hello?"

"Yes, sir?"

"I need a man at the CIA: Mr. Cooper Dewey. Can you hear me?"

"Yes sir. This is a scramble unit and will sound strange to you at first. Just talk normal, slow and even. Do not talk while the other party is talking. Who is calling, please?"

"Robin Warren."

"Yes, sir. One . . ."

"You cut out," Warren said loudly. "I can't hear you."

"Press the damn button, boy," Frankling said.

"Yes, sir, I am."

"We're under the bridge." Smythe lowered his head to see out a window. "That might screw it up. Wait a minute." The huge Wilson Bridge abutments loomed in the darkness.

"Hello, hello," Warren said. "It's still not working."

"Damn things never do when you want them," Frankling exclaimed. "No damn good."

The telephone crackled in Warren's ear. "Go ahead, sir."

"Is this thing working?"

"Yes, sir. Loud and clear. Mr. Dewey is on the line."

"Hello, Mr. Dewey?"

"Yes, hello, Mr. Warren."

"Can you hear me?"

"Yes, you are faint but very plain. Go ahead."

"About *Methodist Missionary*."

"Yes. Do I have a green light?"

"Yes, you do."

"I understand. Your message is affirmative. There is a green light. Correct?"

"Yes, correct."

"Very good. Thank you. Good night."

"Good night." Robin Warren hung up the telephone and stared out the window into the dark. "It must have been the bridge."

"Damn things never work right when you mus' have 'em.

'Member when I was in Korea, Carl, an' I called you up? Phones all screwed up. You could talk 'n I could hear but I couldn't hear and you—"

"No," Smythe said, "I could talk and you could hear, but not the other way: you couldn't—uh—you could hear but I couldn't hear you; right?"

"I don' know if you could hear. How the hell should I know if you could hear? You weren't with us. You were off somewhere on your holiday."

"Bar Harbor."

"What?"

"Tha's where I was. In Maine."

"Sure. How am I s'posed to know if you can hear up in Maine when I'm in Korea, for Chris' sake? What did he say?" The President looked warily at Robin. "What did that spook in the wheelchair say?"

"He simply repeated the message."

"Good; no back talk or argument for once. Tha's good."

"Show's on the damn road," added the Attorney General.

"How about some champagne now, young man? Your day's work is done."

"Yes, sir. Thank you. I guess it is."

Hugh Frankling held his hand high and snapped his fingers. "Champagne," he half shouted, "for Mr. Rob here."

The steward had already begun to move toward the table. He filled the three tall champagne glasses and moved back to the galley doorway.

"I pr'ose a toast, Mr. President," Smythe said heavily. He held his glass in front of his face, both elbows on the table. "A toas' to victory in Yoorguay. May the bes' spies win."

"I'll drink to that," Frankling said. "To victory over the little Commie bastards and their submreens."

"To victory," said Robin with chagrin. To *Methodist Missionary,* and assassination, and to world-shaking decisions that are made without comprehension.

CHAPTER **15**   Later, in the heat of the second summer of the Frankling administration, in that season when everything had turned to trouble, he would be asked to remember and explain why he had gone to Buenos Aires in June.

He would remember then, though he would not explain, how Lani Romera had filled his thoughts in the days after they met at Capron's party. He would feel again the emptiness of that time of impatience and desire.

He had called her often in the late evenings at hotels in the weeks following Capron's party. Her film promotion tour was taking her to medium-sized cities in the South and the Midwest for one-day appearances. Her schedule was jammed with press interviews and parties for film distributors and reviewers. It seemed impossible for her to arrange to be with him. Whenever he was free to fly to her she was booked solid. And the few times she could have met him for dinner in New York or Washington he had a command performance somewhere else.

They both came to anticipate his evening calls; their conversations were always easy and soon became intimate. They talked for an hour or more; neither wanted to cut off the call.

But he chafed at their separation. He was experiencing an emotional and physical need to be with her that was different, stronger, more disabling than anything he'd ever felt for a woman. He admitted to himself that he wasn't handling it very well—it interfered with his work and the rest of his life. He wasn't prepared to call it love; it was physical desire, passion, lust; it was a need to be with her, a need to be made love to by her. And a big part of it was simply the fact that fate had conspired to keep them from consummating their powerful mutual physical attraction.

Lani was in Atlanta one evening when they talked about a way to have a little time together in Washington. She was supposed to fly to New York and catch the Concorde to Buenos Aires to begin some South American appearances. She would come to Washington en route, and they could have an afternoon together.

But not even that worked out. The Council of Economic Advisers rescheduled a meeting with the Petroleum Producers Board for that afternoon, and Robin was obliged to attend. So he and Lani would have only a quick lunch in the White House mess. She came to his office from the airport. He was in a meeting there and kept her waiting for ten minutes. Then, as three men left, staring back over their shoulders, he invited her in.

"Hello, how are you?" He held out both hands to her.

"Close the door and I'll show you," she said quietly. She looked around in appraisement as he closed the door and came up behind her. She turned and put the palm of her hand on his cheek.

"I hate telephones," she said.

He intended to hold her gently, but could not. When he felt her body in his arms he pulled her close to him and they kissed. He felt as if he had come home. At once his telephone chimed and he reflexively turned to reach for it, holding her with one arm.

"Shit," Lani Romera said. She walked away from him to the couch and sat looking at him as he listened to his secretary.

He hung up and walked to her, holding out his hand. "I have exactly forty minutes. Shall we eat or stay here?"

"Can we lock the door and make love?" she asked. Her voice was brittle with annoyance.

"No. This place is like a bus station. I was going to get a room at the Hay-Adams, if we'd had more time. Do you know how much I want you?"

She took his hand and stood, running her other hand up his arm. She was wearing Levi's and a blue work shirt, a silver concha belt, her hair caught back with a silver clip, bare feet in leather sandals. "Can I eat lunch with you, looking like this?"

"You're perfect. Let's go."

They left his office circumspectly, but their hands touched as they walked to the elevator. He took her upper arm in his hand as they rode down, crossed the narrow street and passed the basement cop with a nod.

Everyone in the crowded private dining room recognized her; conversation stopped until she and Robin were seated in the corner at one of the small tables.

"Very nice," she said. "Is it Navy?"

"Right. The staff is all Navy. So are the prices. The food's just fair, but it's cheap. You have all these people bug-eyed, you know. Kings and prime ministers don't faze them, but you've stopped the show."

"Can't imagine why. I'm just another citizen passing through."

"It's probably the way you wiggled your ass as we came in."

"What a thing to say in the White House, Mr. Warren. Let's try to have a high-level discussion, please."

"OK. When do we go to bed?"

"When I get back."

"When is that?"

"Ten days."

"I can't wait ten days."

"I guess you'll just have to, unless you can come to South America. Do you think I can get you into my suitcase?"

"Where are you going to be this weekend?"

"Argentina. I get Saturday and Sunday off. Why don't you come down?"

"Where will you be?"

"On the coast, south of Buenos Aires. I have the use of a villa. It is very quiet—out in the country, on the water." She put her hand on his and looked at him directly. "Why don't you come? *Please.*"

"I have to be back here Monday. Is that possible?"

"Sure. It's six thousand miles, but the Concorde makes Rio in about three hours now—then Buenos Aires is just down the road. Oh, do come, Robin."

And so he had gone to Argentina for the weekend, spending a

fortune on the air fare, taxing Kathy O'Reilly's formidable talents to procure reservations on the supersonic flight, and canceling all his Friday afternoon appointments.

When Warren cleared customs and immigration at Ezeiza International Airport in Buenos Aires, Lani Romera was waiting, more or less disguised behind dark glasses and under a bandanna. She kissed him warmly and took his attaché case.

"How was it?" she asked.

"God, you look good to me," he said. "Do we have a car?"

"Better than that; we have a helicopter."

"No kidding? You don't mess around."

"We go through that door and down some steps and it's just out on the ramp. Do you have other luggage?"

"No. Only this bag and that case. Are we going to the villa? Does it have a bed?"

"Definitely." She laughed and squeezed his arm with hers.

There was a feeling of being alone with her even in the crowded airport. She was the only familiar person in totally strange surroundings. So for him she was all there was. The surroundings, foreign and therefore unreal, did not register. There was only this woman.

The helicopter was large, red and white, of some European manufacture. The pilots sat higher than the passengers, separated by a soundproof wall. A crewman buckled Lani and Robin side by side on a comfortable couch, then climbed out and joined the pilots.

They tilted forward briefly as the helicopter gained airspeed, then leveled out, the torque and vibration of the rotor the only evidence of the machinery above them. Their route took them across the south-central part of Buenos Aires, block after block of white apartment houses of ten or twelve stories.

"You know what that looks like?" Robin asked.

"Los Angeles?"

"No, those graveyards on Long Island that you see on the way to JFK—rows and rows of white headstones."

"There are millions of people down there. I always used to think of Argentina as cows and tall grass and cowboys. But B.A. is a huge place."

He put his arm behind her and drew her close, his hand covering her breast. She turned and looked at him, her lips open a little. He kissed her, found her tongue with his, felt her hand on his leg.

"A helicopter would be a historic first for me," he said quietly.

"Robin?" She leaned back a little.

"Hmmm?"

"The Caprons are here."

"Where?"

"At the villa. It's their villa."

"Shit."

"They were over in Santiago. They came especially when they heard you would be here. They won't stay long."

"Neither will I, dammit. I have to leave Sunday morning." He was annoyed. "I want you alone."

"They're going in the morning. But we will have to see them some while they're here. I'm sorry."

"So am I. When? Dinner?"

"No; you and Auguste are invited somewhere for dinner."

"Without you?" He pulled his arm back. "What the hell?"

"Just for a couple of hours. I'll be waiting for you."

"Where are we going? No one else knows I'm here, do they?" He experienced a fibrillation of fear.

"No, of course not. Auguste wants you to see something or other."

The great federal city sprawled to their left, the white buildings almost garish in the strong morning light. The Rio de la Plata was truly a silver plate in the distance across the rooftops. The helicopter had been flying east. Robin sensed a change of course to the south as the dense hodgepodge of apartment houses gave way to patches of forests and the Atlantic beaches.

Robin turned to look at the shoreline. Lani attempted to make conversation, gradually regaining his tolerance, then his apparent

176

interest. He half faced her, listening. She had tried to speak some Spanish in a television interview, with mixed results; her theater appearance had been a success; she had done some shopping.

But as she talked he was thinking about Auguste Capron's presence. It was, no doubt, as carefully contrived as his first encounter with Capron at the Business Council. Lani did Capron's bidding, certainly, and he began to wonder where her Capron work stopped and her genuine attraction for Robin Warren began. Thinking back, he recalled that she had suggested the trip. Would Capron have turned up if they had gone to Maine or the Vineyard? But he had just flown six thousand miles to have this woman. And he intended to have her. Tomorrow she could sell him out to the Chinese or the Cubans if she wished, but today he would have her in the ways of all his fantasies.

They flew low over the water, in a sweeping arc to the right. A long modern house paralleled the beach. It was angular, white and stark with dark glass, overlooking broad lawns bordered by high white walls.

Two men near the wall watched the landing. Someone stood on the terrace in front of an open door, shielding his eyes. The crewman helped them out and pointed toward the house. Lani and Robin instinctively bent low as they crossed the lawn, moving away from the slowly revolving rotor. The man from the terrace came toward them. It was Mike Meyerson.

"Welcome to Casa Piña," he shouted. Meyerson led them to the terrace to watch the helicopter rise, lower its shoulder and lean out toward the Atlantic, gracefully wheeling east, then northwest, toward the city.

Robin was aware of the pressure of the residual silence. Meyerson's voice seemed tinny and flat.

"It's good to see you, Robin. Was it a good trip?"

"Fine. Very easy. But I'm grubby and sleepy. I'd like to clean up, I think."

"Sure. We'll show you. You know his room, don't you, Lani?"

"I'll show him," she said.

"Auguste and Julie will be back about four. Dinner is at nine. There's plenty of time. You can have a swim later," Meyerson said.

Lani led Robin to a detached casita in a small grove of pines to the side of the house, overlooking the ocean. He locked the door as Lani went to open a wall panel which concealed an impressive array of music equipment. She turned on the amplifier and the reel-to-reel player with evident familiarity; he came up behind her as she adjusted the speaker volume. Speakers, concealed all about the room, made a low snapping noise, then produced a quiet Brazilian rhythm.

He kissed the back of her neck, sensed a slight movement of withdrawal, put his hand on her shoulder and turned her to him. He kissed her mouth. She returned his kiss as if he had interrupted her adjustment of the speaker volume. Sandy had often kissed him like that—preoccupied, even disinterested. He took her hand and led her to a couch which faced the glass wall and the ocean beyond. As she sat he drew her against him.

"Lani?"

"Hmmm?"

"Where are you?"

"Here."

"Is everything OK with us?"

She leaned forward and looked at him. "Sure. What do you mean?"

"I don't know. You've seemed pretty distant."

"I'm right here, Robin. Right where I want to be."

"It's a fabulous place to be."

"I'm glad you're here, too." She leaned back against his body; he brought his arm across her right shoulder and took her left arm in his hand, lightly.

"I've done a lot of daydreaming about being here alone with you," he said quietly.

"Oh? What happens in the dream?"

"I stroke your arm, like this. And kiss your shoulder and neck,

178

so. Then you turn. No, just your head. Mmmm." Her lips parted as they kissed.

"Ah. Then?"

"And then, within a very few minutes, we go to bed."

"Oh?"

He leaned up out of the couch, carrying her forward with his arm. He held her to him as he moved to the side of the windows to draw the heavy curtains across the glass wall. She looked at him sharply, a hint of alarm passing briefly across her eyes.

"Come out on the deck and see the ocean," she said.

"I don't want to see the ocean. I can hear it. I want to see you." There were no other windows in the room. The drapes and upholstery had a light floral pattern reminiscent of Corot. The bed was broad and low, almost Japanese. Reading lights on booms extended from side tables.

He was holding her close, one hand firmly on her wrist, as he looked at her. She pulled gently away from him, then more insistently as he continued to hold her firmly. Unthinking, he crossed a line: He would, by God, have her now, whatever was going on. There was no thought of consequences, aftermath or the future. Holding her wrist, he ran his other hand under her loose blouse and along her back. In one motion he drew it over her head, released her arm and let the blouse drop to the floor. At once he took her, behind her knees and across her naked back with his arms, scooped her up and carried her to the bed. She stiffened, then tried to turn, but he held her close; he knelt and lowered them both onto the turned-back sheets.

She struggled. "You son of a bitch, what—"

He kissed her roughly. She twisted to escape from his arms, but her tongue betrayed her. He felt it dart into his mouth, dance along his lip, meet his tongue and caress it. Then she was fighting him again, stronger than before. Somehow he undressed her, then himself. The first penetration brought a sharp cry of pain from her. She was small and dry. But then, almost instantly, they were one in every sensation and movement, although her eyes were

179

clenched shut and she kept her head turned far to one side until just before she climaxed. Then she drew his mouth to hers, engulfed it in lips and tongue and a shout of anger and rapture and release, both arms tight around his neck. She shuddered, shifted, wrapped her legs around his waist and he drove deep and hard. She was wide, clear, his. He burst within her, then buried himself deep, feeling her belly heave and throb, everything pervaded with her musky odor.

"Am I too heavy on you?"

She tightened her arms around his neck, but released her legs and stretched them to full length along the outsides of his legs. Then she brought her hands to the back of his neck, embedded her fingernails lightly and scratched the length of his back, digging deep into his buttocks.

"You son of a bitch," she growled. "How did you know?"

"Do you always want to be raped?"

She closed her eyes and turned her head quickly aside as if the word caused her pain. Her mouth tightened into a straight, hard line.

"What's the matter?" Robin asked. "What did I say? Rape?"

She shook her head and moved from beneath him. He let her go. The air was cold on his skin where their moist bodies had parted. He drew the sheet over them, then worked his arm under her neck, drawing her to him.

"Lani? What's wrong?"

"Nothing. You are wonderful," she said into the pillow.

"Did I hurt you?"

She shook her head, then abruptly sat up, her fingers combing through her hair. "It's an old war wound, darling. It only hurts once in a while. I'm OK."

"Want to tell me about it?"

"The truth is, I don't know much about it for certain. Sometimes I'm just perverse, I guess. I was put off by something just now, but I also wanted you to take me. I wanted to be raped, I guess. Sometimes I hate it and cry and carry on. But mostly I want to be taken by force." She was stroking his arm. "That was one of our problems—Goldberg's and mine. He was just never up for war games. He decided I am pretty weird—and I guess he's right."

"If you're weird, I'll take a dozen."

"Wrapped or will you eat them here? What was your wife like in bed?"

"Huh?"

"Your wife—Suzy."

"Sandy."

"Yeah. Was she passionate?"

"Oh, I guess. It was a schoolyard romance and we married pretty young."

"What did she do that you liked?"

"Hey, come on. I don't talk about other ladies."

"This?" She moved down his body.

"You're the one who's here now and you're who does that—and I like it. Oh yes. I like it."

"You're ducking my question." She looked at him across his belly. "Did she do this?" she asked.

He put a hand under each arm and pulled her up to him, her head back on the pillow, and he rolled half on top of her.

"You are fantastic," he said.

"Who lays you, now that you're divorced? Do you ever see Sandy?"

"No."

"Who, then? That Mick secretary?"

"No."

"Well, who? You're no celibate, that's for sure."

He didn't answer. She had raised the ghost of Maggie Valle in spite of him, and there was nothing he could say. He sighed and Lani took it for pleasure. He looked at Lani and relaxed. She was falling asleep, her flawless mouth slightly agape, breathing deeply. Beautiful. He withdrew his arm gently, rolled away from her and relaxed. In a moment he too was asleep.

About three they awoke and swam in a white-and-chrome heated pool, then lounged in the pale sunshine. Robin was asleep on a chaise on the pool deck when the Caprons appeared. They had been to shop in the heart of the city. When Julie Capron took Lani into the house to show her a dress she had found, her husband sat down next to Robin.

"I've been over in Santiago this week," Capron said.

"A holiday?" Robin asked, feeling unwilling to make conversation. He was barely hiding his unhappiness at Capron's invasion.

"No. Nothing is ever really a holiday anymore. I was looking at fishing."

"Shrimp?"

"Yes, but bottom fish too. Fish for meal and fertilizer and protein concentrate. Chile has an abundance of fish products for export."

"Interesting."

"Tonight I have a treat for us."

"Lani was very vague. We're going out to dinner?"

"Yes. You must dress in your suit. I am taking you to meet a remarkable old man."

"Who?"

"I'll save him as a surprise. We'll fly; can you be ready at half past eight?"

"Sure. What's the mystery?"

"No mystery. It's a treat—a surprise. So I'll not tell you, but I think you'll like it. I know you will." Capron stood. "You've had your siesta, but I've missed mine. So I'll rest now and see you at eight-thirty. *Hasta luego.*"

Robin found Lani waiting in his room. They showered together, made love wet, on the bed, then slept, twined in the sheet and each other. This time she had been the aggressor.

Only Auguste Capron and Robin Warren flew away to dinner. The same red-and-white helicopter had returned to lift them into the Atlantic dusk. When the pilot reached his airspeed he lowered his altitude to about ten feet above the water and flew northeast, toward the darkening open sea. A few minutes later he turned off the lights—all the lights, even the red running lights on the

182

fuselage. It had become so dark that Robin could barely see the water.

"We are meeting my friend on his ship, Robin. Uruguay is just across there." Capron pointed out the left window. "You can see the lights of Montevideo on the north margin of the Rio."

Uruguay. Of course. Everything began to fall into place.

"Your friend is Uruguayan, right?"

"Right."

"Navy?"

"An admiral. We'll dine on his flagship."

"Auguste, this is—"

"Be at peace, Robin. It is a purely social occasion." Capron put his right hand on Warren's arm. "No business of any kind will be discussed. I promise you."

"Yes, I'm sure that's—"

"Admiral Suárez is a man of complete discretion. I know you'll like him. He's a graduate of Annapolis, you know."

The engine sound changed and Robin sensed that the blackened helicopter was climbing and making a circle to the right. He looked out the window into total darkness. The pilot flashed his landing lights twice quickly. When Warren was once again accustomed to the dark he realized they were hovering over a small square of dim blue lights. As they descended slowly, he could make out the shadows of a warship's superstructure ahead. No other light could be seen.

The helicopter rocked gently from wheel to wheel, then settled onto the landing pad. The engine whined to silence as a swarm of men approached from all sides, tying it down, blocking the wheels. Someone opened the door next to Robin, admitting a breeze coated with wet salt.

"Bien venidos, señores. Por favor."

Warren and Capron unbuckled, deplaned and peered into the darkness.

"This way, Mr. Capron," a tall officer said. "The Admiral is awaiting you in his quarters."

The ship was large; a light cruiser, Robin guessed. As they walked forward in the dark the ship began to make way, rocking slightly, side to side. They were led up two flights of stairs and forward to a square cabin built as if it were an afterthought, behind the bridge. The young officer led the way through a light-safe vestibule into a sizable saloon furnished like a living room, a round oak table set for dinner at one side. The officer offered them drinks in a slightly British accent, relaying the orders to a mess steward in machine-gun Spanish.

A door at the far end of the room opened and a short gray-haired man stepped over the doorsill into the saloon, smiling broadly at them. His face was deeply creased, so markedly lined that Robin was reminded of pictures of Auden. The Admiral was dark-skinned, stout and very short.

"Auguste, my friend! And Mr. Robin Warren. I am deeply honored," he said in a deep voice.

"Admiral Suárez," Capron said formally, "may I present Mr. Warren? Of the White House."

"Of course, of course." Suárez shook Robin's hand vigorously, looking up into his face. The gold bands of rank on Suárez' white uniform sleeve ranged from his cuffs nearly to his elbows. Rows of campaign ribbons began at his pocket and disappeared under his left lapel.

The Admiral turned to Capron. "Please, my old friend, let us sit over here on the couches until dinner is served. It has been many weeks since I have had a chance to talk with you." His English was heavily accented.

Capron explained, somewhat too elaborately, Robin thought, that he and his wife had been in Santiago on business. Robin was on a little holiday in Argentina. They deeply appreciated the Admiral's generous invitation, he said.

"Perhaps you recognize this ship, Mr. Warren?" Suárez asked.

"No, sir, I don't."

"It was formerly the U.S.S. *Boise.*"

"Is it a light cruiser?"

"Yes. Very good. A light missile cruiser." He said "miss*ile*"

184

with the British pronunciation. "We obtained her from you when we were a Western nation. Before the Junta. It is a sound ship. Of course, now it has been modified to fire Soviet missiles."

"Awful," Capron said.

They had now arrived at the topic of Marxism and Uruguay, Robin realized. Very soon he would be put in direct conversation with the Admiral on the subject of the overthrow of the Uruguayan regime by the United States. He would be expected to speak for the President, of course. Capron had lured him into a trap. Robin's lust and stupidity had put him in this spot; not simple, carnal lust for Lani alone, however. He had lusted for the future opportunities that a man like Auguste Capron could provide. He knew that was the reason he had not pressed Capron for details about his dinner surprise. It explained the suppression of his annoyance at Capron's interloping upon his weekend with Lani. He was Capron's patsy. He wanted what Capron could someday give him; he'd been seeking the man's favor ever since they'd met. And now he was thoroughly compromised.

"After we dine, gentlemen, I would like to show you all around my flagship. But I am sorry to say that I cannot." The Admiral made a deep shrug. "It is no longer possible for me to assure you of the reliability and discretion of my crew. I cannot afford to have you seen with me. We've all been made plotters and spies by our tyrants. It is very sad. Very sad."

"I considered suggesting we meet in Argentina, perhaps at my club," Capron said, "or at the villa."

"No, the high seas are better, Auguste. The Junta's people are everywhere in B.A. Perhaps even at your villa."

Suárez pointed to an Annapolis class picture hanging over the Admiral's desk. "There are three astronauts in that class, Mr. Warren. Do you see me at the end, in front? I had to get a dispensation because of my short stature. I was the smallest in the class. My Annapolis classmates still call me Shorty."

Robin walked over to look at the picture. A cadet in the fifth rank on the right side could be seen in a Rockefellerian gesture. Robin and the Admiral talked lightly about the differences in the

185

use of such manual obscenities in various parts of the world.

Then dinner was served briskly by the Admiral's steward. Capron asked questions about the Chilean fishing fleet, about which Suárez was comprehensively informed.

When the plates were cleared, Suárez looked at his watch, stood and pressed a buzzer, and summoned his aide-de-camp. He turned to the Americans.

"Gentlemen, I hope you will forgive my imperfect hospitality. This vessel will shortly rendezvous with other units of our Navy. I must soon light up. It is essential that you effect your takeoff at once."

"Of course." Capron nodded, rising. "We'll be on our way."

"Mr. Warren, it has been my honor and pleasure to have you aboard. I wish it could have been a more leisurely visit."

"Thank you, Admiral. I'll never forget it," Robin said. No more talk about Uruguay at all. Nothing requested, nothing given. He felt as if he were about to miraculously escape execution. They shook hands.

Capron and Robin followed the Admiral's aide back to the landing platform through the dark labyrinth of passages and stairways. A large rocket launcher loomed over the helicopter. Not even the hooded blue landing lights were used for the helicopter's takeoff. Once airborne, the pilot dropped to the wavetops and set a course south toward the brilliant lights of Mar del Plata.

Robin and Capron did not speak during the return flight. As they flew, Robin mentally turned over the question of Capron's motive, trying it, gnawing at it like a dog with a slipper. He found only one explanation for the dinner with Suárez: the Admiral doubted President Frankling's commitment to the coup against the Junta. So Capron produced one of the President's staff as a token. Since it was all symbolic, nothing had to be said. If it was not that sort of pantomime it made no sense at all. He'd been lured by Lani, delivered like a prize pig by Capron and inspected by Suárez. The porcine medium was the message. No grunts were necessary.

186

But the worst thing was that the energy for it all—the locomotion—had been his own desire to ingratiate himself with Capron, with future reward in mind. He could recognize and tolerate their corruption, Capron's and Lani's, but he could not bear to think about his own. He preferred to feel trapped, unwary, even foolish. Lani and Capron had compromised him. That was the explanation.

In twenty-five minutes they had made a dark landing on the lawn between the villa and the Atlantic. As they walked to the house from the helicopter one of the white-jacketed servants handed Robin a telegram from Kathy O'Reilly in a sealed envelope. He opened and read it as soon as he came into the house. Walking quickly to his room, he saw Lani swimming laps in the lighted pool.

Before she returned from swimming, Robin had packed his suitcase and written her a short note:

"Lani—I've been called back. Sorry for the sudden departure. R."

In the courtyard at the front of the house a chauffeur sat behind the wheel of a Mercedes limousine. He turned as Robin opened the rear door, tossed his bags on the floor and doubled into the seat.

"*Señor?*"

"*Aeropuerto, por favor.* Mar del Plata."

Without a question, the driver started the engine and eased the large car around the drive and out the gate.

At the Mar del Plata airport Robin discovered that shuttle flights to Ezeiza airport at Buenos Aries did not begin until nine on Sunday mornings. As he slouched in a modernistic, tube aluminum airport chair which had seen better days, he noticed that the Argentine Airlines ticket counter was open. The sole clerk was coping with the irately described needs of a large family whose connection had somehow been missed. When they were sent on their way, the woman turned to Robin. It became evident that neither her English nor his Spanish was sufficient, but between

187

them he was able to make her understand his change of plans and his need to travel to Miami.

The clerk took his SST coupons and filled out several long forms. More paperwork and his signature and passport number were required before new tickets could be produced. It was nearly dawn when she presented him with a thick ticket envelope, smiling broadly.

It was not until he arrived at Buenos Aires that he discovered he had been booked aboard a Cruzeiro Do Sul flight to Rio de Janeiro and then Varig's milk run from Rio, via three intermediate stops, to Miami. During his three-hour layover in Rio, Robin tried vainly to book a direct flight. The airport was jammed and he could not find a better schedule available on any airline. Everyone in South America was flying somewhere.

It was by then impossible to regain his canceled SST reservation too. He needed Kathy O'Reilly, he reflected with amusement. His muscle with the airlines had been left at home.

The flight from Buenos Aires to Rio via São Paulo was not bad. The lunch was quite decent. But the night flight from Rio de Janeiro to Brasilia, then Manáos and Caracas was deadly.

In Miami, between flights, he tried to call his office. The White House switchboard operator chided him: "Didn't you know we were trying to find you, Mr. Warren? We left messages everywhere. Didn't Miss O'Reilly find you?"

"I've been hiding out to get some work done. Who's calling?"

"Mr. David Hale wants you. One moment." The phone went dead, then made switching noises.

"Robin?"

"Yes."

"David Hale. Where did I find you?"

"I'm down south. I've been fishing this weekend."

"I see. Can you come back? Have you seen a paper today?"

"I haven't even heard any news, no. What's up?"

"A plot to overthrow the government was nipped in the bud in Uruguay last night. The CIA may have been rather deeply involved. The Boss had to go ahead with his press conference

188

today, but there are a lot of unanswered questions. I want to have a senior staff meeting on it very soon, and I think it's important that you be there, too. OK?"

Robin Warren tasted metallic ashes. A leaden realization blighted the center of his mind. He fought it aside, then made room for it. There was a deadly problem; it was not his problem, so he had nothing to feel guilty or concerned about. But it was there, and it would have to be dealt with. It was not going to go away. He could handle it. It would be all right. It would be all right. Hale did not sound upset; doubtless it was not as big a crisis as it seemed. Hale was asking a question.

"Can you get here?"

"Sure. But I don't get to Washington until about four P.M."

"You are coming to the state dinner for the King of Norway?"

"Right."

"I'll see you then. We'll get together with Broderick and Durrien tomorrow morning and see where we go from there, OK?"

"Sure, Dave. I can fill you in on what I know about Uruguay right now if you—"

"No, save it. We'll go over it then, Robin. Don't worry about it."

"OK. See you tonight, then." He hung up, sat still for a moment, thinking, then dialed the telephone.

"White House."

"This is Robin Warren. Please give me Mr. Thompson."

"Surely, Mr. Warren."

"Mr. Thompson's office, Mr. Warren. Can I help you?"

"Is he there?"

"One moment."

"Thompson."

"Bill, Robin. Listen, what's up? I'm invited to the senior staff meeting tomorrow to talk about Uruguay. What is going on?"

"I'm not sure. Hale's office called a while ago; it was little Turley and he was charging hard, as usual. Demanded to know where you were and, when I wouldn't say, he threatened me awhile; it was his little Beaver Patrol number. So I spit in his eye, and hung up on him. Then I called Hale and had to settle for his secretary. She's a friend of mine. She says everyone in their office is very sphinctered about Uruguay, and *you're* it somehow. They want a staff meeting tomorrow morning. I guess you are the guest of honor."

"That or the main course; I'm not sure which. What does the news summary say happened in Uruguay?"

"The CIA blew it, I guess. The summary says they had some big covert plot and it was discovered just before the revolt was to begin. Apparently Uruguay captured a CIA man and a lot of local plotters. The Communists are raising a big stink."

"I'll be in tonight. I'm going to that dinner."

"OK. I'll put the news summary in the car that picks you up at the airport."

"Right. Do one other thing, Bill. Call Cooper Dewey at the CIA. Say that I want a report from him in the car, too. I get into Dulles about four. That should give him enough time."

"Cooper Dewey?"

"He's an assistant director over there. He'll know what I want, but he'll probably refuse to do it. I'll see you tomorrow."

As Robin Warren flew from Miami to Washington on June twenty-first he slept deeply. He did not awaken until the airplane was landing at Dulles Airport.

There was no report from Cooper Dewey in the White House car that picked him up at the airport. As they drove toward Georgetown, Robin Warren asked the driver what the President had said about Uruguay at his press conference. But the driver hadn't listened to the President, either.

Part III

THE CRISIS

CHAPTER **16**   "Good morning, Mr. President," Nick Gurley said brightly. "That was a great press conference yesterday."

Hugh Frankling opened his eyes with a startled movement of his head. Every weekday for months this earnest and enthusiastic young man in his dark-blue business suit dutifully woke him up, but Frankling would never get used to it. In his Senate days he slept until he naturally came alive, the way a man *should* wake up. It was invariably jarring to have someone invade your bedroom, talking to you cheerfully, prodding to get you moving.

Frankling grunted as he sat up. A cup of hot coffee sat on a small silver tray on the night table, as it did every morning when he awoke. The President reached for it, drank slowly, rubbed his right eye with two fingers, then grunted again to show that he was awake. He hoped the young man thereupon would go away.

"General Durrien will be in the small dining room for breakfast in twenty-five minutes, sir."

"Right. Uruguay, eh?"

"Yes, sir. Here's his memorandum. You said you would want to see it when you got up." Gurley handed the President a blue folder.

"Sure. I'll get dressed first. Is Valencio out there?"

"I'll send him in, sir. The NSC meets with you at ten. David Hale said to tell you he was seeing Robin Warren this morning. Warren is coming to Hale's senior staff meeting at eight."

"All right, Nick. I'll see you at the office." Frankling put down the cup and swung to his feet, rumpled and stiff.

"Yes, sir."

Frankling moved woodenly to the bathroom and slammed the door behind him. Gurley waited until he heard the shower start, then opened the hall door and beckoned the valet.

"Make sure he reads that blue file before he goes down to breakfast. OK?"

"Yes, sor," the Filipino said.

When he had dressed, Hugh Frankling took the Uruguay file from the bed where Gurley had conspicuously placed it, sat heavily into the one chair in the room, and read the memorandum. Bob Durrien had sent it into the paper mill overnight to prepare him for their breakfast meeting, and for the morning meeting of the National Security Council. It was all about Uruguay, of course. That damn thing had become a potentially dangerous problem. Dangerous politically and even rather dangerous internationally. All that trouble developed in about thirty-six hours, thanks to television. That goddamned Auguste Capron. Frankling now hated even his name. It had been a mistake to see him, to listen to him. A slimy bastard.

The President sat deeper in the chair and opened the file.

For The President
From Lieutenant General Robert L. Durrien,
      U.S.A., Assistant to the President for
      National Security Affairs
Re: (1) Uruguay
      (to be discussed at the National
      Security Council Meeting)
     (2) United Nations debate
     (3) Senate Select Committee hearings

Synopsis

A CIA operation called "Methodist Missionary," first planned and proposed by that Agency two years ago, updated last month and allegedly authorized by the President on May 31 of this year, was designed to overthrow the ruling Junta and kill the President of Uruguay, Jose Gómez Fellano, a known client of Russia and Cuba.

On June 20 the attempted coup failed. By June 21 written "confessions" were released by the Uruguayan Foreign Office stating that the coup was jointly financed and managed by the CIA and United International, a multinational corporation based in the U.S. and controlled by Auguste Capron.

On June 21 the USSR formally requested the Secretary General and the current Security Council President to convene an extraordinary session of the United Nations Security Council in order to receive the voluntary testimony of several of the plotters: Uruguayan naval officers and a captured American, allegedly a CIA agent, Randolph Sands.

That session is going to be scheduled, and our UN Ambassador reports that the USSR, Cuba, and Uruguay are undoubtedly making preparations for a TV spectacular to embarrass the United States.

Ambassador Cunningham also reports that there is already a noticeable acceptance of the Uruguayan allegations among Security Council members, and a related erosion of support for the proposed Deep Ocean

Resources Trust (on which, you will recall, we are
relying heavily as a source of crude oil, natural gas,
uranium and coal in our National Energy Policy projec-
tions). Unless the United States can make a convincing
rebuttal to the Uruguayan charges, the Deep Ocean
Trust may be a dead letter in the UN for at least a year,
perhaps more.

Another danger: As matters are shaping up, even if
some version of the Ocean Trust were adopted on schedule, the terms now might be so disadvantageous as to be
unacceptable to the U.S.A., and we would be compelled
to reject it.

Purpose of the NSC meeting:

The President will receive recommendations for
strategy to counter the attack on the U.S.A. by the
USSR and its clients in the United Nations. Our ultimate objective is to secure establishment of a Deep
Ocean Resources Trust advantageous to this country.

Probable recommendations:

Based on reactions voiced at the preparatory meeting of the Undersecretaries' Committee of the NSC
yesterday (Monday), the options to be presented to
you, and their sponsors, will be as follows:

Option One: To admit that the U.S.A. sponsored the
coup. We would invoke the Monroe Doctrine, in effect, to justify our action and to call alarmed
attention to Soviet incursions into this hemisphere
in Cuba, Bolivia, and Uruguay.
There is some State Department internal support for
this option, but the Secretary will not sponsor it.

Option Two: To deny U.S. involvement, describing the
coup as a genuine, domestic revolution against the
tyranny of the Marxist regime without any outside
support by the U.S.
The Director of Central Intelligence and Secretary
of Defense will favor this option.

Option Three: To admit CIA involvement but deny that it was authorized. This response requires a detailed and factually supportable explanation of U.S. internal procedures, including the identification of those responsible.

The Secretary of State, the Attorney General and General Durrien will favor this option. The Director of Central Intelligence is strongly opposed.

It is not known how the Vice President and the Director of the Office of Management and Budget will vote.

NSC Staff recommendation: Option Three

Justification: As is always the case when there is a failure, none of the choices is ideal. But there is no merit to admitting U.S. complicity outright. We would get no credit for candor. On the contrary, the cost would be an inevitable defeat in the UN and the probable loss of the crucial advantages we hope to secure from the Deep Ocean Trust.

In comparing Options Two and Three you must consider that Uruguay will probably produce compelling evidence in a dramatic fashion. The burden of proving a total absence of U.S. involvement would be heavy beyond hope.

For your private information, the confessed agent provocateur Randolph Sands is, in fact, a CIA agent assigned to the Western Hemisphere Division. Steps are being taken to interdict any attempt to produce him as a live witness at the Security Council (but the possibility of success is rated at less than 50/50).

The recommended option: The U.S. Ambassador to the UN, Mr. Cunningham, should state that agents of the U.S. acted contrary to established U.S. Foreign Policy and without proper authorization. Further, that a multinational corporation, acting for its own pecuniary interest alone, suborned a young government employee to issue instructions in the name of higher authority, and caused lower-level Central Intelligence Agency employees to plan and attempt to execute the coup, all without any authorization, knowledge or approval of the President, the Secretary of State, or other proper authority.

Obviously, the success of this gambit depends upon the availability of evidence to support the ambassador's statement. It has been suggested that, since the USSR clients will be presenting evidence in personam, a video-taped statement by the President might be carefully prepared to establish that you had no knowledge of the chain of events which were set in motion in your name, and, specifically, that you wholly repudiate and disapprove of this interference in the internal affairs of Uruguay.

David Hale advises that Robin Warren's admission of culpability may or may not be available to be presented during the UN debate. Obviously, it would be most important and helpful.

The Senate Committee hearings:

Chairman Oates called me today to say that a Senate Select Committee intends to begin public televised hearings into "Methodist Missionary" in July, after the Fourth of July Recess. He is determined to beat the Russians and the UN to the punch.

He is requesting all White House, NSC and CIA files on the operation. Your counsel, Elwood Broderick, has not yet approved the release of anything. He is in touch with the chief counsel for the new committee and is trying to work out ground rules without waiving Executive Privilege or classification restrictions.

If you decide on one of the above UN options it will also determine administration strategy at these Senate hearings. Your position will necessarily be the same in each forum, although in determining tactics it must be recognized that the Democrat majority on the Committee will be motivated by a desire to embarrass and impugn a Republican President, while the USSR and its clients will seek to indict the U.S.A., entire.

State is now prepared to follow the White House lead in these Senate Committee hearings, although at first encounter this was not the case.

RLD
R. L. Durrien

Frankling opened the blue folder and pushed the last of the thick pages into the fold, then stared briefly at his shoes. He nodded vigorously, heaved to his feet and walked briskly to the small elevator across the second-floor hall from his bedroom. A grizzled old usher in white tie, wing collar and black hammer-claw coat was waiting, holding open the door.

"Good mornin', Mr. President."

"Good morning, John."

The usher followed Frankling into the car, closed the door firmly and pushed a button. The little car jerked slightly and descended.

The side walls were decorated with narrow mirrors and inlaid wood. Frankling invariably looked at his reflection as he rode down in the morning. He braced his shoulders and put his left hand lightly on his stomach. He held his breath.

"Yes, sir," the usher said. "The Gennel's in the small dinin' room waitin' for you, sir." He held the door.

General Robert Durrien turned as he heard the President come in; he had been looking out the window at the Pennsylvania Avenue traffic. He wore a brown flannel suit and a quiet necktie; a quiet man—a teacher and theoretician, short, stocky, balding. But tough; much more cold-blooded than his round, bland face implied. Hugh Frankling had seen Durrien in action before the Senate Foreign Relations Committee many times, presenting Defense Department testimony. Quiet authority, that's what he had; he took command and he proved relentless in winning. After the inauguration, as the President's new National Security Advisor, he had justified Frankling's confidence by organizing and stage-managing quick Congressional approval of a substantial increase in the defense budget, seven billion dollars over the amount proposed by the outgoing, lame-duck administration. More money for defense had been one of Frankling's campaign promises, one that was important to him.

"Bob, good morning."

"Good morning, sir."

"Let's sit right down. I've read your memo about Uruguay."

"Things are piling up, Mr. President. Elwood Broderick says the Senate hearing will be massively covered by the television networks."

"I'm sure. They remember Watergate. They all got fat on that. This is their first crack at us. What got old Senator Oates so cranked up so fast?"

"He wants to trade for something, I think. That's why he called me himself, to tell me about his select committee. But he's cagey. He's not ready to tell me what he wants. He'll let us sweat awhile."

"Ah, here are the eggs—all kinds." The President used the big fork and spoon to remove poached eggs and bacon from a large silver tray held by a butler. There were fried and scrambled eggs too. Enough for six. The man then moved quietly to Durrien and held the tray low. Another butler poured coffee from a covered silver pot.

"Who is the ranking Republican on Oates's committee, Bob? Or do you know yet?"

"Yes, sir. It's Senator Arthur Brawley."

"Blast. They'll run all over him. He'll be terrible on television. No help."

"I think the strongest Republican will be Senator Larkin. Here's the list."

"Yeah, he's young and tough. But inexperienced. More coffee?" Frankling ran his finger down the committee roster.

"No, thanks."

"I'll go along with your recommendation, Bob. It happens to be true, you know. I never authorized that *Methodist* operation down there. I may have Smythe prosecute that Warren kid. He must be crazy to do a thing like that."

"Well, the CIA people are partly to blame, Mr. President. Cooper Dewey is an old hand over there. He should have checked with me. He knew better. But Warren apparently put on a great act and used your name over and over. Totally fooled Dewey. And the United International people helped to suck him in. Capron is at the bottom of this whole thing, I'm sure."

"I agree. I saw him a couple of weeks ago, you know."

"So I'd heard."

"At Rob Warren's urging. Capron wanted me to pull his chestnuts out of the fire then. Told me how terrible the Communists were in Uruguay. Naturally, I finessed him. Told him to see you, as a matter of fact. Did he ever call on you?"

"No, he didn't, Mr. President. I wish he had."

"So do I. So do I."

"Now," said Durrien, "the question is whether Robin Warren will cooperate. If he will go to the Senate and tell the truth, our United Nations problems will be greatly eased."

"Do you think he will, Bob?"

"I don't know, Mr. President." Durrien looked at his wristwatch. "We should know shortly. He should be meeting with David Hale and the senior staff right now."

Robin Warren pushed open the heavy wood door and stood in the doorway of David Hale's office. His eyes were drawn to the empty coffee cups on the butler's table. The meeting had been going on for some time. They must have started early.

"Come in, Robin," Hale said. He got up from his deep upholstered easy chair and pulled a leather side chair from under the conference table near the south windows. The other three cushioned chairs near the fireplace were occupied. Elwood Broderick, the house lawyer, Les Carew, the President's press secretary, and Murray Tillerman, the Assistant for Domestic Policy, looked at Robin as he sat down.

Hale hosted these three, plus Bob Durrien and the Assistant for Economics, Hill Gossett, every morning for a half hour of gossip and coffee before their phones started to ring. Others of lesser rank were invited from time to time, but Hale seldom included one of his own staff. Warren had never before been invited.

"Sit down, Robin, and tell us what you can about this Uruguay mess," Hale said quietly. "Oh, how was fishing?"

"Very good."

"You go alone?" Elwood Broderick rumbled.

Warren looked from Hale to Broderick. "No," he said. "I went with a friend who knows the country."

"What about this CIA thing?" Tillerman asked. "What started it?"

Broderick glanced sharply at Tillerman. He thought it had been agreed that Broderick would lead the interrogation.

"Sure," Robin Warren began, "Auguste Capron—you all know how he fits in this? His conglomerate owns the telephone company in Uruguay. Anyway, he asked for an appointment with the President."

"I think we're all aware of that appointment," Hale said evenly.

"Right." Warren clasped his hands in front of him and leaned forward. "In that meeting Capron asked that the President do something to prevent the expropriation of his company by Uruguay."

"What did he propose that the President do?" Tillerman asked.

"He didn't say, specifically. After Capron left, the President instructed me to assign the CIA—a man named Cooper Dewey— to recommend what to do."

"So what did you do?" Hale asked.

"I called Dewey over and gave him the President's assignment."

"Robin," Les Carew drawled, "why didn't you let Bob Durrien do it? The CIA is sort of his territory around here, isn't it?"

"Yes, but the President just flatly told me not to. I wasn't supposed to tell him or David or anyone."

David Hale and Murray Tillerman exchanged looks of disbelief.

"Why not?" Hale asked.

"The President said he'd tell you about it. He didn't want any leaks. He told me not to tell anyone. He said he'd tell you himself at the right time."

"When would that be?"

"He didn't say."

"So then what did you do?" Broderick asked. His trousers were too tight. He half stood, pulled them down and eased back into the chair.

"When Cooper Dewey was ready I met with him and listened to his recommendation for this coup."

"And?" Broderick asked.

"And I told the President what the CIA recommended."

"*When* did you do that?" Hale pressed.

"After dinner on the yacht. When was that? I can't remember the date. Well, it's the only time I've been on the yacht with him. Around the first of this month—the same day Dewey and Dooley came in with the plan. During dinner on the yacht the President told me to give them the green light. So I did."

"Who is Dooley?" asked Murray Tillerman. He was leaning forward like a pointer on the scent.

"He's one of Capron's vice-presidents," Robin Warren replied slowly. "But you already know that, don't you?"

Tillerman nodded. "We also know he was with the CIA for twenty years in Latin America. But," he parroted, "you already know that."

"No, I don't. Nobody told me that."

"Well, Robin," Hale said levelly, "let's cut out the bullshit, shall we?"

"There's no bullshit. I've told you what happened."

"Have you taken any money from Capron?" Hale pressed.

"Hell, no. You took care of all of that. You got his money."

"I mean you personally. Has he or have any of his people taken care of you?"

"Absolutely not," Robin half shouted. "What do you think I am? What is this?"

"Who is it you were fishing with, Robin?" Broderick said. It was more of an accusation than a question.

"What has that got to do with anything? Murray, will you tell me what is going on?"

Tillerman tapped out his pipe and was about to speak when Elwood Broderick intervened: "When you told the CIA to go ahead with the operation was there anyone with you—did anyone hear you do it?"

"Sure."

"Who was that?"

"The President and Smythe."

"The Attorney General?"

"Right."

"Where were you?"

"In the dining room of the yacht."

"Where was the yacht?"

"Sailing up the river."

"The same day you saw Dewey and the Capron vice-president?"

"Right."

"And the President heard you do that?"

"Certainly. Ask him. He was a little smashed, but he'll remember. He told me what to say. Have you asked him?"

Hale nodded slowly. "Of course I've asked him, Robin. So did the press conference. Did you see it?"

"No. What did he say to you?"

Les Carew shook his head slowly.

"You mean he couldn't remember?" Warren asked. "He wasn't that smashed. Smythe was there, too. Has anyone asked him?" Warren's voice rose in increments as he looked quickly from Carew to Broderick, then to Hale.

Tillerman blew into his empty pipe. "Look," he said, "this is the way I put it together, Robin: Capron worked on you, one way or the other—money, broads, whatever you like—and you tried to do him a favor. Right?"

"No. Listen, Murray, I recommended his appointment with the President—but not for money or women or anything else."

"No, I mean after that. When the CIA said they could scratch the Junta, you told them to go ahead, to save Capron's holdings down there. Right?"

"Wrong, Murray. I already explained that. ‚The *President* decided that."

"When you were on the yacht, right?" Carew asked.

"Right."

"The three of you. You, Smythe and the President, right?"

"Right."

"Wrong," snapped Hale. "They were on the yacht, but you missed the boat."

"What do you mean?"

"Just that. You never showed up, so the motorcade left without you. You were never aboard that boat with them. Now, where *were* you when you told Dewey to go ahead? In your office?"

Incredulous, Robin Warren banged his fist on the chair arm and stood up. "What are you bastards trying to do? I *was* on the boat! The President gave that order! I *know* it. *He* knows it. I don't know what you people are trying to pull, but I'm not going to sit here and be the fall guy!"

"Robin," Hale began, "let's take a look at what is ahead. There are going to be all kinds of investigations: the Senate, the CIA, the FBI, maybe even a grand jury. Your best strategy will be to tell the truth. I've checked and double-checked. You weren't on the yacht with the President then or any other time. If you will accept responsibility for your actions we can try to protect you. But if you attack the President, try to put the blame on him, we have no choice, do we?"

Warren was clenching and opening his fists in frustration. "David, you son of a bitch, you can't do this. The truth is the truth. I was there. He gave the order. There is no way you can—"

"Robin," Broderick rumbled, "both the Attorney General of the United States and the President of the United States say you weren't there. They waited, but you didn't show up. They were alone on the boat. Those are two pretty credible witnesses, wouldn't you say?"

"You sonsabitches," Warren said. The words were squeezed. "I won't stay here." He turned and opened the door, stepped quickly across the small reception room and into the hallway.

A Secret Service agent stood at his post at the far end of the hall, outside the President's office. That meant Frankling was in there now.

"Oh, Robin, good—I was going to call you . . ." It was Bill Clarkson, the President's tall Assistant for Congressional Affairs, a defeated Congressman from North Dakota. He emerged from the stairwell behind Warren and clapped a big hand on his shoulder. "We've got some kind of tough problem with the Government Employees' Union, on that pay raise bill, young man."

"Not now, Bill."

"Oh. Are you headed for the Boss?"

"Uh, yeah. That's right. I'm headed for the Boss." Robin turned and walked deliberately toward the Secret Service man at the turn of the hallway. At Nick Gurley's room he abruptly sidestepped to his right and pushed open the door. Gurley was not in his office. Warren walked across the room and gently opened the door which gave access to the dark hallway between the Oval Office and Gurley's. He could faintly hear Frankling's deep voice. The President's bathroom and the stewards' galley were on the left, the small hideaway office on the right. Straight ahead was the curved door in the west wall of the President's office. Warren found the brass knob and turned it slowly, pulling the door toward him a few inches. There was no Secret Service monitor on this door; it was assumed that Gurley would keep track of people coming in through his office and act the watchdog.

President Frankling was standing behind his desk looking down at a newspaper, the telephone in his hand at his ear. As Warren watched through the crack the President took off his glasses, looked out the window and gestured with the horn-rims as he talked.

"Well, why the hell didn't you say so?" Frankling said.

Although he couldn't see most of the room, Robin Warren guessed the President was alone; from the tone of his voice, he didn't seem to be on stage. Warren pushed the door, stepped into the elliptical room and looked to his left; there was no one else there. He moved toward the desk, without thinking what he would say. His fists clenched involuntarily. He had never before come into this room uninvited. He was an invader. There were the battle flags festooned with ribbons, the huge eagle and stars in the ceiling fresco and woven into the brown carpet, the Stuart painting, the Lincoln bust, the huge Woodrow Wilson desk, elaborately carved.

This was the Presidency in array and Robin Warren was here unbidden, in violation of the laws and statutes of the United States of America. Intellect told him to turn and leave quickly. Some instinct, perhaps now only fear, held him where he stood.

Frankling heard the soft *tunk* of the door closing and turned. His brows rose, but his conversation didn't break stride.

"You can't keep him in there, in that job, if he's going to take me on like this." His glasses waved at the newspaper. "He knew damn well what he was doing when he said that. I don't care how much you need him." Frankling looked at Warren distractedly, then focused on him, his brows gathering. He swung his heavy glasses onto his nose with a sudden roll of his arm and said, "Will you hold on just a minute?"

Frankling carefully cradled the receiver in both hands, as if afraid Robin might take it from him. After a moment of thought the President spoke to the telephone again. "Ah, Rob is here," he said confidentially. "When? I see. No, I don't think so. I'll let you know." He hung up the phone and gestured Robin to the desk with his fingers. "Sit down, Rob. Sit down. Let's talk."

Robin approached in doubt. He had lost the momentum that had been created by his anger. Now Frankling's quiet invitation threw him off stride. He hadn't barged in here for a friendly chat. "Mr. President, I apologize for—"

"It's all right. I was going to call for you in a minute, anyway. What happened in Hale's office just now?"

"They tried to get me to say I authorized that CIA operation on my own—that I wasn't on the boat; that you didn't tell me to do it."

"And what did you say to them?"

"The truth: that you authorized it when we were on the yacht."

"Well. You know, Rob, that *if* that assassination plot *had* been authorized by the President, some very awesome problems would land on this desk." Frankling patted the desk top with the palm of his right hand, then swiveled a quarter turn in the tall chair to look directly at Warren. "Very awesome: I'd be drawn and quartered by the Senate Democrats, to say nothing of the press, then I'd be pilloried by the Russians in the UN on every television set in the world. More important, the United States would be seriously damaged. I've told my press conference that I did not authorize that operation—from the yacht or anywhere else. Perhaps you knew that?"

"I was told."

"You know that. And you realize the grave consequences to the nation should the world believe I am not telling the truth?"

"No—I—no; I can't agree. Because I didn't do it!"

"Didn't call Cooper Dewey?"

"You *know* I called him. But I didn't do it on my own. You know that, too, Mr. President."

Frankling sat, hands clasped over his belly, staring at him impassively. His eyes blinked slowly. His next words came from miles away, hurtling down a straightaway, aimed for a spot between Robin's eyes: "I did not authorize you to make that call."

Warren jumped to his feet involuntarily. "Oh, sir, that's just not true!"

"I'm sorry, Rob. It *is* true. Furthermore, unless you will immediately accept responsibility for your actions"—he leaned forward, elbows on his knees, hands clasped—"there is no longer any place here for you. If you tell the truth I can try to protect you, but if you fight me, you are on your own. Think about that. On your own; alone." His joined hands chopped downward.

Warren shook his head desperately. "It's not right. You can't . . ."

"I must. It *is* right. I *do*. This is and must be your responsibility and not anyone else's." Frankling stood abruptly, then leaned forward, his hands on the desk. "Do this: take the rest of the day off. I will see you again at four o'clock. Tell me then what you intend to do."

"What can I do?" Robin asked hopelessly.

"You can tell the truth. I need for you to do that; the country needs for the truth to be told."

"The truth? You mean that I did it on my own? That's not . . ."

Frankling nodded, looked up at Warren and opened his right

hand. "Rob, you must come forward and admit that I gave you no authority; you *must*. I cannot tell you how vital it is that you do so. Go home now, and come back at four. Think it over. Help me, Rob."

Robin Warren's face flushed hot. He turned, pulled the door handle and fled down the dark hallway and into Nick Gurley's office. It was still empty.

He stood for a minute, looking blindly toward the table Gurley used for a desk. He was breathing rapidly; his face had gone from hot to cold. His neck and shoulders were taut. He walked slowly to the hall door, retraced his steps along the wide first-floor hallway and climbed down the basement stairs. His thought was suspended at a pinpoint. He needed to sort things out and decide what to do. He was alone. He was in great danger. His mind would not move beyond that primitive realization. Perhaps someone could help him. He did not want to see anyone. He knew he could not talk to Kathy O'Reilly now. Nor anyone. He left the basement, turned toward Pennsylvania Avenue and walked quickly to the exit gate. The muggy air stifled him. He took the wave of the guard in the small white kiosk and hurried to make the green light across Pennsylvania Avenue. In front of Blair House he hailed a cab and woodenly gave the driver the address of his house in Georgetown.

It felt good to run his hands over his face. He rubbed his forehead, pinched the bridge of his nose, massaged his cheeks with both hands. It relaxed him to do that. As the cab crossed Seventeenth Street he realized his hands were wet; he was crying.

CHAPTER **17** Hugh Frankling picked up his telephone and pressed the green button marked "Hale."

"Yes, Mr. President?"

"David, I think we'd better talk. Warren was just here. He's not going to be helpful. He's supposed to come back to see me at four, but I'd guess he will stick to his story."

"He just left the grounds through the northwest gate," Hale replied.

"You'd better give me a rundown on how we corroborate my press conference answer on Uruguay when the time comes. I'll want to talk to you in about twenty minutes—get Carley Smythe to come over, too, if he can. Let's be sure we have all our ducks in a row."

"Yes, sir."

"Oh, and by the way, David, how could Rob Warren just walk in on me—no warning or anything? He could have been a damn Arab with a dagger or something."

"How did he manage that?"

"He came in this door—the one to Nick Gurley's office. Doesn't anyone watch that side?"

"I'll check it. I suppose Nick was out, although he probably would have let Robin in even if he'd been there. But not without telling you first."

"It would have been better if I had avoided him, you know. What could I say to him?"

"What did you say?"

"I don't know. He took me by surprise—I said some damn thing. It was all right. I appealed to his patriotism."

"Did you concede he'd been aboard the yacht? You didn't—"

"Of course not. But I like to be able to prepare a conversation like that in advance."

"Sure."

"Shall I invite Bob Durrien to sit in with us?" Frankling asked. "How much does he know?"

"He doesn't know anything. No, I wouldn't include him—at least not now. As we go along I may need to confide in him to some extent, but the President shouldn't."

"Yes, I guess you're right. I'll see you in a half hour—no, wait a minute; let's say two o'clock. After the meeting with the NSC, I'll lunch and take a nap. You and Carley Smythe come in when I'm done with that."

"Yes sir. Two o'clock."

At 1:45 P.M. the President pushed a button on his console which directly rang his National Security Adviser's telephone.

"Yes, Mr. President?"

"Bob, were you confused by my little charade in the NSC meeting?"

"No, sir, I don't think so."

"You understand which option I have selected?"

"You accepted our recommendation, as we discussed at breakfast, right?"

"Yes. I don't see that we have any other choice. But I must say I don't understand the CIA. That Bill McConnaghay must be crazy. How the hell could we deny that the CIA was involved in Uruguay? They caught his man, for Christ's sake! They'll have him right there at the UN!"

"More likely they'll produce film of him."

"But they might bring him right into the UN, right?"

"Probably not. They fear we'd eliminate him en route."

"Ha! Right. And the CIA would if it could, I suppose."

"I think Cooper Dewey would run over him with his wheelchair if he could. The CIA doesn't encourage spectacular failure."

"No, I'm sure it doesn't. Even though it's had so much of it."

"Mr. President, based on our breakfast talk I've already met with my people and will have Ambassador Cunningham in to begin to plan our UN strategy."

"Fine, Bob, but remember: While the UN is important, it's the Senate hearings that can spill our political lifeblood. Oates and the others can kill us the same way Ervin and that pack of idiots killed Nixon. Never take your eye off of that reality. Do all you must do to put on a good show in New York. But we must be certain that we conclusively make our case here, at those televised Senate hearings. At whatever cost."

"I understand."

211

"David will talk to you more about them. I'm going to try to stay a little ways above the battle. I think I can be more effective that way. But I'll appreciate it if you'll meet with David and keep close to him on this."

"Certainly, sir."

"One thing: Robin Warren. He is the nigger in the woodpile, and his credibility is central to everything. Anything you or the CIA or anyone can come up with that will impeach his credibility . . ."

"I understand. I'm sure Dewey is hard at work on that now at the CIA. What they can't find they'll be glad to manufacture."

"Good." Frankling laughed flatly. "Let's hope that won't be necessary."

"Right."

"Thank you, Bob."

"Certainly, Mr. President."

Hale nodded to Nick Gurley as he opened Gurley's office door. "Busy?"

"Come in, David."

"Were you here this morning about nine when Robin Warren walked through?"

"Through here?"

"He walked in on the President."

"No. I was probably across the hall in the scheduling meeting."

"OK. I'm going to have a lock put on this door. You and I will have keys. They can fix it so the President can open it from the other side without a key, if he needs to come in here."

"He never does."

Hale pulled the door open and looked at the brass latch. "They'll do it tonight. Come get a key from Turley in the morning."

"Sure, David."

Hale traversed the short dark passageway and entered the Oval Office. He walked to the chair at the west side of the desk and sat down, flipping open his note pad. "They are going to put a one-way lock on that door tonight."

"Hmmm?" Frankling looked up from a memorandum he was reading.

"Don't forget that knee button under there. An agent will come on the run."

"I know. But I had a hunch; I thought I might talk him around. If I'd had him thrown out that would have torn it all."

"Yeah. You couldn't do that. Well, no one else is going to wander in here."

"Good. Now, what have you done to establish that Warren did this thing on his own?" Frankling shook his head slowly. He leaned back in the huge leather chair and put one polished shoe on the corner of the desk between them. "You know, this is a sad business, David. It is so sad to have to insist that a young man do the right thing—to impose it upon him when he won't see it."

"Ummm."

"He must do it, of course, David. I'm sure you see that. There was a day in this country when someone in Warren's position would have stepped forward to help his President without even being asked. Something has changed in this nation, though, and it's too bad. Loyalty, a sense of duty, devotion to a cause—those things are laughed at, and the country has lost something important. They tell me it's even gone from West Point. It's a sad thing. Watergate and Vietnam and Kennedy all contributed to that, I guess."

"And," said Hale, "the Korean scandals, and Wayne Hayes and a lot of mayors and governors. Young people refuse to blindly follow anyone these days."

"It's unhealthy. But"—Frankling's voice became crisp, and he dropped his foot to the floor and swiveled toward his desk—"it just means we have to work that much harder. For the welfare of the country. Now, what have you got?"

Hale flipped open a red file folder. "We're going to have some new faces around here in the next few days," he said ironically.

213

"Going to replace the boat crew?"

"Shortly. First, I've sent the yacht to Newport News for a six-month overhaul, and the crew will be disbanded as soon as it arrives there; they'll each be sent to a different post—overseas—without any of them realizing what's happening."

"Is there a log or some record of that cruise the other night?"

"I've got that. It's being amended slightly."

"Anything else—by the way, where is Carley Smythe?"

"He's in a meeting at Justice. He'll be over as soon as possible."

"Is he firm on this?"

"Fine."

"Have you and he agreed on what actually happened?" The President's voice leaned on the word "actually."

"Yes. I want to run through the story with you too, so that you're together on it."

"Do you want to wait for him? Do it with both of us at once?"

"Sure."

Frankling carefully cut the end from a cigar with his penknife. "What else are you doing?"

Hale moved his index finger down a handwritten page. "The Secret Service people who know anything are being kept here as a unit. It's better than dispersing them. I've passed the word through Dunc Billings—they are a highly discreet bunch."

"I know. I know. I'm sure they knew all about Jack Kennedy's girls and they never breathed a word. Of course, the White House press corps knew all about them, too, and they didn't print anything."

"The military drivers in the cars that night are gone. One is on his way to Guam. The other is already in Iran. The military telephone operators involved are gone, too. We're not finished tracking down the various logs and other phone records, but it won't be long. The ship was no problem. Both ends of the phone call, the dispatcher's record at the garage . . ."

"It sounds like you've thought of everything. Did the mess stewards go with the boat?"

The muffled phone buzzer rasped quietly.

"Yes, they did."

Frankling pushed a speaker button on the console.

"The Attorney General is here, Mr. President."

"Fine, Jane. Send him in."

The east door admitted Carleton Smythe before the President could switch off the speaker.

"Let's sit over there, Carley, by the fireplace," Frankling said. "It's more comfortable."

Smythe stopped in the middle of the huge Presidential seal that formed the design of the carpet.

"I was meeting with the Chief Justice, and he went on and on. I just couldn't leave."

"That's fine. How is Brown? Is he still grateful for his elevation or has he forgotten me?"

"He's very cooperative. He says right now we are beaten on the water-rights case, but he hopes to turn one justice around. He's delaying any final vote."

"I hope he understands how vital that case is—we can't use those tremendous oil shale deposits if we lose that case."

"I went over that with him again today. He's all right."

"Carley," Frankling said, shifting on his chair, "I've asked David to run through this yacht trip with us both, to be sure we're together on it." He cleared his throat. "Would either of you like coffee—a Coke?"

"Coffee, please," Smythe said.

Frankling pressed a button on the telephone console, and his valet appeared.

"Coffee, Valencio." He made a circular motion to include Smythe and Hale. "Now, David, before you begin let's be sure everyone understands the importance of this thing. I was in the Senate in 1973 and 1974. I wasn't on Ervin's committee, but I watched carefully what they did. So I am a great respecter of the devastating power of the televised committee hearing. Nixon could not have been forced out if the public had not been conditioned by those Ervin shows. The Presidency is what is at stake here. It's not just me. Oates is out to weaken, if not destroy,

215

this office. Of course, Oates and his crowd are also going to try to sink me personally with this Uruguay crap. Depend on it. He is a venal, partisan old bastard and he's never liked me.

"But it's bigger than mere personalities. It's the same thing they did to Johnson and Nixon and Carter. There's a cabal in the Congress that's determined to pound the Presidency into a secondary role in this government. That's what this is all about." As he warmed to his subject Frankling sat forward on the edge of the chair, lifting himself off a little at times, for emphasis.

The Filipino valet passed coffee and slipped out the west door.

"Now, David, how does this all come together? What should Carley say when he's called as a witness up there?"

Hale pulled out a page of notes and wedged back into the corner of the small couch. "The President and the Attorney General went for a short cruise on the *Sea Island* during the dinner hour on May thirty-first. That's the evening Warren told the CIA to go ahead. Neither one of you had any contact with Warren all that day. The President was at Goddard watching the Space Shuttle mission most of the day. Attorney General Smythe neither saw nor talked to Warren, according to his office logs. It is true that Warren's office was told that he should join you for dinner. His secretary will testify to that, and to the fact that Robin left his office to ride out in the motorcade. But he wasn't there when you were ready to leave the south lawn, so you left without him. No one knows where he was. Perhaps he was keeping a rendezvous with his movie-star lady friend. We don't know."

"What time did he phone the CIA?" Smythe asked.

"Uhm . . . ," Hale glanced at several pages, then stabbed at one with his finger. "At eight forty-five P.M."

"That late?" Smythe asked. "I thought we were back by then."

"You *were*," Hale emphasized. "You had been back for some time. That's where his story is going to fall apart. You'd been back almost half an hour. He couldn't have called from the boat."

"What time did he actually call the CIA?"

"That's the *actual* time, General. The CIA people can swear to that. We haven't tried to change their minds. That's a good time."

"Just so I understand," the President said, "the yacht got back earlier—right? And the CIA got Rob's call after that. So he couldn't have been with us telephoning from the yacht. Is that how it comes together?"

Hale nodded. "The ship's log shows—or will show—that you docked at eight-twenty P.M. You were cruising about an hour and three quarters. Just down to the bridge and back."

"Where did he call from?" Smythe asked. He leaned forward to put his empty coffee cup on the table.

"More coffee, Carley?" Frankling stabbed at the cup with his cigar.

"No, thank you."

"We don't know what secure phone he used, General. I suppose it could have been any one of dozens. The White House Communications Agency records don't show its location, but there are twenty-seven of them here in the West Wing alone."

"What else?" Frankling pressed. "What more do we need to know?"

"I think that should do it," Hale replied. "Understand, sir, this isn't foolproof. Some sailor or garage driver may show up five years from now to say Warren was on the boat."

"By that time it won't matter, eh, Carley? Just get us through the Senate hearings and the UN—"

"And the election," Smythe interjected, standing. "If you'll pardon me, I must go. It's up to you, David, to keep this thing glued together until then. Until after the election. I understand your boat schedule, and there's no problem. Just be sure the records bear me out. And, for Christ's sake, no surprises. I can't stand surprises."

"That's right." The President nodded, holding up his hand. "But wait up, Carley. You've got to stay while we talk about Rob Warren. Sit down there." He pointed at the couch, its cushions barely recovered from Smythe's recent indentation. "What do we do about his credibility? He's liable to go up there and accuse us of all sorts of things."

Smythe subsided reluctantly.

"He's got to be discredited *before* he goes up to the Senate hearings, gentlemen," David Hale said. "If Watergate teaches us anything it is that the credibility of witnesses is made or lost way in advance of their testifying."

"So—what have we got? And how do we use it?" Frankling looked from Hale to Smythe and back.

"David's right," Smythe said slowly. "If we can get the media to tear him up during the next week or ten days it won't matter what happens after that. If he's quickly destroyed, every car driver in the White House can show up to corroborate his story and it won't make any difference later."

"The Capron angle—let's play that up," Frankling urged. "Warren was bribed, or seduced or whatever."

"More than likely he was seduced," Hale offered, "by Lani Romera, the movie actress. She is under contract to Capron. He first met her at Capron's home. They have had several rendez-vous."

"Good. Was he with her that night, when he says he was on the yacht?" Frankling suggested.

"Not likely," Smythe said wryly. "But even without that we can probably put together some very damaging stuff. I'll get what the Bureau has today. Still, all of that won't be as good as Warren's confession. It will be much, much better if young Mr. Warren just admits to the Senate that he did the whole thing without authorization."

"Fine, but how are you going to get him to do that, Carley?" Frankling said with a hint of hopelessness.

"I think there's one possibility we discussed last night: Jep Valle. Warren worked for him for several years. They were, and still are, very close. And Warren is also close to Valle's daughter."

"Was," interjected Hale. "I think they split up."

"Why should he do what Valle tells him to?" the President asked. "And why would Valle ask him to confess?"

"I don't know whether Jep has anything on the boy or not," Smythe replied. He blew a cloud of cigar smoke toward the ceiling. "But, knowing Valle, I'd be surprised if he didn't.

Remember, Valle wanted very much to be in the Cabinet. If you promised him Treasury now, C.O.D., he'd suborn the Pope himself to get the job."

"You may be right, Carley. You may be right. What do you think, David?" The President pushed a button to summon his valet.

"I think it's still a possibility," Hale replied. "We know Valle still keeps his hand on Robin. He just may have leverage we don't have. "Can you live with Valle in the Cabinet? We talked about it before and—"

"The point is," Frankling interrupted, "that we can afford to pay a large price to get Rob Warren to step up and admit what he did. Valle would be a problem, but less trouble than we're going to have with that Senate committee and those TV commentators if they believe Rob. These days I'll go for a nice definable problem like Valle if I can get one."

"You'd give him Treasury?" Smythe asked.

"In a minute—the day after Warren testifies on television. It must be C.O.D., as you said. We'll send old Hurlbut to France. That's still open, isn't it, David?"

"Yes, sir. But I'm not sure Hurlbut will resign Treasury that easily."

Frankling half stood. "He'll damn sure resign if I tell him to! If I need that job for Valle, he'll resign. I guarantee it."

"I know the Attorney General wants to go now," Hale said, "so may I sum up? We will assemble all the ammunition against Warren we can. I'll coordinate that effort. The FBI can send its stuff to me, the sooner the better. Meanwhile you'll contact Jep Valle, General, and up the ante. We'll hold up our media blitz. How much more time shall we give Valle?"

"Two days," Smythe grunted. "Either he has the goods by then or he doesn't."

"That's all of tomorrow and until six P.M. the next day, then," Hale said briskly. "If he hasn't delivered by six P.M. we give what we have to the morning papers for the following day."

"I hope he can make the boy see the light," Frankling said. "For

219

the good of the country, if not for his own good. Appeal to Valle's patriotism, Carley, when you talk to him. He was in the Senate, after all. The man must be a patriot."

Smythe rose to his feet with a small guttural exclamation. "I must hurry along, I'm afraid. I have two of those incumbent patriots waiting over in my office. They want to persuade me to appoint some nincompoop a federal judge out in their state."

"And?"

"And I guess we will—we're now going to need all the friendly patriots we can get up there, aren't we?"

"Indeed we are, indeed we are. Oh, David"—the President stayed Hale's attempt at departure—"one other thing: Auguste Capron."

"Sir?"

"I'm counting on you to keep him in line. It's very much in his interest to cooperate with us now. Let's be certain that his people understand what actually happened, and testify accordingly."

"I'll see what I can do."

"You do that. I feel sure Mr. Capron will be happy to help. Very happy."

Hale and Smythe stood, gathering their papers.

"Carley, stay a minute more," Frankling said, pointing to the couch. Hale was obviously dismissed: "Thank you, David."

"Yes, sir."

Smythe sat, tentatively, unwilling to stay.

Frankling pursed his lips. "What do you honestly think? Can we pull it off?"

"What choice do you have?" Smythe shrugged enigmatically. "You passed the point of no return at the press conference, didn't you?"

"I guess we did."

"Of course," Smythe amended, "you could say that further investigation has disclosed—"

"What? That I did it?"

"No, you couldn't say that. You could still say that Warren was with us on the yacht. You'd avoid all the record-changing and crew transfer. You might avoid the dangers in that. Just admit he was there. Then the only question would be whether or not you approved his call to the CIA."

"You mean, he called from the yacht without our knowing it? How could he do that? Who would believe I had nothing to do with it?"

"You could say he'd called from a bedroom, I suppose. Or while you and I were out taking a breath of air. It's possible."

"But most unlikely. A young man doesn't just get up and leave the President's table when he feels like it. No. If I admitted that much, I've admitted I approved it. No, it's better that he wasn't there at all. That removes any possible doubt that I had any part in his phone call. I thought about the other, but it's not believable. We've gone the best way."

"Maybe." Smythe nodded. "But you now have a full-time job making certain that nothing comes unstuck. I'm with you, of course, and I'll help, but I'm not confident it can be done."

"It must be done, Carley! Goddammit, it's the country's ass that is at stake here—you see that, don't you? It's a row of dominoes: if we lose this thing in the UN we lose the treaty too. And our energy situation is most precarious. We must have that gas and oil. Ten more years and we'll be OK. But we need the deep-sea oil until then."

"And if you get bloodied up in the Senate?"

"Sure, I have something at stake, too. Sure, it affects the election. But it also affects the Deep-Sea Treaty ratification. Be certain of that: if they can, they'll weaken me and defeat the treaty just to reestablish Congressional supremacy."

"As I say, I'm with you."

"I knew that."

"However, today is obviously the last day you could decide Warren really was on the boat if you were going to. In case you change your mind."

"No."

"All right. He wasn't on the boat. So be it." Smythe stood. "I really should get back."

"You go ahead, Carley. I'm glad we had this chance to talk."

"I am, too, Mr. President. I needed to know that you were aware of what you were tackling in all of this."

Frankling nodded as he slowly stood. "I'm aware, Carley. I'm aware. It's a loser, either way. My answer at the press conference was a shot from the hip, in a sense, but I think I chose the best of two bad alternatives, instinctively. In any case, the choice has been made now. I have to hope that you and David will stick with me and see it through."

"Of course," said Smythe.

"Thank you, Carley," Frankling replied.

Robin placed a call to Jep Valle, and was not surprised that Valle's secretary said he was out of the office. He guessed a lot of people would be out of the office when he called from now on. Impulsively he dialed Maggie Valle's office number in New York. As it rang he began to hang up. He decided he didn't really want to tell her about his encounter with Frankling. She had been right about Hugh Frankling and it was going to be hard—nearly impossible—for him to admit it to himself, much less to her.

"Margaret Valle."

Even after she answered, it was still not too late; he could hang up and she wouldn't know he'd called. But her voice brought him a familiar warmth. A familiar need. He wanted to hear her tell him that things would work out. He needed her assurance of loyalty. He wanted her to tell him that he was valuable, and that she loved him. It was a kind of emotional anoxia that brought him to talk to her, as he might have taken a deep breath, involuntarily.

"Maggie?"

"Robin? Is that you, Robin?"

"Hi."

"What's the matter? You sound terrible."

"Frankling. He put the screws to me a little while ago."

"That son of a bitch. What did he do, Bird? Are you all right?"

"I guess. He expects me to be the fall guy for the Uruguay mess. He told me to take the blame for it."

"That's crazy! What do you have to do with Uruguay, for Christ's sake?"

He told her, quickly, objectively, relieved at last to have the story off his chest, out in the open. When he had finished, there was a long silence.

"How do you feel about it?" Maggie asked.

"I hate to admit it, but I'm pretty scared."

"Sure you are. But what's the worst they could do to you? Smear you?"

"Yes."

"But if you knew it wasn't true, could you live with that?"

"I guess so."

"Could they throw you in jail?"

"Maybe."

"Could you take that?"

"I suppose; others have."

"OK. So what will you do?"

"I won't go back. If I don't show up at four, he'll know. The President will know, and he'll call Hale and tell him to turn all the dogs loose to get me. That's how they work."

"Listen, I've got an idea, Bird. Go and spit in his eye at four. Tell him where he can put Uruguay. It's the only chance you'll ever have to tell a President what to do. You owe it to your grandchildren. Then hop a cab and catch the shuttle up here, and we'll figure out what to do. We'll go to Oscar's for a lobster. OK?"

"Look, Mags, this isn't drama for drama's sake. If I don't show up, he'll get the message."

"Maybe. But you said yourself that this was going to be a dirty fight in the papers and on TV. Right? You want people to believe you're innocent? What does an innocent man do now? Does he hide in his apartment, or does he charge in and slam his fist on the desk and raise hell?"

"OK. You're right. I'll be on the six-o'clock shuttle."

Nick Gurley told him to wait in the Cabinet Room. No one offered him coffee or tea; that was symbolic, he thought.

At ten minutes after four David Hale walked in and sat down next to him in the empty room. He was carrying a yellow pad.

"Hello, Robin. Sorry you had to wait." Hale was subdued, almost laconic.

"Hi, David."

"I'm going to sit in with you."

"No, David. No note-takers. Just him and me."

Hale looked nonplussed; not because of Robin's defiance, but because note-takers were Procedure. No one violated Procedure.

"Yes, Robin," Hale insisted. "I've got to be there."

Robin stood. "Well, then you tell him why there isn't going to be a meeting. Either he and I are in there alone or there's no meeting. Which is it?"

"Look, you understand why there has to be a note-taker." Hale was conciliatory. "Sit down."

"Which is it?"

"I don't know. I'll have to ask."

"No. *You* decide. Now."

"Look, in the mood you're in, I'm not sure it would be safe to let you in there alone." Hale stood up.

"OK. Then that's it?" Warren took a small side step toward the door.

"No. I know he feels he has to talk to you. But he specifically asked me to be there."

"I'm sure he did. But you can't be. If you're there, there won't be a talk at all." Warren sensed he had the initiative. "So you decide now and tell me, David."

Hale smiled bleakly. "All right. I'll just go in and explain why I won't be with you."

"Don't bother. I'll tell him. Is he ready now?"

"Go ahead." Hale shrugged.

Warren walked quickly through the secretary's office and shoved open the curved white door. He liked the feel of that brisk little encounter with Hale. Frankling was at his desk, writing a note on the heavy pale-green stationary with the gold embossed seal. He looked up when he heard the door close.

"Mr. President, David won't be with us," Robin began. He felt confident.

"That's fine. We don't really need him, do we?" Frankling was using the genial, deep voice usually reserved for large contributors and children under the age of eight. "I hope you've had an opportunity to think things through, Robin. I want you to see this problem from my standpoint. We've got to do what's right for the country."

Robin was standing in front of the desk, waiting to be invited to sit down. As Frankling paused in his argument, Robin walked around to the yellow side chair at the President's right and slowly settled into it. The hell with invitations and niceties.

"It is not right for me," Frankling resumed, "to ask you to come forward without considering the effect upon you. Naturally, you can't stay in your present position. But there are several men who have expressed their willingness to have you with their law firms when you leave here."

"Who?"

"Well, you'll have to get their names from Hale. Actually, he talked with them. But they are all prestigious firms and high-paying positions."

"Why?"

"Why what?"

"Why are you finding me a job?"

"Well, naturally, out of gratitude. You are coming forward in a manly fashion and I'm gratified that you are."

"I see. I thought perhaps it was a bribe."

"Nothing of the— Wait; first, perhaps you'd better tell me what you've decided to do." Frankling opened his middle drawer and slipped the notepaper in as if to insure that Warren would not read it. Now he was on guard. "I assume you've given it thought. Can I count on you, Rob?"

Warren realized he was not in awe of this man. Even surrounded by the trappings of office, in spite of the personal consequences, he was in control of himself.

"I have decided to tell the truth, Mr. President."

"Meaning?"

"You and I know what's the truth."

"Perhaps no one has explained to you . . ."

"Explained to me what can happen to me? I think I realize what you may try to do."

"Explained to you," Frankling repeated, "that you are placing yourself in jeopardy of a criminal charge."

"Look, sir, there's nothing you can offer me and nothing you can threaten me with that is going to make any difference. It's very simple: I'm going to have to stick to what I know. I'm afraid to do anything else."

"Then I guess we have nothing more to say to each other now," Frankling said with acceptance. He looked and sounded tired. "I'm sorry, young man."

"No you're not," Warren said. The firmness of his voice surprised him a little.

Frankling's eyebrows rose. "You think I *like* being in this situation?" He shook his head. "There are no good choices. No good choices."

Robin stood, moved around behind his chair and put his hands on the top of the leather back. He leaned forward a little, looking at Frankling's face.

"*Bullshit*, Mr. President," he said.

Warren left by the hall door and crossed to the Roosevelt Room, a shortcut to the lobby of the West Wing. He glanced at his watch; it was four twenty-five. If he could find a cab he might still make the five-o'clock shuttle.

He intended to walk to Seventeenth Street to hail a southbound taxi, but as he swung around the post of the northwest gate and started along Pennsylvania Avenue he came face to face with Mike Meyerson standing beside a black limousine.

"Robin, how are you?" Meyerson held out a hand. "Can we give you a ride? Mr. Capron would like to talk to you."

Warren glanced at Auguste Capron, deep inside the Cadillac. Capron smiled. Meyerson opened the door and nodded. "Get in," he said. "We'll take you wherever you're going."

226

Warren thought quickly: *Capron could be an ally. Whoever arranged this little rendezvous, it could be turned to my advantage.*

"Thanks, Mike. I'm trying to catch the shuttle at National."

Meyerson shut the door behind him and slid in beside the chaufieur.

"Hello, Robin." Capron extended his hand. "I understand we need to talk. Please forgive the kidnapping." He smiled broadly.

"Do you know what's going on?" Robin hooked his thumb at the White House as the car accelerated, then turned right into the narrow street between the Treasury Department and the East Wing of the White House.

Capron nodded. "I hear you've been nominated to assume responsibility for Uruguay. What did you decide?"

"I told the President I wouldn't."

"I see." Capron nodded.

"Not only that I wouldn't, but that I can't. I've got to be true to myself."

"Very commendable. What is your situation there now?"

"I suppose I'm fired. No one really said so, but I'm sure I am."

"What will you do?"

"I don't know."

"Robin, I would like you to consider coming to work for me."

"Now?"

"No, I think we both realize that a decent interval must pass. The smoke must clear. But I'm sure it will."

"What sort of job are you talking about?"

"I have in mind a new position, as director of European operations for the holding company. You can pick your city; it's a new position. A hundred and a quarter to start."

"Well, that's very attractive, Mr.—"

"Auguste."

"Auguste. But God knows how long this mess is going to drag out. How soon will you need to know?"

"I hope we can agree immediately. If you need to borrow money to live in the meantime, a bank can be found to provide for you. But you should let me know tomorrow, if you will."

"That soon?"

"Yes, I'll be away for the next six weeks or so. Call me tomorrow, Robin." Capron handed him a card.

"You move fast."

Capron smiled. "I consider you a valuable talent. I don't want you to get away."

"That's really very kind, Auguste." Warren glanced at a clock inlaid in the back of the front seat. Quarter to five.

"I'll call you tomorrow," he said to Capron.

"Unless you can give me your answer now, Robin?"

"No, I'd like to sleep on it."

"Of course."

Nothing more was said until the terminal was in sight. As the car pulled in front of the shuttle entrance Robin offered his hand. "Thank you, Auguste, I'm very grateful."

"Goodbye until tomorrow." Capron smiled.

Robin told Maggie of his Hale and Frankling encounters as they rode to Oscar's in the cab.

"How did you feel afterward?" she asked.

"Euphoric. A little lightheaded. I could have run to National."

"Who else do you know who says 'Bullshit' to the President?"

"Capron was waiting for me outside."

"Outside the White House?"

"Yeah. Like in a movie. The limousine at the curb, The Big Man inside, his lackey on the sidewalk to lure me in."

"What did he want?"

"He offered me a job. This was a big day for job offers. I forgot to tell you: the President said I had four or five offers if I went along with him. Four or five law firms."

"What did Capron offer?"

"Director of European operations. A hundred and twenty-five thousand to start. Pick my city to live in."

Oscar's was jammed to the walls. Robin and Maggie worked their way to the bar and then stood guarding their drinks from passing waiters and impatient diners. When the host called

Robin's name, he pushed a way for the couple through the crowd to a table in the front corner.

"What does Capron want, Robin?" Maggie covered his hand with hers.

"He didn't say. He put it that I'm such great talent he just didn't want me to get away."

"I wish I believed that that was his motive. But it's so transparent! Imagine the reaction to that announcement!"

"He suggested we delay any announcement until the smoke cleared."

"I'll bet."

"Meanwhile he'll arrange a loan for me and I'll just sit quietly in his hip pocket."

"He's in cahoots with Frankling, isn't he?"

"Hale must have called him. I just wonder if they talked before or after I went in to see the President. It must have been before. They had it set up that Capron would pick me up either way—whether I said yes or no."

They gave their orders to an overworked waiter and finished their drinks.

"Frankling threatened me, Mags. He talked about a criminal prosecution."

"That was no surprise, was it?"

"No. But I've got to get some advice. I have no idea what comes next."

"You're as bad as Jep. He couldn't even handle the sale of our own house. What kind of lawyers are you, anyway?"

"Hybrids, of a very rare species. We know nothing about the law. Sort of legal geldings. Very beautiful and sleek, but not much for pulling milk wagons."

"Who can you get? Do you need a criminal lawyer? Criminal lawyer! You'd think in two thousand years that attorneys could have come up with a descriptive phrase that didn't amount to an admission against interest."

Robin smiled. "I need a trial man, I think. I need someone with me in that hearing too."

229

"Do you know Leonard Weil?" Maggie grinned.

"What's so funny about him?"

"He's my Uncle Lenny. Our next-door neighbor in Washington. I used to ride around on his shoulders. He's the man to go to when you have big troubles."

"The Great Weil? Do you think he'd take me?"

"If I asked him to he would."

"Then ask him, please, Mags. I have a strong feeling that big trouble is just around the corner."

"In that case, my dear, you and I are flying back to Washington tonight!"

Part IV

THE STRATEGY

CHAPTER **18**   An inevitable first impression of Leonard
Weil was one of unconcealed wealth. As the cab left Maggie Valle
and Robin Warren in front of Weil's elegant building, a chauffeur
in black livery leaning against the fender of a black Bentley
greeted her by name.

"Evenin', Miz Maggie."

"Oh, Harley," Maggie exclaimed, "how are you? I haven't seen
you in so long! You look wonderful."

"Thank you, Miz Maggie. A little older, but gettin' along fine."

Harley wore gold-rim glasses high on his nose. If he had been
dressed in a conservative gray or brown suit he could have passed
for a thoughtful and prosperous banker, a little overweight
perhaps, but keenly aware of everything going on around him.

"Mistah Weil is waitin' for you upstairs, Miz Maggie. I'm to
bring you right up."

"This is Robin Warren, Harley."

Harley put out a huge paw. "I'm most glad to meet you, Mr. Warren."

"How do you do?"

The chauffeur led them to the elaborately latticed double doors of the entrance, centered among four narrow windows in the gray stone façade. A brass plate discreetly disclosed that the entire building—once a fashionable town house—now housed the Weil law firm:

1775 N Street N.W.
Law Offices
Weil, Mahoney, Defilbriss & Currance

"Remember the way, Miz Maggie? The elevator is here, behind this door."

The ground floor was given over to a formal reception room. Robin guessed that the firm's bookkeeping and filing were hidden behind the paneled walls at both sides. The lobby was a Williamsburg reproduction; the furniture, chandelier and accessories came straight from the catalogue. Harley led them off the elevator on the sixth floor and walked to a door at the end of a richly furnished hallway. Robin had seen law offices in San Francisco, New York and Los Angeles that had been expensively decorated, but he'd seen nothing to compare with this. The senior partners of this firm had collected around them antiques, paintings and carpets of obvious authenticity and enormous value.

Leonard Weil answered Harley's quiet knock.

"Maggie, my dear," he said with delight, "please come in here!" He reached out to Maggie Valle with arms wide and embraced her. She was three or four inches taller than the little lawyer.

Weil released her, reaching out around her for Robin's hand. He had a strong grasp, in spite of his apparent frailty. Warren could not help but react with surprise. This small, birdlike man had the reputation of a warrior; Warren had imagined a person of more imposing physique. He mumbled his gratitude that Weil would see them so late at night on such short notice.

234

The old lawyer gave Harley some instructions at the door and sent him on his way. "Sit here, Mr. Warren, close to me. Maggie, dear, you sit there where I can look at you. What a pleasure to be able to see you! You know, Mr. Warren, I've known Maggie since she was a child. We were next-door neighbors then. In Cleveland Park. I bought a great many Girl Scout cookies from this charming saleslady!"

In contrast to the opulent hallway outside, Weil's office was furnished with an elegant simplicity. The desk was a narrow curved antique table. Weil's dark leather chair was not massive. On the wall above his head, in a thin frame, was the Medal of Freedom mounted upon its blue ribbon. Flanking it in both directions were framed photographs of four Presidents, each with long and friendly handwritten inscriptions. There were no other decorations or hangings in the room.

"Well, Mr. Warren, Maggie says you are having employment problems."

Robin grinned at the understatement. There was just the trace of an accent to Weil's inflection that amused him. "I'm not sure, but by now I've probably been fired. I'll probably be indicted, although—"

"Why don't you tell me briefly what this is all about. Then I'll tell you what I think you should do next."

Robin nodded and began to recount the President's meeting with Auguste Capron. Weil lifted a hand.

"One moment, Mr. Warren—may I call you Robin? There is one problem, with Maggie sitting here, as beautiful as she is." He looked at Maggie. "It is like wounding myself, my love, but I should ask you to step outside. What Robin tells me as his lawyer is privileged and confidential, and that secrecy is lost if a third person is present during his communication. Don't you think we should ask Maggie to excuse us, Robin?"

Warren nodded at the girl.

"I'm sure there's no use in protesting," she said. "I'll go and read old lawyers' magazines."

"Just down the hall, dear," Weil said. "We won't be long. We'll be very brief, won't we, Robin?"

When Maggie had closed the door behind her, Weil leaned forward intently. "I wanted to ask you how that meeting was arranged. Did Frankling shake Capron down for a contribution?"

Robin looked surprised. "Not directly. David Hale over there—he's the—"

"I know Hale, by reputation."

"He took care of the money. Two hundred and fifty thousand, I think."

"And Capron paid?"

"I assume so. Hale took care of it and gave me the impression it was paid, but I don't know for sure. Capron never said anything, one way or the other."

"All right. So what did they say to each other? No—wait! Don't tell me! I want one or two other people from the firm to be here. Can you come back in the morning?"

"Sure . . ."

"Do you have memoranda, or a diary or notes of what happened?"

"Some. I took notes in the Capron meeting but not on the boat."

"But your diary, your desk book—does it show you were on the boat that evening?"

"Yes."

"All right, go by your office tomorrow—those things are at the office?"

Warren nodded.

"Go get them, then come here. We will be ready for you at nine-thirty. Too early?"

"No, that's fine."

"For now, say nothing to anyone. Not press, colleagues, neighbors. Only to me—no one else."

"Sure."

"We'll put it all together in the morning. Come here prepared to spend the day."

"All right. What about your fee, Mr. Weil? Shouldn't we talk about that?"

"How can we, young man? How can I guess the dimensions of the problem? No, we'll take your measurements tomorrow. Then we'll see what the suit of clothes will cost."

"All right."

"One bit of advice, and then we'll find Maggie. Remember what happens when a man contrives a story in this town—sooner or later the truth will out. I assume you are prepared to stick with the truth. Right?"

"Right."

"Good. Pennsylvania Avenue is littered with the bleached bones of the liars and perjurers. Come tomorrow prepared to tell us the whole truth."

"I will."

"Good, good." Weil stood quickly and headed for the door, talking back over his shoulder at Robin. "Now let's find Maggie." He stopped and turned before opening the door. "I'll represent you, of course. It goes without saying, but I should say it. You need help, I can tell. I will help you."

"Thank you," Robin said.

"Yes, Mr. President?"

"David, I'd hoped to hear from you. Since you didn't call I thought I'd better phone you. Before I go to sleep."

"There's really nothing to report. Robin Warren is probably still in New York with Valle's daughter."

"Are you tailing him there? Keeping track of how long they are alone in her apartment? How long the lights are out?"

"The Attorney General says the FBI can't find them up there. They aren't at her apartment."

"Well, where the hell are they?"

"We don't know."

"Has the girl been talked to?"

"Yes. Jep called her."

237

"Is she all right?"

"I don't know."

"Well, let's find out, David. Are we ready to go tomorrow if Valle strikes out?"

"Yes, sir."

"We made a mistake giving Valle so much time—didn't we? He won't help, will he?"

"No, sir, I don't think so. But I feel better having the yacht's crew all dispersed before we go public, anyway."

"How is the investigation coming?"

"Turley is over in Warren's office now. I haven't had a report from him yet. I do know we had to get a locksmith to get into a safe and one desk."

"That's the way. Let me know in the morning what he's found. We want to be ready to go at once if Valle strikes out."

"We will be."

"All right. Good night, David."

"Good night, Mr. President."

CHAPTER **19**   The Old Executive Office Building, a great gray palace of a building, yields over half of its regal interior to wide hallways, courtyards, high ceilings and sweeping stairways. It's a huge old pile of porches, columns, chimneys and variegated window styles which has been reduced to only three working entrances. The others have been sealed in the interest of security. One is the formal front door, topping a flight of steps above Pennsylvania Avenue; the others are nondescript basement entries. White House police are supposed to check everyone at these three doors. But the White House staff regulars who come and go are usually recognized and waved by without any police scrutiny of their plastic passes.

So the fact that he was admitted to the building was no certain test of Robin Warren's employment status. Mornings were quiet there, especially in the lull between the rush of arrivals for early staff meetings and the first outside visitors with appointments.

Warren waved to the policeman in the kiosk outside the easternly basement entrance. The return wave was perfunctory. It implied neither Presidential forgiveness nor custodial cunning.

He rode the elevator up one flight with a man he didn't know and a young secretary he often had seen. She seemed unusually reserved. Perhaps it was his imagination. The place was a rumor mill, but it didn't seem likely they had spread the word about him all the way to the stenographers in only sixteen hours.

When he turned north from the end of the east corridor, he could see his office door at the far end, some two hundred and eighty feet away. A slim, middle-aged man in a narrow business suit stood to the right of his door, some kind of identification card hanging from his breast pocket.

Robin looked behind the man, at the placard on the wall. He was surprised to see that the blue sign still said "Robin Warren, Special Counsel to the President."

"Good morning, Mr. Warren. I am Special Agent Gerold Manning, Federal Bureau of Investigation. May I please look in your case before you enter?" The man held out the little leather case that had been hanging in his pocket. Behind plastic Robin saw the man's picture, the blue seal of the FBI, paragraphs of tiny type, and the words "FEDERAL BUREAU OF INVESTIGATION," bold and black.

"Case? This? You want to search my briefcase? What for?"

"To know what you are bringing in this morning, Mr. Warren. The Director has instructed that you will only be permitted to remove whatever you bring in."

"The Director? What the hell?"

"If you wish to leave your case with me, I will not open it. But I cannot permit you to remove anything from inside the office."

This maneuver was not among the possibilities he'd anticipated. Search and seizure? Perhaps he should talk to Leonard Weil and get some legal advice.

"Here—you keep it," he said to the agent.

The FBI evidently trains its men to open doors without looking at them. As he received the case with his right hand the man easily reached behind him with his left and turned the knob, giving the door a shove so smoothly that it looked rehearsed.

Kathy O'Reilly and Bill Thompson stood in Robin's office with another FBI man, watching as four men in coveralls packed papers, books, pictures—everything—in large brown cartons. Kathy O'Reilly's fists were clenched white; she had been crying.

"What the hell?" Robin repeated quietly.

"They just barged—" Kathy O'Reilly began.

"Mr. Warren, I am Inspector Tom Moore, Federal Bureau of Investigation. We have been instructed to place the contents of these offices in safekeeping."

"Bill, I'd like to use your office for a minute," Robin said.

"Sure, Robin," Thompson said.

He closed Thompson's door, punched an outside line on the phone console, then realized he didn't know Weil's telephone number. Bill Thompson apparently had no phone directory. Robin opened the door and called across the reception area: "Kathy?"

She came to the door of his office, flushed with Irish fury.

"Get Leonard J. Weil on the phone for me, will you?"

In a moment Thompson's buzzer sounded.

"Hello, Mr. Weil?"

"This is Mr. Weil's secretary, Mr. Warren. Could I have him call you?"

"I'm afraid it's an emergency. My office is crawling with FBI agents."

"He's in a meeting; let's see if I can get a note to him." Robin sensed the phone go dead as she pushed her hold button. It was a long wait. He could hear wheels squeaking in the reception area. Boxes were being trundled away.

240

"Robin, sorry to keep you waiting."

"Mr. Weil, I'm at the office and there's an FBI agent on the door and others boxing up all my stuff."

"Then we're too late."

"The guy on the door says I won't be permitted to remove anything."

"What do they have—a warrant?"

"I don't know."

"No matter. I doubt it; they'd have told you. All right—is there someone there to watch them for you?"

"Yes—my secretary and my deputy, Bill Thompson."

"Tell them to find out where the stuff will be kept. You get out of there fast—come over here right away. Just start now and keep moving. The next White House trick will be to tell the press you're there, and we don't want you giving statements now. So get over here, pronto."

"All right, thanks. I'm on my way."

"I've asked two of our young associates to join us this morning, Robin." Leonard Weil pushed a button twice and walked to his door. Weil was a dresser, Robin noted. Even in his shirtsleeves he had a dapper elegance: the tailored shirt was a beautiful fit, and the tie expensive, with gold accessories, and a thin leather belt matching handmade shoes. A small, dapper old man.

"Robin Warren, this is Sarepta Kahn, and here is Bernard Sheffleman. They are going to help me. You can talk to them as though—well, hell, I don't need to tell you all that. You are a lawyer, after all. Sit here, Bernie. Sari, you come closer. Now, Robin, I'd like you to tell us about yourself—right from the beginning. These two will interrupt when they wish to. Just begin at the top. Where were you raised?"

"I grew up in the Napa Valley, north of San Francisco. My father had a store in St. Helena. I went to school there."

"Wine country," Sarepta Kahn said. She was short, plain, with close-cropped black hair, bright black eyes and wide mouth. About twenty-six, Robin guessed.

"Right, lots of grapes and wineries. I worked in the vineyards, played high-school sports. A very normal life. I got a football scholarship to Stanford, played four years of varsity ball, went to law school there and took the California bar exam."

"Are your parents still living?" Weil asked. "Any brothers or sisters?"

"No brothers or sisters—an only child. My father died when I was in high school. My mother still lives in the valley."

"You were with a San Francisco firm?"

"Right. Six years in a big firm in the city."

"Married?"

"Yes. During my first year of practice. Divorced just before I moved to Washington to work for Jep Valle."

"Children?"

"No children."

Sarepta Kahn was taking notes. She looked at him intently. "Hard feelings?"

"What?"

"A hard divorce? A bitter lady?"

"No, not bad."

"Why did you come with Jep?" Weil asked.

"Oh, partly to get away from San Francisco, from a dull life, from my wife's family, who are all over the place there. And I was looking for adventure, I guess."

"Now, Robin, you must be full and frank with us. It's important that we know everything. What about Maggie? Maggie Valle, Jep's daughter," Weil explained to the two young lawyers.

"I'd met her before the divorce. I had her in mind when I moved here. No doubt of it."

"Do you see her now?" Bernie Sheffleman asked. He was in his late twenties, short, dark, fat, his hair in short, tight ringlets.

"She lives in New York. And things have cooled off some. I've been seeing another lady—Lani Romera."

"*The* Lani Romera?" Sarepta Kahn implied the improbability of it all.

"Right. I met her at Auguste Capron's."

242

"We're getting ahead of ourselves, I fear. More coffee, anyone? Tell us what you did when you were with Jep Valle." Weil leaned back, his hands folded over his belt buckle.

Robin spent three hours answering their questions. They examined his relationship with Auguste Capron in minute detail. Sheffleman, especially, questioned him about the evening cruise with the President on the yacht. They asked him to describe Hale, Broderick and the Attorney General, what they were like, how well he knew them, the nature of his contacts with them.

Weil began to ask him about his final meeting with the President. As Warren was describing his hasty retreat from the Oval Office, Weil's secretary came in, put a folded newspaper and a note in front of the old lawyer, and left. Weil read the note, opened the paper flat on his desk and looked quickly at Robin and the two young lawyers. Robin stopped talking.

"It's begun," Weil said. He held the note and shook it slightly. "There are two network news film crews waiting for Robin outside the front door of this building. How do they know he's here?"

Sari Kahn shook her head in sympathy. Bernie Sheffleman rubbed his hands on his trouser legs. He was excited.

Weil stabbed the front page with his finger. "The afternoon edition. Pictures of Robin and his movie star. 'Young White House Aide Fired. Implicated in Uruguay Plot,' " Weil read.

"Jesus," Robin said.

"It gets worse: 'Link to Capron Companies Established.' "

"Sure," Bernie Sheffleman said quickly, "that would be their angle of attack. They'll say he sold out to Capron."

Weil read:

"The White House today announced that the President has fired a top aide, Robin Warren, as a result of his part in the Uruguayan coup scandal.

"Sources close to the President disclosed that Warren, until today Special Counsel to President Hugh Frankling, is the high official believed to have used the President's name to set in motion the abortive coup against the Uruguayan Government June 20.

"Documents discovered by the FBI establish that Warren's motive for launching the CIA plot apparently was his close relationship with Auguste Capron, wealthy international industrialist, whose holdings in Uruguay were believed threatened by the Marxist government there. Warren, 37 and divorced, is said to be romantically linked with Lani Romera, a motion picture actress under contract to Capron's Superior Studios.

"President Frankling has consistently denied authorizing the CIA to launch an assassination plot against the Uruguayan leader. . . ."

"There's more," Weil said, "but you can read it later. It's obvious where this stuff came from, isn't it?"

"Sources close to the President," Sari Kahn said.

"So, I'm fired," Robin said flatly.

"Apparently." Weil handed Robin the *Star-Post.* "Read it now. You'd better know what the party line is."

Centered in the top half of the front page were separate large pictures of Lani Romera and Robin. But they were looking at each other and laughing, as a result of the way the two pictures had been arranged on the page.

"What's this 'powerful White House aide' stuff in the caption?" Robin asked Weil. "What power did I have?"

"Stop and think. Can the janitor be held responsible for a CIA coup? Whom the gods would destroy they first describe as the second most powerful man in government."

"Let me read this," Robin said. The story was carried down the right column and continued on page ten. That inside page also had a biographical sidebar headline:

ROBIN WARREN, AN OBSCURE,
POWERFUL WHITE HOUSE
STAFFER

When he'd finished reading, Robin handed the paper back to Weil.

"In a way, this comes at a good time," Weil began. "It reveals the Frankling line of attack, for one thing. And it will permit us to prepare for those film crews downstairs."

"Can't I duck them?"

244

"Perhaps, but do we want you to?"

"If this is going to be a PR fight," Sarepta Kahn said, "the battlefield is going to be the evening news each night."

"But, for the long run, shouldn't he be silent because we are looking at a criminal prosecution?" Weil asked rhetorically. "How far are they prepared to go to try to prove Frankling had nothing to do with the coup?"

"I'd guess they'll go all the way," Robin said. The onslaught he'd just read had shocked him. He was feeling it in his nerve ends. He felt defensive and defeated. "What should I do?"

"Did you notice how they almost ignored Capron in the *Star-Post* story?" Weil pointed to the paper Sari Kahn was reading. "No comment by him, no picture."

"It says he was unavailable," she said.

"Suppose he were to come forward. He could help a great deal," Weil said. "Robin, why don't you telephone him?"

"Now?"

"Now. Let's see what sort of reaction we get. Surely he's heard of the story by now. Then I want you to call the young lady."

"Lani?"

"Yes, Lani. Her help, while not as conclusive, may be important. Bernie, will you have Miss White reach Auguste Capron for Mr. Warren?"

"Sure. Be right back."

The calls were placed, but neither was completed. Mr. Capron's secretary reported that he was abroad and could not be reached for several days. She would tell him of Mr. Warren's call. Lani Romera's answering service said she too was out of town.

"We'll try again, tomorrow, if they don't call back," Weil said to Robin. "We have two remaining items to cover: do you talk to the film crews and do you submit to a Senate staff interview?"

"What is that all about?" Robin asked.

"Professor Anschults, the Senate committee staff director, called. They want to send a couple of fellows to talk to you and me."

"He called you? How did he know . . . ?"

"To call here? I suppose the press told him. Be sure of this, Robin: we will have few, if any, secrets from the press for the next two months. Don't let it upset you. They will harass you, dog your tracks, disgust and offend you. It will be very difficult. But we need them. Never forget that. If we win, it will not be because of the fair-mindedness of the Senators or some federal judge. It will be because we have manipulated the television and the other press better than Hugh Frankling has."

"My God, the White House has all the guns in this fight," Bernie Sheffleman muttered.

"Not really," Weil replied sternly. He disapproved of his young lawyer suggesting defeat. "Robin will be a constant center of attention from now on."

"But," Robin countered, "he's right: I have nothing to trade. The White House can influence a reporter—they have so much inside stuff to peddle. And Les Carew plays those guys in the Press Room like a piano."

"Ah, we have goodies, too," Weil countered. "*Time* magazine would give a lot for an exclusive interview. So will CBS."

"But—" Robin began.

Weil held up a finger. "Let's not waste time speculating now. May I suggest that you and I go out for a late lunch, Robin? We'll go out through the front door. Sarepta will go with us. She is very photogenic, and it won't hurt to have America see you with a wholesome Jewish girl who is not a movie star. We will stop, smile, and I will promise them interviews with you. Later, of course. We will answer no questions today."

"Whatever you say. That sounds like a good way to avoid them for now."

"And at lunch we can discuss what you will tell the committee staff people."

"You think I need to see them?"

"Oh, yes. Bear in mind, they are as close to allies as you have in this war. The Select Committee is heavily Democratic and will be out to prove Hugh Frankling is a villain and a liar. I think you will find these Senate people very friendly to you."

"OK."

"Now I want you to brush your hair, straighten your tie and wash your face. We are in a beauty contest, among other things. A great deal will depend on your appearance and demeanor. Let me see you smile."

"Now?"

"Yes, of course. You will be called upon to smile a great deal, often when you least feel like it. Let's see your smile."

Robin Warren smiled at Leonard Weil.

"That's terrible. We will have to work on your smile, young man."

"The chairman, Senator Oates, wants to meet with all the staff in the morning. Everyone—secretaries, the investigators, the whole bunch."

"When?"

"I'd guess around twelve; he doesn't come in much before that. He wants to warn everyone not to leak."

"Ha!" The tall, angular woman twitched. "Only Senators can leak?"

"Sure. Can't have the peasants handing out the goodies, can we?" Professor Irving Anschults pushed his glasses up onto his round forehead and wiped his eyes with a wrinkled handkerchief. "Damn, I'm tired. How much more is there?"

"You'd better look at these nine files, Irv. They are all subpoenas that need to be served tomorrow. The other stuff can wait."

The telephone rang loudly.

"Mr. Anschults' office," the girl answered. She put a hand over the mouthpiece and looked at the short rumpled man. "It's your wife."

"Shit. What time is it?"

"Ten."

"I'm in trouble. Here, I'll take it. No, don't go. Hi—I'm sorry it's so late." He listened, shaking his head slowly, then scratching his cheek. He rolled his eyes. "Look, there's just a hell of a lot to

247

do." More listening. "I had a sandwich. I know, I know. It can't be helped, Rebby. Tell them I'm sorry—OK?"

He caught the tall woman's glance of sympathy, smiled thinly and shrugged. "In an hour. Right. Eleven. Don't wait up. OK. OK. Do what you want, Rebecca. Anything you want. Up, down, whatever you want." He hung the phone slowly.

"OK. Let's see the subpoenas. White House, CIA, Commerce, Warren, Capron, Dooley, United International, Smythe. Who is Grosvenor?"

"White House Transportation Office."

"Sure. Looks fine. Let's go with them. Oates can actually sign them when he's here tomorrow. Why don't you go home, Anne Marie? Can I drop you?"

"If it's not too much trouble. I'll get my coat."

"Right. I'd like to stop somewhere for a drink, but I'd catch pluperfect hell if I did."

"I'll be ready in a minute. I'll just lock up."

The offices of the staff of the Select Committee on Assassinations of the United States Senate were temporary and inelegant. The windows opened onto a light well of the Old Senate Office Building. The furnishings were castoffs, there were too few filing cabinets, chairs and telephones. Even ashtrays were in short supply.

Irving Anschults—Professor Anschults—had to let others worry about such details; there weren't enough hours to haggle with the clerk of the Senate over ashtrays. Anschults was having his full measure of trouble with the chairman of the committee, Senator Harley Oates, and with the evidence. Time was much too short to do a workmanlike job on the facts. Everyone was in a rush to start the hearings before the summer TV doldrums set in, and they were hurrying things too much. The ragtag committee staff had been hurriedly thrown together—Anschults from Maryland Law School, the others from Senators' office staffs, a couple of teachers on summer leave, Anne Marie Himmel from the American Civil Liberties Union. Too little help, too little time, too much to do.

He'd been foolish to take the job, Anschults realized that now, but it was too late.

"Irv? You coming?"

"Right now. Just closing up."

"What about the Warren kid, Irv?"

"I'm not sure. Teddy and John are going to try to see him tomorrow. I don't suppose he'll talk to them, but it's worth a try."

"The more stuff I read, the less I believe he acted on his own."

"Sure. But who will believe Warren? Frankling says flatly the coup was unauthorized, and everyone in the Executive Branch backs him up. Except the kid. Why should anyone believe him?"

Anne Marie Himmel and Anschults signed the log at the guard's desk inside the door, pushed out into the warm night and walked toward his car.

"Well, Harley Oates believes him," she said.

"I'm afraid not even he does, really—he's just using Warren to get Frankling. Oates doesn't care where the truth lies."

"You're getting cynical in your old age, Professor."

"No—it happens to be the case. Oates would use any witness at all to sink the White House in this thing. If the boys come up with anyone, no matter how awful, Oates will insist we put him on."

"That could lead to big trouble if a witness folds up, couldn't it?"

"Possibly. But I don't look for much rigorous cross-examination of our friendly witnesses. I think Oates will try to protect anyone who helps him make his case."

She put her hand on his arm as he held the door of the Toyota for her. "We'll be all right, Irv. We'll find the truth and sink Frankling and probably get the Maryland Good Government Award."

"Yeah." He shrugged. "Listen, I've got time. The hell with it. Let's stop somewhere for a drink?"

"If you don't mind vodka, we can go to my place. It's cool there in the evenings anyway."

"It just so happens I don't mind vodka at all. Not at all."

CHAPTER **20** Leonard J. Weil's informal Saturday attire was exactly the same as his weekday outfit. Few clients were invited to his office on weekends, but Weil and his associates were always suited, tied and polished, nevertheless. His only concession to weekend informality was a light breakfast, elaborately arranged on a table in the hall outside his office for his secretary and the young lawyers working on his Saturday projects.

Weil carried a plate of eggs and a bagel into his office and called Sari Kahn and Bernie Sheffleman to join him. "So, my dear young people, let's take stock of where we are. It is now the twenty-sixth day of June; we have exactly fifteen days until the Senate hearings begin. What do we know, so far?"

"Well, we know the President's boat is gone and no one will tell me where it is," Sheffleman replied.

"It's a United States Navy ship, is it not? Can you call the Navy Department?"

"Not until Monday."

"Suppose they won't tell you," Weil said. "What will you do next?"

"I don't know. Freedom of Information Act demand, maybe."

"No good," Sari Kahn said. "Too slow; the whole thing will be over before they have to answer."

"I don't know, then," said Sheffleman.

"I'm to see the Attorney General the early part of the week," Weil said. "I'll ask him if he knows."

"The Navy aide!" Kahn snapped.

"Who?"

"The President's naval aide; ask him."

"Good idea."

"What about the Secret Service?" Weil asked. "Do they have records that help?"

"They flat out refuse," Sari Kahn said.

"How far up did you go?" Weil pressed.

"The head of the White House detail."

"Call the Assistant Secretary of the Treasury for Law Enforcement."

"OK."

"If you strike out there, then the Secretary."

"Secretary Sample?"

"Right. Tell him you're calling at my insistence."

"I got nowhere at the White House garage last night," Sheffleman said. "There are all kinds of dispatcher's records in that office, but they wouldn't show them to me. They wouldn't even talk to me. That is an Army post, did you know that?"

"So?" Weil suggested.

"So I call the Secretary of the Army, right?"

"Or the President's Army aide, maybe?" Sarepta Kahn added.

"Both. By midweek the Senate staff will have subpoenas out for those records, I think, but we should keep trying all the same," Weil said. "Now, how about the CIA, the Capron people, the movie star and the rest of the list?"

"We're moving through it as fast as we can, Mr. Weil," Sari Kahn replied. "We have Charlie Hellman and his merry men on the job, but I won't even have a preliminary report from their investigation until next Tuesday or Wednesday. We'll have to be patient."

"What's your impression of our client, Sari?" Weil asked.

She smiled broadly. "He's beautiful. When we close the file can I keep him?"

Weil didn't smile. "Do you believe him?"

She nodded. "Partly because I don't ever believe a word Hugh Frankling says. And Robin comes across honest to me. And he's gorgeous."

Weil shook his head. "Bernie, I'm afraid we're going to have to

251

remind Ms. Kahn that today she is a professional person, not a woman."

"That's exactly what she tells me all the time to keep me at a distance. I guess I should have been a quarterback."

Sari Kahn made a face.

"What about you?" Weil asked him. "Do you believe him?"

"If I were on the jury I'd probably vote for the President, the Attorney General and the CIA, not some young guy who is in a jam."

"So, there it is. I would, too. Who wouldn't? We must have that corroboration of the key fact: he was on that boat when he said he was!" Weil hit his desk with his fist. "What have we overlooked? Is there something in this that we have not seen? How do we prove it?"

"Did the movie star ever call him back?" Kahn asked.

"No, nor did Capron. But they were both away this week. Perhaps we should try them again now. Try the young lady's private number, Sari."

Sari Kahn's eyebrows raised suddenly when a woman answered the telephone after one ring. "Miss Romera, please. Leonard Weil is calling," she said.

"Who is Leonard Weil?"

"He is Robin Warren's attorney. We are calling from Washington, D.C."

"This is Lani Romera," the voice said flatly.

Sari handed the receiver to Leonard Weil. "She answers her own phone," she said.

"Hello, this is Leonard Weil, Miss Romera. How do you do?"

"I'm wondering why you are calling me."

"I represent Robin Warren, Miss Romera. He badly needs your help."

"I can't think how or why."

"He must appear before the Senate in a few days and he will be questioned about his motive in ordering the CIA to attempt a coup in Uruguay. He will say the President instructed him to do so.

252

Some Senators will imply that he had been seduced to do so by you and Auguste Capron."

"By me? That's ridiculous."

"It will help him greatly if you will say so publicly."

"You mean come there and testify?"

"Yes. That's the only way."

"I couldn't do that, Mr. . . ."

"Weil."

"Mr. Weil. That's totally out of the question. Robin is a wonderful man and I'd like to help him, but I couldn't do anything like that."

"Your career?"

"Yes, that's part of the reason. A big part. You could say it's career."

"You might be subpoenaed. You might be required to—"

"No," she interrupted. "It wouldn't matter. I won't show up. You can call Mr. Capron's lawyer if you want to. He is—"

"I don't think so, Miss Romera. If you aren't willing to come to help your friend, there is no point in calling a lawyer." Weil's tone was accusatory.

"Tell Robin I'm sorry, please. I would help him if I could." She hung up abruptly.

Weil looked at his associates and shook his head. "She says there is no way she will help. She is very fearful, I think."

"We have only an office number for Capron," Sari said.

"Please try him on Monday. Capron could be of enormous assistance."

"How about that Dooley?" Sheffleman asked.

"What do we know about him?" Weil turned to Sari Kahn.

"He's only been with United International for six or seven years," she said. "Before that he lived in South America."

"And did what?"

"Worked for several American companies. Most recently for a pharmaceutical manufacturer. I'm trying to get more details."

253

"Did Warren bring in his bank records and tax returns?" Weil asked.

"I sent a messenger to his house for them," Sheffleman said. "I'll go through them this morning."

"Where is our client today?" Weil asked.

"I'm not sure," Sheffleman replied.

"Fifteen days. He could deteriorate badly in fifteen days with nothing to do. We must put him to work. Call him, Sari, and tell him to stay home this weekend and reconstruct the months of April, May and June. On paper. Day by day, hour by hour, where he was, who he saw, what business he did. That will exercise his memory. If we can't get his date book from the FBI at least we'll have his reconstruction. And it's good to keep him busy. Next week have him come here every other day for an appointment. Check over what he's done, then bring him in to see me. I'll tell him the progress we're making."

"Fine."

"He's in for a rough two weeks in the press, I'll tell you. Did you see the paper today?"

"Is that true, about his father?" Sheffleman asked. "I don't recall Robin saying he was a suicide."

"He didn't," Kahn replied. "He said his father was dead. That was all."

"Only the beginning," Weil said. "From here on in it gets dirty. You've never seen dirty like it gets in one of these things. We've got to help the boy get through these next two weeks. It won't be nice."

CHAPTER 21

To: Leonard J. Weil
From: S. Kahn/B. Sheffleman
Re: Warren, Robin

Status report as of June 30

The client: Robin Warren has been in twice this week. He is making some progress on the diary. The press are hounding him wherever he goes and that is having its effect upon him.

Some thought should be given to hiding him somewhere before and during his testimony so he can relax and get some sleep.

The general status of the case:

In general, it's bad.

Our investigation is coming up empty on all fronts. Specifically:

a) The yacht: The Navy refuses to disclose its whereabouts. The Naval Aide at the White House says that such information is classified and is never, ever revealed. The Secretary of the Navy refuses our calls.

A search of newspaper files gave us the name of the commanding officer of The Sequoia (Nixon-Ford yacht), but there is no record of the Sea Island's C.O., and the Navy won't tell us his name.

255

b) <u>The White House garage:</u> Same kinds of negative answers from the Army.

c) <u>The Secret Service:</u> One of the investigators at Charlie Hellman's knows an agent on the S.S. White House Detail. He is sympathetic to Robin Warren and hostile to Hale, Turley and the White House Beavers. The friendly agent did some checking around to see if there were trip reports and shift notes for May 31. He was told to stay away from the subject. The White House Detail has a code word for a case or subject that is absolutely too hot to discuss (as in LBJ's brother Sam, Nixon's brother Don, etc.). The subject is said to be "in the freezer" or "frozen."

    The agent was told that the yacht trip of May 31 was "frozen." He feels he is obliged to cease any inquiry or checking once he is told that. He backed away from the whole thing immediately.

    Isn't that interesting!?

<u>Capron:</u> Refuses to answer calls from our client or us.

<u>Lani Romera:</u> Refuses to help.

<u>The CIA:</u> Refuses to grant any of us an interview <u>re:</u> Methodist Missionary.

<u>The President:</u> His Appointments Secretary says his press conference answer on Uruguay precludes the necessity of involving himself in the controversy.

<u>The Attorney General:</u> His answers to you during your appointment with him were straight party line, and adverse to our client.

    Since then we have done our best to find someone to whom he might have said something different. Either his acquaintances won't talk to us or they say they have not discussed the subject with him. We have exhausted the list you prepared. Anyone else we can try? How about his wife?

<u>The Senate Hearings:</u> The networks have decided to pool and rotate their coverage each day. The first hearing day is Monday, July 12, as you know. All three networks

will devote their Sunday panel shows July 11 to the subject of the Uruguay coup and the hearings. The lineup is:

Meet the Press: Chairman Harley Oates
Face the Nation: The Attorney General
Issues and Answers: Gen'l Robt Durrien

A little one-sided!
Provision is being made for seating 120 press in the hearing room. Tickets for the public are available only through the Select Committee staff.
The tentative order of witnesses is:

1. Ex—U.S. Ambassador to Uruguay
2. Uruguayan desk man, State Department (actually a woman)
3. The Secretary of State
4. D. E. Dooley, United International V.P.
5. The Attorney General
6. Robin Warren
7. Senate staff investigators
8. Capron
9. CIA people

The Senate Committee staff
    Something odd is going on within the staff. We had expected subpoenas to issue to the Navy, Army, etc., by this time.
    Staff people we have talked to say these papers have been prepared for a week but they have not yet been signed. Oates must sign them.
    Middle—level staff there is especially partisan. They think they have a chance to fatally nail Frankling with Robin's testimony if it is corroborated. They are bitching that Anschults, Oates and the other Democratic Senators on the committee are not moving fast and hard enough. These staff people signed up to pillage the White House and are not being given the free hand they expected.

Recommendations:
    We think you should see Senator Oates and Prof. Anschults again, to urge them to issue the subpoenas at once. Only twelve days remain.

At the same time, press them for a reading of their commitment to a full-scale attack on Frankling. It may be that we are in for a disappointment there. If so, we should know it as soon as possible.

SK
BLS

"Professor Anschults, this is Leonard J. Weil."

"Yes, Mr. Weil?"

"I'm amazed! I got right through to you. It's the first time." Weil laughed.

"It's good to hear we're getting better at something. What can I do for you?"

"I would like to ask you for a few more minutes of your precious time, Professor, you and Chairman Oates."

"What seems to be the trouble?"

"No trouble. But as we get closer to the twelfth—just ten days now, eh?—as we get closer, there are some urgent questions that arise. I'd like to come see you both about them."

"Such as?"

"Well, I still don't have the chairman's final answer on immunity for Mr. Warren—"

"I can take care of that right now. The answer is no."

"Well, the other day, when we were together, Senator Oates indicated he would think it over, and—"

"He did think it over, Mr. Weil. He told me the answer is no. Is there anything else?"

"Yes, sir, I have several other items."

"Well, Mr. Weil, the Senate is in recess for the Fourth of July, as you know. I don't expect to see Senator Oates again until the morning of the twelfth. I suppose he has already left for Arkansas by now. So, unless it's something I can answer, you'll just have to wait until then."

"I see. Can you tell me one thing, Irv—all right that I call you Irv? Call me Lenny."

"Of course."

258

"One thing: did he sign the subpoenas for the Navy and Army records before he left?"

"He took them with him. I assume he will send them back when he signs them."

"When he signs them. Of course. All right. Thank you so very much. Goodbye."

"Goodbye—Lenny."

There was only one light on in the President's refuge in the Old Executive Office Building. With the other lights off it seemed cooler. It was a very hot Friday outside.

The President was slouched deep in the brown chair in the corner. A cloud of cigar smoke wreathed the brass reading lamp, rising slowly toward the high ceiling where the air conditioning carried it away. He looked up as David Hale pushed open the door for Attorney General Smythe.

"Come in, Carley," Frankling said to the Attorney General. "Take this chair here. I had David call you over when he told me you had heard more from old Oates. Do you know now what he wants?"

Carleton Smythe smiled. "More every day. He's like a kid in a candy store, now that he realizes we'll probably deal with him. The only specific I know is that he's looking to get some licenses for deep-sea nodule mining for some contractor he's whoring for. But that's only the opening number.

"I was afraid of that. Can we meet his price?"

"And can he deliver?" Hale added.

"Mr. President, I honestly don't know. Art Brawley is the ranking Republican, you remember. He thinks Oates has no stroke with Laughlin Lincoln, for instance, because Oates is still pretty much of a racist. All the blacks in the Senate distrust him, Lincoln included. The same for the Chinaman from California. So there's two he probably doesn't have. And there are only six Democrats."

"Well, if Oates can't throw this fight, why are we dickering with him?"

"I'm not saying he can't. I'm only saying I don't know if he can." Smythe tucked in his chin and shrugged.

"It seems to me," David Hale said, "that we have very little to lose and a lot to gain. What does he want? Some licenses. Suppose he wants an Army base? Or a defense contract? Cheap enough. And if he doesn't deliver, we're no worse off." He gestured, hand out, palm up—a self-evident truth.

"I agree with that." Smythe nodded.

"All right, so we deal," Frankling muttered. "Who does it, Carley, you?"

"I guess I do. The old turd has gone home to Arkansas for the Fourth, but I can probably call him tonight and cut the deal. I'll let David know if there are any problems."

"You do that. Carley?"

"Yes?"

"Thank you."

"You're welcome, Hugh. You're welcome."

The Attorney General's long Cadillac eased from West Executive Avenue into the heavy Pennsylvania Avenue traffic. In thirty minutes Carleton Smythe was at the front door of his block-long apartment building. He had bought two condominium apartments there the year before, had the wall between them removed, and allowed Jane Smythe to decorate them to her unique taste. He liked nothing about it.

Smythe had his mind on Harley Oates as his FBI bodyguard opened and closed doors, operated the elevator and took his briefcase into the small den off the living room.

"We won't be going out tonight, Fred," Smythe said to him. "I'll see you at the regular time Monday."

"Good night, General."

"Good night."

The agent closed the door firmly behind him.

Smythe noticed his wife standing in the dining room, a drink in her hand. "Good evening, dear," he said.

" 'We won' be goin' out t'night, Fred,' " she mocked. "Tha's for damn sure. We nevah go anywheah. Another won'erful Friday evenin' at home! With the won'erful Attorney Genn'l of the 'nited States! Hot damn!"

"I'm sorry I'm late, Jane. The President called me over unexpectedly."

"Oh, sure, honey. Well, it's too goddamned bad, Carley. You missed a nice, delicious meal." Jane Smythe swayed as she walked toward the bar in an alcove off the living room.

"Perhaps the cook could fix me some eggs and toast," Smythe said in a conciliatory tone.

"P'rhaps the cook could. But the cook ain't heah, deary. I sent the cook home. How d'ya like that?"

"Look, Jane, I have some calls I must make now. Why don't you lay off the sauce now? Fix me some eggs—nothing fancy?"

"Ah'll jes bet you have some calls to make. Goin' to get all lined up with some slut for up in yoah lil' bedroom there at the office? Gonna have a lil' sweet talk tonight 'fore you go to bed?" She minced a two-step, holding her glass in both hands.

"Don't be foolish, Jane. Please don't drink any more."

"I'll fuckin' well drink if it pleases me, Carley. You don' even come home or call, so I drink. Tha's a trade: you play aroun', I'll drink. Don' you tell me not to drink, fat ass, an' I won' tell all the people how you run aroun'. All the people that think what a big man y'are." She poured gin into her glass, held it in both hands and drank deeply. "You can jes' lay your own eggs, big man. I ain't yoah servant girl." She moved unsteadily down the hallway to her bedroom. The door slammed behind her.

Smythe shook his head slowly as he entered the den. He closed the heavy door, then turned back to lock it. At the desk he picked up the White House telephone and asked the operator to find Senator Harley Oates for him.

The "Admin Board," the White House switchboard of a dozen skilled operators, keeps extensive card files of the telephone numbers of thousands of prominent persons around the country. They found Oates on the first try.

"Evenin', General."

261

"Evening, Mr. Chairman, I hope I am not disturbing you."

"Oh, no. Miss Marianne and I were just sittin' out. We were on the porch listenin' to the night sounds. It's a beautiful evenin' here."

"The President suggested I call, Mr. Chairman."

"Yes. Well, that's jus' fine."

"I want to be sure just what it is we're talking about, once and for all. On my side we are suggesting that your hearings not attack President Frankling. What is being asked on your side, Mr. Chairman?"

"Well, you know, General, a pearl of great price, as the Bible says, is not had for the askin'. Nor do I seek anythin' for myself. I'm like the old farmer who was feedin' the rooster because he loved his hens, if you see what I mean." Oates chuckled.

"You want that contractor to get the nodule mining license?"

"Well, that seems only fair. Those people have spent millions . . ." Oates's voice trailed off.

"And what else?"

"I'm very concerned about the possibility that the Montrose Electric Manufacturin' plant might close in Little Rock. They are good people an' they truly need that contract from the Department of Energy, the one we discussed."

"And poultry prices, I believe?"

"Yes. Tha's very important to my chicken farmers. That price jus' must be stabilized."

"Is that the list? I'm taking notes—"

"Well, there is one other thing. It's rather personal, rather close to home. It's Miss Marianne's brother, you know. Ted T. Smith."

"What about him?"

"He tells his sister he is bein' harassed somethin' terrible by the IRS down here. You all have a very unpleasant district director in this locality, you know. I've spoken to the Treasury people before, about him—I disremember his name, but you can find it out."

"And you want?"

"Let's move that IRS district director, General. Promote him and put him somewhere else. He's very bad. And let's have those

IRS boys stop pickin' on Mr. Smith. He's well known here, a very reputable man."

"I see. Anything else? Nodules, poultry, Montrose Electric, the IRS district director and T. T. Smith's taxes. Is that the list?"

"Yes, General, that's the list."

"All right. Consider it done. We have a deal."

"Well, that's very gracious of you, General. Please extend my compliments to the President. A fine man, Hugh Franklin'."

"I'll do that, Mr. Chairman. I'll do that. Good night."

Smythe flashed the operator four times.

"Yes, General? Are you through?"

"Yes, I'm through with Senator Oates. Has the President retired?"

"No, sir, he's talking on the telephone now. Shall I tell him you wish to speak to him, when his call is down?"

"Yes, please. I'll wait here for him."

"He's just hung up, General. One moment."

"Yes, Carley?" Frankling said.

"I've just talked to Oates. We've got a deal."

"What did you have to give—the mining license?"

"And also the kitchen sink—even his brother-in-law's tax problems. He's an old bandit. An energy contract, poultry prices and an IRS man's head on a plate."

"Well, at least he'll deal."

"Now it remains to be seen how he'll deliver."

"Follow it closely, Carley. Keep checking with Brawley."

"They're all in recess up there now. No one's around except the committee staff. Brawley's not going to know. His little minority staff isn't worth a damn to him."

"Well, follow it the best you can. Keep me posted. That's a good night's work, that deal with Oates. A good night's work."

"I hope so. How about the boat?"

"David says it's hidden away at Newport News and the crew is scattered far and wide. The captain is at Guantánamo, poor devil. Good night, Carley."

CHAPTER **22** When he first moved to Washington Robin Warren had found the two-story town house, built in the late sixties in the Colonial style. Brick, shutters, false dormers, white trim, built flush with the sidewalk, kitchen and narrow living room down, two bedrooms and bath up, $510 a month unfurnished. It was a good place to live. Reservoir Street dead-ended in Thirty-second Street N.W., so traffic was one way and light in that short block. The neighbors minded their own business. A quiet, well-maintained area, worth the money.

From the day he was fired Robin Warren was besieged behind the shaded windows of that house. The narrow street, the alley across the street, the sidewalks and most of the driveways were usurped by reporters, cameramen and technicians, with their cars, tripods, motorcycles and messengers, from dawn until their respective assignment editors decided to end their vigils for the day, often at some hour far into the night.

If he drew back a front-window curtain to look into Reservoir Street film crews would hoist equipment to their shoulders and shuffle to his doorstep. They watched his door and windows constantly.

His telephone quickly became an enemy within the walls. Finally he couldn't stand the constant ringing any longer; he took little wires off their terminals inside the wall box until he found the combination that stilled the bells.

He was awakened early each day by the slamming of car doors. When the arriving cameramen, sound men, light men, photographers and reporters gathered, conversations floated up, film boxes clashed on pavement, men and women laughed down in the street. Walkie-talkies and car radios rasped and growled.

Robin set up a card table in the bedless, box-littered spare bedroom at the back of the house. He had never used that room before. Now he thought it the best room in the house, away from the street. He drew calendars on plain white paper and tried to fill in the squares. Kathy O'Reilly remembered many of the events and sent him notes from which he filled in the blanks for April, May and June. Bill Thompson supplied some others. But Warren's memory did not perform well. He was rattled and jangled by the street noises, by his imprisonment in his own house, and by a kind of involuntary rumination that distracted his mind at times. Thoughts flowed through his mind in spite of his efforts to concentrate on his assignment. He found himself daydreaming about how the Senate hearings would be. He pictured men questioning him, microphones and crowds of people. He heard questions and saw himself answering them.

Slowly the reconstruction of the occurrences of the previous three months took shape, but it was hard, discouraging work because he knew himself to be unable to recall events he should have remembered. He worked on the calendars until ten Monday morning. Sarepta Kahn expected him to call at ten. On his hands and knees, with the screwdriver on his Swiss Army knife, he connected the telephone in his bedroom. Before he could dial out, the phone rang.

"Yes?"

"Mr. Warren?"

"Who is this?"

"McCauley at the *Star-Post,* Mr. Warren. Have you seen the story about you and Lani Romera that is running?"

He pushed the receiver button several times to disconnect the call, then quickly dialed Miss Kahn's direct line.

"Kahn. Good morning."

"This is Robin Warren."

"Hello. How are you today?"

"Not too good. I'm feeling very hounded at the moment."

"A lot of them out there?"

"Looks like about fifty."

"We have some press hanging around here, too. How is the calendar coming?"

"Pretty well. There's not that much that's relevant to Uruguay, actually."

"But Mr. Weil wants everything you did, whether you think it's relevant or not. Everything."

"I know. That's what he's getting."

"Can you come in this afternoon?"

"I guess so. I may have to climb over the back fence to get out of here."

"Is there a back way out?"

"No, not really. I have a tiny terrace out back. The fence belongs to my back neighbor. He has a bigger yard; there's no gate or anything."

"Have you seen the paper this morning, Mr. Warren?"

"Robin."

"Right. Robin."

"No. What now?"

"The lead is that Justice Department sources predict you'll be indicted right after the Senate hearings."

"I suppose that's right."

"Not necessarily. First the committee refuses you immunity; now this. It sounds to us like someone would like you to refuse to testify on grounds of possible self-incrimination."

"Makes sense. Maybe I should take the Fifth."

"That's one of the things Mr. Weil wants to cover with you this afternoon. I know he feels you must make that decision for yourself. But we'll talk about it. You probably have some questions."

"Well, I may have by then. Right now I'm a little numb. I've never been indicted for anything."

"Sure. Look, would it help if I came by to pick you up?"

"I'd appreciate that. It's hard to get a cab up here and I don't want to walk over to Wisconsin with this mob trailing me."

"I'll be there exactly at two. As close to your door as I can get. I'll beep three times. It's a little Mercedes."

"They must pay pretty good down there."

"Not bad. But the 450 SL is a gift from a grateful client."

He whistled.

"My father, dummy. My lovely, rich father. Barry Kahn. Ever hear of him?"

"Sure. In fact, I've met him. I just didn't put it together."

"Three beeps at two. See you then."

"Right." He kneeled and unscrewed the yellow wire. Then he stretched full length on his bed, his eyes closed, the heels of his hands on his forehead. They were talking out there; a woman laughed. Someone was taking something metal apart or putting it together, making a scraping sound. They were noisier than usual.

Indicted! And tried. Jep said the Justice Department could get anyone if it wanted them badly enough. No doubt old Attorney General Smythe wanted him, enough to make sure he was put in jail. Robin thought of his mother. There had been a letter from her Saturday. She obviously didn't understand what was happening to him. He had tried to explain it on the telephone on Sunday. But she couldn't accept the idea that her son's interests were adverse to those of the President of the United States. Ever since he'd gone to work at the White House she'd been telling people what a wonderful man Hugh Frankling was. When they talked on the phone Sunday Robin told her that the President was a liar. Mrs. Warren couldn't shift her mind that quickly. He finally gave up and asked about his aunt and his cousin's children.

When they had completed a series of high-speed turns and were moving downhill on Wisconsin Avenue, Sari Kahn handed Robin an envelope. "Came this morning," she said.

267

Robin recognized Jep Valle's personal stationery, unusually heavy and very expensive. He tore open the small, bulky envelope.

DEAR ROBIN—

Since you've disconnected your phone this seems the best way to reach you. I'd have come by your house—in fact, I drove by—but neither of us needs any more publicity than we're already getting. So I didn't stop.

Lenny Weil tells me that he'd like to get you out of that mob scene for a while. I'd like to help.

I have the use of a farm place out near Middleburg for the next month—very secluded and quiet. There's a guest cabin which is yours to use any time; today, tomorrow, next week. Just let my office know.

Maggie and I will be there next weekend and we both hope you'll join us. No one else will be there except the very discreet help.

If I can assist in *any* way at all, please call.

I know you are strong, and that you feel you're right in this fight. If anything can help in a situation like yours, strength of spirit will.

Your friend, always,
JV

The Monday afternoon session with Weil produced a decision: Robin Warren would not plead self-incrimination. He was innocent and truthful, and so he'd testify. Weil prepared him to be questioned by the committee staff. And they decided against giving any press interviews. If the U.S. Attorney intended to get him indicted, the less said the better.

Midweek, Leonard Weil took him to Irving Anschults' office for more interrogation. The professor seemed nervous and disorganized, but not hostile. No new ground was covered. Within twenty-four hours the *Star-Post* quoted sources which described Robin's answers to Anschults' questions in great detail.

As Friday approached, Robin debated whether to go to Valle's farm for the weekend. His week had been vacant: shoddy frozen dinners at home, television—even daytime shows—to divert and relax, he told himself. He couldn't remember the last time he'd

268

laughed. It would be good to be with Maggie Valle, touch her, amuse each other.

On Friday, Leonard Weil read the draft opening statement and urged him to completely rewrite it. So instead of weekending with the Valles in Virginia, Robin sat in his bare back bedroom, his air conditioning on full blast, drinking iced tea and typing.

Robin talked with Maggie Valle on the telephone every evening. He quit reading the papers. He could not stand to read everything they were printing about him. She read the *Star-Post* and *Times* coverage and gave him a summary when they talked. He watched television news and wondered if he should. He felt soiled by the notoriety that the secrets of his life were given.

He had always been ashamed that his father had killed himself. That bulky redheaded man and his mother had been miserable together, and his father was evidently the weaker of the two. He had shot himself when Robin was fifteen. Neither Robin nor his mother ever talked about the suicide. But it lay between them all the rest of Robin's years in Napa. He had no father, because of her, and they both knew it. He was ashamed of his father for killing himself and resentful of his mother's part in it. Now, for some reason which only the editor of the *Star-Post* knew, the fact of Tom Warren's suicide was a part of Robin's biographical summary, worked into the buildup coverage every day of the week between the Fourth of July and the first session of the hearings.

Maggie Valle coolly summarized the Lani Romera stories for him, refusing to stop for his explanations or rationalizations. She read him the adulatory stories about the Senators who were members of the Select Committee. Harley Oates was apparently granting interviews in Arkansas to anyone with a pencil or a camera. Every issue of every paper or news magazine had a picture of Oates on his Arkansas porch in his hickory rocker.

Telephone conversations with Maggie Valle that week always ended with her assurances of loyalty. "You know I love you, don't you?" she always said. "I love you, too," he replied. Even as he said that to her, each evening, he realized that it was not true. Whatever love he had felt for her had been cauterized by his attraction to Lani Romera and by the subsequent trauma of the White House events. He'd been fired, hounded, humiliated and exposed. He now felt only beaten—incapable of loving anyone.

He slept badly, tensely, dreaming active, demanding dreams he could never remember, awaking to street noises under his window. The press refused to go to bed on the hot nights of the weekend and refused to let him try to sleep. But he dared not get up and go out; they waited all night outside his door. So Robin lay looking at the ceiling, his thoughts skittering from subject to subject, out of control. He was on the brink, and he knew it.

CHAPTER **23**   Professor Irving Anschults went to the big Senate Caucus Room for a few minutes every day to check on arrangements. He was glad to be able to get a feel of the room. Several times he sat in the chair next to the chairman's place; that's where he would be next Monday. There were dozens of details to be ruled on. Would the still cameramen be allowed to roam freely during testimony? Where would visiting Senators be seated? How about their families? Foreign ambassadors? For three days, on Friday and over the weekend, most of his logistic problems were centered in the rotunda just outside the Caucus Room door. The round lobby area surrounded an open well from roof to basement. Each television network had been allocated space in this lobby for its technical apparatus. Everyone complained about the lack of space, a shortage of electrical capacity and the temperature.

As the time for preparation of the hearings diminished, Anschults fully realized that Chairman Harley Oates was playing some little game of his own, and that he, Irving Anschults, could be hurt in the backlash of whatever it was.

Oates stayed in Arkansas until the Saturday before the hearings were to begin. During that week Professor Anschults called him repeatedly to urge Oates to sign the subpoenas which required the military to produce garage logs, ship logs and telephone records. Sometimes the old chairman said he was too busy to talk with Anschults; at times he pleaded fatigue or forgetfulness; twice he merely described the beauty of the view from his porch, deflecting Anschults with rural non sequiturs. On two occasions he said there were reporters present, so he couldn't talk. Saturday night, when he returned to Washington, Oates couldn't see or talk with Anschults because he had to prepare for his Sunday appearance on *Meet the Press*. On Sunday he was not available to take Anschults' calls, before or after the telecast.

It was no accident that one of the *Meet the Press* panelists asked Oates about the subpoenas. The reporter had been given the subpoena question by Anschults the night before. But neither Anschults nor the others listening really learned anything from Oates's artful answer.

Oates did reveal, however, by the essence of his evasions on that Sunday program, that he'd gone soft on President Hugh Frankling.

When Irving Anschults went to bed that Sunday night he couldn't sleep. About thirty minutes after midnight he made an extraordinary telephone call to Senator Thomas Stapleton at home to ask Stapleton for an early-morning meeting the next day. Fortunately the Senator had not yet retired.

"About the chairman and what he said on *Meet the Press*, I assume?" Stapleton asked.

"Yes, Senator. And what he didn't say, too. I wasn't able to reach the chairman all day. There are a hundred loose ends."

"I tried to reach him, too, Professor. All right. My office at nine?"

"I'll be there," Anschults said.

Rebecca Anschults rolled on her side and looked at her husband. "What kind of chairman do you have that won't talk to you?"

"I didn't choose him."

"Is that a right way for a chairman to act?"

"No, it's a very devious way to act. Something's not right at all. Now let's sleep."

But he didn't sleep. At four he got up and went out into the back yard in his pajamas. He put the kids' toys away, watered the flowers and covered the barbecue grill. At five he dressed and drove to the office without breakfast.

Before nine Irving Anschults was ushered into Senator Thomas Stapleton's large office in the New Senate Office Building. The Senator was tall, spare and balding, athletic and handsome. His office was decorated with huge color photographs of Connecticut scenes—covered bridges, white churches, even a factory. Anschults was offered an old horsehair-stuffed leather chair salvaged from another era. Over coffee he described to Stapleton the importance of the subpoenas.

"This was crazy, to start these hearings immediately after a long recess," Stapleton said. "There's been no chance for the members of the committee to stay abreast of things. We've been scattered all over, some of us overseas, out of touch."

"Well, it was the television . . ." Anschults began.

"I know; Oates said he was afraid no one would watch if we scheduled them any later in the summer. With all this confusion, maybe it would be better if no one did."

"It's still not too late to get the subpoenas out, Senator. But I wonder if Senator Oates is willing to put them out now."

"I wonder, too," Stapleton said. "I think the best thing for me to do is go and see old Harley before things begin. What do you intend to cover at the hearing today?"

"Just scene-setting. We have two Uruguay experts for today— the former ambassador and the State Department desk man—uh, desk person. It's a woman. They should run about two hours, then we'll adjourn. I've sent everyone on the committee a briefing packet. I hope you got yours. It has a list of witnesses."

"It's probably here somewhere." Stapleton waved at his crowded desk. "I'll read it before I come over."

"Shall I come with you to see the chairman?" Anschults asked.

"No, Professor, I'd better see him alone. Thank you anyway."

Senator Harley Oates was nowhere to be found until a few minutes before twelve. Then, walking the circuitous route necessary to go from his office to the Caucus Room via the south hallway, unnecessarily escorted by two Capitol policemen in full regalia, he appeared.

Oates was wearing a white suit and white shoes. His gray hair appeared whiter than usual, his face more tan. People who crowded near him, as he stopped to shake hands and sign autographs for those in the line, could see that a makeup man had missed a small patch of pale skin behind his right ear. Otherwise the cosmetic job was flawless.

"Ahm raht pleased to see y'all this mornin'." Oates beamed. His accent was thicker, his voice a little deeper than usual. As he shook hands his wattles quivered. "Goin' to be late 'less ah move along now. Hope y'all git in there to see our system wuhk. God bless y'all."

He stopped four times along the line to permit himself to be adulated. Then he moved into the rotunda lights' blinding glare. His arrival was forecast by a policeman, who was sent ahead to the rotunda for that purpose by Oates's press secretary. The old Senator, live and in gleaming white, moved slowly about the doughnut-shaped lobby, stopping at each television network area to answer a few questions.

In the high-ceilinged Caucus Room a flock of still cameramen moved about, eyes on the door, ready to abandon the Senators who were now standing at their places, waiting behind the long curved dais. As more time passed, Stapleton and the other committee members made wry remarks to one another about the delay. Anschults sent a staff employee to the rotunda to find Oates and say that everyone was ready and waiting.

At last, at 12:32 P.M., the spectators sitting near the large double doorway began to applaud. Senator Harley Oates, nodding genially, waving as if a little embarrassed by the applause, moved

273

slowly into the room toward the end of the long, elaborately carved and polished wooden structure behind which the Select Committee would sit.

Tom Stapleton went quickly to intercept Oates at the end of the dais. Cameramen, seeing his movement, rushed to gather a step below them in the no man's land between the committee and the witness table.

"Ah, Senator, good mornin'," Oates said loudly.

"Mr. Chairman, I think you and I should talk a little before things begin," Stapleton said quietly.

Automatic cameras clack-clacked, strobe flashes winked and cameramen jockeyed for position.

"Tom, I apologize foah bein' late," Oates exclaimed so that the reporters at the press table could hear. "Ah had no idea it would take so long to walk up here. They's quite a crowd out there and they slowed me."

"Mr. Chairman . . ." Stapleton began. His bald pate gleamed in the television lights.

"Ah, Senator Wong." Oates took the hand of the little California Senator and pumped it vigorously. Then, turning away from Stapleton, Oates moved through the line of waiting committee members, shaking some hands, patting a shoulder, saying a word to each. When he reached the center of the dais Oates was facing Irving Anschults.

"Ah, Professor! Shall we begin? Just take yoah seat an' we'll start."

The eleven camermen were clustered in the well below Oates's place, calling to him to hold up the large wooden gavel that lay on the counter top. Oates grinned broadly and took it up. As he held it, as if to pound it, the cameras whirred and clicked. Oates struck the gavel for the cameras, then as the cameramen called more directions Oates looked left, then right, striking the gavel over and over.

The chairman's charade caused the talking in the room to subside to a light murmur which was echoed up into the vast reaches of the high ceiling. Several of the Senators at the far ends of the curved dais sat back in their chairs and watched Oates perform with his gavel.

At last the chairman struck a loud blow. "The committee will be at odah, please. Be at odah. Be at odah."

The other Senators took their places. Stragglers moved into the few empty chairs at the six press tables which were ranged across the room behind the witness table.

"Ladies and gent'men," Oates said.

The loudspeakers in the room became imperfectly loud during the third word, then subsided. A technician checked his dials and connections.

"Members of the public an' you people of the press, ahm goin' to expect you to be very quiet all through these hearin's. Ah guess ah don' need to say any more." Oates looked to his left, leaned forward and looked to his right. "Ah'll introduce the Senate Select Committee on Assassinations, which is convened this mornin' . . ."

"Afternoon," Senator Stapleton said quietly.

Oates shot him a glance. ". . . convened pursuant to Senate Resolution Twelve of this session. Ah'll start down on my right." Oates drawled out the names of the Senators and their respective states, starting at the far end of the long table. When he came to Senator Wong of California he paused, then chuckled loudly. "He's the only one on the committee who is always Wong. Heah on my left is the director of our staff, Professor Irving Anschults of the University of Maryland Law School. Now, I think that covers everyone, doesn't it?" He looked left and right again. "At the outset I want to say that everyone, Senators and the professor, will be given a chance to question each witness in rotation, ten minutes at a time."

Stapleton leaned toward Oates, his hand over the microphone in front of him. "Mr. Chairman, do you intend to state the object of our inquiry?"

Oates shook his head quickly. "I want to get started now. That's in the authorizin' resolution, anyway." Oates turned to Professor Anschults.

"Professor Irving, who is the first witness?"

"Anschults," the staff director said very quietly.

"Who?"

"My name is Anschults."

"Ah know that. Who is the first witness?"

"Ambassador Samuel Thurmont."

A small gray man in a double-breasted blue suit had taken the witness chair during the introductions. He opened a thin notebook and looked at Anschults expectantly.

Harley Oates abruptly stood and raised his right hand. Anschults looked at him with surprise, then looked at the witness and signaled him to stand. Oates raised his hand and the still cameras clattered. The witness was sworn and Oates sat down.

"Mr. Chairman, a point of order."

Oates looked down the line to his left. "Who is that? Senator Larkin?"

"Yes, Mr. Chairman. I'm wondering about these photographers down front. I feel they should not occupy this area between us and the witness, especially when someone's trying to testify. They will be extremely distracting."

"Oh, ah think they will be all right there, Senator. You see them; they are all scrunched down out of the way. They don't bother you, do they, Ambassador?"

The witness looked up from his notes in confusion. "Sir?"

"No, I thought not." Oates smiled. "You can rely on me, Senator Larkin, to keep mah eye open for any lack of decorum in this chamber. Ah thank you for your suggestion. Let us be at odah now. Mr. Ambassador, do you have a statement to give?"

"Yes, Mr. Chairman."

"Then give yoah name and address, and read us what you have."

Ambassador Sam Thurmont had been in Montevideo at the time *Methodist Missionary* aborted. He was immediately recalled by the State Department, just ahead of his expulsion by the Uruguayan Foreign Ministry. Knowing nothing of the CIA's coup in advance, he was understandably critical of the attempt. He

276

explained all of this in his opening statement, along with his impression of the Uruguayan political situation, geography, demography and economy.

Midway in the little man's statement Senator Thomas Stapleton rose, motioned to his staff assistant to follow, and walked behind the curtains at the left end of the dais, disappearing into an anteroom. Their passage was scrutinized by the line of aides seated behind their Senators, and by the hundred and twenty reporters, most of whom were not listening to the ambassador.

In less than five minutes Stapleton returned to his place. Irving Anschults reached behind Oates to hand Stapleton a note. The Senator read it, folded it and handed it back, looking at Anschults with raised eyebrows.

The questioning of Thurmont was brief and desultory, in spite of his being the first witness in a highly publicized hearing.

As Ambassador Thurmont was yielding the witness chair to Mrs. Columbia Meeghan, the desk person for Uruguay at the State Department, Stapleton's aide returned with a handful of papers. He walked the length of the dais, placing one of his papers in front of each Democratic Senator. They read:

To Democratic members of the Select Committee:

I request you attend an urgent meeting of the Democrats on this Select Committee in my office (221 NSOB), immediately following adjournment today.

There are some matters which must be discussed and decided upon at once.

Thomas Stapleton

Harley Oates put his hand over his microphone and turned to Stapleton. "What the heck is this, Tom?"

"We need to talk things over, Mr. Chairman. I'll explain later," Stapleton whispered.

Stapleton handed his copy of the letter to Irving Anschults. He had written at the bottom: "You come, too, and bring that press inquiry. T.S."

277

The next witness, Mrs. Meeghan, was even less exciting than Ambassador Thurmont. All up and down the press tables the leads for the day's stories were being composed, using the words "slow start," "disappointing," "nothing new or sensational."

By two o'clock the lady had been excused and Oates had adjourned the hearing until noon Tuesday, the next day. Within thirty minutes the six Democrats and Irving Anschults were seated in Tom Stapleton's inner office, listening to Harley Oates recapitulate the day's events, somewhat defensively.

"Ah think it's best to start slow and finish with a bang. Not the other way aroun'. Pace is everythin' in one of these things. Pace, timin' an' an eye for the cameras. That's the secret."

"I'm sure no one will accuse us of starting with a bang today," John Goldmark, the rumpled old Senator from New York, said wryly.

"May I put a problem to you, gentlemen?" Stapleton was seated behind his desk. He gently rested his palms on the desk top and looked at Harley Oates. "Mr. Chairman, I've suggested this discussion because I feel, instinctively, that we are headed for trouble."

Oates looked as if he was about to speak. Stapleton held up one hand. "Let me tell you the signs I see. Then you tell me, and the others, where I'm wrong."

Oates sat back, nodding slightly.

"In the beginning this assassination plot looked open and shut." Stapleton brought his hands together for emphasis. "A CIA agent is caught red-handed. Then Frankling says he knew nothing about it. He blames it all on young Warren. Warren, on the other hand, says Frankling and Smythe knew *all* about it." He spread his arms wide. "So, either way, we win. Either Frankling was in on the plot or he runs a loose and sloppy White House. We can't lose." Stapleton looked around the room, gauging his colleagues. "Whichever way we want to go, however, we are going to need a certain body of evidence. It is essential. We must receive and analyze the records in the White House to drive home—to prove—our thesis, whichever alternative it is. However, when I arrived back at the office this morning from the recess, I discovered to my surprise that, so far, nothing has been done to get the White House records."

"Can't they be subpoenaed?" Laughlin Lincoln asked.

"Sure they can," Stapleton replied. "Perhaps Chairman Oates will explain to us why they haven't been."

"Haven't been what?" Oates said with a broad smile. "I don' understand what all the fuss is about, Tom."

"Subpoenas, Mr. Chairman. White House and military records. To prove or disprove the conflicting stories we're going to get."

"May I ask," interjected John Goldmark, "whether there are such subpoenas?"

Stapleton looked at Anschults. "Professor?"

"Yes, Senator, I prepared them before the recess. I gave them to the chairman for signature."

"Now, just a blessed minute!" Harley Oates exclaimed, his face reddening. "This is too much! Ah am the *chairman* of this Select Committee, not some professor's errand boy. It is not for him or anyone else to tell me what to sign and not to sign. As a United States Senator, and this committee's chairman, ah reserve to myself those decisions. That is mah prerogative and mah duty. There is nothin' to discuss about that. I'll not remain here and be criticized"—he heaved to his feet—"for not obeyin' some damn professor's instructions. 'Sign here, sign there.' I have more worthwhile ways to spend mah time." Oates stepped quickly to the door without looking back. As the door slammed behind him he could be heard faintly: "Goddamn' professors!"

Senators Stapleton, Goldmark, Wong, Speers and Lincoln looked at one another with amazement.

"Tom, what the hell is going on?" Gurley Speers asked. "There must be somethin' more to this that I don't see."

"Sit down please, Senator," Stapleton said to Lee Wong, who had risen as Oates walked out. "There is evidently quite a bit to this, as Gurley says. We need to talk it out."

"Of course," said Wong.

"Professor, tell them about that reporter's call," Stapleton said.

Anschults nodded. "Just before the hearings opened today, I took a call from a reporter whom I know. The question I was asked was whether or not I am aware of an agreement—a deal—between the chairman and the Attorney General. The chairman is supposed to have agreed to go easy on the President. The administration would do a number of things for Senator Oates in return, including taking care of his brother-in-law's tax problems. I said I knew nothing of any such deal."

"I see." John Goldmark nodded. "And I gather the subpoenas never went out."

"No, sir, they didn't," Anschults said. "The chairman never would sign them."

"Tom, can't you sign them, as vice-chairman?" Laughlin Lincoln asked.

"I wouldn't do that, so long as Harley is functioning; at least, not without the consent of a majority of the committee."

"I'll circulate a letter among all the other committee members today," John Goldmark said. "We've got to have that evidence, it seems to me."

"But isn't the situation very dangerous for everyone if the reporter's hypothesis is true?" Senator Wong asked. "If we take no action to learn the truth, and merely permit events to take their course, we will all be accessories to corruption."

"What are you suggesting?" Gurley Speers asked.

"We must know if the chairman made such a deal," Wong replied.

"Suppose he did?" asked Speers.

"Then we must each repudiate it," John Goldmark interjected.

"You mean make it public? Destroy Harley Oates?" Gurley Speers looked at the others for support. "Haven't the Democrats in the Senate enough trouble already?"

"It's a question of which would hurt worse, Gurley," Tom Stapleton said.

"Harley Oates is a national hero now, by God. You bring him down and you'll damn near destroy the Senate!" Speers exclaimed.

Wong pursed his lips behind gathered fingers. "I confess I've been troubled with the role we've been cast in, on this committee—we Democrats. Everyone expects us to destroy the President if we can. But when we do, we expose our country to censure in the UN, and I don't think that's wise. I'd rather let Frankling off the hook than put the country in that position. Suppose this young aide of his is a liar? Suppose the President had been victimized by this boy and by Capron's multinational corporation? I find that to be a believable possibility, you see. If Frankling is telling the truth, we may be led to do the Presidency great harm and, worse, open the United States to attack in the UN, on the basis of one young man's lie."

"So?" Lincoln urged him on as Wong's words slowed.

"So—I don't know. Perhaps there is a way to have it both ways. If we assume the chairman sold out to the President, that is bad for the chairman, but it is also bad for a President who attempts to suborn a Senator. I would much prefer to attack Frankling for that. If he is hurt on such a charge, it does not weaken us internationally. And, if the chairman *joined* us in exposing and condemning the President's attempt to corrupt a venerable and honorable Senator, then we are free to find the truth wherever it is. We all stand for virtue."

Stapleton smiled. "Let's go one step more. If we were then to defend the President against the multinational corporation, we could cut the legs out from under Uruguay and Russia in the UN in an extremely credible way. We attack Capron and the boy, and uphold Frankling's version of the facts."

"But," asked Goldmark, "if Frankling is innocent, why would he try to fix the chairman?"

"Why, indeed?" added Lincoln heavily.

Stapleton held up a hand. "That, it seems to me, is a question better asked at a White House press conference than in the Senate. As I'm sure it will be. If we can get Senator Oates to go along, there need not be insurmountable problems in the UN Hugh Frankling is sure ready to blame us for bad UN results if we attack him. But this way we will have stood up for him—shoulder

281

to shoulder with him against the Russians. We'll only attack him for trying to corrupt our incorruptible chairman."

"They'll ask us why we stood with him on Uruguay, if he tried to buy Oates. Why did we?" Lincoln asked.

"Because, Lucky, that is where the truth led us," Lee Wong said. "We are with him where he's right—versus Capron; and we are against him where he's wrong—in trying to buy a United States Senator. This way frees us from Frankling and from Oates, both. We are not the blind allies of anyone."

"Only simple seekers after truth and justice," Goldmark said wryly.

"Who among us is best able to persuade the chairman to be righteously indignant in his denunciation of the President's effort to buy him off?" Stapleton looked around the circle of his colleagues with amusement. "Gurley? You're closer to him than any of us."

"I'll be glad to try, Tom. But I think you should come with me."

Goldmark nodded. "You should be there, Tom."

Stapleton looked at Lincoln. "Is everyone agreed that this is the way we go?"

Lincoln, Wong and Gurley Speers nodded.

"All right," Stapleton said. "Let's go see if we can find our distinguished chairman."

Above all else, Harley Oates was a realist. When Senator Thomas Stapleton and Oates's friend Senator Gurley Speers explained that a reporter had the story of Oates's agreement with the Attorney General, Oates's pragmatic mind leaped to a realistic decision with uncharacteristic speed.

Stapleton's proposed maneuver was a clever one, but it would work only if Oates could turn on the President and attack him before the reporter's story broke. If Oates could accuse the White House and the Attorney General first, then he was off the hook. Timing was everything, though; he had to move quickly. He'd never catch up with the story if it got out ahead of him.

The chairman smiled at his visitors and assured them that he thought their proposal was "just fine." Two phone calls established that the reporter with the rumor had not yet found anyone to confirm it. So Oates agreed that he would hold a press conference in the Caucus Room, where it could be televised live, at nine the next morning, Tuesday. Anschults would tell the press that the chairman would discuss a matter of great importance.

Well, Oates reflected, he had done his best for Frankling. It was no fault of his if Smythe couldn't keep his mouth shut.

Robin Warren watched the ambassador and the lady from the State Department on his little black-and-white television set, at the card table in the back bedroom. He saw the witness chair in which he would sit. He identified the men who would question him. He watched the swirl of action behind the seated Senators. At the adjournment he watched the Senators move out into the rotunda to give interviews, saying nothing.

As they gave way to equally vacant network commentary, he hooked up his telephone and called Leonard Weil. There had been no call back from Capron, Weil reported. Sheffleman was still trying to reach him. Weil's investigators had produced nothing new over the weekend. He still couldn't prove that Robin had been aboard the yacht. A reporter had called asking about a deal between the White House and Harley Oates. Robin read to Weil the opening statement he had written and they agreed on several changes.

Weil passed along messages from a few people who had tried to reach Warren but were told his telephone was out of order. Among them was a call from Mrs. Sandy Warren in California. Against his better judgment, Robin called his former wife.

"I've been thinking about you," she said. "They say you are going to have to testify pretty soon."

"That's right. On Wednesday or Thursday. How are you?"

"Very well. I'm working, in Menlo Park. For a decorator. But I'm going to take some time off to watch you. I'll be praying for you."

"Thanks. We don't think it will be too rough. This bunch is out to hang the President, you know."

"The news," she instructed, "says that you will say you were on the President's boat and he says you weren't. Were you?"

"Yes, I was."

"Well, can't you just prove that?"

"We're trying."

"It seems to me if the President is actually lying about that . . ."

"You're right; I've got to make them believe me."

"Have you talked to your mother? She called me the other day."

"Yes, last week. She doesn't get the picture. She seems to think the President and I are still pals."

"You'd better call her. She's worried."

"Sure."

"Really, Robin. She's in a state."

"OK."

"Is your phone broken?"

"No. I unhook it. Too many press calls and cranks."

"How can I reach you?"

"I'm not sure you can."

"Don't you want me to call?"

"Sandy, you've no idea what it's like here. I'm trapped in this house; there's a mob of reporters outside the door. If I didn't turn the damn phone off, it would ring off the hook. Why the hell would you take it personally that I won't take your calls?"

"All right, Robin. I'll call your lawyer's office. You're in my thoughts all the time. Just remember."

He said goodbye and hung up, feeling the old resentment at her assumption that she knew what was "best" for him. He felt even more alone and depressed.

CHAPTER **24** The President's press secretary, Les Carew, was the last to arrive at the early-morning staff meeting in David Hale's office. He hurried in with a handful of tear sheets from the news wire machines.

"That necktie!" exclaimed Murray Tillerman. "The worst so far! You look like you are—"

"Shut up, Tillerman," Carew said tensely. "Have any of you seen this? Oates is having a televised press conference in an hour." He proffered the wires.

"So?" Hale asked.

"There's a story moving on one of the wire services that he'll charge the White House with trying to bribe him," Carew said.

"That's all we need now. Who in the White House?" Elwood Broderick rumbled.

"I don't know. Has anyone a clue about this? Did anyone here talk to Oates?" Carew seemed badly shaken.

"The A.G. was negotiating with him," Hale said calmly. "The President knew all about it."

"Jesus wept," Carew said quietly. "That old fraud will get up there and preach about the Constitution and the Bible and he'll murder us."

"Has anyone talked to Smythe this morning?" Hale asked. No one had. He reached for the telephone on the floor beside his chair.

"The Attorney General, please, operator."

"Does he testify today?" Broderick asked.

Carew shook his head. "Tomorrow."

"General? This is David Hale. I think you'd better come over

285

right away. No—Les Carew says Oates is going on television in an hour, probably to claim you tried to buy him off. I don't know. That's only rumor. Right. I'll tell him. OK."

Hale click-clicked the receiver button. "Nick Gurley, please. Nick? What is he doing in there now? How long have they been in with him? OK. Thanks."

Hale looked at the others. "Smythe is coming over. Les, you'd better talk to him. Maybe you can put him on in the Press Room to reply to Oates. Right now Durrien and one of his people are still in there with the old man. I'm going to go run them out. Les, stick around. He'll probably want you in a minute. Be thinking of what Smythe says in rebuttal." Hale went out the door.

"Hell, that's easy," Broderick grunted. "He denies it. What else could he do and live?"

Senator Harley B. Oates of Arkansas ambled briskly into the Caucus Room precisely on the stroke of 9 A.M. The front half of the room was full; reporters and still photographers had taken every seat at the six press tables. A makeshift camera platform was installed behind the tables for three film cameras on tripods. A mixture of Senate employees, technicians and stray tourists filled the back seats and most of the standing room.

Television announcers minutely described Oates's entrance. All the networks had decided to carry this event live, following their regular morning shows. They would all use the pool feed once Oates began, but now each network's own man was establishing the individual identity of his news organization with a dramatic lead-in.

A rostrum had been placed in front of the witness table, slightly off center, a thicket of microphones taped to it. Oates seized the sides of the podium and squinted into the piercing television lights.

"Is ev'body ready?"

Without waiting for a reply he began, slowly, quietly, gradually building the cadence and volume.

"It saddens me to tell you that there has been a grossly improper attempt to influence the chairman of the Senate Select Committee on Assassinations. In a moment ah will tell you exactly how this thing took place. But first, ah must make it clear to you that the work of the committee will go forward, as the Senate intended for it to. Our inquiry will not be influenced or deterred by fear or favor."

Someone at a press table said something out loud.

"Ah will take your questions when ah am done, friends. Be patient. Now the facts. The facts are: that the Attorney General, Mr. Carleton Smythe, approached me and offered me several valuable inducements to deflect the committee's investigation away from President Frankling." He looked up for effect. The gallery buzzed; it was, indeed, a Big Moment. He slowed his pace.

"Since the President is the Chief Magistrate under the Constitution of the United States, and the Attorney General the principal law enforcement officer, ah have nowhere to turn for redress, except to turn to the people." He nearly shouted the word "people." "That is what ah am doin' this mornin'. What was attempted was reprehensible, but it was also doomed to failure. *This* United States Senator is not for sale!"

The big room echoed Oates's climax. He looked into the lights, his eyes darting. After a dramatic pause he said he would take questions. One answer described Smythe's telephone calls to Oates in detail. He told with great particularity what everyone had said, including what the White House operators had said in completing the calls. Yes, Smythe had been his only contact. He had only Smythe's word that the President told Smythe to call him. No, nothing of value—nothing whatever, in fact—changed hands. He had rejected the subornation. No, he did not withhold the White House subpoenas. They were now issued, he explained. Once the committee majority had met and considered them, they were signed and served. Even now the records were being produced. What did Smythe offer him? Oates told with relish the Bible story of the Devil tempting Jesus. The Attorney General had implied that he too was offering the whole world, Oates said.

Yes, it was up to the entire Senate to decide if contempt charges should be brought. Oates would wait until the hearings were over to submit that issue to the Senate.

Yes, he was flatly accusing the Attorney General of attempted bribery.

Wire service reporters ran for their telephones. Oates walked slowly toward the door to the rotunda, nodding, engulfed in a knot of shouting reporters and photographers. He acted as though he did not hear their questions. At the door two policemen moved in to help him through the narrow entrance. Oates shunned the network reporters in the rotunda who called to him. A waiting elevator took him away, leaving the boiling aftermath of journalists. There were too few phones. Some reporters darted into Senators' offices nearby. Others ran off down the halls.

Ten minutes later Les Carew assembled the White House press corps. Some had arrived early, in anticipation of a White House reply to Oates's charges. Not everyone was there, but there were enough: the wire services, the *Star-Post,* the *Times* and the networks. With a few words of introduction, Carew offered up Carleton Smythe, the Attorney General, to answer Oates's charges.

Smythe's hand trembled. He gripped the podium, cleared his throat and looked at Carew. Carew nodded encouragement.

"The fact is," Smythe began, "that Senator Oates's allegation is wholly false. Absolutely . . . false." Smythe cleared his throat again. "Senator Oates approached me, asking *quid pro quo* to stall the Uruguay investigation. Oates called me. I turned him down, flatly. I refused to stop the tax case against his brother-in-law and refused all the other stuff he wanted. That was the end of it."

Smythe answered questions as the cameras in the back of the Press Room ground out the footage that would appear on the evening news, along with the clips of Oates's charges.

Yes, Oates wanted other specific things: mining permits, price supports for his friends. No, Smythe hadn't told the President about it. Yes, he might file charges, but had decided to wait until the hearings were over.

Yes, he supposed he would still be a witness before the committee. Yes, he was sure the chairman would have some tough questions for him now.

Whom had he told about Oates's call? No one. No, he hadn't tape-recorded it, but his recollection was very clear.

No, nothing of value had changed hands. Nothing at all.

Yes, he was charging the chairman with soliciting a bribe.

Les Carew then cut off the questions. The networks had all the film they would use. And Smythe's denial was categorical. It would move clearly on the wires, so nothing could be gained by leaving Smythe up there for them to gnaw at. Carew led the Attorney General into his office, opened a cabinet behind his desk and poured some gin into a glass.

"Thanks." Smythe drank deeply. "Was that all right?"

"Excellent. I think you neutralized the thing beautifully. Now, when you get over to your office, say nothing to your regular Justice Department press. Johnny Tashlen can just tell them you stand on what was said here. I'll call him, too."

"Fine." Smythe was feeling sick. "Where's a toilet?"

"Out there, first on your right."

Smythe left Carew's office hurriedly. Carew followed him, motioning to his secretary.

"Look out for Smythe when he comes out. I'm going to tell the President how things are going."

Professor Irving Anschults fidgeted in his chair. The television lights were beginning to bother his eyes; they shone straight at him from the back of the room. He had a slight headache, and he would have preferred to spend that afternoon in his office. The White House records—or at least some of them—had come in, and Anschults wanted to examine them in detail. Instead, he had to be there on the dais beside Harley Oates. The initial inspection was assigned to a young man on his staff.

The Secretary of State was a distinguished but *pro forma* witness leading off the Tuesday lineup. He deplored any interference in the internal affairs of the other nations of the hemisphere. The Administration abhorred political assassination, as a matter of policy. He knew nothing of the Uruguayan plot.

Senator Larkin asked the Secretary some general questions about the Department of State's ability to work with the CIA. They batted back and forth the question of who should be informed of the CIA's covert operations. Other Senators chimed in, but the rest of the questions were predictable and uninteresting.

Donald Dooley then took the Secretary's place with two lawyers, one to sit behind him and take the long view, the other to occupy the second chair at the witness table. Dooley declined to make an opening statement. He had been subpoenaed; he was volunteering nothing. So Irving Anschults questioned him at length. In fact, Anschults was still at it at four o'clock when Senator Stapleton passed Chairman Oates a note and Oates declared a recess until noon Wednesday.

At the recess Anschults still had two pages of questions he wanted to ask Dooley. He gathered his papers into a briefcase while trying to talk with three reporters who were standing below the dais, asking about Dooley's apparent connection with the CIA.

"You heard his answers," Anschults said. "Draw your own conclusions. I don't have any evidence one way or the other."

"But," one of the reporters said, "why not subpoena CIA employment records? You can do that, can't you?"

"If it's vital. I'm not sure it is, at least at this juncture. We'll see."

Anne Marie Himmel tapped Anschults' arm. "Sorry, Irv, but you'd better come down to the office right away. Clark needs you."

Anschults brushed off the reporters, hefted his briefcase and followed the tall woman.

"What has been going on?" he asked.

She was moving fast through the crowded noisy rotunda. She dove down the curving stairway and he lost sight of her. A reporter with a tape recorder was moving beside the professor, yelling questions at him, holding a microphone toward him. The headache was getting worse. Anschults clumped down two flights of stairs, displayed his pass and opened the briefcase for the policeman at the checkpoint, then moved quickly down the guarded hallway to his office door.

Clark, Anne Marie and another woman were standing by his desk.

"What's the rush? What have you got?"

"The ship's log." Clark pointed to a pile of photocopies on the desk.

"So?"

"So Robin Warren wasn't aboard the boat."

"Bullshit. Let me see."

"This is the one for May thirty-first. See: here's where the passengers came aboard. Frankling and Smythe."

"How about other dates?"

"Nope. He's never been on that boat when Frankling was, all the way back to January."

Anschults sat heavily into his chair, took off his glasses and rubbed his eyes. "Anne Marie, could I have some coffee?"

"Sure."

"So?" He looked at Clark. "Is Warren that big a liar? What have we got here?"

"I don't know. I believed him."

"So did I," Anschults said. "Maybe I wanted to." He looked for his coffee, then back at Clark. "Do any of these records help us?"

"Nope, there's no corroboration of Warren's story anywhere in there. Nothing."

Anne Marie came back with a Styrofoam cup of coffee. "You'd better read this about Capron." She pointed to a memorandum. "He has skipped. Also, your wife and daughter are out there."

"Yeah. I was going to take them to dinner. You'd better tell her—"

"Whoa, Irv. Wives I don't tell."

"What?" He looked from the memorandum to the tall woman distractedly.

"I said, I've worked on the Hill long enough to know better than to tell wives that their husbands are too busy to take them out to dinner."

"Why not?"

"Somehow, wives don't understand such things coming from a woman like me."

"They don't?"

"They don't."

"OK. So ask her to come in, then, and I'll tell her myself."

"With pleasure."

He reached for the telephone as Anne Marie and Clark walked out.

"This is Anschults. I need to talk to the chairman. Already? Well, where can I get him? OK."

He dialed another five-digit number.

"Senator Stapleton, this is Irving Anschults calling. We have a problem with subpoenaing Auguste Capron."

"Oh?"

"He's left the country."

"Where is he?"

"The Bahamas—Lyford Cay. He has a house there."

"We missed him, eh?"

"I'm not sure. We've served an adult at his New York residence, and he's been personally served in the Bahamas. His New York lawyers have moved to quash both of them."

"Who is right?"

"He's probably right about the New York try—it's no good. But I think we got him in the islands. The fact that he was in another country shouldn't make any difference."

"Can we get a decision in time?"

"Oh, I think so. But I'll need to assign a couple of the lawyers to these motions, full time."

"Do that. Let's get him."

"Yes, sir."

"What about the actress?"

"She's in Australia. The FBI man in the embassy there will serve her. We should get her any time now."

"Okay, Professor. Keep me posted."

"I will, Senator Stapleton. One other problem. We have the White House records now and they are bad news. Robin Warren is a liar."

"In what respect, Professor?" Stapleton asked. He smiled at the young reporter seated beside his desk.

"The ship's log indicates Warren has never been on the yacht with the President—at least not this year any time," Anschults said.

"I see. Is there anything—?"

"No, no corroboration anywhere. I can't reach Senator Oates until ten tonight. He's gone to New York."

"All right. I'd suggest you call Wong, Goldmark and Speers. I think we should caucus in the morning and decide what to do. OK?"

"Fine. I'll do that." Anschults hung up. His wife and fourteen-year-old daughter were standing in the doorway.

"Hi. Come on in."

"So, we didn't want to disturb the busy man," Rebecca Anschults said. "Are you about ready?"

"What did you think of the hearing, Marcie?" he asked the girl.

"I could barely see," she said. "We were way over at the side."

"That's too bad. I saw you there."

"Elizabeth Taylor was there. I saw her. She was sitting right in the front in the middle."

"Could you hear me asking the questions?"

"Sure. But I didn't understand it. What's a farm-suital?"

"Pharmaceutical. That's a drug. The man said he worked for a drug company. I'm not so sure he did."

"Are you about ready? We can visit at dinner," his wife urged.

"I have to make three calls," he said wearily. "It will be thirty or forty minutes, anyway. Maybe we shouldn't try it tonight."

"Is that any way to have a family?" Rebecca's voice rose. "Always the work before the family?"

"Look, you can wait or you can go. Either way." He ran his fingers through his hair. "I've got to make these calls quickly, before the Senators leave. Just sit there. I'll call while you wait."

"Well, Marcella," his wife said loudly, "how does it feel to be so loved and wanted by your father? It must feel wonderful. He drops everything and takes you to the best place in town when you come in! Lucky girl."

"Momma." The girl was embarrassed.

Anschults dialed a phone number. "It's all right, Marcie. We'll go in a minute," he said.

"Come in, Robin. Did you watch Dooley?" Leonard Weil stood behind his bare desk, a yellow note pad in his hand.

"Yes. I took a bunch of notes. Sari said to tell you she'll be right in."

"All right. I think the most important thing he said was that the CIA made a lot of recommendations, not just one. Is that right?"

"He's wrong about that. There were no other options—just *Methodist Missionary*."

"He says the coup took him by surprise. Wasn't it discussed?"

"In great detail. He talked about the people his company could get to participate."

"All right, let's go down the list, Robin: He admits Capron's big worry was expropriation of the telephone company down there. He says Capron talked to the President about that—hearsay, but rules of evidence don't count in one of these things. No question, so far. Then, he said he had a call from you to come to a meeting. Did you call him?"

"No. The CIA called my secretary to say he was joining Cooper Dewey and me."

Weil made notes in the margin of his pad. "And I tried to get his exact words on this next: 'I sensed that Mr. Warren had had prior conversations with the CIA about Uruguay.' Was that his testimony?"

294

"Yeah. His implication was that it was all cooked up before he got there. That Dewey and I staged a charade for him."

"Exactly. And?"

"And, it's not true."

"He denies making any recommendations to you. The CIA man gave you six options and Dooley just sat there. Did you know he was a former CIA agent?"

"Not until several weeks later. After the plot failed."

"How I wish I could cross-examine Mr. Dooley," Weil exclaimed. "What fun we could have with him!"

"Isn't there some way? Anschults or someone?"

"John Goldmark." Weil nodded. "I will call him, now. I think he'll put the questions for us. First I wanted to talk with you." He summoned his secretary. "I'll have Senator Goldmark now, please."

Weil reviewed his notes, line by line, until a buzzer sounded, then picked up the phone, still looking at his pad.

"John? Lenny. Good to hear you."

"Hello, Lenny. Is this about the Uruguay hearing?"

"Yes, I represent Robin Warren, you know, John. This fellow Dooley you have on the stand does not have the truth in him. I thought perhaps you'd like a few clues."

Goldmark sounded humorless. "I don't think I can help you, Lenny."

"Have I offended you by calling, John? If so—"

"No, no. Not that. But your client is in serious difficulty with the committee, in case you didn't know."

"How's that?"

"We've just had the return from our subpoenas, Lenny. The military records you wanted us to get."

"And?"

"And your man has not been telling us—you and us—the truth."

"In what regard?" Weil looked at Robin Warren, who had walked to the window.

"Well, for one thing, he wasn't on the yacht at all that night."

"How do you know?"

"The ship's log, Lenny. And the garage records for May thirty-first show he was taken home from his office at six-thirty P.M., not to the boat."

"Can you arrange for me to see those things, John?"

"I don't know, Len. Perhaps you should talk to Oates about that."

"I see."

"Be cautious, old friend. I wouldn't like to see you go too far out on the limb for that boy. I fear he has deceived you."

"Thank you, John. I hear your advice."

"All right, then. Good night."

Weil put down the phone and stared at his note pad, then looked up at Robin.

"Trouble?" Robin asked.

"Trouble is right," Weil said grimly. "They've cooked the books."

CHAPTER **25**   The Wednesday morning *Star-Post* escalated the confrontation between Chairman Harley Oates and Attorney General Carleton Smythe with a banner headline and front-page pictures of the two aged gladiators. Senator Thomas Stapleton read the two-column account of Oates's charges and Smythe's countercharges as the musty elevator eased its way to the fifth floor.

The hallway leading to Harley Oates's apartment needed light bulbs and paint. Someone on the fifth floor was cooking sausages for breakfast. A radio could be heard delivering the morning traffic report through the thin walls. He knocked on the door marked "5-A."

Harley Oates came to the door in blue pajamas and a wine-colored bathrobe.

"Tom! Miss Marianne, it's Senator Stapleton of Connecticut! What a surprise—on our doorstep at dawn. Ah'm delighted. Come right in!" The old Senator was so obviously embarrassed and upset Stapleton almost closed the door and walked away. "Jes' come in the livin' room and Miss Marianne will be right in." Oates hurried out of the room into some back hallway.

The living room had been furnished forty-seven years before, when Harley Oates was a newly married third-term Congressman. The heavy overstuffed furniture was counterpointed by hundreds of small china figurines, dishes and bric-a-brac. Every level surface in the room was jammed with Blue Boys, candy dishes, Disney animals, bud vases, Eiffel Towers, and filigreed plates in profusion. The Oateses had moved to this building only four blocks behind the Capitol when the neighborhood was a fashionable area. When "respectable" people began to move to the big deluxe apartments out in the northwest section, the Oateses had gone to look. But neither of them drove an automobile, and the old Moorish Towers Apartments was still an easy walk to the Senate, the train depot and a long-since-vanished grocery store. So they stayed where they were, as the neighborhood, then the apartment house itself, deteriorated around them. But behind their door life remained as they had always lived it.

"Miss Marianne, I have the signal honor to present my distinguished colleague, Senator Thomas Stapleton of Connecticut." Oates was highly excited. The folds of his face flushed and jiggled. He turned quickly from his wife to Stapleton and back.

"How do you do, Mrs. Oates?"

"An unexpected pleasure, Senator. I hope no unpleasant emergency brings you to our door this mornin'." She was small in all dimensions, a head shorter than her short husband and twig-thin under a quilted housecoat. Her regular features once had been very beautiful, Stapleton could see. Her eyes were jet black, now the only strong points about her.

"No, ma'am, no emergency. I do apologize for coming here like this, but I am concerned about the chairman's situation with the Attorney General today. I felt we must talk."

"Yes, indeed you must," she said. Almost a whisper. "Senator Oates didn't sleep much last night, thinking about all that. It worried me."

"Let's all sit down, Tom." Oates motioned to a large mohair chair. "Have you had your breakfast?"

"Yes, thanks. Look, I'll come right to the point, Harley. I think you should open the hearing today by announcing that you will not take part in the interrogation of Smythe. Turn the gavel over to me."

"What the hell for? That scoundrel has slandered me. He called me a liar and briber. I cannot turn the other cheek! My honor requires me . . ."

"Hush, Senator Oates," his wife said quietly. "I think the Senator has more to say."

"I do, thank you, ma'am. I'm thinking of the long-run outcome of these hearings, Mr. Chairman. If you and Smythe have a big run-in today, there will be two bad results. We'll all be forced to go on the attack, to join with you—to support you—against the administration. That's exactly the opposite of what we agreed to do. And, second, the press will murder us all. We'll be using the committee to adjudicate your dispute. We can't do that. We've got to stay on the high road."

"But, Tom, this would be seen as my own committee supplanting me. That would be taken as censure—a finding that Smythe is innocent and ah am guilty."

"Not if you did it, voluntarily, yourself. Then it would be statesmanship."

"He's right, Senator Oates," Mrs. Oates said, nodding. "Right as can be. If you step forward and suggest it, that will be an act of high purpose."

"Will you interrogate that slanderer rigorously?" Oates asked.

"Not about your controversy, no, Harley. If I were going to do that, then you might as well take him on yourself. We'd have the same bad result. The reason for me to question him is to be able to gracefully avoid the subject entirely."

"Ah understand." Oates turned and looked at his wife. "Why don't you let Miss Marianne and me discuss it, Tom? You've caught us with the day barely begun."

"I think you'd better decide now, sir. If I'm going to do the interrogation this afternoon, I'll need the morning to prepare. That's why I've come here so early."

"Of course."

"You must do it, Oates," the lady said.

The old Senator seemed to lose his inner bracing, slumping in the old chair. "Yes, ma'am, I guess you're right. All right, Tom. Why don't you write out what you think I should say?"

"No, Mr. Chairman. I have great confidence in your ability to find the right words." Stapleton stood. "Mrs. Oates, I apologize for this unannounced intrusion."

"Why, not at all, Senator. I'm afraid you found us unprepared to receive you. I hope you'll forgive my appearance."

"You look charmin', as always, Miss Marianne," her husband said. He grunted as he pushed up and out of his chair. "I'll show you out, Tom."

It was already hot outside. As he followed Oates into the little entry hall of the apartment Stapleton was perspiring. He realized what he'd been missing: there was no air conditioning. Above a narrow table in Oates's entryway was a faded color print of the Egyptian Pyramids. A pair of women's white gloves lay neatly beside a silver calling-card dish on the table. The dish held one card.

Senator Laughlin Lincoln had been questioning Donald Dooley for about five minutes. In the middle of a long, evasive answer Dooley sensed some commotion behind him in the Caucus Room, back to his right. As soon as he could, he turned to see where the photographers were going. They had abandoned their nose-shot vigil on the floor in front of the witness table and were moving back toward the main door, swinging cameras into their hands, checking their settings as they went. A hand-held camera light snapped on, a few spectators stood for a better view and those at the press tables turned and craned their necks.

Just inside the doorway stood Attorney General Carleton Smythe, apparently calm and impassive, flanked by two FBI agents and preceded by two attorneys, both in blue seersucker.

"Be at odah," Oates said, leaning into his microphone. He reached for the gavel as he turned to Stapleton. "What is it?" Oates asked. "Ah can't see what that is back there. What's going on?"

A staff man leaned forward between them and whispered Smythe's name.

"Why don't you finish up your interrogation, Senator Lincoln?" Oates leaned forward and looked to his right. "Are you nearly finished?"

"Well, Mr. Chairman, yes, I'm nearly done. Mr. Dooley, are you saying that your company—ah, ah . . ."

"United International, Senator," Dooley supplied.

"Are you saying that company did nothing whatever to support the assassination of the Uruguayan leaders? In any way? No money at all?"

"That's correct, Senator."

"I have nothing further, Mr. Chairman," Lincoln said.

"Very well," Oates said. "While the witnesses are exchanging places ah have something ah would like to say for the record."

Stapleton shielded his microphone and said, "Mr. Chairman, why not wait until Smythe sits down? There's too much confusion."

Oates grunted. "Very well."

Smythe's entourage moved down the side, along the wall, then turned in front of the press tables, preceded by the photographers walking backward. Some reporters stood to get a better view. It took several minutes for the Justice Department lawyers to get settled, to open briefcases and notebooks, and for the photographers to recede.

Smythe sat, expressionless, wary, waiting for Oates to show some sign of how he was going to attack.

"As ah was sayin', ah have a matter to put on the record," Oates began.

"Mr. Chairman?" The Justice Department lawyer seated next to Smythe leaned forward, his lips nearly touching the microphone in front of Smythe. "Mr. Chairman—"

Oates glared at him. "Ah'm talkin' now, mister. Please don't interrupt me."

"I have a point of personal privilege, Mr. Chairman. My name is—"

"You're out of odah, mister. Be still, now!" Oates thundered. "Ah'm going to say what ah have to say, then everyone else can talk all day long, for all ah care." He paused until the hubbub subsided. "Now, everyone knows that ah have made serious charges against this next witness, the Attorney General. They tell me he has denied them. Ah don't propose to detour this inquiry to air our differences in front of this committee now. There are more appropriate forums for that, later. To be sure nothin' gets off the straight and narrow now, ah'm goin' to hand the gavel to the vice-chairman, Senator Stapleton. He'll preside an' ah don't intend to interrogate this witness at all. Any questions ah think are left unanswered at the end ah will give to the staff to follow up on. Are there any questions about what ah've said?"

He handed the gavel to Stapleton and shoved his chair back six or eight inches. Smythe's lawyer whispered in his client's ear at length.

"Are you ready to proceed, Mr. Attorney General?" Stapleton asked crisply.

"Yes, Mr. Chairman. I have an opening statement I'd like to read."

"Very well."

Smythe opened a thin notebook. "Mr. Chairman and members of the Select Committee on Assassinations," he began.

"Mr. Chairman!" Senator Gurley Speers called out.

Stapleton held up a cautionary finger toward Smythe. "Senator Speers?"

"Mr. Chairman, as a point of order may I point out that the witness has neither made a record of his name and address, nor has he been sworn to tell the truth."

"Thank you, Senator," Stapleton said. "You are quite right. Under some circumstances an oath is not required of a member of the Cabinet, but as I think of it, it should be administered to all witnesses appearing before this Select Committee. Thank you for making the point, to which the chair acquiesces. General, will you please stand and raise your right hand?"

Smythe was sworn, resumed his seat and gave his name and address.

His opening statement was punctuated by the loud click-whine of the automatic cameras; the photographers maneuvered from side to side in front of him, shooting from every angle. Smythe was a dry, uninspired reader. His statement was categorical and carefully written, but hardly dramatic.

He was the President's only guest aboard the *Sea Island* on May 31, he read. He had never been on that vessel with Robin Warren, at any time. Nor had he ever been present, anywhere, when Robin Warren had discussed Uruguay with the President—or when anyone else had discussed Uruguay with the President, for that matter. When Smythe finished reading he closed the notebook and took a drink of water.

Irving Anschults pulled his microphone two inches closer. He started Smythe's interrogation with a series of questions about the legality of the expropriation of Americans' property by foreign governments. It was a subject Smythe knew something about, and he relaxed.

Then Anschults inquired where Smythe had been during the day of May 31. Smythe replied that in the early afternoon his office received the President's invitation to join him for dinner aboard the *Sea Island*. He was driven to the south grounds of the White House about 5:30 P.M., but the President sent word that he should come to the Oval Office. Smythe waited alone in the Cabinet Room for ten minutes or so, then joined the President for a brief conversation. About six they walked to the President's waiting limousine and were driven to the boat.

Q. Where was the yacht?
A. At the Old Navy Yard.
Q. On the Anacostia River?
A. Yes, sir.
Q. What route was driven there from the White House?
A. We went by the Tidal Basin, then a short distance on the freeway.
Q. Who was aboard the yacht?
A. The crew, the President and I.
Q. No one else?
A. Not that I saw.
Q. Did the yacht leave—ah, when did it leave?
A. As soon as the President arrived.
Q. What time was that, General?
A. I'm not positive. I would estimate it was about six-thirty.
Q. P.M.?
A. Yes. But the ship's log doubtless will show the time exactly.
Q. And how long was the boat gone from the Navy Yard?
A. About an hour and forty or forty-five minutes; under two hours.
Q. So, if you left at six-thirty P.M., you returned about eight-ten or eight-fifteen, is that right?
A. Yes.
Q. Do you know the exact time Robin Warren telephoned the CIA the evening of May thirty-first?
A. I've been told. It was at eight forty-five P.M.

"Mr. Chairman," Anschults interjected, "I will show the exact time of that call by extrinsic, firsthand evidence later. It was, in fact, eight forty-six P.M., according to CIA records."

"Very well," Stapleton said.

Q. So, to state the obvious, Mr. Smythe, if you cruised from six-thirty to eight-fifteen P.M., and Warren's call was not made until eight forty-six P.M., then his call was not made during that cruise. Correct?

A. That's correct. Our cruise had ended about thirty minutes before that. And, I should add, Mr. Warren was not with us.

Q. To be clear, you say he was not a passenger during that cruise, is that correct?

A. That's correct.

"Mr. Chairman," Anschults said, "I have here"—he waved a document—"Exhibit Eighty-seven, marked for identification, which is the official U.S. Navy ship's log of the *Sea Island* for May thirty-first. The one Mr. Smythe referred to. I offer it."

Senator Stapleton looked at him sharply, then took the document. He put his hand over his microphone and asked in a low voice, "Are you going to *prove* the document, Professor?"

"Sir?"

"Prove it—authenticate it? Is the captain going to identify it?"

"Oh. No, sir. It's certified, by the Navy."

"That makes it admissible?"

"Well . . ." Anschults motioned to Clark from his staff to come over.

"Never mind. We'll discuss it later," Stapleton growled. Clark was waved away.

"Go ahead," Stapleton said.

"This log shows that the *Sea Island* departed the Navy Yard dock at 1837 hours." Anschults looked up. "That's six thirty-seven P.M. It docked upon its return at 2020 hours. That's eight-twenty P.M. The total elapsed time was one hour and forty-three minutes.

The log shows the President debarked five minutes later, at 2025 hours."

"I guess I was fairly close," Smythe said.

"Mr. Chairman?"

"Senator Brawley."

"May I ask a question about the log at this juncture for clarification of the Attorney General's testimony?"

"Very well."

"Does the log show the identity of the passengers and crew aboard the *Sea Island* that night?"

"Professor, can you answer that?" Stapleton asked.

"Yes, sir. The crew is not listed. But the passengers are named." He read from the exhibit. " 'The President and the Attorney General.' "

"No one else? Not Mr. Warren?"

"No, sir."

The press tables broke into excited conversation. This was their first exposure to the contents of the log and its significance. A few reporters left the tables and headed for the telephones.

Neither Democrats nor Republicans on the committee subjected Smythe to much cross-examination. Senator Larkin began to ask about Smythe's knowledge of CIA covert operations in South America, the Middle East and Africa. Smythe offered to answer those questions, but only in private, in executive session, so Larkin withdrew them. The television cameras were an inseparable part of this committee, under all circumstances.

Carleton Smythe was off the witness stand in time to take a late lunch at the Metropolitan Club. Harley Oates recovered his gavel from Stapleton as Smythe disappeared through the Caucus Room door.

"Mr. Chairman," Anschults began, "the Central Intelligence Agency has objected to the appearance in public of certain of its employees who had been subpoenaed. In lieu of their appearance, we have been provided with affidavits containing the substance of the testimony they would have provided had they appeared."

"What exhibits are those?"

"Exhibits 102 through 104."

"Without objection, they will be received," Oates intoned.

"Mr. Chairman!" Unnoticed, Leonard Weil had slipped into the chair at the witness table. Now his voice boomed to the corners of the room as he shouted into the microphone.

"Who is that?" Oates demanded.

"Mr. Chairman, I am Leonard J. Weil, an attorney of this city, and I appear for Mr. Robin Warren, who has been subpoenaed by this committee."

"You are out of odah, Mr. Weil," Oates said. "We are receivin' certain exhibits at this time."

"Yes, Mr. Chairman, and I am objecting to their introduction. The identity of the persons making those affidavits does not even appear." Weil flourished legal-sized documents. He read from one:

" '(122), being first duly sworn, deposes and says: that he/she was on duty at the switchboard of the Central Intelligence Agency between six P.M. and midnight May thirty-first . . .' Nowhere in all of this is this person identified. The other so-called affidavits are the same kind of smoke screen. I believe I have standing to object to them because these statements appear to be damaging to my client. Mr. Chairman, we should be permitted to know the names of these people. And we should have a right to cross-examine them. Otherwise they are just spooks—just ghosts here."

Oates scowled at Weil. "Counselor, in my view you have no standing here to make objections. This isn't a trial, you see. It is a legislative inquiry. The only persons competent to raise procedural questions are the members of this committee. Now, ah don't hear any member of this body raisin' any such—"

"Mr. Chairman," John Goldmark said.

"Senator Goldmark." Oates's voice dropped in disappointment.

"Mr. Chairman, this CIA procedure has always troubled me, and it bothers me today. I have no way of weighing the value of the statements made in affidavits of this kind. I don't get to see the witness. I can't test his veracity by cross-examination. My sense of equity and fairness is offended. How is an adversary to meet such so-called evidence? No, Mr. Chairman, on points of order and personal privilege I object to these exhibits."

"Very well, Senator. Although this is not an adversary proceeding, ah think this is what we'll do on this," Oates replied. "The committee will stand at recess until noon tomorrow. In forty-five minutes we will convene in executive session to consider this procedure, to which an objection has been made. Recess." He hit his gavel lightly on the counter top and lurched to his feet. "Tell them to come to my office, Professor. An' you be prepared to say who those CIA numbers are. I want to get this all straightened out. A thing like this should never have happened. There are tares in our wheat this afternoon, and I don't like it."

Leonard J. Weil walked slowly from the Caucus Room, purposely attracting reporters as he went. By the time he reached the rotunda he was surrounded by a mob of journalists twelve deep. At once someone passed a chair overhead and the short lawyer bobbed up, steadying himself with one hand on the shoulder of a huge bearded reporter. Microphones of all kinds were thrust at him. "Shut up!" someone yelled. "Quiet!"

"You are all asking me about these CIA documents," Weil yelled. "I have never seen them before today."

The crowd quieted.

"But I have practiced law many years, before courts and commissions of all kinds, and many times before Senate committees. My sense of legal fairness tells me you don't let a person hide behind a number—conceal his identity—make allegations, and then not be subject to cross-examination by anybody. That's not the American legal system.

"In there"—Weil pointed at the door—"is the Committee on Assassinations. It's well named, I think. By this number device someone is trying to bushwhack my client. But I'm not going to permit some CIA agent to snipe at him from concealment. We *demand* the right to cross-examine! It's a fundamental right in this country that not even the CIA, the White House or the Senate can take away from Robin Warren! Or any citizen!"

Weil stood down from the chair and worked his way through the noisy crowd of reporters without answering any of their questions. His car was double-parked outside the basement entrance to take him back to his office. At the office Bernie Sheffleman was waiting at the curb to open the car door. As Weil got out, his young associate began to talk nonstop.

"Mr. Weil, I have two things before you go in: I've found a documents expert, a former FBI man, who is available. He can go look at the ship's log this afternoon. Also, Robin is upstairs and he's pretty nervous. He watched Smythe on television and it's all piling up on him."

"Naturally. All right, bring him in to see me in fifteen minutes. Come, walk with me, Bernie. Let's think about this documents expert. If we use him, everyone is going to know it. It's going to be printed in the paper and it will be on TV that he examined the exhibit. Suppose he won't give us a good opinion? What if he says he can't tell, or he thinks it's genuine? When we don't put him on the stand, everyone says, 'Aha! The log is genuine!' Right?"

"Sure, but what else do you have? Smythe and Dooley killed us up there. You only have Robin's *ipse dixit,* and that ain't much."

"We also have the fact that the yacht and its crew were sent away from here in the dead of night."

"Circumstantial."

"Yes, you're right," Weil said. "It's not much. So, how do we prove Robin Warren was aboard that boat? We must prove the log's been doctored. And the garage records. All right. You get your man lined up. I'll call Anschults and arrange for an inspection."

They had walked slowly up to the corner and back. Sheffleman held the front door for Weil, then followed him into the elevator.

"We'll examine the documents," Weil continued, "but that's not enough. The best testimony we can get may be only a disputed opinion. We need more."

"We need the ship's captain to testify he saw Robin there," Sheffleman said.

"Come into my office," Weil directed, leading the way. "Bernard, can you find the captain?"

Sheffleman shook his head slowly. "So far we're not even positive of his name. I wouldn't know where to begin."

"Keep pressing the investigators. They must find us someone from that boat."

Sheffleman nodded.

"Now," Weil said, "I'll call about those documents. You go line up your expert."

Irving Anschults was not available for Leonard Weil's telephone call. He was in Chairman Oates's office listening to the ebb and flow of the continued debate between Oates and John Goldmark. Finally, Oates impatiently cut off the discussion and asked for a vote of the whole committee. Only Goldmark voted in favor of permitting Weil to cross-examine any committee witness. Only Goldmark and Larkin voted to require the CIA to identify the agents who made the affidavits.

At Senator Wong's suggestion, there was implicit agreement that someone had to go before the cameras to explain the reason for denying cross-examination. "No one can explain it convincingly," Goldmark said, "because it's so unfair. Everyone will see through you."

"It's the difference between an adversary judicial proceeding and a legislative inquiry," Oates said. "Anyone can understand that."

Thomas Stapleton pointed to Arthur Brawley. "The vote was bipartisan; I think the explanation should be. Arthur, why don't you and Harley do it?"

There was a murmur of assent. As Oates and Brawley were sent off to the cameras in the rotunda, Irving Anschults excused himself; he half ran to his office. He felt desperately pressured. Tomorrow was Robin Warren Day, and Anschults knew he needed more time for preparation. As he went through his outer office he asked his secretary to reach Leonard Weil. The buzzer was sounding by the time he got to his desk to pick up his telephone.

"No cross-examination, Mr. Weil," he announced.

"I'm disappointed, but not surprised, Irv. Call me Lenny. What about the CIA names? Do we get to know who the affiants are? Who's accusing us?"

"No. Just the numbers. It's a legislative inquiry, not a trial."

"One other question—about Exhibits Eighty-seven and Eighty-eight: I'd like to send a couple of fellows up to look at them this afternoon. There's no objection, is there?"

"Who?"

"Bernie Sheffleman from my office and another man."

"Who?"

"A documents man."

"You think the log's a fake?" Anschults' voice rose a little.

"I don't know. That's why I want them to look. I'm no expert. I can't tell."

"I'm not sure about that. It's a Navy document. I'll talk to Senator Oates."

"I'll tell you what—I'll take a chance, Irv. They'll be up there at four. You talk to Oates. But on this one, if you exclude us you'd better have a damned good reason. It won't be enough to say it's a legislative inquiry. I'll raise such hell you wouldn't believe."

"I'd believe," Anschults said wearily.

"So, how's my client today? We made some headway up there this afternoon; did you hear?" Weil's enthusiasm was strained.

"Yes, I heard," Robin Warren said. "I was in a cab coming down here. I heard you on the radio. In case you're interested, the cab driver disagrees: he doesn't think you made any headway. He thinks I'm a liar and you're a shyster."

"Did he recognize you?"

"Not until after he'd said that. Then he tried to bluster his way through. As far as he's concerned, I'm guilty, and he doesn't even know what I'm charged with!"

"I hope you didn't tip him! Did you watch Smythe?"

"That son of a bitch. They hardly asked him a single tough question. I thought the Democrats were going to go after him."

"I think the ship's log and the other records have scared them off. They don't want to appear totally irresponsible."

"Things are really stacking up against me, aren't they?"

"It's darkest before the dawn, so they say. I'm sending an expert up to examine the log. I think he'll find it's a fake."

"How can we prove it?"

"The ink. Usually a falsified book of entry shows all of the entries in the same ink. Ultraviolet rays show that. Authentic entries are normally made at different times with different pens or pencils. They should appear different under the light. Experts take photos that expose falsification."

"Will they let your man take pictures?"

"I'll know in a little while. Bernie should be there very soon."

"My opening statement is ready to go," Robin said.

"Good. Leave it with Sari and we'll have it duplicated." Weil looked at his client intently. "Listen to me, young man. I know you are feeling the pressure. There is just one antidote for it: be confident. In the beginning I asked you to promise me you would only tell the truth. Right?"

"Yes."

"All right. If you are telling the truth you have a right to be confident. Does that sound old-fashioned and unrealistic? Well, it's not. The liar has to worry that maybe he can't keep his false story straight. You don't have that problem. You just tell it the way it happened."

"OK." Robin's mouth was dry. This was a typical pretrial pep talk he'd heard given a dozen times at the Butler firm in San Francisco. It came with the yellow pads and the form book.

"Look, Mr. Weil—Leonard. I'm beginning to realize how much all this is costing. The documents expert has to be paid up front, I know. And you are putting in your full time—all three of you. The fact is, I don't even know how I'm going to pay my rent at the end of the month. I'm sorry, but it's going to be a long time before I can begin to pay you."

"Robin, if your morale were better today I wouldn't tell you this; I am not supposed to. But I don't think Jep will mind, under the circumstances. The fact is, my retainer is paid in full. And all our expenses are guaranteed. Your friend Jep Valle has taken care of everything, so you are not to worry. That should brighten your outlook."

"It does, of course, but I . . . I hate to be in this position."

"Jep is a generous man. So you must be gracious."

"Right. Sure. Where and when do you want me in the morning, Leonard?" Robin's mind was jammed with reactions. He needed to get out and walk and think. Perhaps he could call Maggie. He wondered if she knew. He stood up restlessly.

"I want you here at nine. The blue suit, remember. We'll talk over the questions you'll probably get, eat a little something, then drive up in my car. Nine sharp."

"OK. Good night."

Warren rode the little elevator to the basement and left Weil's building by the service entrance. A narrow lane led to the street to the north. As he emerged, a mailman was emptying a mailbox at the curb. The man looked up and smiled.

"Good luck t'morra, Mr. Robin. Give 'em hell!"

Warren was not yet fully accustomed to the public's acute awareness of his identity. His picture was on the evening news almost daily now, and it had become impossible for him to go anywhere in the city without being recognized. Some, like the mailman, spoke; usually, almost invariably, those who did said something friendly. Others, mostly whites, were elbow grabbers. Robin would be walking along a street, eyes straight ahead, and he'd peripherally see a passing woman grab the arm of her companion—she'd recognized him. He was beginning to notice the relationship between recognition and eye contact, too. If he avoided eye contact with people in a crowd he might not be recognized. But, for a reason he did not understand, if he met someone's gaze he increased by a substantial percentage the probability of being recognized by that person.

He smiled and nodded to the mailman. A half block away he

found a phone booth. He called Maggie Valle at her office, person to person, collect.

"Robin, how are you?"

"OK, I guess. I have opening-night jitters, of course."

"Sure you have. Listen, I'm going to come down tomorrow morning. Can I get in—get a seat?"

"I suppose. I really don't know. But please come down. I'll be glad to see you."

"We can have dinner together tomorrow, after the session?"

"Sure. But bring money. I'm nearly broke. Unemployed people have a chronic shortage of money, I'm discovering."

"Sure. Don't worry."

"Your father paid Lenny Weil's retainer."

"Well, I'll be damned."

"Did you know that?"

"No. Is that good, sweetheart?"

"I don't like it. I'm sure he meant well, but I wish he'd talked to me first."

"No one did?"

"It was a secret, I guess."

"Sort of typical of Jep, though. *La geste grande.*"

"I'm going to talk to him about it," Robin said.

"Wait until you're finished at the committee, Bird. Keep your mind clear. Are you sleeping?"

"Sure. Well, not much."

"Why not take a pill?"

"No."

"Up to you. Look, for heaven's sake don't get involved in a ticket for me. I'll get in, don't worry."

"Call Lenny now. He's still there. I just left him. He'll take care of it."

"OK, I'll do it. 'Bye, Bird. I love you."

"I love you, too, Mags. It'll be good to see you."

He thought of calling someone to have dinner with. Kathy O'Reilly, perhaps. But he had no appetite for food or conversation. It would be awful to sit and watch someone try to cheer him up. It was about a mile to his house on Reservoir from Weil's office. It would feel good to walk, even in the heat. He took off his jacket and tie, rolled up his shirtsleeves and began to walk vigorously, passing pedestrians, oblivious to their recognition and surprise.

CHAPTER **26**   Leonard J. Weil took his wife's brown dog for a walk every evening after work while Myra Weil prepared dinner. His dog-walking route was always the same: down Dexter to Forty-ninth, right to Fulton Street, up the hill to Foxhall, right to Dexter and back to the white brick house.

As the poodle sniffed and tugged her way toward the front walk, Weil more than casually examined a tall young woman in a wheat-colored sleeveless dress who stood at the curb in front of his house by an old Fiat. She was neither beautiful nor plain, by ordinary definition, but he thought her attractive. Weil liked her bearing. Alert. Straight caramel-colored hair. Sensuous wide mouth.

"Mr. Weil?" Good green eyes too.

"Yes?"

"I apologize for waylaying you this way at your home, but I must talk to you." A husky voice.

"Are you a journalist?"

She smiled at the idea. "No. I'm a schoolteacher. Elementary school. In Bethesda."

"What can I do, Miss . . . ?"

"I am Carla Simpson, Mr. Weil. I think I may be able to tell you something helpful about the Robin Warren case."

"Well." He looked down and shook the leash impatiently. "Damn dog. Will you come in, please, Miss Simpson? I'd like to hear what you know."

She waited on the porch while he wiped the dog's feet with a towel, removed his shoes and released the poodle. It ran into a hallway and headed for the kitchen sounds.

"Come in, please. Getting all these details taken care of with the dog is the most important thing I do all day. Especially cleaning the dog's feet."

"Shall I?" She lifted a shoe.

"Oh, God, no, my dear. You're company. It's only family that can't have dirty feet. Myra?" he called. "Myra? We have a guest!"

"What?" from the kitchen.

"A guest. Miss Simpson."

"Miss who?" Footsteps, the dog leading the way.

Myra Weil was two heads shorter than Carla Simpson and half again as wide. "Miss?"

"Miss Simpson, dear. This is Mrs. Weil. Miss Simpson was out front. She may know something important relating to Robin Warren."

"Where to hide should be the most important thing to that young man this evening. How his mother must feel!" Myra Weil wiped her hands on an apron. "Well, show Miss Simpson in, Lenny. May I give you some coffee, dear?"

"Thank you."

"Lenny?"

"Please. We'll go in the den. This way, Miss Simpson."

Myra Weil followed with mugs and a coffeepot, then returned to her kitchen.

Carla Simpson sat on the front of a large leather chair, her long legs together tightly, her hands clasped. Weil sat across the small room in a cane chair, balancing his coffee cup on his knee. He liked her sensible looks.

"Now, what can you tell me, please?"

"I know a young man who was second officer on the *Sea Island*."

315

Weil put his cup on the floor, drew a thin pen from an inside pocket and asked, "His name?"

"Martin Slinde. He's a Navy lieutenant; a full lieutenant."

Weil wrote on a pad he took from his desk.

"Was he aboard on May thirty-first?"

"I think so."

"You're not sure?"

"No. I only deduce he was. He was on duty that day. Before he was shipped out he told me about a trip that sounds like the one you all have been arguing about."

"Where is he, Miss Simpson?"

"In Italy. Naples, I think. Under some kind of tight restriction."

"Have you heard from him?"

"Indirectly. He sent me a message by someone. Orally. He's not permitted to write."

"Why?"

"I don't know."

"What was the message?"

"Only that he's OK, and not to worry. He will call me as soon as he can. That's all. I'm only guessing. I don't know if any of this will help you or not." She swung her tight knees from left to right, shifting her weight.

"Tell me what Lieutenant Slinde told you about the yacht trip."

"He was very upset at the President for being so drunk that he disrupted the Washington Salute."

"The what?"

"The formal Navy salute opposite George Washington's grave at Mount Vernon."

"I'm afraid I don't know about that."

"Marty has told me about it. Every U.S. Navy ship is required to stop, lower its colors, play the national anthem, and have a deck parade when it goes by there."

"Without exception?"

"I think so. I think it's a law."

"And were there people with the President?"

316

"He said it was Mr. Smythe and someone else. Smythe was drunk, too. Marty was very disillusioned that they would act that way. He's—he was—very proud to be on the President's yacht crew, but it was an eye-opening experience for him. For both of us."

"Are you and Lieutenant Slinde engaged?"

"Not officially; I don't have a ring yet. But we have an understanding."

"Have you any idea why he was transferred?"

"The yacht was sent to some Navy yard for dry-docking. He was to come right back here once they got it up out of the water. But I didn't hear anything from him for a long time. Then this fellow called with that message. That's all. That Marty is all right. No reasons. But when I watched the Senate hearings this week, I began to make the connection. It's because he knows your client was aboard, isn't it?"

"It must be. It must be! Can you come to the office with me tonight, dear? I may want you to tell some friends of mine about the Mount Vernon"—he looked at his notes—"the Washington Salute."

"But not testify!" She made a mock grimace.

"Oh, no. Don't worry. No surprises like that. You have arrived in the nick of time, thank God. Just let me make a phone call now, and find out about this ceremony."

Weil dialed his office number and asked for Sari Kahn.

"Sari, ever hear of the Washington Salute? At Mount Vernon? Navy ships?"

"No," Sari replied.

"Find this for me, please: a statute or regulation requiring every Navy ship to stop in the Potomac and salute Washington's grave at Mount Vernon. We need an authenticated copy."

"What do they do? Shoot a cannon?"

"No, they play the anthem, and line up on deck. But find this for me: when they have this ceremony, must it be entered in the ship's log?"

"OK. Anything else?"

"Yes, please have Bernie and our client in my office in one hour. You be there, too."

"I'll see you in a few minutes."

"Goodbye." Weil smiled at Carla Simpson. "That's a fine young woman, Sarepta Kahn. She does good work. Shall we have some dinner? I'd like to take you to my office tonight, if you don't mind. This information is crucial. Can you spend the evening? You could leave your car and we'll bring you back here."

Carla Simpson looked surprised, then a little pleased. Diminutive elderly men can get away with things like that, of course. "Well, I hadn't planned to."

"We may be able to bring your lieutenant home, my dear. I think we can if we work together. Myra," Weil called to his wife, "Miss Simpson is staying for dinner."

Warren was in a chair in Weil's office when the lawyer entered with Carla Simpson, trailed by Sari Kahn and Bernie Sheffleman. Weil introduced the girl to everyone, seated them and pointed at Robin.

"Put down the coffee, young man, and think about your May thirty-first boat ride."

"OK, I'm thinking."

"You sailed along, south?"

"Yes."

"By the airport?"

"Yes."

"Then what did you see?"

"The flames from Blue Plains."

"What next?"

"The bridge."

"The interstate—the Woodrow Wilson?"

"Right. Then Fort Washington."

"All right."

"Then, nothing much until Mount Vernon."

318

"George Washington's home. All right. Then?"

"Well, then the yacht stopped briefly before we turned around and went back."

"Back north?"

"Yes."

"Tell us about what happened when you stopped." Weil shot a glance at Carla Simpson.

"The crew all lined up on the foredeck and saluted Mount Vernon. They rang their bell and played 'The Star-Spangled Banner.' "

"Had you mentioned that before?"

"I don't think so. I totally forgot about it."

"No," Sheffleman said. "I'm sure he didn't mention it. We haven't gone through the trip step by step that way before."

"Why did they do that, Robin?" Weil asked.

"A crewman said they always salute 'Ol' George.' "

"Bernie, I want that big map of D.C.—make sure you get the one which extends to Mount Vernon. And a ruler!"

"Robin, how fast did that boat cruise that night?"

"I don't know; not fast."

"What time did you turn at Mount Vernon?"

"I'm not sure. It was just dusk. You could barely see Washington's house up there on the hill. Around eight, I'd guess."

"Bernie— Isn't he back?" Sheffleman came in with a map five feet square. "Give Carla the ruler, please. Now go find out what time the sun set here on May thirty-first. Quickly!" Weil commanded. "Carla, I need a measurement. How far is it from the Navy Yard—going on the river now—to Mount Vernon? Sari, help her find the Navy Yard there."

The women spread the map on the floor and traced fingers up the Anacostia River.

"Here it is," Carla said.

"Robin, think," Weil insisted. "Your ground speed becomes very important. Can you estimate your downriver speed?"

"I'd guess no more than eight or nine miles an hour. Maybe ten."

"And slower on the return trip, eh? Against the current, of course."

"No, I think they speeded up to compensate for that."

"So, about the same?"

"I don't know. It was dark."

"Fifteen inches, Mr. Weil." Carla looked at him, then at Robin. "That's fifteen miles. One way."

"Sari, fifteen miles at ten miles an hour? Quick!"

"Ninety minutes," she snapped.

"What time did it leave the dock?"

"Robin says about six twenty-five."

"Add ninety minutes. That's seven fifty-five." Weil computed. "How long did the salute take?"

"Five minutes," Robin replied.

"So you start back at eight. Fifteen miles back—you're not back until nine-thirty! Nine-thirty P.M.!"

"That sounds about right."

"All right, now, Robin, let's figure this out. *Where* were you on the river when you phoned?"

"I don't know. It was dark. You couldn't see anything once we turned around. Really dark. The only thing I saw—"

Sheffleman burst in. "Sunset was at 2010 Daylight Time, official."

"Good," Weil said. He rose and walked to where he could see the notes Sari Kahn had made on a tablet on the floor. "Now, Sari, assume the same speed on return, on the next line. That's right. Good."

Weil turned to Robin. "What was the only thing you saw, you were saying?"

"The bridge. The big supports loomed out of the dark as we went under. That's—that's where we were when I phoned!"

"Are you sure?"

"Yes, the bridge overhead interfered with the phone transmission!" Robin hit a fist into a hand. "That's exactly where we were. At eight forty-six, didn't they say?"

320

Weil craned to see the map. "Carla, what is the distance from Mount Vernon to the Wilson Bridge?"

"About—between seven and eight miles."

"Sari, seven and a half miles in forty minutes?"

"Eleven-plus miles per hour."

"It fits," Weil said with satisfaction. "Under the bridge at eight forty-six P.M."

"Do you want to hear about the ceremony?" Sari asked.

"We all do." Weil nodded. He sat in the chair by his window.

Sari opened a thin file and read from her notes. " 'Regulation 1801. Ships Passing Washington's Tomb. When a ship of the Navy is passing Washington's tomb, Mount Vernon, Virginia, between sunrise and sunset, the following ceremonies shall be observed insofar as may be practicable: The full guard and band shall be paraded, the bell tolled, and the national ensign half-masted at the beginning of the tolling of the bell. When opposite Washington's tomb, the guard shall present arms, persons on deck shall salute, facing in the direction of the tomb, and "Taps" shall be sounded.' "

"That's right," Robin said. "They played a terrible, tinny recording of 'Taps.' "

" 'The national ensign shall be hoisted to the truck or peak and the tolling shall cease at the last note of "Taps," after which the National Anthem shall be played. Upon completion of the National Anthem, "Carry on" shall be sounded.' "

"Fine. Now," Weil said to Carla Simpson and Sari, "suppose a boat went all thirty miles in less than two hours, leaving about six-thirty and returning at eight-twenty. How fast would it have to run?"

Both women performed computations, then looked at each other.

"Sixteen point thirty-nine?" Carla asked.

"That's what I got," Sari said. "Sixteen and a third miles per hour. Pretty fast for a boat."

"And that allows no time for turnaround, or for the ceremony

321

or slowing. To go to Mount Vernon and back in that elapsed time they'd be going over twenty knots at times," Shefieman said.

"It didn't happen," Robin said flatly.

"Sari, if a Navy ship performs this Washington ceremony, must it be entered in the ship's log?"

"The regulation doesn't say. I'll try to find out tomorrow."

"Yes, you do that." Weil turned to his client. "I have not explained to you about Miss Simpson, Robin. Her bancé is a young Navy officer who was aboard the yacht the night you were. Perhaps you saw him. She tells me he is tall and thin. He was the second oficer."

"I saw several officers at that ceremony," Robin said. "I remember talking to one about the President."

"Martin is quite blond, about six foot one, with a short haircut. Martin Slinde," Carla Simpson said.

"He may have been the one I talked to. I don't know," Robin replied.

Leonard Weil pointed to Carla Simpson's purse. "I'll bet you have a picture of him, don't you?"

The girl smiled and opened her bag. "As a matter of fact, I have three." She produced the snapshots and handed them to Robin Warren.

He nodded. "I remember him."

"The question is," Weil corrected, "will he remember you?"

"I think so. He made some crack about the President. I said something back. He should recall it."

Weil took the photographs and examined them closely. "Carla dear, may I photocopy these? We won't damage them."

Carla Simpson nodded. Weil handed the photos to Bernie Shefieman.

"Bernie," Weil said, "I want you to go to Naples. Tonight, if possible. You find this young man; then, once we know exactly where he is, I promise you, we will raise so much hell they will release him and you will bring him back. Go get a reservation and pack some shirts. Let Sari know where you are at all times. Be on your way now. This must be done at once."

"I'd like to talk to Miss Simpson a little," Sheffleman said. "The more I know about him, the better."

Weil nodded. "All right, you two use your office. I expect to hear that you've found him tomorrow, but certainly within thirty-six hours. Is that clear?"

"Yes, sir."

"Go with God," Weil said solemnly.

The narrow Georgetown house was too warm, so most of the guests had moved out to the garden. The warm night lay on the city like a wet pillow; it was a fire escape night, Sari Kahn thought to herself. In Baltimore, fifteen years ago on hot nights like this, she and her brother were permitted to sleep on a mattress out on the fire escape. That was, of course, before the family moved to Columbia and had air conditioning.

A deputy to the deputy assistant of something had been coming on to her all evening at the party, but it was too hot. She couldn't get very interested. He was tall, with curly hair and money—a nice Jewish boy that her mother would love.

". . . we were in that sort of terrace room," he was saying, "and who should come in? Three sheets to the wind?"

"I give up—who?"

"The A.G.'s wife—Smythe's wife. Ever see her in person?"

"No. Drunk?"

"Very. Very blowsy and loud. Everyone in the place watched her. She had a couple of drinks alone, then left. She looks like a big tough broad. I'll bet she gives him hell!"

"He deserves it." Sari Kahn sipped her drink.

"She was talking to the waiter about him. And even the busboy got an earful. The poor A.G. has no secrets, I guess. Boy, how she ran him down!"

"I guess." Sari Kahn looked at a treetop, then back at the young man. "Myron, you are a beautiful creature! Remind me to rape you sometime when it's cooler. Do you know where our hostess keeps her telephone?"

"In the den, near the front door. What did I do?"

"You just gave me a hell of a thought. Hold my drink, OK? I won't be long."

Obviously there was no listing for the Attorney General Smythes in the D.C. phone book. Sari Kahn turned to the U.S. Government pages. Her finger found the number she wanted.

"White House," the operator said.

"Attorney General Smythe's residence, please. This is Mary Klein, his secretary." She shielded the mouthpiece against the party noises behind her.

"One moment, please."

"'Lo?"

"Mrs. Smythe?"

"Who's this?"

"Sari Kahn, Mrs. Smythe. Do you know that Carleton Smythe tried to bribe that Senator Oates but now he denies it?"

"Yeah, ah know. Carley was on TV. Lied like a fuckin' rug. Who did you say you are?"

"Sari. Sari Kahn. Listen, I'm just downstairs. Isn't that nice?"

"Lovely, honey."

"Why don't you and I have a big drink together? Would you like that?"

"Lovely. Where we goin' t' have that drink?"

"How about right up there? I'll bring my champagne and be right up, OK?"

"Lovely. Sarah? Sarah?"

"I'll spell it for you when I get there, OK? I'll be the girl at your door with the big, big champagne bottle. See you in a minute!"

She dropped the phone on its cradle and ran to the patio.

"Myron! Let's go for a fast ride in that Porsche of yours. Here, I'll take those." She took his drink and hers out of his hands and put them on a brick wall. "I have to get something; I'll meet you at the door, darling. Quick!" She pushed him, then grabbed his hand. "Come on, baby."

"Where are we going?"

"About ten blocks—1601 Cathedral. Let's haul ass!"

As they went by the bar Sari reached into a tub of ice behind the bartender and snagged a bottle of Schramsburg Blanc de Blancs, 1976.

"Come, Myron. What makes you so slow?" Sari dragged him out the front door.

"Oh, I don't know," the tall deputy to the deputy assistant said. "I guess it's glands."

CHAPTER **27** Elwood Broderick sipped his coffee distractedly, reading the front page of the *Star-Post* spread out on his lap. David Hale played the host, filling cups for Murray Tillerman and Les Carew.

"Not too bad," Broderick mused. "Smythe had a pretty easy time of it up there at the committee, didn't he?" He looked up at his senior White House colleagues with satisfaction.

"Didn't you watch?" Les Carew asked.

"No, I had to see some people from Justice right then. I figured I'd see the PBS rerun last night, but we had to go out. My wife's parents are in town."

"It was perfect," Murray Tillerman said. "Old Oates retreated—he virtually conceded to the A.G., right on television—then Smythe banged Robin hard, and the yacht's log cinched it. We had a very, very good day up there. Couldn't have been better."

"Well, today may not be as good," David Hale cautioned. "I think you all better take the afternoon off and watch young Mr. Warren's performance. We may need some bright ideas by nightfall. The Boss is going to want everyone's reactions." He showed concern; it tarnished the easy tone of his voice.

"Is he watching these things?" Tillerman asked.

"He watched the A.G. I don't know if he can sit all the way through Robin Warren or not," Hale said.

"What about the CIA agents?" Tillerman asked.

"It says here the committee voted they don't have to appear." Broderick pointed to his newspaper.

"That's a break." Hale nodded. "I think we may come out of this in reasonably good shape now. We've been incredibly, incredibly lucky so far. We've won everyone's first impression; the phone polls are good. We've got to make sure Robin Warren gets on and off, and that the hearings end quick with no delays."

"It just may be out of our very competent hands," Tillerman observed with a snort.

"Maybe," Hale said elliptically.

Carleton Smythe read the front page of the *Star-Post* with satisfaction as he ate his breakfast. They'd run a decent picture of him, taken while he was reading his statement. The story was straight, even favorable. He was turning to the inside continued story when he noticed his wife standing in the living room, looking at him through the double doorway.

"Good morning, Jane."

"Hello, Carley." Her hands were together, working, in front of her.

"Breakfast?"

"No."

"Have you seen the paper?"

"No." She gave a quick head shake.

"Things went well yesterday. Good coverage."

"Nice." She wore a long sleeveless nightgown, open at the neck; her hair was tousled.

"I was tired last night," he said. "I went straight to bed. Your light was out."

"That's OK." She was subdued.

"Did someone come here late? I woke up and thought I heard voices."

"Someone?"

"Did you have a late visitor?"

"No." A quick shake of her head.

"Odd. I'm sure I was awake."

"There may have been someone, I guess." She looked away, out the window.

"Who?"

"A woman. Don't know her name. She had a lot of questions about you." She looked at him briefly, then down at her bare feet.

Smythe put down his paper and got up. "You let her in?"

"Just for a while. A little while. We had one drink."

He walked to her. "What was she asking about? Who was she?"

Jane Smythe rubbed her cheek slowly in aid of recollection. She turned to go to the bar; he grabbed her roughly by her bare upper arm.

"No, goddammit, no booze. I want to know—what woman? What questions? A reporter?"

"You're hurting me, Carley." She tried to pry his hand off her arm.

He gripped her tighter. "I'll hurt you a lot worse, lady." He shook her arm side to side.

"I can't remember. Champagne isn't good for me, you know. There was a lot about Oates."

"What do you know about Oates?"

"Nothing."

"Were you listening on the phone?"

"When?"

"You bitch! Tell me what you heard!" He took her other arm. Her head bobbed side to side. "Tell me!"

"Don't—Carley—don't. I'm—sick."

Smythe had an aversion to overt illness. She must not vomit here, he resolved. Still gripping her arms, he lowered her to a chair. "I'll get you some water."

As he poured a glass at the bar in the alcove he continued: "I

327

know you have listened on the extension before, Jane. Did you hear me talking to Oates? Do you recall what you heard? Did you listen to my call to the President?"

He handed her the water. She sipped slowly. It was an excuse not to answer. She looked at the red blotches his fingers had made on her arms. She touched the marks on her left arm with the fingers of her right hand, then looked up at him.

"Jane, I've never struck you, have I?" He was furious. "Now listen to me; and listen good: if you don't tell me what you told that person I am going to hit you in the face now." His voice was low and controlled. He spoke slowly, a tremor lifting the words. "With my fist. And I will keep hitting you until you tell me. Or you fall unconscious. Do you understand?"

She understood, in spite of her fear and surprise. She had never seen him enraged like that. Her head throbbed and her stomach ached. She began to cry quietly. He had never hit her; she was quite certain that if he hit her she would die.

"I don't know who she was," she mumbled, "but she knew all about you and Oates. I didn't tell her anythin' she didn't know." She put the glass on an end table and touched her arm again.

"Like what?" he asked through gritted teeth.

"Like you tried to—buy him off." Jane Smythe swallowed the words. "She didn't know about his brother's taxes, or the other stuff you gave him. But she did know for sure that you bought him."

"Did you hear my talk with Oates, Jane?"

"I thought you were callin' a girl. I know you're meetin' someone."

"So you listened."

"I liked his Down South talk, so I stayed on. I didn't know why you called him. I thought it was a girl you was talkin' to." She buried her face in her hands.

"And the President? You listened to that?"

A muffled "Yes."

"You told the woman about that?"

328

Jane Smythe looked up. A thin line of mascara had run down her left cheek. She disgusted him and he showed it.

"She knew the President knew," she said quietly.

"Did you *tell* her?"

"Sure. She already knew."

"You stupid cow."

He moved quickly to the living-room phone extension and picked up the telephone book. She didn't look up until he began talking into the phone.

"This is Carleton Smythe. I have a bit of an emergency. May I speak with Dr. Kargianis?"

"Carley . . ." she protested. "Please. You mustn't . . ."

"Doctor? I apologize for calling you at home so early. I'm afraid Mrs. Smythe is showing very disturbing symptoms this morning. Yes. Yes, she's been drinking heavily lately."

Jane Smythe stood and came to him. He looked up as she reached for the receiver. He moved back into his chair, dodging as he talked. Then he put his other hand on her belly and pushed her with all his strength. She fell back to the rug on her buttocks, crying out in pain.

"She's somewhat violent, Doctor," he said. "She just tried to grab the phone to prevent me from talking to you. Yes, I'm afraid so; you know I've not wanted that. But I'm afraid I can't help her anymore."

She rolled onto her side, pulling up her knees, covering her eyes with her palms. "No," she crooned. "No, no, no."

"Doctor, it must be done very quietly," he said. "With this Senate hearing going on, there are reporters all around. Can you come now? Bring some help? She may not want to go, you know. What time? I'll keep her here until then. Please hurry."

"Carley, no. You hurt my back just then. Don't send me to that place again." She was crying steadily.

"Just lie there, Jane. The doctor is on his way. Just don't move. I'm going to sit here with you until he comes. You are very sick, my dear. He will take care of you." Smythe sat back in his chair.

He looked at Jane Smythe with detached interest as he prepared a cigar, rolling it between his fingers, wetting it carefully, cutting the tip with a silver tool. He struck a flame with the table lighter and pulled deeply, exhaling smoke. He examined the beginning ash with approval. " 'Thy clouds all other clouds dispel,/And lap me in delight,' " he murmured.

Part V

THE HEARING

CHAPTER **28**   When Robin Warren went home Wednesday night there was only one photographer; the man was leaning against the fender of a parked car, reading a paperback book. When he saw Robin he put his book down, took the usual putting-his-key-in-his-front-door pictures, and went his way.

But Thursday morning they began arriving at four, the whole regular army: television, print, and still photographers, and technicians; station wagons, slamming tailgates, coffee cups, litter and loud talk. A man living in the house across the street came to his front door about five. Standing in his open doorway, in pajamas and robe, he looked down on the crowd around Robin's entrance and shouted, "You inconsiderate bastards! I have a family trying to sleep in this house. Either shut up or go away!"

A couple of television reporters snickered. A still cameraman took pictures of the householder.

"Ever hear of the First Amendment, buddy?" a reporter yelled.

The man went back into his house and slammed the door.

Warren looked at his clock: five-thirty. He stretched out on the bed on his stomach and pulled a pillow over his head.

At seven his alarm sounded. He woke easily and sat up. He'd slept well until the street argument awakened him. He'd needed no pills to sleep; just good old exhaustion. And the extra nap helped. He had a pregame sensation; he was a little keyed up—too early to be nervous yet, but he had the beginning of feeling combative. He showered, shaved and carefully dressed. The *Good Morning America* show contained a lot of coverage on Smythe and Oates, then a long speculative piece on Robin, Leonard Weil and Senator Thomas Stapleton by ABC's man-in-the-rotunda. Stapleton would be the Democrats' designated hitter; he and Irving Anschults had been assigned primary responsibility for interrogating Robin, the reporter said. Senator Timothy Larkin would carry most of the burden for the Republicans. Then came the stereotypes. Weil was a fox. Robin Warren was probably a liar. The climax was approaching; seating tickets were impossible to find; it was the best show in town; Oates was a cagey country lawyer and Constitutional expert; Stapleton was a slashing prosecutor.

Listening, Robin tensed. He pulled out three neckties before he decided on one; it would be the gray-and-white one he usually wore with blue. In an unstated way, there was a tradition of good luck about wearing that particular tie and he had the feeling that luck could make some difference today.

At precisely eight, Leonard Weil's car pulled up in front of Robin's house. Robin opened and closed his door quickly, half ran through the question-shouting crowd of reporters to the car, and slid in beside Harley, the chauffeur. Before Robin could close the door the car was moving, the camera crews scuttling for position, still filming as the car rounded the corner.

Harley drove to Weil's office via Du Pont Circle. It was a humid morning, fair, about to be too hot. Some of those walking to work were already carrying their suit coats over their shoulders.

Weil was waiting for him in a dark-blue suit, blue shirt, blue tie, his desk top clean.

"Have you eaten?" Weil greeted him.

"I'm not really hungry, Leonard. Just coffee."

"Hear the news this morning?"

"Yeah. Stapleton is the DA, right?"

"What's that? What about Stapleton?"

"ABC says he's going to question me for the Democrats. Larkin for the Republicans."

"What about the others? They won't?"

"That wasn't clear."

"Let's find out." Weil called Sari Kahn in.

"Good morning." She was wearing her navy-blue jury suit, too.

"Call Irving, your professor friend, and find out if Robin will be questioned by everyone or just by Stapleton and Larkin and him."

"OK. Bernie gets to Naples in a couple of hours. He got a seat on a flight to Rome out of Dulles last night. I hope he can sleep on airplanes."

Weil nodded impatiently.

"I had an interesting evening after I left here last night," Sari Kahn said.

"Sari, I really must go over this redirect material with Robin; unless you—"

"Sure. Remind me to tell you what Jane Smythe told me, sometime when you aren't so busy."

"You talked to the Attorney General's wife last night?" Weil asked with disbelief.

"Sure. She and I are old drinking buddies now."

"What did she say?" Weil pressed. "Does she know Robin was on the yacht? Did Smythe tell her?"

"No, but she eavesdrops on Smythe's telephone calls. She heard him bribe Oates."

"Ah," Weil said.

"The Attorney General offered Oates a mining license, some commodity price supports and help with Oates's brother's tax troubles. Some IRS agent gets fired, too."

"So it's true. And Oates agreed?"

"Right."

"Bless my soul," said Leonard J. Weil. "Where did you see her?"

"I went to their apartment. There's more." Sari Kahn smiled broadly.

"Yes?"

"The A.G. then called the President."

"And?"

"Frankling authorized the deal."

"She heard him?"

"Yes."

"And she freely told you all this?"

Sari laughed. "Some women are just looking for a chance to clobber their husbands. And she's queen of them all. I just furnished the audience. And the champagne."

"What can we do with this?" Robin asked Weil.

"Who knows? Maybe get Smythe to tell the truth. After the hearing today I might go have a chat with him. Robin"—Weil leaned back in his chair, glanced out the window and returned—"this shows that there's nothing harder than keeping a contrived story from falling apart. As time passes, it begins to flake off, little bits here and there fall away, then some major piece of goods is exposed."

Sari got up to leave. "How does that Shakespeare couplet go? 'What tangled webs we weave,/When first we practice to deceive.' "

"Not quite." Leonard Weil smiled. "Not Shakespeare and not exactly a couplet." He leaned back in his chair and looked up at the ceiling.

> " 'O what a tangled web we weave,
> When first we practice to deceive!
> A Palmer too!—no wonder why
> I felt rebuk'd beneath his eye:
> I might have known there was but one,
> Whose look could quell Lord Marmion.'

"That's *Marmion*, by Sir Walter Scott, my dear. It's quite long. Do you want to hear more?"

"I know when I'm topped," Sari said. "He's all yours."

A sense of detachment had been building all day. By eleven it was pervasive. Robin felt he held none of the controls. What was to occur was totally out of his hands. He was on a raft, going down a river. He couldn't stop and get off, nor could he steer. He must ride it out. So he would take the ride—he knew his part—but he felt no involvement.

A football game was different: a man's skill and strength could effect an outcome there. He was never detached in ball games. There was the sense of precise execution, the feel of the ball in his fingers, the impact with other bodies.

But this Senate hearing was so ungraspable, unreal, very correct, civilized, yet so deadly. Like fencing from the roofs of adjoining buildings. But killing.

They rode up to the Hill in Weil's car and Robin felt as though he were sitting far off in the branches in the top of a big tree, watching the tumbrel roll on its way to the guillotine.

They stopped near a side entrance to the Senate Office Building. Fifty or sixty tourists bunched around the doorway to look at Weil's car. Three policemen, one a captain, came to the curb. When Robin followed Weil out of the car onto the pavement there was frantic picture-taking—a couple of pros and thirty Instamatics.

Robin, Weil and Sari Kahn walked in slowly, following the leading policeman's pace. A couple of women murmured "Good luck" as Robin passed; someone laughed. An elevator waited inside the door. No one told the operator which floor. He didn't ask.

The police led them down a long hallway. For two hundred feet, people were standing against the right wall, two and three abreast; a few sat on the floor, reading. As the little phalanx of police approached, people turned to watch the procession. Robin was aware that they recognized him. He heard his name being passed from the tail to the head of the line: "It's him." "Here's Warren." "Here's the kid—the witness."

"Hey, Robin, how about an autograph?" A longhair held out his paperback and a pencil.

"No stops," Weil said to the police.

"Sorry," Robin said to the kid.

"You'll be sorry, all right," a square-built gray-haired lady said sharply. People laughed.

Someone softly whistled a funeral march in time to the policemen's cadence.

"Traitor!" a tall man halfway up the line said. "Turncoat! We're for the President here!"

Robin slowed, nearly stopped, fists clenched. Weil put his hand in the small of Robin's back and shoved. "I don't think you really want to punch out that citizen, my client. Save your best shots for inside."

Up ahead the rotunda area was bright with television lights. Four minicams on cameramen's shoulders were waiting for him. Behind them he could see a profane confusion in the marble lobby: blue screeds on scaffolds, a big camera on a platform eight feet above the floor, men and women walking about rapidly, others at tables covered with metal control boxes. And wire: wires and cables twined and snaked everywhere, tied in bunches along the baseboards, running in crazy patterns across the floor, overhead on two-by-four racks, some tied, some loose, some as big as a baseball bat, black wire mostly, some white, here and there yellow and red.

Taking in the scene ahead, Robin was no longer aware of the people in line, although they became bolder, calling to him harshly, louder. Leonard Weil muttered his astonishment; then they were swept away from the people into the rotunda's whirlpool of light and noise along with the flotsam of press people who flowed counterclockwise around the rotunda well. Robin, his lawyer and the three policemen walked rapidly through the television area, its territorial claims demarked by rope fences. Robin recognized a commentator who stood in front of a blue backdrop facing a huge camera on a wheeled tripod. The man was describing Robin.

A technician's table held four tiny television sets. Robin saw himself on three of them, walking along, seen from different angles, but he didn't feel any identity with the images. Now, more than ever, that feeling of disembodiment pervaded. Through television country, then radio city—earphoned men hunched at tables pushed against the railing along the margin of the well, talking into microphones, saying his name, their backs to the procession, which by now was halfway around the circle—he felt himself to be apart from that entire lit-up madhouse.

To the right, Robin was drawn to look through a pair of doors twenty feet high; the huge room was more bright than the rotunda. He knew it was the Caucus Room, crowded to the doors, people standing. The procession went on by, noise drowning all but instinct. No one could talk and be heard. He had no awareness of moving the parts of his body. He rolled on wheels, pulled by a string.

They curved to the left, following the railing. A policeman stood in front of a rickety faded-green wall built across the marble floor from the railing to the permanent wall. As they approached, the old wooden door was opened by someone. Near dark by comparison was a cube of a room, fashioned out of gypsum board and located across the well from the television territory. One of its walls was the building's wall; a dirty window gave a view of the Capitol dome. The low ceiling was mottled with grime.

Weil and the police captain were beached just inside the door. Robin was vaguely aware of Weil thanking the policeman and pushing him out.

The room was filthy. An old metal desk, four spavined wooden chairs and a swivel chair were gritty with prehistoric dust. Two empty file cabinets supported a platoon of used Styrofoam coffee cups, ashtrays, a pile of paper towels and a D.C. phone book.

Robin picked up the telephone and listened to the dial tone. The earpiece was moist.

"It works," he said.

"That was fine; that's an unbelievable mess out there and you stayed out of trouble," Weil said. "We will be called at noon or whenever they are ready for you to begin. Would you like a coffee, a Coke? The policeman says he will get it."

"Sure. A Coke, please."

Weil poked his head out the door and gave an order to the waiting policeman.

The lawyer sat on a straightback and gestured at the swivel chair. "Might as well be comfortable."

Robin sat behind the desk, nearly capsizing. The swivel chair was broken in such a way that it swung back and to the side when weight was put upon it. He rested his arms forward on the desk, trying to balance. No one talked. The crowd around the rotunda well created a low roar that could be heard and felt.

Robin realized momentarily that it was he, sitting in this grubby space, who was soon about to enter that klieg-lighted theater they had walked by. For what purpose? For the truth? For spectacle and entertainment? In punishment? Surely not by his choice. No, not quite true. He could have confessed and been everyone's hero.

The Coca-Cola arrived. He took the bottle and receded from the experience. He looked at Weil, flipping through his notebook, then tying his shoe. Then an atom of thought stuck to his consciousness. Then another. He wondered if his hair was combed.

"Did Maggie get a seat?" he asked.

CHAPTER **29**   "I'm going in to visit with our journalist friends," Leonard Weil said. "I think I can plant a few seeds. The committee should be calling for you any time now. It's ten minutes to twelve. I'll join you when you come in there."

340

Robin Warren nodded.

"I'll send Sari in to wait here with you."

"OK."

Weil opened the door and quickly closed it behind him. In that eyeblink Robin received a retinal flash image of a small group of people in a semicircle facing the door, standing quietly in glaring, yellow-blue light. That glimpse shocked and unnerved him; especially the sight of the small committee outside the door. When Sari Kahn came in he was looking out the window.

"Who is that out there?" he asked. "By the door?"

"Reporters," she said.

"Sure."

Automobiles drove by at a normal speed. A few pedestrians moved along the sidewalk, the heat damping them to slow motion. Everything out there was normal.

Sari Kahn came to stand beside him.

"Hot day out there; poor tourists."

"That depends on your point of view," Robin said ironically.

The door opened and a police lieutenant leaned in.

"Come this way, please, Mr. Warren," the policeman half shouted.

Robin tugged at the hem of his jacket to pull out the wrinkles.

"Your notebook," Sari reminded, pointing. "Best of luck. You'll do fine."

"Sure. Let's go."

The seven reporters stood silently in front of the door. They watched the policeman lead Warren and Sari Kahn into the maelstrom. Other police officers had formed a loose aisle past the radio tables, holding back a sizable crowd standing in a hallway which came into the rotunda from the left.

Robin felt awkward. It was the uniformed police, barring people so that he could walk by, that embarrassed him particularly—that and other stimuli he did not then identify. He was stiff and unnatural as he walked. It would have been a good thing to smile, perhaps. The still cameramen were moving with him. A TV camera on a high scaffold was turning to follow him. No smile came. He told himself to stand up straight. The policeman was moving very slowly, for no apparent reason. Robin wondered if people would think he was sleeping with Sari Kahn. He followed the policeman through the door into the beam of a spotlight that hit him straight on. He instinctively began to raise his hand to shield his eyes, then pushed it down.

Leonard Weil stood between two of the long press tables, holding court. A circle of men and women reporters were smiling as he regaled them, gesturing extravagantly.

Robin stopped momentarily, unsure whether to join his lawyer or go to the witness table. Men were standing on the dais behind the counter. He recognized Senators Wong and Lincoln, familiar television-star faces. There was a thick and noisy hedge of people sitting and standing to his left, all the way to the distant back wall. A velveteen rope separated them from the press area in front of him. An aisle ran along the wall to his right, to the end of the dais, where a short flight of steps could be seen. But the entire scene—the people, the space, even the atmosphere—had been given over to television. He could *feel* the televising. There were the extrinsic aspects, of course: wires, boxes, lights, heat pipes, scaffolds, workmen, camera platforms, cameras. But television was, more, an *intrinsic* presence in this huge, high, wide, ugly Doric room. The scene was being cut into little squares and sucked out of this cube full of people and light, through some metaphysical pipe, and he could feel parts of it going, as one feels the bath water running out of the tub. Everything in the room was going to be vacuumed through those conduits and hurled at the mind-pans of millions of people; the people in the Caucus Room could tangibly feel it as it went, somehow. At least he could, as he stood there. He felt it, as he had felt sand eroding from under his feet as he stood in the ocean—it made him insecure, unfooted.

"To your right," Sari Kahn said. The policeman had disappeared somewhere and she was now in command. They moved along the wall, the narrow space between the reporters' chairs and the marble, half filled with people trying to move around each other. He heard a few people hissing at him from the rear of the room. At the corner of the nearest press table Leonard Weil stood waiting for him.

"Just go over, sit down and get used to the chair, Robin. Get comfortable and relax and sit still. They want to take your picture, the boys do." Weil had adjusted his voice, sharpening it to be heard in the echoes and roars.

Robin nodded, worked his way around several knots of reporters, and finally sat down in the leather chair at the left, the one the Attorney General had used. On the table was a thick packet of Mailgrams in a rubber band. He looked up at a thickset man in a cheap suit who was grinning and nodding.

"Yours. Look at the address."

Robin turned the packet on the green baize table top and read his name. He slipped the top telegram from under the rubber. It was addressed: "ROBIN WARREN, C/O SENATE COMMITTEE HRG., WASHINGTON, D.C."

He debated whether to open it. A crowd of reporters and photographers was gathering around him, in anticipation of an unusual picture, a possible story. He decided to take a chance. The telegram was from a woman named Erma Horton of Palatine Street in Odessa, Texas.

ROBIN WARREN, HAVE YOU MADE JESUS YOUR PERSONAL LORD AND SAVIOR? I MADE JESUS MY SAVIOR FOUR YEARS AGO AND MY LIFE HAS COMPLETELY CHANGED. YOU DON'T KNOW ME BUT I AM PRAYING FOR YOU TODAY: LUKE 27:1.

ERMA HORTON

Photographers took dozens of pictures as he read the wire. He folded it carefully and put it in his pocket, reached back behind his chair to hand Sari the remaining bundle, then turned back to watch the committee members and staff standing, posing self-importantly, moving about, a level above him.

Senators Oates and Stapleton emerged from behind the blue screed at the right-hand end of the dais and went quickly to their chairs. Oates picked up a sheaf of papers and squinted at the top one. Irving Anschults leaned over to whisper in Oates's ear. Oates nodded and looked up quickly.

"This committee will be at odah."

Robin felt the surge of excitement in the room.

Leonard Weil slipped into the chair beside him. "God, aren't those lights awful!" Weil exclaimed. "They could actually burn you. Feel that!"

"The next witness is Mr. Warren," Senator Oates said. "The Select Committee would like to finish his interrogation today and Friday so that he need not return on Monday. So, in the interest of dispatch, the majority and minority have selected one of their number, respectively, to carry the major responsibility of examinin' the witness. This does not bar any Senator from askin' any question he desires to, of course. But we will all endeavor to avoid repetition, in the interest of time.

"The odah of interrogation will be: Professor Anschults, then the chair for ten minutes, then Senator Stapleton for the majority for thirty minutes, then Senator Brawley for the minority for thirty minutes. At that juncture I will allow any Senator ten minutes. We will then return to the original rotation and continue that sequence until all questions have been put. Are there any questions?" Oates looked to his left and right.

"Mr. Chairman," Leonard Weil said.

Oates looked up in surprise.

"Mr. Chairman?"

"Yes, Mr. Weil?"

"Mr. Chairman, am I to be given an opportunity to interrogate my client, on redirect examination so to speak, when the committee has completed its questions?"

"Mr. Weil," Oates said with mock patience, "we are not tryin' a lawsuit here, as I told you before. I see no reason for you to ask your own client questions in our presence. You can do that back in your own office."

The audience laughed.

"Mr. Chairman, I don't need to ask him questions for my

information. I believe I know exactly what happened. I am concerned that this record will be incomplete—that important questions may remain unasked."

"Ah have more confidence in the members of this committee than you do, ah guess, Mr. Weil. You may be surprised at how thoroughly they will interrogate your client. Why don't we wait and see? Now let's be movin' along. Mr. Warren, please stand up and be sworn."

The still cameras gnashed and whacked as he stood with his hand raised.

"If you have an openin' statement, will you please furnish the clerk with copies and proceed to read it into the record?"

Weil signaled Sari Kahn to deliver the required fifty copies to a woman clerk. Robin sipped the paper cup of water which some functionary had poured from the carafe on the table. It was tepid and sour. Behind him he sensed the restless crowd, feral, crouched in hostile anticipation.

"OK," Weil said softly. "Remember, now: slow and distinct."

Robin had clipped the typed statement into a light-blue notebook. He opened the cover and looked at Oates.

"Mr. Chairman," he read, "I am Robin Warren, I reside on Reservoir Street in Washington, and until last month I worked at the White House.

"I went to work at the White House right after President Frankling was inaugurated. My job was to provide an open door there for people in all walks of life—individuals, groups, rich, poor, organized or not. I was to listen to their needs and concerns, decide who in government might help them, and try to cause the Executive Branch to respond. This is not a new function in the Office of the President. Midge Constanza for President Carter, Bill Baroody for President Ford, and Charles Colson for President Nixon were my recent predecessors, although they each had a somewhat different job description. . . ."

The first section of the statement was intended to summarize his first encounter with Auguste Capron at the Business Council meeting, Capron's meeting with the President, and how Warren was instructed to call the CIA. Near the end of the narrative, the chairman interrupted.

"Mr. Warren," Senator Oates said.

Warren looked up, momentarily surprised.

"Mr. Warren, ah've just been told that the members of the committee must now go to the Senate for a roll-call vote. We'll stand in recess for fifteen minutes." Oates stood and walked off the dais, followed by Stapleton, Archuleta and Larkin. Robin noticed, for the first time, that Goldmark and other Senators had disappeared.

"Where did the others go?" he asked Leonard Weil.

"They began drifting off, one at a time, about five minutes ago. Since they're on television they'll go vote on everything that comes up. You'll see Senatorial diligence to duty like no one has ever seen it before. You can't let it bother you. Just go ahead, as if they were all hanging on every word."

"Do we have access to a toilet?"

Weil leaned back and turned to ask Sari Kahn, who shrugged and went off to find out. Robin stood to stretch, his every movement followed by the still cameras' lenses.

"I suppose if I raised my arms to stretch that would be a front-page picture," he said to Weil.

"Not unless you made an ugly face." Weil laughed. "The shots that make you look human will never get past the photo editors' wastebaskets. We are not exactly the critical favorites in these proceedings."

A photographer in the front rank heard them. "You want pictures for your Christmas cards? How many you want to order?" he deadpanned. There was laughter from the rest.

"Why, I didn't think you fellows could be bought." Weil smiled.

Sari Kahn returned, breathless, to report she had commandeered an Oklahoma Senator's private facilities in the first office down the hall. She led Robin to and from without incident, while Leonard Weil stayed at the witness table bantering with a couple of reporters. When Robin returned there was still no sign of the Senators.

346

"Plenty of time," Weil reported. "They stayed for another vote. These gentlemen have been asking me some interesting questions, Robin."

"I'm Sammy Roth, Mr. Warren. UPI."

"And I'm Jervis Calicott of the Baltimore *Sun*."

"How do you do?"

"Mr. Warren, we were asking Mr. Weil here what the White House is afraid of in your notes? Why won't they make them available?"

"I explained," Weil said, "that the Nixon case holds that they are the President's property to furnish or withhold. But I think their question is: Are they just preserving prerogatives or is the President trying to hide something?"

"Well, I took very detailed notes of his meeting with Capron," Robin Warren said. "They will show that the President told me to get ahold of Cooper Dewey at the CIA, and they show that the President had decided that something had to be done in Uruguay."

"What about your date book?" Weil prodded.

"That shows I was supposed to go on the yacht on May thirty-first. It isn't a diary, of course. It only looked ahead."

"Do you have notes from the yacht?" Roth asked.

"No. I didn't take any."

The reporters looked at each other.

"Any notes of your talks with the CIA?"

"No."

Chairman Harley Oates, once again in his place, leaned into his microphone.

"Now, if everyone is ready," Oates said, "we'll proceed. Go ahead, Mr. Warren."

"Give them a summary of what you've read," Weil said *soto voce*.

"Mr. Chairman, I had just described my White House duties and how they had led me to meet Auguste Capron. I explained he requested a meeting with the President which was held in mid-May, after which I was instructed to contact the CIA to determine if a threatened takeover of American property by Uruguay could be prevented." He then began to read once again. "I followed the President's instruction; I told none of my colleagues about the Capron meeting or its consequences."

He read an account of his meetings with Cooper Dewey and a detailed description of the dinner on the President's yacht.

"I was instructed to call Mr. Dewey right then. There was a red telephone in the main room of the boat—where we had just finished dinner—and I used that.

"I told Cooper Dewey exactly what I had been instructed. The President and Mr. Smythe were in the room with me and heard me speak to Dewey. I know they heard, because they commented on the conversation when I was finished.

"When the yacht returned to the Navy Yard I returned to my home in a White House car, alone. It was about ten P.M. when I got home.

"There were no conversations with the CIA or the President about Uruguay after the boat trip. The next I heard from anyone about it was after the CIA operation failed."

Warren looked up to indicate that he was finished. Several Senators were standing in a group talking at the end of the dais.

"Very well, Mr. Warren," Harley Oates said. "You are a lawyer, are you?"

"Yes, sir."

"Went to a good law school?"

"Stanford, yes, sir."

"They teach you about the United States Constitution there, Mr. Warren?"

"Yes, sir."

"Where, in the Constitution, is there any mention—a syllable or a word or a sentence—that vests in a member of the White House staff the right to conduct foreign affairs?"

"I'm sure the staff is not mentioned."

"No, it's not to be found in our Constitution, is it? Not anywhere. That's the prerogative of only one man, isn't it?"

"The President."

348

"That's right, Mr. Warren. Very good. You show a fine grasp of the Constitution, on that point. The President. Of course, under the doctrine of several Supreme Court decisions, a President may delegate certain of his Constitutional powers. But, if he does *not* delegate his powers to a staff person, what powers does that person have, Mr. Warren?"

"A White House staff person has no authority unless the President gives it to him."

"Very good, Mr. Warren. So, if it should appear that a staff person arrogated to himself some of the President's prerogatives, without the President's knowledge or consent, that staff person would be *ultra viries?*"

"Yes, sir."

"And guilty of a loathsome breach of the confidence reposed in him by his President?"

"Don't answer—rhetorical," Weil muttered.

"A breach of confidence, Mr. Warren?" Oates repeated.

"Yes, sir."

"Can you explain to this Select Committee, Mr. Warren, how it is that the Chief Executive and Attorney General of the United States have no recollection of your being aboard the President's yacht on May thirty-first when you have just testified, under oath, that you were there, in full view of everyone, for the whole time? Were you invisible?"

"No, they saw me, sir. They spoke to and about me."

"Can you think of any reason why someone would wish to *lie* about whether or not you were authorized to call the CIA that evening and order the killin' of the leaders of a neighbor country with whom we are at peace?"

"Well, sure; a failed operation of that kind is an orphan. No one wants to take responsibility for it."

"And you think that justifies a high-rankin' official of our government to come before a select committee of the Senate and take a solemn oath to tell the whole truth, and then lie?"

"No, I don't, Mr. Chairman."

"But, Mr. Warren, you're obviously an intelligent young man.

The Attorney General, a member of the President's Cabinet, has sworn to one thing. The Counsel to the President has sworn to the opposite. Would you say there is room for an *honest* difference of opinion between you?"

"No, sir, I would not. The difference between us is not honest; the Attorney General is lying."

Leonard Weil leaned forward. "I should like the record to show, Mr. Chairman, that in this very room, early in the morning of Tuesday of this week, the chairman of this committee described the credibility of the Attorney General to the nation in almost those exact same words, plus some stronger ones."

"That was in a very different context, Counsel," Oates growled. "Professor, you may inquire."

Irving Anschults pulled his chair closer to the counter and edge-tapped a sheaf of papers on the counter top. "Mr. Warren, have you ever practiced law in the District of Columbia?"

"Yes. I worked for a law firm here."

"What was the nature of your duties there?"

"I assisted one of the partners."

"Senator Valle?"

"Yes."

"Did you try court cases?"

"No."

"Draft contracts? Leases? Negotiable instruments?"

"No, I usually represented the firm's clients before legislative and regulatory bodies."

"Is that called lobbying?"

"Yes."

"So you were a lobbyist, not a lawyer?"

"In this case they were one and the same."

"Mr. Warren, at some time you went to work at the White House. When was that?"

"During the Presidential transition."

"Did the President personally hire you?"

"I flew to Ohio and met with him."

"At the White House did you meet with him frequently?"

"Not every day."

"Every week?"

"No. I'd say perhaps ten times in the first year."

"Were you one of those people in the White House who sometimes gave the President advice?"

"Yes. One of my functions was to advise him on the concerns and attitudes of the people I was in contact with."

"Did you do that in private meetings with the President?"

"Rarely."

"Well, then, how did you give him this advice?"

"In written memoranda."

"I see. In all the seventeen months before this May meeting with Auguste Capron and the President, had you and the President ever met together alone, just the two of you, so that you could advise him?"

"Just the two of us? No."

"But you say you two, you and the President, did meet alone after Mr. Capron left the office that day?"

"Yes."

"And he discussed this Uruguayan matter with you then—it was a very, very sensitive matter of foreign intelligence, was it not?"

"Well, in the beginning it related to the expropriation of property—Capron's company and other American properties there."

"But he decided to call in the CIA then, you say?"

"Yes."

"Had you ever been a part of any CIA operation before?"

"No."

"Whose area of responsibility is the CIA normally, in the White House?"

"General Durrien's."

"But it's your testimony that on this occasion in May—I don't have that date—when did you say the Capron meeting was?"

Warren looked at his May calendar, the day-by-day reconstruction, laboriously compiled on the back-room card table.

"May twenty-sixth."

"You say that on May twenty-sixth the President met alone with you—for the first time in seventeen months—and asked you to administer a CIA operation to kill the leaders of a friendly country and destroy their government, and—"

"No."

"To what part of that question are you saying no?"

"The part about my taking over a CIA operation to kill."

"The *Methodist Missionary* plan was to kill the President of Uruguay?"

"Not on May twenty-sixth, it wasn't."

"Did the President say, 'Don't kill anyone'?"

"Killing wasn't discussed."

"Just ends, not means? To stop the expropriation?"

"Yes."

"Well, you were to be the White House man in charge of the Uruguay problem, right?"

"No. I considered the President in charge. I was just his conduit to the CIA."

"You spoke for him?"

"Yes."

"The President told you, 'You use my name'?"

"No, but it was implied; he told me to get the CIA to do certain things. I told Mr. Dewey at the CIA that the President had given these instructions. Which he had."

"What was Mr. Dewey's response?"

"He agreed to come to my office to discuss it."

"Did he ask for a letter from the President showing that you were authorized to speak for him?"

"No."

"Did he ask you, 'Mr. Warren, are you authorized to instruct me in the President's name?' "

"No."

"You called him on the White House phone?"

"Yes."

"He came to your office?"

"Yes."

"Mr. Cooper Dewey uses a wheelchair, doesn't he?"

"Yes."

"Can he walk?"

"I don't know. Apparently not."

"So he gets around in his chair with some difficulty?"

"I don't know . . . How do you mean?"

"Well, Mr. Warren, would you say it would have been easier for Mr. Dewey to make the trip to your office or for you to make the trip to his?"

"Are you asking me why I asked him to come to the EOB rather than to meet in the CIA building?"

"Not exactly; but was there a reason?"

"Yes. I had been told the CIA had all its offices bugged. I felt more comfortable about doing business in my own office."

"So what did you do?"

"I phoned him; then he came over and I gave him the President's questions. The next time, he returned with Mr. Dooley, and, finally, I spoke to him on the phone from the yacht."

"In all those conversations, did he ever challenge your authority to relay instructions? Instructions to kill four or five men and overthrow a friendly government?"

"No."

"Did you ever show him any sign of authority—a note or letter from the President?"

"No."

"If he had raised the question, suppose he had said, 'Look, no offense, Mr. Warren, but I don't know you'—incidentally, had you and he ever talked or met before May twenty-seventh?"

"No."

"So he says, 'I don't know you, and before I dispatch our killers to stage a coup in Uruguay, perhaps I'd better be sure you really do speak for the President.' What did you have that you could have shown him?"

"Nothing."

"Nothing. Will you please tell the committee what in the world you said and did to convince an experienced, skeptical, hard-bitten

353

CIA man to accept your word that the President wanted Uruguay's government overthrown?"

"I've told you. I told him what the President's instructions were."

"And that's all?"

"Yes."

"He didn't think it a somewhat out-of-the-ordinary assignment?"

"I don't know what he thought. His only statement was that he thought it unusual that I was the conduit, not General Durrien."

"So what did you say or do to vitiate his doubts?"

"Nothing, really. I wouldn't say he actually doubted me. He just remarked that the General was his usual contact, that's all."

"When did you first fully realize, Mr. Warren, that you were in a position to exercise the power of life or death over people thousands of miles away by simply invoking the President's name?"

"Well, not—no, I guess I did realize it in a sense, at the meeting I had with Dewey and Dooley. Not exactly that I had the power, but that I was involved in such a decision, a life-or-death decision, acting for the President. But I always felt it was the President's decision, not mine."

"And that was May twenty-first?"

"No, the morning of May thirty-first."

Anschults looked over at Senator Oates, his eyebrows raised.

"All right," Oates announced. "Senator Stapleton, you may now inquire for thirty minutes; then Senator Brawley in behalf of the minority for the same period."

"Mr. Warren, you are a single man?" Stapleton asked briskly.

"Yes, Senator."

"You are divorced?"

"Yes."

"Do you know a woman named Lani Romera, also known as Lenore Douglas Goldberg?"

"Yes."

"She is the motion picture actress?"

"Yes."

"How long have you known her?"

"Since the end of April."

"How did you meet her?"

"At a dinner at Auguste Capron's home in New York."

"Did Mr. Capron introduce you?"

"Mrs. Capron did."

"Have you seen Mrs. Goldberg since that party at Capron's?"

"Yes."

"On what occasions?"

Robin Warren looked quickly at his attorney. Weil did not turn or acknowledge his plea. The lawyer was slumped impassively, his hands folded on his lap.

"She has been my guest for lunch here in Washington. And I saw her on one subsequent occasion."

"Where?"

"In South America."

"Where?"

"Buenos Aires."

"Argentina?"

"Yes."

Warren felt his face flush.

"Is Mrs. Goldberg a friend of Mr. Capron's?"

"She is under contract to one of his companies."

"She works for him, then?"

"Yes. At Superior Studios, as an actress."

"You are an experienced lobbyist, Mr. Warren. Let me ask you: In these various appointments you had with Mrs. Goldberg, did you ever think that she was lobbying you in behalf of Mr. Capron's business interests?"

"No, Senator."

"You didn't realize it?"

"I don't think she was. She never discussed Capron's business."

"Did Mr. Capron ever offer you a job, Mr. Warren?"

"No, sir."

"Or any other form of inducement: money, gifts, anything of value?"

"No. Wait, I take that back. He paid my hotel bill the one night I went to his dinner in New York."

"Where?"

"The Carlyle."

"How much was the bill, Mr. Warren?"

"I don't know."

"Please think: any other favors?"

"He sent his car for me."

"From the hotel to his home?"

"Yes, via my date's house."

"Mrs. Goldberg?"

"No."

"Another Capron employee?"

"No."

"Any other favors?"

"No."

"Under her contract Mrs. Goldberg grants Mr. Capron's company full claim upon her time, I presume?"

"I don't know."

"Did Mr. Capron direct her to spend time with you?"

"No. I don't know."

"He may have?"

"Not that I know of."

"Did he release her from other duties to spend time with you?"

"No."

"Are you sure?"

"Yes."

"Was there anything in Mrs. Goldberg's attitude, or conduct with or toward you, which tended to make you feel gratitude to Mr. Capron?"

Leonard Weil went into action, holding up one hand to stop Robin from answering. "Senator Stapleton, I have exercised all the patient restraint of which I am capable. I cannot sit silent any longer and permit you to commit these lurid speculations."

"Well, Mr. Weil, perhaps you'd rather answer for your client, then. Just explain this to us, will you? The President of the United States says and his Attorney General swears they didn't authorize this CIA operation. Your client admits he made the call to the CIA. Now, he did so either because the President told him to or for some other reason. Even you will find it forgivable that some of us do not wish to believe the President and the Attorney General to be liars. If they are truthful, then is it lurid to speculate on Mr. Warren's motives for unleashing the CIA upon a foreign country, with orders to kill? If you were in this chair, Mr. Weil, could you overlook that question without doing your best to explore every conceivable possibility? What would cause this young man seated beside you to do such a thing on his own?"

"Since you ask me, Senator, I will reply: *nothing.* There is no logical explanation for his call to the CIA except that he was under orders from the President to do so."

"But you see the problem with that, Counsel. To arrive there I have to determine the President a liar and the Attorney General a perjurer. I can't do that easily."

"There is some recent precedent—in both parties," Weil said coldly.

"Will you answer the question, please, Mr. Warren?"

"Nothing tended to make me thankful to Mr. Capron; that's not why I called the CIA."

"Very well. You mentioned a red telephone on the yacht?"

"Yes."

"Where was it?"

"On an end table near the stern door of the saloon. Next to a lamp."

"Anything else on the table?"

"An ashtray and matches."

"Had you ever met Mr. Dooley before the day of your meeting with the CIA man, Cooper Dewey?"

"No."

"Can you think of any reason why Mr. Dooley should have attended that meeting?"

"I don't know of any. Mr. Dewey invited him."

"Is he a CIA agent?"

"Dooley? I don't know."

Stapleton leaned to whisper something to Senator Oates.

"Senator Stapleton reserves the balance of his time and yields to Senator Brawley."

Brawley, a square man with a short haircut, asked questions in a deep, strangled voice laced tight with pomposity like a corset.

"Mr. Warren, your normal duties at the White House have nothing whatever to do with the CIA, do they?"

"That's correct, Senator."

"You are supposed—you *were* supposed to be a contact man, available to people who need to be heard, with a particular point of view?"

"Yes."

"You realize, from working there, that the White House maintains various books and records?"

"I don't understand the question."

"Records. You know that the garage, for example, keeps a record of when you use a White House car—who uses it, the origin and destination, the hour of the day, that sort of thing?"

"Yes."

"I have here a certified copy of the garage records for May thirty-first. Have you seen this?"

"No, but my attorneys have."

"Then you know it shows you used a White House car at six-thirty P.M. to go from the Old Executive Office Building to your home and used another at eight-five P.M. from your home to that building?"

"I know there is such a piece of paper, but that's not a record of what occurred."

"Mr. Chairman," Leonard Weil said loudly, as if to attract the attention of the press, "are we to be given an opportunity to hear the testimony of the man or men who allegedly made those entries? I want to hear someone swear that they are true. Because we know they are false!"

"Mr. Weil, those records are certified to be accurate and kept in the ordinary course of business," Irving Anschults said. "We don't plan to put on any more witnesses about them."

"Well, Mr. Chairman, I'd like to put on some testimony about those." Weil was angry. "I don't suppose you'll loan me your power of subpoena?"

"You suppose right, Mr. Weil," Harley Oates drawled. "Things are goin' too slow here as it is. A certified business record is good enough for any court of law ah know about. It ought to be good enough for you. Let's move along now. Senator Brawley?"

Brawley cleared his throat importantly. "Have you or your lawyer also seen the log from the President's yacht? Are you aware it lists only two passengers and does not list you?"

"So I hear; that's wrong, too."

"Is it also wrong that the yacht returned to the dock at eight-twenty P.M.?"

"Yes, that's wrong."

"And the Attorney General is wrong when he says you weren't there?"

"He's wrong; I was there."

"Was anyone at your residence with you between six forty-five P.M. and eight P.M. on May thirty-first?"

"I wasn't there then. I was on the boat."

"Was anyone there?"

"Not that I know of. No."

"Was there a young lady there—a stewardess for National Air Lines?"

"No. Absolutely not."

"Are you certain?"

"Yes."

"Isn't it a fact that on May thirty-first at eight forty-six P.M. you phoned the CIA from a telephone in the Old Executive Office Building?"

"No. I phoned from the yacht."

"You say that, in spite of the Attorney General's sworn evidence to the contrary and these certified records?" Brawley held up a sheaf of papers.

"I phoned from the yacht."

"Mr. Chairman, I'll reserve the balance of my time," Brawley said.

"Very well. Senator Goldmark?"

"Yes, Mr. Chairman. I have a few questions on a topic that does not appear to be covered by the prior interrogation." The old man flashed a creased smile at Robin Warren and leaned forward, his chin cupped in his hand. The metal buttons on his blue blazer caught the television lights.

"Mr. Warren, let me test your recollection. Please cast your mind back to May thirty-first. That's less than sixty days ago, is it not?"

"Yes, Senator."

"Let's assume you were aboard the *Sea Island* that night. When you went aboard the yacht whom did you see first?"

"The captain."

"What was his rank?"

"Three stripes. Commander, I think that is."

"Did you go indoors?"

"Just for a moment. Then we had drinks up on the top deck."

"Is there furniture there?"

"Yes."

"Describe it."

"It's white plastic; molded seats and a white coffee table."

"What did you drink?"

"I had white wine."

"Were the President and the Attorney General drinking?"

"Yes; double martinis. Quite a few."

"Were they drunk?"

"Later they were obviously affected, but not out of control."

Robin could hear the press tables behind him buzzing. They liked that one. It gave them the day's lead.

360

"Where was dinner served?"

"In the one big room. The saloon."

"Describe the table."

"A long table. We sat at the stern end, the President at the end, Mr. Smythe on his left, I on his right. No other places were set. A big basket of cut flowers was to my right in the center of the table. The tablecloth was white. Lots of glasses, wineglasses. Three or four kinds."

"What was served?"

"Dungeness crab that someone had sent the President, a salad, fresh vegetables on a big tray in little nests, about four or five kinds. Some kind of meat. A Baked Alaska for dessert."

"Meat? What kind of meat?"

"I don't know. But I remember the dessert; the President made some jokes about Wally Hickel, relating them to Alaska."

"You went to a telephone at some time that evening?"

"Yes."

"Next to a table, did you say?"

"No—on an end table, next to a couch."

"What color was the couch?"

Robin Warren closed his eyes tight. "Blue, I think. Dark blue. Solid."

"Not patterned? Are you sure?"

"No, I'm not positive. I remember some solid blue, but it may have been on the stern deck area outside the saloon. I could be wrong on the couch."

"Do you know any of the White House drivers—the chauffeurs?"

"Yes, some of them."

"Do you know the identity of the man who drove you to the Navy Yard, May thirty-first?"

"No."

"What was the President wearing on the yacht?"

"Gray pants and a blue windbreaker with a Presidential seal on the left side. White shirt. Striped tie."

"What color tie?"

"Blue and green."

"What was Mr. Smythe wearing?"

"Blue blazer, slacks, white shoes."

"Time's up, Senator," Oates said with displeasure. "We have to go vote once again, I see. I believe we may be a while voting this time, so without objection we will stand in recess until tomorrow. To be certain of finishing on time with this witness I suggest we convene at eleven A.M. tomorrow. Recess."

Weil grabbed Robin's arm. "Say nothing to the press, boy. Not a word. Let me handle them."

"What got into Goldmark?"

"I went to see him last night. I cashed a lot of chips."

"He was great."

"It's not over yet; here they come. Now, remember: not one word. Let's walk on out. Keep moving."

Robin Warren and Leonard Weil were engulfed by reporters as soon as they stood. Sari Kahn was hopelessly separated from them as she struggled to collect Weil's briefcase and her own.

The questions the journalists asked, then shouted, demonstrated that Goldmark's questions had raised some doubts. Weil smiled owlishly, waving his hand back and forth in front of his face.

"No questions now. It's been a big day. Catch us tomorrow."

Robin wondered if Maggie Valle was there. He looked back over his shoulder as the mob moved slowly toward the door. He couldn't identify anyone. The heat was oppressive. A woman with a reporter's pad had his arm and was shaking it, trying to get him to answer her question.

"Was the President drunk, Robin? Was he drunk? Robin? Was Smythe drunk?" she repeated.

He turned back and silently followed Weil through the door and toward the elevator. Two policemen appeared at last, cut a path for them to a waiting lift, then escorted them out the side door to Weil's car. Harley waited behind the wheel, his wide grin displaying an array of gold teeth. Weil led Robin into the car, and a policeman closed the door. Reporters and photographers pressed against the side of the Bentley as Harley eased it forward.

"You showed 'em good that time, Mr. Warren." Harley grinned. "I heard you on the radio. They ain't no doubt now that you was there. You *must* of been on that boat."

"Drive the car, please," Weil snapped. "Watch that cab pulling out. How about going back on Fifteenth?"

"Well, they's doin' all that pipe work up there, Mr. Weil. Still dug up pretty bad. Thought I'd go across on K and up behind the Mayflower."

"I forgot." Weil tapped his forehead. "I have a message for you. Maggie said she'd meet you there. Did you know?"

"Yes," Robin said. "Yeah, I guess I knew."

CHAPTER 30   Friday was muggy and wet. Overnight, the tip of Hurricane Abigail had lashed a mere flick of its rainy tail upon the capital. Elwood Broderick disliked the rain. Years before he had moved to southern Arizona to escape such meteorological inconveniences, and on mornings of inclement weather he cursed his decision to come to Washington.

His bulk precluded an actual run from his car to the basement door in the rain. Instead he shambled at a more rapid pace than usual, grumbling his displeasure, glancing at the sky, once feeling his inside pocket to be certain he had the FBI report to share with the others at the senior staff meeting. He muttered his greeting to General Bob Durrien at the door to David Hale's office. Carew, Tillerman and Hale were already on their second cups of coffee.

"Morning, Woody," Tillerman said as Broderick and Durrien found chairs. "This is a meeting of the Bad News Bearers. Have you any shitty tidings to contribute?"

"Coffee first," Broderick said dourly. "Then I have one or two suitable items."

"Disaster is the word of the day at the UN," Durrien said. "Have you heard that our Uruguayan friend is coming up personally to lead the parade? General José Gómez Fellano himself will represent the prosecution."

"Figures." Carew nodded. "That's the guy we had the contract out on?"

Durrien grunted. "Not 'we.' What's this 'we'?"

"When is that show due to start?" Hale asked.

"August twentieth, give or take a day." Durrien lit a cigarette and blew smoke at the ceiling. "Since it's an emergency session, the President of the Council canvasses everyone. Not all the preferences are in. But around that date. We have urged a delay until October, but we're not getting any support for it."

"Well, how did you like our very own Robin Warren, Woody?" Tillerman smiled.

"We may have won the battle and lost the war up there yesterday," Broderick said slowly. "What got into John Goldmark? We were doing fine until he fed Robin all those marshmallows."

Tillerman swung to look at the press secretary. "What sort of reaction was there, Les?"

"My phone's been ringing ever since. The wires led with the drunk-President angle. We'll see a bunch of columns speculating that the Uruguay decision was made while he was smashed. I'm saying to all of them that Robin wasn't there, so what does he know? And Warren's resorted to character assassination. And ask Smythe, who *was* there. That sort of stuff."

Broderick took a folded paper from his inside pocket and opened it carefully. "The Director says a former FBI documents expert has been examining the White House records the committee subpoenaed."

"Who is he working for?" Tillerman asked.

"Leonard Weil."

364

David Hale put a hand out to Les Carew. "Cigarette."

"I thought you quit!"

"I started again." Hale shook the pack, tapped the cigarette on the coffee table and struck a match. "What did the expert conclude, Woody?" Hale lit the cigarette and dropped the match into a cloisonné dish.

"He concluded he should resign the assignment. He'll write to Weil today and say he's been called away."

"Who pressured him?" Carew asked lightly.

"No one. He didn't like the feel of it after a preliminary look. Didn't want to be in the middle of a mess."

"Wise man," Hale said.

"What do we do about Robin Warren, Les?" David Hale's voice had an impatient edge. "What's our counterattack?"

"I'm going to have Johnny Solomon see the key bureau people plus the *Star-Post* and *Times* after Robin is finished testifying. Johnny will have them in for drinks. Durrien is coming over to talk to them. You should come, too. We'll try to get some good stuff running for Sunday and Monday."

"Anything else?"

"No. Is there any way to get old John Goldmark straightened out?"

Murray Tillerman swung a leg over the arm of his chair. "How important is it?"

"Very," Hale snapped. "Have you got a lever with him?"

"Sure. The New York Relief Act expires in October. In ninety days. He'll have to beg all over town to get it renewed. It won't be long before he's around to see me."

"Call him this morning, Murray. That's the most important thing you have to do all this year. If you can't phone, go up there and wait for him. Get him. And shut him off." Hale lit another cigarette.

"Two," Carew counted. "You're an addict."

"Fuck you," Hale said. "Woody, when this committee is finished, what becomes of the exhibits?"

"I've no idea. Archives? No, maybe the Library of Congress. I don't know."

"Stay after, this morning, please. I need to ask you to do something."

"Sure."

The President had time to finish scanning the *Star-Post* and the front section of the *Times* before the telephone operators were able to reach the Attorney General for him. "Where the hell were you, Carley? I've been calling for an hour."

"Sorry, Mr. President. Jane's back in the hospital, and I went by to make sure everything is all right."

"My God, what now? The same problem?"

"Yes, only worse. She just cracked up the other night; let some stranger into the place and was talking wildly, then tried to assault me the next morning. It's really torn me up."

"Well, you probably didn't get to see young Robin yesterday, then, did you?"

"Oh yes."

"Were we all that drunk? I don't recall having more than one or two. The press is bombarding poor Les about it."

"I think you are about right. One or two. You were in full possession, I'd say. I thought that, on balance, the committee handled Robin Warren very well yesterday. The net impression was that he's a young opportunist—a lobbyist and a lecher."

"I suppose they'll get into more of that today," Frankling said with anticipation, his voice rising.

"Stapleton has stuff he hasn't used yet, I know. I'm sure he's going to use it."

"Does Jane need anything?"

"No, thanks. They have her in seclusion for a while. Drying out is always very tough for her. She won't be down off the ceiling for a week or so."

"Isn't that too bad? Why do people allow themselves to be taken over by a habit like that?"

"Weakness," Smythe said flatly. "It's a question of character. Character is the whole ball game, Mr. President."

"I suppose you're right. I am wondering about Jep Valle, Carley. I know you and David and the others feel that young Warren is being destroyed up there in the Senate, but I'm not so sure. Is Valle doing *anything* to help us with him?"

"You can never tell with Valle, Mr. President. He says he's trying. But I have no way of knowing."

"We should have tapped the boy, Carley."

"No, I don't think so. That's too dangerous."

"Well, can you build a fire under Valle? Get an answer from him, one way or the other?"

"I'll try."

"I know you're doing your best, Carley, I know. Just don't underestimate Warren's ability to harm us. It would be better if he could be brought to corroborate your testimony up there."

"I understand, but it may be too late for that, Hugh."

"Yes, I know. It may be too late. Too late for anything. But do your best, Carley. This goddamn thing could sink my administration—our administration!"

"Did you get some sleep last night?" Leonard Weil greeted his famous client.

"Not much."

"Did you ever locate Maggie? I'm sorry I forgot her message."

"She was at the Mayflower. She watched the hearing on TV instead of using her ticket."

"What did she think?"

"She thought I was too stiff and grim." Robin smiled.

"Did you get the message that your former wife called here?" Weil asked.

"Yes. She said I wasn't on the attack enough. She assures me that truth always prevails and that everything is going to be all right. But she'd like me to take Oates on—head on."

"No, you can't do that. I'd say you were fine yesterday."

Sari Kahn knocked and came into Weil's office. No blue jury suit today—a lemon-yellow summer dress instead, bare in many of the right places.

"Excuse me, Mr. Weil. I have two things. First, Jane Smythe has disappeared."

"Oh? How do you know?"

"I decided to see if I could talk to her again, so I went over there. I waited until Smythe left this morning and rang the doorbell. They have a maid, and Mary Lou and I got to chatting. Seems Jane was gone when Mary Lou came to work yesterday. She thinks the A.G. has put her back on the funny farm."

"Has she been in one before?"

Kahn nodded. "Twice. Jane has told her all about the horrors of an alcoholic sanitarium."

"Which one?"

"Mary Lou doesn't know."

"Any leads?"

"Nothing good. How about letting the press find her for us?"

Weil smiled. "Why not? Who do you give your business to these days?"

"*Star-Post* or *Times*? Take your choice."

"Why not both?"

"I might lose an admirer unless it's exclusive. I think the *Times* fellow would work it harder, don't you?"

"In this case, probably."

"I'll go and call my friend Al. Good morning, Robin, how are you?"

"Good morning, Sari Kahn, Girl Detective. Go get 'em!"

"The other thing is that Bernie has been refused admission to the Navy base at Naples. But he's found someone who knows Lieutenant Slinde. He'll call this afternoon. I'll go call the *Times*." She closed the door behind her.

"That Smythe!" Weil exclaimed. "He must have found out that his wife talked to Sari. The poor woman! Drying out is a bad time for people like her."

"What about the documents expert?"

"I have a sad little note from him. Here."

It was handwritten:

DEAR MR. WEIL,

I looked at the records. I would need to see the originals to tell anything at all. The Senate showed me only photocopies.

But I have been called to Richmond to testify in a court case. There will be no charge. I am sorry I can't help you.

Sincerely,
DENNIS LAWRENCE

"I suspect they bought him off," Weil said.

"Where are the originals?" Robin asked.

"The White House picked them up. The President has them." Weil nodded. "I have asked John Goldmark to try to get them back. Incidentally, you made a believer out of him—he accepts the fact that you were there, on the boat."

"Well, that's one, anyway."

"Where the hell is Goldmark?" Robin muttered to Leonard Weil, his hand over the microphone.

"I have no idea; perhaps he's just late."

"Everyone else is here."

"If he doesn't show up I'll ask Sari to call and find out. Don't worry. Just listen to the questions. And keep your answers short. Relax."

"If I were any more relaxed I'd be sound asleep." Warren smiled.

"Good. It doesn't hurt to smiie a little."

"I'm smiling! I'm smiling!"

"The committee will be at odah," Oates said. He'd taken his round of applause as he entered, spoken briefly to Professor Anschults and Senator Stapleton, then read a memorandum he'd found at his place.

The gallery, and even a few of those at the press tables, had greeted Robin with hissing again when he followed Leonard Weil into the huge room.

"Ah wish to admonish those in the room"—Oates squinted into the rear lights—"that there will be no more expressions from the audience. Either of favor or disfavor, neither one. We can conduct this inquiry without an audience if need be, and ah won't hesitate to enforce the chair's rulin' on this."

"Mr. Chairman."

"The distinguished Senator from the state of Washington, Mr. Brawley."

"Mr. Chairman, I wish to join you in condemning these displays of emotion from the back of the room. They have absolutely no proper place in a hearing of this kind."

"Thank you, Senator." Oates nodded. "We are a few minutes late in starting. I ask each member to keep his inquiry concise. Senator Wong?"

Wong looked down the curved desk at the chairman. "Mr. Chairman, I believe my distinguished friend and colleague, Senator Keene, is my senior in the rotation."

"You're correct, Senator, but he advises me that he passes this round."

"Oh, thank you, Mr. Chairman. And I also thank the Senator. I have a few questions. Mr. Warren, I must tell you," Wong began, "I was most favorably impressed with your responses to Senator Goldmark's questions yesterday. It was obvious to me that you are familiar with the President's yacht."

Robin Warren nodded. Wong spoke in an easy West Coast accent, not the clipped syllables of the stereotype Chinese. He was short, stocky, gray-haired, with horn-rims over a broad nose, bushy gray eyebrows, wide mouth, black button eyes, J. C. Penney suit. Somebody's grocer on Geary Street.

"The obvious question is: When did you gain that familiarity? Please tell us, Mr. Warren, the first time you saw the President's yacht."

"About a year ago."

"And what was that occasion?"

"The Congressional liaison people at the White House had a party aboard for freshman Congressmen."

"And you were a host?"

"I was supposed to circulate around and get acquainted."

"Did the boat remain tied up or did it sail somewhere?"

"It cruised upriver to the Key Bridge, then down to Alexandria and back."

"Did you see the captain of the vessel then?"

"Yes, he greeted everyone as they boarded."

"How many stripes did he have then?"

"Three."

"Did you go on the upper deck during that cruise?"

"Yes."

"White plastic furniture?"

"Yes."

"Did they serve dinner?"

"No. Just drinks and hors d'oeuvres."

"Were there bouquets?"

"Yes, spring flowers in baskets."

"You saw the blue furniture then?"

"I can't say for sure."

"The brass lamp and red telephone?"

"Not that I recall."

"I see. When was the next time you were aboard the yacht?"

"Last September or October."

"For what purpose?"

"Some of the White House staff were invited on a cruise by Mrs. Frankling."

"Was the President aboard when you were?"

"No. Not either time."

"Did you dine with Mrs. Frankling that time?"

"Yes."

"At the long table?"

"No. It was a buffet. I took my food upstairs."

"To the white plastic furniture?"

"Yes."

"May I ask the occasion?"

"There were fireworks off Haines Point. Some municipal celebration."

"Frederick Douglass Day?"

"It may have been."

"Did you notice the red telephone on that cruise?"

"Not that I can recall."

"The brass lamp?"

"No."

"The blue couch?"

"No."

"Did you drink wine?"

"Yes. And there were spring flowers in baskets."

Leonard Weil shot him a glance that caused the waiting photographers to press the shutter buttons on their automatics. Weil leaned to his ear.

"That was smart-ass. Watch it, or you'll lose your shirt," Weil whispered.

Wong quit while he was ahead. Speers, Lincoln and Archuleta passed. Senator Timothy Larkin of Minnesota preened briefly, shuffling a packet of five-by-eight cards, pursing his lips.

"Mr. Warren," Larkin began, "I didn't understand your testimony yesterday with respect to your profession. Did you say you had never practiced law?"

"No, sir. I worked for the Butler firm in San Francisco from the time I graduated until I moved to Washington."

"Did you do the normal things? Research, drafting, try cases?"

"Yes."

"So you realize that what you are charged with doing in the President's name, without authority, comprises several crimes?"

Weil spoke up. "Senator, I will not permit my client to answer that, lest his response be misunderstood. Having in mind the leaks from the Justice Department, I wrote this committee to ask immunity for my client in connection with his testimony here. But the professor tells me that request has been denied, although I still haven't received an answer to my letter. Mr. Warren insisted on testifying in spite of the threat of prosecution, confident that he has nothing to fear from telling the truth. But I can't let him respond to questions of the type you put, for obvious reasons."

"Very well, Mr. Weil. Mr. Warren, what instruction or orientation or legal advice is given a person when he goes to work at the White House? Are you instructed on do's and don'ts?"

"Not really."

"Is there a book of rules?"

"No."

"Well, did anyone ever tell you how far you could, or could not, go in invoking the President's name in telling underlings what to do?"

"Time's up, Senator Larkin," Oates intervened.

Larkin looked incredulous, then amused. He knew he'd been given a short count. He also realized that everyone else knew it. He smiled.

Oates went on quickly. "Chair recognizes Senator Stapleton."

Warren sensed a tightening of the mood behind him at the tables. The gate had swung open and the lion had trotted into the arena, his tail twitching.

"Mr. Warren, with whom do you live?"

"I live alone."

"You have a bachelor apartment?" Some grease he put under "bachelor" made the word slide around until it said "orgy."

"No, I rent a house."

"A whole house?"

"Yes, a small house."

"Do you entertain there?" Read that "orgy," too.

"Not often."

"Did you divorce your wife, or she you?"

"Oh, Mr. Chairman!" Weil exclaimed. "What is the legislative purpose of a question like that? I object to these innuendoes."

The press tables had stopped writing and were sitting back, enjoying the show.

"Senator?" Oates smiled at Stapleton. "Would you justify your line of inquiry?"

"Mr. Chairman, it is clear to me that this highly placed young man, in a position of the President's trust and confidence, was importuned, lured, seduced, or induced at least, to do the bidding of persons outside government. I feel it is my duty to explore the circumstances. It is our obligation to propose remedial legislation to insure that unauthorized instructions will never again set CIA killers after victims at home or abroad. The question that hangs above this case is: What was Robin Warren's motive? Motive, Mr. Chairman, is often complex. To understand Mr. Warren's motive we must try to understand Mr. Warren. Yes, such an inquiry is personal—as personal as a man's motive. But to do our job we must know and understand this man—the main actor in this drama. That is the basis for my question."

"Mr. Chairman—"

Oates cut off Weil's reply. "No, Mr. Weil. I think we all understand Senator Stapleton's objective now. Without objection, we'll proceed."

Sari Kahn leaned over and spoke rapidly, quietly, in Weil's ear. Weil, in turn, whispered to Robin, "Goldmark's office says he was called up to New York today. A matter of great importance."

Robin nodded. He looked at Stapleton, his eyes narrow. "My wife sued for divorce; we dissolved our marriage by mutual agreement."

"Her grounds were what, sir?"

"Irreconcilable differences, I think."

"It was extreme cruelty and infidelity. Those were actually the grounds, were they not, Mr. Warren?"

"No, I don't . . . It was a default divorce. I didn't appear or contest it. I'm not sure . . ."

Stapleton held up a long document. "This is a certified copy of her complaint in San Mateo County, cause number 21237, Mr. Warren. *Warren versus Warren.* Would you care to refresh your recollection? A copy was served on you, wasn't it, at the time it was filed?"

"Yes. But I believe she amended it to irreconcilable differences; dropped all that other when we agreed—"

"Were you philandering during your marriage, Mr. Warren, as your wife, Sandra, says in this document?"

"Oh, Senator, shame on you!" Weil exploded. "With all your years as a lawyer you know only too well, you must know, how very twisted and unfair that question is. The unproved allegations of a divorce complaint! I will instruct my client not to answer."

"On what possible ground?" Stapleton shot back. "If the lady's statement is untrue, he has only to say so. This is his chance to make a public denial to her public charge. On the other hand, if it is true it will tell us something we need to understand about the gentleman's, ah, shall we say *a priori* susceptibility to the blandishments of someone like Lani Romera."

"Don't answer," Weil muttered.

"Very well, evidently Mr. Warren pleads nolo contendere to that question. He stands mute." Stapleton smiled thinly. "Who was your companion at Mr. Capron's dinner party?"

Robin looked at Weil. The old lawyer shrugged in response. What's the use? the gesture said.

"Miss Valle."

"Senator Valle was your former employer?"

"Yes."

"The boss's daughter?"

"I wasn't working for him then."

"What was your relationship with Miss Valle as of early this May?"

"She was and is my friend."

"Only your friend?"

"I don't use the word 'only' in connection with the word 'friend;' Senator. A friend is a wonderful thing."

"Oh, very true, Mr. Warren. But there are friends and *friends,* aren't there? What was the nature of your friendship with Miss Valle?"

"None of your business, Senator," Robin replied grimly.

"Were you lovers?"

"At one time we were in love. I wanted to marry Miss Valle. I still love her, very much."

"Well, then, where does Mrs. Goldberg fit in? Did she replace Miss Valle as the sun in your constellation of friends?"

"I was very attracted to Miss Romera. Briefly. We had two or three dates."

"Two or three dates. Malts and roller skating? Oh no, you and Mrs. Goldberg went—ah—abroad, didn't you?"

"One time."

"All the way to Buenos Aires?"

"Yes."

"Shared a bed?"

Warren looked at Weil again.

Weil struggled up from his disgusted slouch. "Yes, Mr. Warren, you are right," Weil said. "This has gone much, much too far. In all my years of proceedings with the United States Senate, there is only one incident that even comes close to the subterranean level of this interrogation. Mr. Stapleton has picked up Joseph McCarthy's mantle from the slime and—"

"That's enough, Mr. Weil," Harley Oates shouted into his microphone. "I'll not countenance your vilifying a member of this committee, sir. We will not hear from you!"

"Mr. Chairman—"

"No more, Mr. Weil. Put another question, Senator Stapleton."

"Thank you, Mr. Chairman. Mrs. Goldberg worked for Auguste Capron's studio, correct, Mr. Warren?"

"Yes."

"Did you invite her to Buenos Aires or did she invite you?"

"She was there promoting a film. I went down for the weekend."

"Where did you stay?"

"In a private home on the coast."

"Miss Romera's home?"

"No, Mr. Capron's."

"Auguste Capron's?"

"Yes."

"At his expense? Meals, servants, cars, all those things?"

"Yes. I paid my own air fare both ways."

376

"How discreet of you. That must have been a sizable air fare. How much did it cost?"

"I don't recall exactly; about fifteen hundred dollars."

"How long were you there?"

"Two days."

"Two nights?" Stapleton smiled his innuendo.

"No, not even one night; actually, just an evening. I left after dinner to return to Washington. I was only there Saturday. I returned Saturday night."

"What was the reason? Were you called back in a rush?"

"I was uncomfortable being Mr. Capron's guest while the Uruguayan operation was pending. So I left earlier than I had planned."

"That's all, Mr. Chairman—no, wait." Stapleton leaned forward on his elbows, his forearms on either side of his microphone, his hands together as if in prayer. "One more question: Mr. Warren, I think the committee must know this to understand why you acted as you did for Auguste Capron and his company. Mr. Warren, at any time did you *fornicate* with Mrs. Goldberg?"

The press tables roared. Leonard Weil put a restraining hand—a fist—on Warren's arm, then stood, hollering. "Mr. Chairman!" He could not be heard. He sat down and put his mouth against the microphone: "Mr. Chairman!"

"No, Mr. Weil," Oates replied. "I will not require your client to answer—unless he desires to."

"Mr. Chairman!"

"Yes, Mr. Weil?" Oates was enjoying himself.

"Mr. Chairman, in view of the extraordinary misconduct of Senator Stapleton I ask leave of the committee to put some questions to my client. I ask leave to examine on redirect, so to speak."

"Mr. Weil, I am sure you withdraw the word 'misconduct.' Now, we find ourselves in the same situation as yesterday." Oates looked to his left. "We are bein' called to a vote in the Senate now. Since it is a vote on the Department of Defense supplemental appropriation it will doubtless consume time beyond our normal adjournment. Ah am goin' to recess this hearin' until ten A.M. tomorrow, Saturday, there bein' no objection. The committee will caucus on your request and staff counsel will advise you of our rulin'. Until ten A.M. tomorrow. Recess."

Pandemonium. Every one of the one hundred and twenty reporters moved to secure a reaction from Weil or his unhappy client. Some headed for the witness table, others rushed to wait astride the path between the table and the only door. A few went out into the rotunda.

Weil climbed up on his chair at the witness table. "Ladies and gentlemen," he shouted, "I am as shocked and disgusted as you are. We will have no comment until after the committee rules on my request. I *may* have a statement later at the office." He stepped off the chair and clapped a hand on Robin's shoulder. "On your feet, son. We'll get out of this cesspool."

Robin allowed himself to be pushed and guided out into the hall, blinded by flashbulbs, deafened by questions.

"Look this way, lover boy," a photographer shouted, but Robin stared ahead like a man on his way from his own execution.

CHAPTER **31**   Sari Kahn burst into Leonard Weil's office. "They've got Bernie," she said. Robin Warren and Carla Simpson had just begun to gather themselves to leave for the Saturday session of the Senate committee. Weil was standing behind his desk sorting through his Saturday mail.

"They've got Bernie," Sari Kahn said again loudly.

"Who?" Weil asked.

"The Navy. I've got a Navy lieutenant on my phone calling from Naples. He's someone Bernie found. He's a friend of Slinde's. It's awful. Slinde has been shipped out to sea and they've arrested Bernie."

"Where is he?"

"This fellow isn't sure. On the base, he thinks."

"What ship is Slinde on?"

"I don't know. Ask him. He's on line four."

Weil picked up the telephone. "Lieutenant, this is Leonard Weil. Lieutenant Slinde's fiancée is sitting here. Can you tell us what ship he is being held on?"

"Hello, Mr. Weil," the distant voice said. "I'm not positive, but I think it's a destroyer, the *Flanigan*. They flew him out yesterday when they discovered Mr. Sheffleman."

"Where is the *Flanigan?*"

"Near Crete."

"In the Mediterranean."

"Yes."

"What was Bernie Sheffleman arrested for?"

"Resisting a military policeman."

"Is he on the Naples base?"

"He was, but now I'm not sure. He was picked up last night in a restaurant."

"What was he doing?"

"Eating dinner."

"What happened?"

"Two ONI agents sat down at his table and began asking him questions."

"ONI?"

"Superspies; Office of Naval Intelligence."

"And?"

"They say Mr. Sheffleman became agitated and assaulted one of them."

"Were you there?"

"I was late to meet him. I was just inside the door when they took him."

"Did he assault anyone?"

"No. They didn't give him a chance. They just cuffed him and led him away. I had to disappear; I didn't want them seeing me there."

"Sure. Thank you for calling us."

"He guessed something like that could happen so he gave me Miss Kahn's numbers."

"I'm glad he did." Weil hung up the phone and wiped his eyes with a handkerchief.

"All right, friends," he said. "They have just made their first big mistake. We're going to be late if we don't leave now, but I have a good feeling about how things are going to go up there today. Let's go to war!"

Senator Stapleton's interrogation had provided *Star-Post* readers with titillating Saturday morning reading. "Did You Fornicate?" was the subhead.

The Caucus Room was jammed to the doors, the waiting line longer than usual. Leonard Weil led Carla Simpson, Sari Kahn and Robin Warren rapidly through the hallways and around the rotunda, brushing aside insistent demands for comment or reaction. Reporters had been waiting at the curb and moved with them. Robin walked erect, his eyes unswerving, as if he could not hear the reporters' questions or the taunts from the loungers in line.

In the refuge of the gypsum-board cubicle, Weil pulled two chairs close and motioned Robin into one. Weil leaned forward and spoke spiritedly.

"Listen, young man: This is *your* day. This is the day we shift the whole burden of this event to Hugh Frankling. Understand?"

Robin nodded.

"All right, here's what you do. There may be more questions from Senators. Get through them with flat, short answers. OK?"

"Sure."

"Don't give them *anything* to sink their teeth into. Right?"

"Fine."

"Then I will take you on redirect. I want to festoon that room with unanswered questions. See?"

"Sure."

"Let the White House pick it up from there, if they can. So, you listen to each question and give me something to go on. Will you?"

"Sure."

"Then we'll meet with the television people out here afterward. Right?"

"Right."

"This may be the last day, or you may have to come back Monday. They gave us this redirect but reserved the right for some rebuttal of their own. So I'd guess they'll adjourn after I finish, without telling us. They'll decide over Sunday."

"OK."

The next hour passed quickly. The walk into the Caucus Room, Oates's applauded entrance and the desultory, anticlimactic questions of Senators Lincoln and Archuleta blurred the time.

Chairman Harley Oates watched the small clock carefully.

"That's your allotted time, Senator." Oates broke into a hopeless, convoluted question to rescue Archuleta from himself. "The committee has agreed to extend to Mr. Weil the, I might say the rather extraordinary, right to question his own client, both in the interest of adducin' all relevant evidence in this matter and as a matter of fairness. I admonish you, Mr. Weil, that you have only twenty minutes. Be concise and limit yourself to matters relevant to this legislative inquiry."

"Thank you, Mr. Chairman. I am grateful for the courtesy of the committee. I will not abuse it." Weil moved his chair to the side of the table, half turned toward Robin and arranged a stack of yellow foolscap between them.

"Mr. Warren, who saw you in the car which drove you from the White House to the yacht on May thirty-first?"

"A Secret Service man told me to get into that car. And the driver, of course—an Army sergeant."

"Who saw you board the yacht?"

"That driver, Secret Service agents and crewmen of the yacht."

"The captain?"

"Yes, he greeted me."

"Stewards?"

"Yes."

"They served the drinks and dinner?"

"Yes."

"Who heard you make the phone call to the CIA?"

"The President and the Attorney General. A male telephone operator connected us, and then I talked to Mr. Dewey at the CIA."

"Who knows that you debarked from the yacht?"

"Secret Service agents and the same sergeant. He drove me home."

"Very well. Senator Wong established you had been on the yacht before."

"Yes."

"Have you ever sailed below the interstate bridge—the Woodrow Wilson Bridge—on any cruise?"

"Only May thirty-first."

"Never before?"

"No."

"What occurred when the yacht proceeded south of that bridge on May thirty-first?"

"After a while the steward disappeared and the engines stopped."

"What did you do?"

"The President wanted more drinks, so I went to find the steward."

"What did you observe?"

"The crew, lined up and saluting on the foredeck. We were just opposite Mount Vernon; they were saluting George Washington's grave."

"Did you hear music?"

"Yes; they played a recording of 'Taps' and 'The Star-Spangled Banner.' "

"Mr. Warren, was this before or after sunset?"

"Just before."

Weil turned toward Oates. "Mr. Chairman, I have here a copy

of Navy Regulation 1801, duly certified, which I offer. It governs Navy ships passing Washington's tomb after sunrise and before sunset."

"Ah don't see the materiality of that, Mr. Weil."

"I will show that the President's yacht, a Navy ship, complied with this regulation in the minutes just before sunset on May thirty-first, Mr. Chairman, and therefore that it could not have returned to the Navy Yard at the hour shown in the log you have in evidence."

"When you do all that, Mr. Weil, I'll reconsider your regulation. But as of now it's not material."

Weil shrugged. "Very well. Now, Mr. Warren, at my request did you ascertain the hour and minute of sunset in this longitude for May thirty-first?"

"Yes, 2010 hours; eight-ten P.M."

"How long was the yacht stopped at Mount Vernon?"

"About ten minutes. Five to ten minutes."

"Then what did it do?"

"Cruised back toward the Navy Yard."

"Do you know where it was when you telephoned the CIA?"

"Yes."

"Where?"

"Under the Woodrow Wilson Bridge. It interfered with the radio telephone transmission for a while."

"May I have Exhibit Eighty-seven, the alleged copy of the log of the yacht *Sea Island,* please, madame clerk?"

Weil waited until a young woman brought him the exhibit.

"Examine the log entries for May thirty-first, please, Mr. Warren. Especially the hour prior to sunset—1910 to 2010 hours."

Weil leaned up and over the corner of the witness table toward Robin. "Now, Mr. Warren, do you see any entry indicating that the Navy vessel you were on complied with Regulation 1801 by stopping its engines and saluting the Father of Our Country?"

"No, this indicates that at 2010 hours the captain ordered 'Engines stop' but that at 2020 it docked at the Navy Yard, and five minutes later the President debarked."

"How do you explain that, Mr. Warren?"

"The exhibit must be false. Any member of the crew will remember this particular ceremony."

"Why?"

"Because the President and the Attorney General were talking and laughing so loud in the dining room that the crew heard them out on the foredeck during 'Taps.' "

"Did you hear them, too?"

"Yes, I did."

"How do you know the crew heard them?"

"I overheard their comments."

"What did they call the President? As a result of his conduct?"

"One of them called him a son of a bitch. Another, an officer in the wheelhouse, spoke to me about it as I walked by."

"Now, Mr. Warren—"

"Your time has expired, Counsel, and, by agreement, the committee stands in recess until noon on next Monday." Oates was obviously glad to cut this off.

"I have only a couple of additional questions, Mr. Chairman," Weil insisted. "And my exhibit."

"No, Mr. Weil. We are at recess."

"Then I'll ask them out in the lobby!" Weil shouted. He turned to Sari Kahn. "Get Carla; she's over there, at the second table! I want her with us. Come on, son."

Weil and Robin plowed their way to the rotunda, shaking their heads, Weil pointing to the lobby. "I'll answer all the questions out here," he shouted to the surrounding mob of reporters.

By the time someone had found Leonard Weil a chair, Sari had shoved Carla Simpson through the deep ring of reporters to Weil's side. She stood there, pushing her hair into place, clutching a large leather purse, looking at Robin Warren in appraisal. He glanced at her; she looked away quickly.

"You journalists," Weil bellowed for attention, "you journalists are probably wondering where the crew of the *Sea Island* is right now. Well, I can tell you!"

The din subsided. Weil resumed with some modulation. "I can

tell you that the yacht has been sent to a Navy yard for dry-docking. It's a top-secret deal. The Navy won't tell where it is. And the crew—the crew has been sent out of the country, scattered all over the world. Why?"

"What are you saying?" a reporter yelled from the back. "Tell us. Why?"

"So they can't be here. So they can't testify that they saw Robin Warren, can't say they served him dinner, maybe even overheard his phone call."

"Where are they?"

"We don't know for sure. This attractive lady by my chair is the fiancée of the second officer—the second mate?—a Lieutenant Martin Slinde. I'll spell that, S-L-I-N-D-E. He's not allowed to write or phone her. But he smuggled her a message. I sent a man from my office, Bernard Sheffleman, to find him. They had hidden Lieutenant Slinde in Naples, Italy. When the government discovered what I'd done they arrested Mr. Sheffleman on a trumped-up charge. And they have Lieutenant Slinde hidden on a ship in the Mediterranean. We think it's the *Flanigan*. Why? Because *he* is the man who spoke to Robin Warren on the yacht on May thirty-first and could testify that Robin was aboard."

"What's her name?" A reporter pointed.

"Carla Simpson."

"Let's talk to her!"

"In a minute." Weil held up a hand, excited. "The questions are: Where is the yacht crew? Where are the Secret Service men? Where are the chauffeurs? See—that's all they'd have to do! Bring in the ship captain or the fellow who served the President his dinner May thirty-first. Let them say Robin wasn't there. But they haven't done that. *Why?* I think you know as well as I do. Where's the real ship's log? Why isn't the ceremony at Washington's tomb logged in? Where are the answers to all these questions?"

Weil eased down off the chair and turned to Carla Simpson. "Get up and tell them, dear. It's the quickest way to bring your young man home."

"But what . . . ?"

"Just tell them the truth. They'll love you."

She stood on the chair and answered questions; spelled her name, Slinde's name, furnished home towns and ages, told of the message she'd received.

"Ask her about the ceremony," Weil shouted.

And then she recounted Lieutenant Slinde's reaction to the President's drunken indifference to the Washington Salute.

"That's a full plate for the Sunday papers," Leonard Weil exulted. "And the cameras got it all for TV! Watch that bastard in the green car, Harley. He's not going to stop for the light."

"Ah see him, Mr. Weil. He ain't goin' to get us. Mr. Warren, you goin' to the Mayflower or the office today?"

"The Mayflower, Harley. Thank you. Carla—I can't thank you enough." Robin turned to the girl beside him. "Do we know how to reach you?"

"Mr. Weil has my number. Gee, this has been exciting. I'm so glad I did it. Do you think they'll send Martin back now, Mr. Weil?"

"I think they have no choice but to produce him now. They must let Bernie and your lieutenant go. What other choice do they have?"

CHAPTER **32**   "Come in, Tony!" John Solomon greeted the latecomer. "The bar's over here. What can Marcia fix you?"

"Something cool—vodka Collins, I guess. It's terribly hot out there." Tony Hamlin, the bureau chief of *Time,* was damp and rumpled, his tie a little off center. "I walked across the park and that was a mistake. Sorry to be late."

"You know everyone?" Solomon gestured around the large

room. The bureau chiefs of *Newsweek,* NBC-TV News, CBS-TV News, ABC-TV News, the *Times* White House correspondent and the national-affairs editor of the Washington *Star-Post* were perched or seated, talking with General Robert Durrien, David Hale and Les Carew of the White House staff.

Solomon's secretary handed Hamlin his drink on a napkin on which was printed "Solly's Soliloquies," the sobriquet for these Friday afternoon sessions in the conference room adjoining John Solomon's office in the Old Executive Office Building, down the hall from the President's hideaway office.

The room was typical EOB: parquet floor, elaborate plaster wainscoting, sixteen-foot ceiling, hardware and other vestiges of the nineteenth century. But the furnishings were by W. & J. Sloane out of GSA, plush carpet, heavy chairs and tables. Two walls were covered with framed political cartoons collected by Solomon in his years as a political hanger-on and sometime newsman.

John Solomon took a seat near the door and motioned to the secretary to look for needy drinkers.

"Gentlemen, now that Tony has had a chance to cool off, I'd like to introduce a couple of my colleagues who have to be leaving us shortly." Solomon looked like a golf pro: wavy gray hair, deep tan, big hands and a million dollar wardrobe. "Director of Public Information," it read on the door. His job was to peddle the White House line, aggressively, uncritically. And peddle he did, without discretion or shame.

"I talked the President's chief of staff into coming by for a minute. You all know David Hale," Solomon added unnecessarily. "David? Anything special on your mind today?"

Hale nodded. He'd been nursing a 7-Up since four-thirty, waiting for Hamlin to arrive. "I imagine everyone saw the Senate hearings today. Perhaps Mr. Weil was successful in planting some seeds of doubt. So I'd like to tell you how the President feels about cooperating with the Select Committee."

"Tony," Solomon interjected, to Hale's obvious annoyance, "I said before you came that, as usual, all this is on deep background.

These gentlemen are 'knowledgeable White House sources,' OK?"

Hamlin nodded.

"The President," Hale continued, "has instructed that we give Chairman Oates's committee everything they ask for. Everything—documents, people, whatever they need. Check with the staff up there; I think they'll tell you we have done so."

"What do you say," the CBS man asked, "to the suggestion that you've hidden the boat and its crew?"

"The yacht is in dry dock in Newport News and has been there the whole time. It's there for a routine hull inspection. No one has asked Les about that or he'd have told you. Right?"

"Correct." Les Carew nodded.

"I don't know about personnel. That is purely a Navy function. Perhaps Bob Durrien can tell us how that works."

Durrien shook his head. "As far as I know that's also been a routine matter. The Bureau of Naval Personnel could help you with that."

"If the committee wants those crewmen, it can get them. I'm sure you all know that. But there is little reason to haul a seaman back from his duty station to corroborate the testimony of the Attorney General of the United States unless there were something more than Mr. Weil's rather wild innuendo. By the way, did you know Lenny Weil had a documents expert look at all the records? Not a word from him either."

"Who was it?"

"A former FBI man. Get his name from Weil. We don't have it. Well, that's all I wanted to say, gentlemen. We have nothing to hide here. Whatever Senator Oates or his colleagues want, they get." Hale smiled, clapped his hands lightly together for emphasis, and stood. "If no one else has a question, I'm going to sit in the corner and listen to Bob Durrien. Thanks for the drink, Solly."

"Thank *you,* David." John Solomon was obviously afraid of David Hale. "Bob, I know you have to go soon. We have all the heavy hitters with us today, men. General Bob, what do you have on your mind this Friday?"

Durrien stood and gripped the back of his chair. "Gentlemen, I think we can now make some forecasts. And I am deeply concerned about what I see ahead." As if unaccustomed to loose-fitting civilian clothes, Durrien gave his trousers a hitch. "The UN extravaganza on Uruguay is now scheduled for the third week of August. We may see prisoners in chains brought there to testify. General Gómez Fellano of Uruguay is coming to New York to testify, with an unusually heavy security force. There will be filmed confessions, piles of arms and other equipment of United States manufacture, all presented to attempt to persuade the world that this country is a threat to smaller nations everywhere."

"How are you going to answer all of that, General?" the *Star-Post* editor asked.

"We can only tell what happened as honestly as we know how: a CIA operation was started without proper authorization. That's the truth and we're stuck with it, so to speak. If people don't believe us, our relations with South and Central America will deteriorate badly. You've already heard of the riots in Bolivia and Peru, protesting the Uruguay operation. We have reason to believe those were carefully staged."

"By whom?"

"Communists; the FPR. I think you can look for more of that, including staged demonstrations here and in New York. We fear a deterioration of relations in Africa and other Third World countries too, if we can't put this fiasco in its correct light."

"What do you foresee as the effect of that?" the NBC man asked.

"On the surface, the usual: embassy demonstrations, burned USIA libraries, and that sort of thing. But, more vitally, there will be a loss of Third World interest in the Deep-Sea Mining Treaty. Without their solid support we will lose all our years of work for that agreement." Durrien shook his head slowly. "And it is so close; just within reach now."

"What's the effect of Warren's testimony? Will he be at the UN?" Hamlin asked.

"I don't know. Potentially, this young man can hurt his country very badly while he tries to save his own ass. It depends, in part, on how you and your organizations treat his unfounded accusations.

"So far only Warren and his lawyer contend that this Uruguay operation had any official sanction. There is only their unsubstantiated claim, against overwhelming evidence to the contrary. If your news coverage gives them some standing or dignity—in spite of the absence of corroboration—then they will have hurt the country."

"Are you telling us how we should treat the story?" the editor challenged.

"Of course not. I simply hope you realize the consequences of this thing. I'm sure you will do whatever you feel you should. I've never yet been able to dissuade any of you from doing what you wanted to." He smiled. "But Warren and Russia want to pin this coup on the President and on this country. It just comes down to that. They have made a great many charges, and proved none of them. I can tell you that assassination and overthrow are not U.S. policy."

"Are you saying," Hamlin pressed, "that there will be no evidence of Hugh Frankling's involvement other than Robin Warren's testimony?"

"As a matter of fact, I'm not, but I want you to listen very carefully to what I say about that: I know how these things work. In time, I have no doubt, there will appear an allegedly corroborating piece of evidence or a witness. When the Soviets are trying to prove a case, things like that have a way of happening. When these things show up, I hope you all will thoroughly scrutinize them, and take them with a grain of salt. No, I wouldn't be surprised at *anything* that might turn up in this case."

"Are you saying that Warren is a Russian plant?"

"Absolutely not. He has his motives, Russia has her motives. They are not the same, but they are coincident in result. It is unfortunate."

David Hale stood. "Gentlemen, I must be going. I'm glad we

were able to answer your questions. You and your companies bear a very heavy responsibility in this situation, as Bob indicated. I know the President is confident that you will handle yourselves with wisdom. All he asks is that you find the proper balance in your reporting. The President knows he has told the truth. His word has been challenged by a desperate and, obviously, personally motivated young man. It will soon be challenged by the Communist bloc in the UN."

Hale looked around the room slowly. "At root, I am to blame for this. I made a bad choice when Warren was hired. And our system was not tight enough. An operation like Uruguay should have required either the President's signature or Bob Durrien's. If Bob had been at the checkpoint this all would not have occurred.

"Obviously a chain is no stronger than its weakest link, in this case Robin Warren," Hale continued. "But we have to recognize, too, that the media can make the situation monumentally more serious by giving undue weight to Warren's allegations, or Russia's, when the evidence doesn't warrant it. The President is confident that you'll keep your balance in this. That's all he asks. Thanks."

"Look, fellows, let the girl get you a fresh one," Solomon said, smiling. As the door closed behind Durrien and Hale, Solly Solomon once again took charge:

"Let's put this thing into some perspective. I have lucked onto a transcript of Robin Warren's phone call to the CIA which I'm prepared to share with all of you on a not-for-attribution basis. No source given. For your background information, the party he called at the CIA had just recorded another call. The CIA person didn't stop the device from recording and it took the conversation with Warren too. The CIA didn't even know they had it. It was found by accident when the tape of the earlier call was played. There's only one thing new in it and that is Warren's reference to when he talked to the President. Remember, Warren now says he got the President's OK at the dinner table, walked six or eight feet and called; right? OK, now listen to this:

391

"'RW: Hello, (287)? This is Robin Warren.

(287): Yes.

RW: I reviewed Methodist Missionary with my principal today, and you have a green light.'"

Solomon's secretary distributed copies of the CIA transcript.

"Remember, gentlemen: the President was at Goddard Space Center all day in NASA meetings on the Space Shuttle return. Warren was here. At the office. They didn't talk on the phone. And in his call he says 'today,' not 'tonight.' Not conclusive, of course, but it's one more thing."

"He might have said 'today' even if he were on the boat," ABC said.

"Oh, sure. He might." Solomon shrugged. "But when you stop and think about his lunch and dinner with Auguste Capron, and those lovely times with Capron's cutie, it's got to make you wonder who the boy was really working for. Well, who's for another?"

"I've really got to push," Tony Hamlin said, folding the transcript carefully.

"I've got to go, too. Thanks for the drink," the editor said.

The others stood and eased toward the door, too. Solomon shook hands with the *Newsweek* bureau chief. "Stay a second, Sy. I want to show you something."

In a moment only the secretary remained with them, collecting glasses.

"Excuse us a minute, will you, dear?" Solomon commanded. Without a look back the girl left.

"Sy, I thought you might like to have these."

"What are they?"

"Love notes from Lani Romera to Robin Warren."

"Where the hell did you get them, Solly?"

"I've got a friend at the FBI. One of them . . . this one, I think . . . no, this one here, is pretty good stuff."

"Ha! I'll say. But we can't use this. You want the *Star* or the *National Enquirer*. We're a family magazine."

"They're yours. Do whatever you want with them. I owe you one."

"That's right, you do. OK. Maybe there's something here. If not, I may give them to a friend."

"But no source. The handwriting is easy enough to identify. So is the content."

"No source. Thanks for the drinks."

"Don't mention it. We'll do it again. Soon."

Part VI

A MOMENT OF TRUTH

CHAPTER **33**   "Are you receiving company, Mugs?" Jep Valle asked through his daughter's door. It was after midnight.

"Sure, Jep. Come on in. I'm just reading."

He opened the crooked wood door and took two steps up into the dormer bedroom. "Well, don't you look cozy!"

"I'm just lying here in air-conditioned eighteenth-century simplicity. Isn't this nice?"

The reconstructed farmhouse room had been furnished with a massive maple bed, an antique armoire and a washstand, all in keeping with the old home's vintage. However, soffit lighting, central heating and cooling, and an elaborate adjoining bathroom spared Maggie Valle the discomforts which had been known to other, earlier tenants.

"Your friend the Sheikh has good taste in antiques."

"I think he had a big budget and a talented decorator," Jep Valle replied. "Let's talk a minute, OK?" Jep was serious.

"Sure. Come sit here on the bed. His highness's decorator couldn't figure out how to fit a chair in here; the bed is your only choice."

"I have a tough assignment from the President, Margaret. I just talked to the White House."

He used her given name rarely. She knew she was about to receive a message from close to the bone.

"Are you talking about Robin?" she asked.

"Yes, the President wants Robin to help salvage the Presidency. If he refuses, the nation may face very serious problems."

"After what Frankling has done to Robin?"

"Perhaps he had no choice. And, on the other hand, some people feel it's Robin who is pulling the Presidency down. They say that Robin may hold all the cards."

"Meaning?"

"Meaning that if our friend Robin doesn't come out with some support for Frankling now—this weekend—I think we are going to have a full-scale Constitutional crisis in this country next week."

"I don't understand, Jep. Why is that?"

"Because the seeds of Frankling's downfall were planted up there at the Senate hearing this morning. They won't sprout for a while. Oates will try to end the hearings quickly now. But the story won't go away. Congress will be in recess. The President won't be making any news. What will they use to fill thirty minutes of network news every night? Uruguay. And Lenny Weil's show today gave them an agenda."

"Maybe they'll find the answers to some of Uncle Lenny's questions."

"Maybe they will."

"You think that those answers can pull Frankling down?"

"There will be a huge attack on us in the UN next month, remember. Robin will be right in the center of that. The Russians will be trying to prove that Frankling ordered the Uruguay thing. The President will be under fire every day."

"It's his responsibility. He deserves it."

"And the Oates and Smythe bribery fight will be heating up as the summer goes along. That also will weaken Frankling; it's bound to."

"So his job is no bargain. I see what you— But wait; what if you persuade Robin to help him? What do you get as your reward?"

Valle smiled. "Ah. My analytical daughter. Yes, that does have to be considered, doesn't it?"

She straightened her legs and folded her arms over her breasts. "You keep Frankling afloat by persuading your young cat's paw, Robin Warren, to change his story; to say that he's guilty and heinous Hugh Frankling is innocent. Then comes the payoff. Right?"

"Not that he's guilty."

"Oh. Pardon me, dear father. What is the delicate phrase you've chosen for him to utter?"

"I have the feeling—it's just a hunch—that you are not entirely with me in this."

"Did you come up here just now—listen, you've got to level with me now, Jep, I'm deadly serious—did you come up here to make me persuade Robin to recant?"

"Not recant, Mugs."

"What?"

"To call off the fight. Nothing more. Robin could go on the cameras tomorrow and ask the country to stand with Frankling."

"Never mention Uruguay?"

"He wouldn't have to."

"Right; he wouldn't. A four-year-old kid would understand what he was saying. Every reporter in town would write that Robin was pleading guilty."

"Not necessarily."

"Oh, Jep! Yes they would. *You* know they would. Don't try to bullshit your daughter. Did you *really* think I would help you persuade him to do that?"

"Yes, I guess I did."

She shook her head, looked at him, began to say something, and shook her head again quickly. A deep breath restored some of her control.

"Look, Jep, I'm not his keeper. I'm not even his lover anymore. Maybe he's lying awake over there in the cabin right now just waiting to hear your *fantastic* offer. I suppose there's a high-paying job and lots of fringe benefits that go with this statesmanlike act he's going to perform for the country. Right?"

Her father nodded.

"He's a free man," she continued. "Why don't you go and proposition him yourself? He has round heels for every good-looking woman in this town; maybe he's a pushover for slimy deals too."

Valle stood up, straightening his bathrobe. "You're a pretty tough cooky."

"I'm your daughter, remember? Are you going out there? Because"—she swung back the covers—"if you are, I'm going, too. Just to watch. I've never seen you smooth statesmen work, right up close."

"I wish you wouldn't."

"Oh, I promise not to queer your act, Jep. I'll be as quiet as a mouse."

"Why don't we wait until breakfast?"

"Ha! You're worse than I thought. You'd sneak over to the cabin without me, wouldn't you? Really, Jep, I won't influence him, one way or the other. I'll just sit there. If you think about it, that's probably to your advantage; maybe he'll think I'm there to lend you moral support."

"Maybe. All right. Do you have a robe?"

"Those of us who ride the Eastern shuttle use our raincoats for dressing gowns on weekend parties in the hunt country. Didn't you know that?"

Jep found the yard light switch by the back door. A garden floodlight cast long shadows as they crossed the boxwood terrace and walked down a flagstone stairway to the damp lawn by the side of the stone farmhouse. A hundred yards away they felt their way onto the wooden porch of the log-slab cabin. Jep rapped on the Dutch door, then tried the knob.

The cabin had been slaves' quarters on a nearby plantation. The clever Southern lady who restored the big stone farmhouse bought the old cabin, razed and removed it, piece by piece, to this farm. Reconstructed, it was surely the most luxurious slave quarters in the county.

Maggie found a living-room lamp next to the doorway.

"I'll get him," Jep said. He started down the narrow hall.

"I'll go with you."

"It must be my honest face."

"I must have learned something during our long and meaningful association. I may be blind, but I'm not dumb."

The bedroom air conditioner was on full blast. Robin was sprawled on his face, the light of an electric blanket winking on the side table. He did not move as the Valles stood over him.

"Robin," Jep Valle said softly.

"You'll have to kick him," Maggie said with familiarity. "Hard."

Jep shook Robin's bare shoulder. "Hey, boy. It's Maggie and Jep."

Robin stirred, raised himself on one hand and blinked at the dim light from the doorway. "What's wrong?"

"Nothing. We need to talk to you a little."

Robin dropped to the bed, eyes closed, as if to return to sleep. "Mags," he said, "is that you?"

"Yes, Bird."

Robin opened one eye, rolled over and sat up, naked, the covers over his waist and legs. He looked at them, squinting in the dim light.

Maggie sat on a chaise longue in the corner of the room. She swung her feet up and wrapped her light raincoat around her legs. "How about turning off the winter?"

Jep punched a button on the air conditioner. It was suddenly country-still in the room.

"Hmph. What's up?" Robin asked, completely awake now.

"I've had a call from the White House," Jep said. "They need your help. They are concerned about the United Nations hearings on Uruguay."

"Yeah, they could be rough."

"Rough on this country. And rough on the President. But rougher on you. Will you be going up there?" Jep asked.

"What for?"

"The Russians will want to present you as a witness."

"Me? Hell, no, not unless I have to."

"They can't subpoena you. But they'll show the video tape of your Senate testimony, anyway."

Robin hit the bed with his fist. "Shit!"

Maggie smiled thinly, in spite of herself.

"You've got Frankling boxed into a terrible corner," Jep said.

"*I* have? Why are you trying to lay this on me, Jep?"

"Because you've weakened him—really weakened the United States—badly."

"I'm only defending myself, Jep. You know that."

"But the secondary effect may be to pull down the Presidency. We have to think about that: Jack Kennedy killed, Johnson and Nixon hounded out, then Carter. Now this. We have to wonder if the country can stand it—whether we can survive another one."

"Jesus, Jep."

"Have you given any thought to trying to stabilize things?"

"How do you mean?"

"What if you were to go on television and support the Presidency? Not Hugh Frankling, personally, but the institution?"

"What could I say that might help?"

"I'm not sure. Does the general idea appeal to you at all?"

"Well, sure, if it would help. You know the bind I've been caught in. I don't want to cause damage; I've just been trying to answer the charges against me. What do you think, Mags?"

"I'm not here." She shook her head.

"Do you like the idea?" he pressed her.

"What idea?"

402

"That I'd go on TV and urge people to support the country—no, that sounds ridiculous. Is that what you meant, Jep?"

"I think," Jep Valle said, "you'd have to trace the fall of the recent Presidencies and urge people to rally around the institution—not attack it—and stand with the President in the UN battle."

"What do you think, Mags?"

"Why would people listen to you, Bird? Frankling says you're a fucking perjurer."

Jep Valle shot his daughter a look. She clapped her hand over her mouth.

"What is this?" Robin looked at her, then at Jep.

"The President wants to deal, Robin," Jep Valle said. "He simply can't go into the UN with you sniping at him. The country will lose the Deep-Sea Treaty and God knows what else."

"What do you mean, 'deal'?"

"He can arrange for you to lead a full and prosperous life. You can strengthen his hand, perhaps save the Presidency. He feels the two of you can strike a bargain that's good for the country and good for you."

"What's he offering?"

Robin heard Maggie make a sudden movement. He looked over at her but found her looking back at him without expression.

"An overseas job in industry that pays a hundred fifty thousand a year plus fifty thousand dollars of tax-free expenses. A banked retirement fund. White House exculpatory statements that will make it easy for you to become accepted anywhere."

"For this I go on TV and say the President is a good fellow?"

"Essentially."

"Maybe I should talk to Leonard Weil about this."

"No," Maggie snapped.

Robin looked at her again. She sat with her arms folded, her mouth-compressed into a strong line.

"Why not?" Robin asked.

"Never mind," she said.

"I think what Maggie is saying is that you ought to come to your own decision on this. It's too important to delegate. *You* are the one who will have to live with it, either way. I think that's why she won't give you advice now. You might end up hating the result and the person who urged it."

"Maybe I just don't understand what I'd be expected to say on television. Maybe that's my problem."

Maggie rustled her raincoat. "All you have to say is that you lied and Hugh Frankling told the truth, you jerk!"

Jep Valle turned slowly to look at her.

"I'm sorry, Jep. I can't sit here and watch you do this to him."

Valle said nothing. Robin took his part: "That's not what Jep said, Maggie. It would be a general statement; about the Presidency."

"Jesus, Robin darling, are you that stupid? Don't you see what Daddy-dear is up to? He's selling you out, you dummy! He'd like to deliver you to Hugh Frankling all trussed up like a Christmas goose, then he'd get his big payoff." She turned to her father. "Why don't you tell him what they'll give you, Father?"

Valle shook his head slowly in amazement. "You were going to be the mouse in the corner, remember? For a mouse you sure have a big mouth." There was a humorous façade on the words, but he was furious. "Perhaps you'd permit Robin and me to talk this through now."

She held up her hand. "You haven't told him the price yet. Tell him what he's worth, at least. What will they give you—the Court of St. James's?"

"Shut up, Margaret," Valle snapped.

She recoiled as if he had struck her. As she moved to stand she said, "I'll go now. There's no reason for me to stay."

"I want you to stay," Robin said. "Maybe I am dumb; maybe I'm going to be used, but you've got to stay and help me think this through."

"What's there to think about?" she asked impatiently. "You can't go on television and say that crap. Every paper in the country would write that 'the young former Presidential aide literally admitted that his allegations of Presidential wrongdoing were groundless.' Think, Bird! If they couldn't get stories like that printed, why would Frankling offer you such a huge bribe?"

Robin turned to Jep Valle. "Listen, Jep, if I went on TV I'd insist on making it clear that Frankling told me to call the CIA."

"Why?"

"Because it's the truth."

"Let's add it up, Robin," Valle said. "The truth, as you call it, has you in the crisis you're in: just you and the Russians against the rest of the United States. You can get out of that jam. But not by going on television and blasting the President. Why should he agree to that?"

"I guess he shouldn't. But if I do a big turnaround, what does that make me?"

"The *Flying Dutchman*," Maggie snapped.

Robin frowned. "What do you mean?"

"You'd be a political ghost ship—a freak—blown overseas and back before the wind. You'll be an empty vessel with no insides. A ghost. An exile."

"You obviously have your mind made up what he should do," Jep said sarcastically.

"No. Because I don't think he should do anything. Why should he? He didn't cause Hugh Frankling's troubles. Robin didn't decide to kill those Marxists, and he didn't lie about it. Frankling dug the hole."

"So we just let the country fall into the hole? Robin happens to be the only person who can keep us out."

"Bullshit, Jep. First, maybe Frankling shouldn't be President anymore. If he's so stupid as to get into such a spot, he ought to quit. And, as much as you want to be an ambassador or in the Cabinet, I don't see how you could destroy Robin to get there. I don't understand how you could do that."

There had been a flicker of reaction when she said "Cabinet" and she had not missed it. "That's it, isn't it?" she pressed. "They've promised you a department, haven't they? You'll be in the Cabinet if only Robin will play ball—right?" She began to weep, in spite of herself. "I've been hoping it would never come to this, Jep." She wiped her eyes on her sleeve. "But I guess I knew it would. You really don't give a damn for anyone else, do you? Tonight it's Robin. Tuesday it could be me, if the price were right. I guess I've known for a long time that you are like that, but I've tried to be careful not to make it a thing between us. Tonight it's between us."

"Wait, Maggie . . ." Robin could sense what she was about to say.

"Jep," she said loudly, "I can't approve of you. I don't want to be here with you now. I'm going back to the house."

"Wait, Mags," Robin said.

Before his daughter could get off the chaise, Jep Valle stood.

"Wait, Jep," Robin said sternly. "Goddammit, don't walk out. *You* started this; let's talk it through."

"What's there to talk about? I think Margaret has expressed your point of view for you very clearly." Valle had stopped just short of the door. He leaned against the side of the jamb, hands in his bathrobe pockets.

"I want you to hear it from *me,* Jep, and I want you to understand it," Robin said. "I'm not sure I completely understand it myself, but I want to try to tell you how *I* feel, as best I can. I've had plenty of opportunities to tell the same story as Frankling. The President and Capron and you have all promised big rewards if I did. You know why I didn't? Mainly because I was scared to." Warren wrapped his arms around his raised knees and looked at Maggie. "I was afraid of getting caught in the lies, and I was afraid of losing your daughter. No high-mindedness or purity involved at all—just fear."

Valle grunted.

"If I were merely moral," Robin continued, "you probably could have bought me long ago. But I've been like a rabbit caught in the headlights: I haven't known what to do except stay where I was. I was afraid that either way I ran I'd get run over. I suppose it's stupid as you see it, but I don't know what to do about the whole thing—except tell the truth. So I'm dead center."

"Monday," Jep Valle began, "they'll start in on you again."

"I know. They are holding the Buenos Aires trip for the big windup, I suppose."

"What more is there to that?" Maggie asked.

"Robin met a Uruguayan admiral on his ship down there just before the coup," Jep Valle said.

"Why the hell would you . . . ?"

"I went down for the weekend to be with Lani. But Capron showed up and took me to dinner on this cruiser."

"My God, they'll kill you, Bird. Just kill you. Did you plot the overthrow with this admiral?"

"No one will believe it, but we didn't discuss it once. We talked about Stanford football."

"You're right; no one will believe it. You, Capron and an admiral, and you don't talk about it? Not too good a story, Bird."

"It's merely true."

"Can't help it."

Valle nodded. "There it is. You and the truth are going to be sunk without a trace."

"Shall I agree to tell Frankling's story, Mags?" Robin asked.

"Do what you want, darling. You've got to live with it."

"We've both got to live with it," he corrected.

"Well," she said, "you know me. I wouldn't lie for Hugh Frankling for a billion dollars. I'd fry first."

"Not very practical," Jep Valle observed.

"No, I guess I never was very practical," she agreed. "Stuff like honor and love and friends have always been more important to me than the practical things. That's a flaw in my character, I'm afraid."

"I think you must weigh the consequences," Jep said to Robin, "and come to your own decision."

"Your reaction is important to me," Robin said to Maggie.

"I love you, Bird. That won't change."

"Jep," Robin said, "I'm going to stand pat. I can't do anything else."

"Is it cowardice or conviction?" Valle asked.

Robin smiled wryly. "Take your pick."

Valle nodded, standing clear of the doorway. "I'll see you in the morning."

They heard him close the front door and walk across the porch.

"Stay with me, will you, baby?"

"I'll turn out the lights," she said. "Poor Jep. Now he'll never be President."

"What will he do?"

"He's going over to the house now to call the President or someone at the White House to say you won't play ball," she said. "Then he'll get drunk, I'd guess."

"Better lock the door or he'll be back."

"I will. Poor Jep."

"Poor Jep?" Robin said. "What about poor me?"

CHAPTER **34**   "Come in, David. I appreciate your being here on a Sunday."

"No problem, Mr. President. There is a great deal to do."

"Do you have the speech draft?"

"Right here. It's actually three different ideas, each one a little unique."

Frankling took the file from David Hale.

"Before you start on that, sir, there is something else: Carleton Smythe called a few minutes ago. About Ambassador Cunningham."

"At the UN?"

"Yes, the Honorable Francis Lowell Cunningham has called here six times this morning. I told him you were preparing a

speech, so you couldn't talk to him. But he's absolutely determined to come in here and talk to you today."

Frankling's eyebrows shot up. "Talk to me? What about?"

"Uruguay."

"Today? Is he crazy? I've got to get this thing written. I can't see
him. Doesn't he understand anything?"

"He's very uptight."

"Well, he's on the spot. So am I. But he can wait until Tuesday,
can't he?"

"He says not. Maybe he gave the A.G. more reasons than he
gave me. Smythe would like a call on it."

"All right." The President reached for his phone and asked for
the Attorney General.

"Mr. President."

"What is it, Carley? Why is Cunningham raising hell?"

"He has tried to reach Slinde."

"Who?"

"The second officer on your yacht—the one Lenny Weil made a
fuss about. He's also asking questions about Weil's associate."

"Why did he . . . ?"

"Cunningham says Weil's questions have to be answered. He
tried to call Slinde last night. Cunningham won't talk to anyone
but you about it now."

"I have to write a speech today, Carley. How about
tomorrow—no, it will have to be Tuesday?"

"He'll resign today, he says."

"Why?"

"That's what he wants to tell you."

"That he's resigning?"

"No. About the call. If you won't see him today, he'll resign.
Then he'll tell the press his reasons."

"The bastard! Listen, we can't have him resigning. He's got to
handle that fight up there. There is no one else with his credibility.
I guess I have to see him, don't I? We need him there. What choice
do I have?"

409

"Unless you could send the Secretary of State or someone else to the UN."

"Cunningham just can't be permitted to quit and blast me. I can't take much more."

"Let me bring him over," Smythe said. "I will sit in and take the heat if he bears down on you."

"You do that. Bring him at four."

"Fine."

Frankling slammed the phone down.

"Why, David? It is all piling up at once. I've got to see him or he'll resign."

"Do you think he really would? I don't."

"I can't risk it. He's the best one to carry that UN fight. So I'll write the Machinists' speech now and see him, and then work on the final draft. Will you have the writers stand by?"

"Sure."

"Let's see this." Frankling opened the file and flipped through one draft, then the second.

He pushed the file toward Hale. "I'm not going to use any of those. I'll prepare my own draft and have Mary type it. Tell the writers to go home."

David Hale stood. "Do you want Bob Durrien to prepare anything before Cunningham comes?"

"No, that's all right."

"I'll be in my office," Hale said.

Frankling was writing. He did not notice Hale leave.

Francis Lowell Cunningham had been a Boston Democrat. But years of service to Presidents of both parties had slightly blurred his ideological baggage tags. He was, first, a politician—a practical man who could count votes and sniff the wind. And he had the ability to fit the part, flexibly, whatever the role happened to be. In the Age of Image this was not an inconsiderable talent.

As a new ambassador he found the UN to be not unlike a Boston political club. He set about at once to cause the diplomatic equivalents of sacks of coal to be delivered to the doorsteps of his new colleagues, with Bostonian results. He won the heart and mind of the ambassador of Mauritius with an elaborate eight-millimeter motion picture camera. The delegates from Sri Lanka soon learned that their new friend Cunningham was an encyclopedic guide to the whorehouses of Manhattan. The British liked girls, too. The Frenchman was harder to win, but Cunningham had discovered his linchpin by July. In the first year the new ambassador was winning high marks for his dramatic progress toward a Deep-Sea Treaty.

Cunningham compared well. His predecessors at the UN lacked his physical presence. Yost looked like a sour fundamentalist preacher, Scali a barber. Andy Young was a hip high-school teacher trying to make friends with the toughest kids in the class. But Francis Lowell Cunningham obviously was the Ambassador of the United States. He spoke Boston Irish when at home and the most elegant, even elaborate, rhetorical English on the job. Most of his speeches were painfully dull, but his conversation could be a delight.

Franny Cunningham was usually diplomatic, but he had a renowned temper. On Sunday he was furious. His limousine was not large enough to contain his anger. Nor was the Cabinet Room, where he was asked to wait. When the Attorney General appeared there to wait with him, the altitude of his dudgeon was obvious.

"Carleton, good day," Cunningham said tightly.

"Afternoon, Franny. The President has asked me to join you."

"A damn good idea, General, because I suspect you may have to arrest someone. It saves me telling the story twice. It's monstrous! Simply monstrous!"

"What's that?"

"It can wait."

A red-jacketed mess steward wheeled in the tea table. He offered tea or coffee, passed sugar and cream on a silver tray, then took up his vigil in the hall outside the heavy door.

"How does the Uruguay thing shape up now, Franny?"

"I'll tell you about it inside, General. It's what I'm here to say."

"Let me ask you about Massachusetts, then. Who will the Republicans put up in November to—"

The door behind them opened. Nick Gurley leaned into the room and nodded. "Mr. Ambassador, General, the President will see you now."

They followed Gurley through the secretaries' area to the Oval Office door.

Hugh Frankling was waiting for them in the center of his office, hands folded in front of him, teetering from heel to toe. The President looked up as the door opened. He extended his hand and came to meet the ambassador.

"Franny, how are you?"

"Fine, Mr. President. Absolutely furious, but fine."

"I hear you're upset. Come sit in this chair and tell me. Carley, sit there on the couch. Coffee?"

The President took orders and Gurley sent in the steward with fresh cups.

"Mr. President"—Cunningham appeared ready to burst—"I am extremely concerned and upset. I have insisted upon intruding at this time, knowing that you had other pressing concerns. I would not have done so except that this matter is extraordinarily urgent."

"Uruguay, eh?"

"Yes, but not directly. It concerns the refusal of the military to accede to your ambassador's legitimate requests for information necessary to my preparation of our defense to the Uruguayan charges." Cunningham clipped his words in anger.

Frankling glanced at Smythe, then back. Smythe was slowly lighting a cigar, examining the ash carefully.

"What military, Franny?" Frankling asked.

"The Navy."

"What do you want?"

"I want to talk with Lieutenant Martin Slinde. I want information about Sheffleman, the lawyer. The Navy refuses."

"Who is he? Why does the Navy say no?"

"Lieutenant Slinde served on your yacht until a few weeks ago.

Lenny Weil says he's been sent to Italy now. The Navy refuses to permit the United States Ambassador to the United Nations to speak to him."

"Why?"

"I'm goddamned if I know, sir! I have been horsed, maneuvered, finessed and disconnected. No one, clear up to the Chief of Naval Operations, will give me a straight answer. The more they bullshit me, the more certain I become that Leonard Weil is correct: the young man is undoubtedly quarantined because they are afraid he will tell something he knows."

"Very strange," Frankling said. "Is he ill, do you think? Maybe some loathsome disease or something? Where is he?"

"I don't know, Mr. President. Weil says he's at sea out of Naples. I called there and got a huge runaround. I'm not sure he's there, and the CNO won't tell me."

"You think he's important?"

"I don't have to tell you, sir, that your credibility is at stake in this. Robin Warren claims he was on the yacht that fateful night. Weil says Slinde will prove it. I've got to have Slinde to prove that Warren wasn't there."

"To prove I'm not a liar. And Carley here isn't a liar. Is that it?" Frankling reddened.

"I'm sorry, but I fear it's come to that. The stakes are immeasurable. And Lenny Weil sent a man to find Slinde. Weil now claims the Navy arrested his man and has hidden him away somewhere. But I'm not willing to believe the Navy would be that stupid."

Frankling stood abruptly. "Franny, I'm glad you've told me about this. I will call the CNO and find out what's going on."

Smythe nodded and pushed to his feet. Cunningham, hands on his knees, remained seated.

"I'm deadly serious about this, Mr. President," he said. "If they don't produce Slinde for me to talk to, in my office in New York, no later than the day after tomorrow, I shall hold a press conference and announce my resignation. I cannot remain and defend you and the country unless I'm allowed all the facts."

413

"Fine, Franny," Frankling said. "I'm sure that won't be necessary. Carley will get you the information. Stay in touch with him."

It was a dismissal. Cunningham stood, shook hands and followed Smythe out. The secretary was not at her desk.

Smythe took Cunningham's arm. "Let's go in the Cabinet Room and talk a little, Franny. There's something that occurs to me. Something you should think about."

They settled in the outsized Cabinet chairs at the near end of the brown oval table. The room lights had been turned out. Afternoon sunshine reflected off the white walls of the Rose Garden portico, but the room was still dim. Cunningham watched Smythe's cigar glow as he pulled on it.

"Well, General?"

"Well, Franny, you kind of twisted his tail in there."

"He seemed to take it with equanimity."

"I think not. I know the vital signs. He's very annoyed. He's going to want to make things even. I'd hate to see that happen."

"What can he do to me? I don't need the work."

"Oh, it's not that. You have been making some real progress up there in the UN. You're a national figure. The press love you. I know for a fact he's had you right at the top of the list to move up," Smythe lied.

"Ha! You've got to be joshing!" Cunningham reacted. "I've been a Democrat since I was weaned. Hugh Frankling would be ridden out of the Republican convention on a rail if he nominated me for anything."

"You know the kind of trouble we're in down here, Franny. It's not just Uruguay or Oates. We have other terrible troubles in the Congress, especially in the Senate. We can't get any of our people confirmed. Our legislation is stuck. That's not news to you. We need a man like you either in the Cabinet or here in the White House. I'm trying to tell you to tread softly for a few days."

"What are you telling me about Lieutenant Slinde?"

"Nothing. I'll have to find out about that. But don't put a gulf between you and Hugh. That's all I'm saying. I have great hopes for you. I don't want to see the Uruguay thing get in the way of the bigger chance here. Don't do anything to jeopardize it. I'll call you when I know about the lieutenant."

Cunningham stood. "I'm going back to New York. Call me tonight."

Smythe stood with him. "It may not be that quick."

"You can move fast. The UN proceedings begin in four weeks. I need to know this week."

"All right. I'll do my best. Stay cool, Franny."

"Goodbye, General."

Smythe sat down again in the quiet room, looking out the French doors toward the Rose Garden. When his cigar was half smoked he stubbed it out and walked back to the Oval Office and shoved open the door. Frankling was at the desk, writing. He looked up. His coat was hung on the back of a chair, his shirtsleeves rolled up one turn. He had loosened his tie.

"Did you talk to the son of a bitch?" Frankling took off his glasses and cleaned them with the end of his tie.

"I dangled the Cabinet at him."

"He didn't believe you, did he?"

"He said he didn't but he may have. It's pretty plausible, the way I put it. He extended his deadline until the end of the week. That must mean something."

"Is that Slinde fellow in Naples?"

"He was. He's on a destroyer in the Mediterranean now."

"Does he damage us?"

"I assume so."

"Can he be kept on ice?"

"Not indefinitely."

"What about Valle? Did he do any good with Warren?"

"He hasn't called me."

"Call him while I finish this."

The White House operators found Jep Valle at the farm. Carleton Smythe talked to him in low tones on the telephone by the fireplace while the President worked at his desk. The conversation was brief and one-sided. When Smythe hung up he sat quietly in the wingback, waiting for Frankling to finish.

"What did he say?" the President asked at last.

"He struck out. Warren and Valle's daughter, Maggie, walked out on him. Valle's very upset."

"So Warren is still going to hurt us."

"Valle says you're washed up," Smythe said.

"He does, eh? Is that what you think, too?" Frankling asked.

"Certainly not. But maybe it's time to take another look at your hole card, Hugh. If Franny Cunningham gets ahold of that second officer from the yacht, the press will be out after you in full cry again. That fellow will say Warren was aboard. You can bet on it."

"The Navy *must* keep him on ice. Goddammit, can't the Commander in Chief *make* the Navy keep him on ice?"

"That won't really help, Hugh. If that one man is kept away, Franny will resign. There'll be hell to pay. And there are other crewmen. Sooner or later . . ."

"I know. So what do I do? Resign, like all the others?" Frankling clenched his fists in defiance. "You want the Vice President in here?"

"*President* Gorsuch? Awful." Smythe shook his head.

"Sure. Awful."

"Resignation is a last resort; the least desirable option." Smythe said it grimly, then relaxed, smiling. "How about the Nixon formula: Throw a few babies out of the sleigh?"

"Like who?"

"Like me. David Hale and me."

"What good would that do?"

"Blame the yacht story on us—admit Robin was aboard. Charge us with falsifying the log and making up the story."

"First, no one would believe it; second, you'd both go to jail. Try again."

"All right, how's this? Go on television tonight and admit everything. Say you lied as a matter of national security, but now you want to set the record straight. Be totally truthful."

"Then *I'd* go to jail," Frankling snorted.

"Why? For what?"

"For . . . well, not perjury, I guess. I didn't testify anywhere under oath. Obstruction of justice?"

"In what case? For that crime there's got to be a pending investigation, and there's not."

"How about Congress? I've obstructed their damn Senate hearing. Right?"

"Contempt of Congress? Think they'll put you in that cell in the basement of the Capitol? Not likely. They won't."

"Impeachment. They could try that," Frankling said.

"What charge? Lying? If that were grounds they'd have impeached every President there ever was. No; think about it. You go on television, confess every falsehood, make a total admission of wrongdoing and then *don't* resign. Sure, you can't run for reelection. That's a given, so say so. But be realistic; you'll spend the balance of your time here climbing your way up out of this hole."

"They'll kill us in the UN."

"Sure. They are going to, whatever you do now. There and on TV and in every paper in the country. Every self-righteous bastard with a typewriter will call for your resignation. You can just have Carew go out and say, 'Hugh Frankling's not a quitter. He's not resigning.' Period. Big crowds will gather out front and hang you in effigy. So what? Letters will pour in. Let them. You stay here and do your job."

"Rough."

"Not as rough as resigning in disgrace, refusing to admit your wrongs, going through what Nixon went through."

"I'll think about it."

"Not too long. If you do it, it's got to be tonight. Monday is another day of hearings. And Franny Cunningham has a short string."

"I'll call you in thirty minutes."

Frankling watched Smythe leave, then swiveled his chair to look through the curved green windows behind his desk. The trees hid the Washington Monument and the other landmarks. The south garden was full-blown now, every leaf out wide in the exuberance of summer.

He really had no choice. Resignation was out of the question. As long as they couldn't force him out—impeach him—he wouldn't resign. My God, look at what resignation had done to the others.

Resignation of the third elected President in a row couldn't be tolerated. The American institutional membrane could be stretched only so many times before it would break. He owed it to the next man not to resign. To the next *men*. What he decided now would affect all of them.

He didn't want to resign. He genuinely liked all this—the comfort and trappings and the heady confidences. Who wouldn't? Someone—some President—hadn't. Who was that? The fellow said the White House was a prison or something. Well, Hugh Frankling didn't agree.

He nodded once and picked up the telephone.

"Give me Les Carew, please—no, wait, operator. No. Give me John Solomon. Yes. Solomon."

John Solomon was not often called by the President. He sounded out of breath and excited when he came on the line.

"Good afternoon, sir."

"John, I want you to do something for me."

"Yes, sir."

"I want you to clear twenty-five minutes on the networks for me at nine o'clock. You can tell Les Carew about it, but I want you to do it, not him."

"Right, Mr. President," Solomon said. "Nine P.M."

"Yes."

"Which day?"

"Tonight."

"Jesus, Mr. President, it's nearly five now. And it's Sunday! I'm at home! I hope you're going to declare war or something good and big."

"I'd rather not give my reasons in advance, John. If there are

418

any delays or leaks, the level of anticipation might get so high that anything I say will be less than enough."

"I've got to tell them something, Mr. President."

"All right. Say it's about Uruguay."

"I'll need more than that, sir."

"Uruguay and Robin Warren."

"Is it an emergency? Could you take the time tomorrow?"

"No. The timing is vital. It must be tonight."

"May I call you back, sir? I'll call them now at the networks. I should know where we are in thirty minutes. You'll be able to hear them crying without a telephone, though."

"I know. I wouldn't ask if it weren't important to the nation, John."

"I'll tell them you said that."

Frankling called Carleton Smythe and told him he had decided to go on television. "Carley, I want you to tell David Hale and Les Carew. They mustn't bother me until it's all finished. I don't want you to even hint at what I may say. Only tell them to watch. Will you do that?"

"Certainly," Smythe said. "May I make a suggestion?"

"One."

Smythe grunted in amusement. "All right. In your talk you should say that I have resigned."

"No."

"The letter already has been sent over there. I mean it."

"Damn."

"It has to be, Hugh. You realize that."

"All right. I'll consider it. I'll see you after the broadcast, Carley. Please come by."

"I shall, Mr. President. Tell them the truth."

"As Pontius Pilate asked, Carley, 'What is the truth?' "

Frankling hung up the telephone abruptly and walked out the French door. The afternoon air was thick and warm, difficult to breathe. He walked along the portico, toward the residence, head down, oblivious to the afternoon colors of the flowers in the Rose Garden.

CHAPTER **35**   The press secretary dropped his feet from his desk to the floor and sat erect.

"Goddammit, David, you must know something," Les Carew insisted. "Didn't he give you a clue? How the hell am I supposed to do my job if I don't know what is going on?"

Hale grimaced. "He obviously doesn't intend to tell either one of us."

"Which means . . ."

"Which means he's about to do something he knows we'd argue him out of if we had the chance."

"He's going to resign?"

"I think he'd have told one of us if it were that."

"What, then?"

"I don't know. Smythe says he doesn't know. If you believe him, no one knows except the President."

"We'll all know in twelve minutes, I guess. Along with the rest of the world."

"What's the press guessing?" Hale asked.

"Resignation. Let's see what the bastards at NBC are saying." Carew nodded at the commentator pictured on the middle of three small television sets on a shelf opposite his curved desk. He pressed a button on a remote control unit and the sound came up on the middle tube. The other two offered silent pictures.

". . . White House requested this network time for what the communications director, John Solomon, described as 'a Presidential statement of utmost importance.' No one on the President's staff will speculate on what he will say tonight. The President has been under heavy fire in the United States Senate—in the Oates Committee, especially—and in the press, for his alleged part in the

420

Uruguayan revolution that failed. This has been a hard year for Hugh Frankling . . ."

Carew buttoned the television into silence.

"Look at CBS," he said. The set on the left displayed the CBS Sunday magazine program that was its one strong weekend rating.

"The bastards refused to clear time for us," Carew said.

Hale nodded. "But the others will carry it?"

"Right. ABC has been plugging it since seven at every break. They are determined to wipe out *Sixty Minutes'* ratings tonight if they can."

"Where are you going to watch from?"

"Here. You want to stay?"

"No. I think I'd rather be alone for this one." Hale stood and walked to the door. "Have you got a cigarette?"

Carew laughed, reached into his drawer and found an unopened pack. He tossed it to Hale. "Keep the pack. How're you fixed for matches?"

"I'll use my heavily embossed souvenir White House matches given to me personally by the President of the United States and bearing his seal," Hale said.

"You do that," Carew said grimly, "while you still can."

At 6:00 P.M. the President's secretary, Mary Nordhoff, had been called to her telephone at home. Her seven guests had just begun to eat spareribs and potato salad in the small yard of the narrow house she rented in Georgetown.

The President needed her at once, he had said. A car was on its way to pick her up. He was sorry, but she was the only one who could do this job—he needed his speech typed on the old machine with the extra-large type. She would know exactly how he wanted it.

The secretary made a brief explanation to her guests and urged them to stay. One of the women volunteered to be substitute hostess and took Mary Nordhoff's apron.

Within twenty minutes, Miss Nordhoff was in her office transcribing the President's dictation. As she rapidly typed she shook her head slowly. She had worked for Hugh Frankling for nearly fourteen years, and she was loyal. For a moment she considered going into his office to urge him not to deliver these words. But it was not her role; she gave him advice when it was asked for, but not otherwise. She couldn't bring herself to cross that line unless invited. Even now.

When she took the first draft to Hugh Frankling she half expected him to ask for her reaction, but he didn't.

He was in the lavatory when she delivered the second draft on heavy bond paper. She put the speech in the center of his desk and left. It was 7:10 P.M.

At 7:45 the Filipino steward came to Mary Nordhoff's office with the manuscript.

"Presdent says preeze do this in big letters," he said.

She realized Frankling was hiding from her. She took the pages and quickly looked at the revisions he had inked in. He's making it impossible to survive, she thought. Do I have a duty to prevent a political suicide? She gathered the papers in a pile and walked down the silent hall to the President's door. It stood open. The President was gone. Seven GSA men were moving the furniture to make room for the television equipment. Mary Nordhoff turned, walked back to her windowless office, and put heavy paper in the big old typewriter.

"MY FELLOW AMERICANS," she typed, "I HAVE DECIDED TO TELL YOU THE TRUTH."

When Hugh Frankling sat at his desk for these televised speeches it was necessary for him to sit propped on a thick foam cushion to be high enough. It was a very uncomfortable and unnatural arrangement, and he had complained to the television people about it. But no one paid any attention to his bitching. Tonight, again, they had the same damn cushion on there, and it made him feel awkward and insecure. And it was hot and itchy.

He was not confident of the speech, either. He had not had help or advice on it, had spent only an hour or so writing it, and it was a

422

huge, fateful gamble. It might well be the only thing about him that historians would record; a speech he'd slapped together between five and eight on a summer evening. But he was really not in control of things; perhaps some astute student of the period would realize that and write about it. He had no good choices. He wondered briefly if any history book would ever say *that* about him.

He hadn't thought of it until just then, sitting at his desk, waiting for the red light on the camera to come on, but suicide had been an unconsidered option. He could have killed himself this afternoon. Interesting that he hadn't even thought of it. He wondered why.

"Ladies and gentlemen," an announcer was saying somewhere, "from the White House, the President of the United States."

The red light went on. He had decided to leave the pages of the speech on the desk, but when the light went on he forgot. He picked up the first page and began to read.

"My fellow Americans, I have decided to tell you the truth." He looked at the camera for a moment. Perhaps, he thought, he should have looked up at the people a little longer.

"I come before you tonight as a man whose honesty and integrity are under attack. The usual political thing to do when charges are made against you is either to ignore them or to deny them, without giving any details." Shaking his head slowly, he continued, "But I believe we have had enough of that in the United States.

"To me, this office—the Presidency—is a great responsibility. I feel that the people must have full confidence in the integrity of the man who holds this office.

"I have a theory, too, that the best and only answer to a personal attack is to tell the truth."

Frankling looked up quickly, wet his lips with his tongue, then looked down at the paper.

"I regret to say that I have not always told you the truth. I suppose there never has been a President who has found it possible to always tell the American people the whole truth. Often the national interest seems to require the President to conceal facts or say things which are not true. The fact is"—he looked up, not reading, as if speaking a vagrant thought—"it's not always possible for the man in this office to *know* what the whole truth is. . . ."

Robin Warren looked at Maggie Valle, beside him on her couch, and squeezed her hand. "Did you hear that?" he asked. "Did he say he'd lied?"

"I think he's already weaseling, Bird," Maggie said. "He's saying now that he didn't know what was true. He's a shifty son of a bitch. You have to listen carefully to what he's saying." She leaned forward a little toward the small television set in her living room.

". . . Several weeks ago, I was asked a question at a press conference about the CIA operation against Uruguay. My answer to the question was that I had nothing to do with the attempted overthrow of that country's government. I tried to give the impression that any action against Uruguay was unauthorized by me.

"If my answer to the reporter's question was literally untrue, as it was, is there any more to be said? I believe there is. I believe that is not the end of the matter. The more fundamental question is: Was what I did wrong? It isn't only a question of whether it was legal or illegal for me to give a misleading answer at a press conference; that isn't enough. The question is: Was it morally wrong?"

The Oval Office was full of equipment and technicians, but Hugh Frankling felt very much alone. The brilliant lights shining toward him made it impossible for the President to see who was in the room. He was unaware that his wife, Gloria, and his secretary, Mary Nordhoff, had come in at the east door and were standing, close together, their backs resting against the wall near the fireplace.

"I say it was morally wrong for me to answer as I did if that answer covered up some wrongdoing—some action on my part which was contrary to the best interests of the United States.

424

"It was morally wrong for me to answer as I did if someone improperly gained or profited as a result.

"It was morally wrong if someone was irreparably harmed by my actions.

"To answer those three questions, let me say this:

"I had a reason for answering as I did. I had three choices, but when you see what they were you will realize that none of them was ideal.

"I could have ducked the question entirely. But it is contrary to my nature to avoid an answer—I feel that the people are entitled to answers. Moreover, had I refused to answer, most people would have assumed that the premise of the question was true. They would have believed that this country had officially mounted an attack upon the Uruguayan dictators.

"My second choice was to state that I had directed the CIA to bring about an overthrow of those dictators who rule that country, to help liberate the Uruguayan people. I did not say that, for several reasons.

"For months our representatives at the United Nations have been laboriously trying to win support for an agreement among all the nations, governing how oil and valuable minerals could be taken from the floors of the deepest oceans of the world.

"At the time of the press conference we were very close to a breakthrough—we had a real chance to secure agreement. That would have gone a long way toward solving significant economic and energy problems in this country.

"I felt that if the United States were charged with the Uruguayan plot, our chances for obtaining agreement on the Deep-Sea Treaty would be seriously jeopardized. . . ."

"David? Les. This is really pretty good! He's got a fair chance of pulling this off," Les Carew said into his telephone.

"It's a big risk," David Hale replied. "We can't afford to just let it ride. You are going to have to hype it like hell with the press. I'll get the wires and phone calls started. Round up some friendly comments from Senators, will you?"

"Right now." Carew pushed a button to summon his deputy press secretary as he hung up.

". . . When I was suddenly confronted with the reporter's question I had to make a quick judgment among the choices available to me. In my mind, the right decision was plain: I had to do what I could to save the Deep-Sea Treaty. I knew that if I took responsibility for the CIA's actions in Uruguay, the enemies of the United States would use that admission to try to ruin the treaty negotiations. I felt I had no choice but to deny I had authorized the CIA operation."

Frankling laid the manuscript flat on the desk and folded his hands.

"The Deep-Sea Treaty is vital to everyone in the world. It is our main chance to unlock much of the remaining energy buried beneath the earth's surface.

"It has been charged in the televised Senate hearings that my purpose was to financially benefit just one American company by sending the CIA into Uruguay. That is not true. One businessman brought me the information that the Uruguayan dictators were about to seize and confiscate the property and businesses of all Americans there. But that businessman's company represents a small fraction of the total investment of all Americans in Uruguay. If we had knuckled under in Uruguay, other petty tyrants around the world might have considered American lives and property to be fair game in their countries. I believed then and I believe now that I acted in the interest of all Americans who own property or do business anywhere in the world. Our government cannot sit idly by while lawless countries take Americans' property. I cannot believe that any citizen of this country disagrees. The Uruguayan operation was in the broad national interest—not for anyone's personal gain. . . ."

Auguste Capron leaned back in the patio lounge and smiled at his assistant. "Very noble of him," Capron said. "He is performing very well."

426

"He should," Mike Meyerson said. "Frankling has every reason to show his gratitude to you."

Capron stood, pulled down the lower margins of his swim trunks and stretched. "You listen to the rest of it. I'm going to swim a few laps."

President Frankling's voice dropped and his cadence slowed.

". . . In response to the third question let me point out—and I want to make this particularly clear—the people who have been most directly hurt by my decision to answer as I did are a few people closest to me: the Attorney General, Carleton Smythe, and a young man on my personal staff, Robin Warren.

"No Uruguayans were harmed in any way.

"When I gave that untrue answer at the press conference I then had to resort to a whole series of subsidiary falsehoods. I blamed Mr. Warren for starting the Uruguay operation. I said *he* lied. He has been subjected to the most intense and unfair attacks, particularly the partisan attacks of certain Senators during the televised hearings. While it is true that the young man made obvious mistakes in the conduct of his personal affairs, I bear a substantial measure of responsibility for what has befallen him. . . ."

Maggie Valle shook her head. "The bastard. What a left-handed way to exonerate you. It's not enough."

"I wonder why he's doing it," Robin Warren said.

"Somebody's got the evidence to nail him, and he knows it. It must be that," she said.

". . . The Attorney General loyally came to my assistance, corroborating my false story in his Senate testimony.

"I cannot calculate the harm I have done these two men. As a direct result of all of this, the Attorney General has resigned his office today. I am not willing to see him suffer further for what has occurred. And so I shall pardon Mr. Smythe for any criminal charges which may arise from his conduct in this matter. I know his

427

motive was entirely selfless; he believed he was assisting me in acting in the national interest.

"I do not know what I can do to repair the damage done to Robin Warren, but I shall do my best to make amends to him. This explanation tonight begins that undertaking.

"To summarize"—Frankling wiped his lips with his finger—"I made the press conference answer that I did having in mind the larger interests of the United States. The effort in Uruguay was in behalf of all Americans with property, jobs, or businesses in other countries. And, in the main, the only ones directly damaged by my actions were people closest to me and, of course, myself. . . .""

Carew was on the phone again. "Jesus, David, he's pardoned Carley Smythe. How do I handle that one? It's Ford and Nixon all over again."

"Not necessarily," Hale said. "This whole speech is about motive. Talk about Smythe's good motives when they ask you. Nixon had bad motives; Smythe had good motives. They're different."

"Let me think about that one," Carew said doubtfully.

". . . But then, some of you will say, and rightly, 'Well, how can we ever believe you again, Mr. President? How can we trust you?'

"Let me tell you my philosophy. In my actions in this office I will always place the interests of the United States paramount. I will set aside fear of personal criticism, personal harm or political loss. In deciding the great issues which come to this desk I will always set aside a chance for short-run personal or political gain. I will always strive for the long-run well-being of the entire country. That is my philosophy.

"I think I can best discuss how a President must decide the great issues by asking you some questions:

"Do you think that I should make such decisions on the basis of what newspapers will praise me for doing? Or should I try to achieve progress for the nation regardless of how I may be criticized?

"When confronted with a choice of telling the world facts which might aid our enemies or, alternatively, misleading everyone for a time, which should I choose?

"Do you want me to wink and look the other way when a Communist dictator threatens the liberty and jobs of Americans?

"Well, I know what your answer is to these questions. It is the same answer audiences all over the country give me when I discuss with them the great issues. The answer is that the President must consider what is right for all the people and do his best to make decisions measured by that criterion. The President must disregard carping criticism and do what is right for the nation. The President must even conceal the facts from the world at times when, in his judgment, to tell all the facts would only aid our enemies. . . ."

"I think I'm going to throw up," Maggie Valle said. "That's the most supercilious, self-righteous garbage I've ever heard."

"Yeah, but I'll bet they are eating it up," Robin replied. "They are sitting in their split-level recreation rooms nodding to each other and whispering about what a great and dedicated man he is."

"God save us all," Maggie muttered.

". . . I am proud of the fact that this whole Uruguayan episode was undertaken in the defense of American lives and property.

"I am proud of the fact that the Deep-Sea Treaty, so vital to our long-range economic well-being, was my motive for answering the press conference question as I did.

"I am proud of the fact that there was no consideration of gain to myself or any other individual in my decisions in this matter.

"Some of you may say, 'Well, that's all right, Mr. President; that's your explanation, but how can you expect to stay in office now that you have admitted telling a lie?'

"I'd like to be able to assure you today that good Presidents don't lie to the American people, but I'm sure you don't expect me to. I'm confident that every American listening to me realizes that there are times when his best interest and the vital interest of the nation require that a President withhold the truth, just as Lincoln

429

and Roosevelt and Kennedy and Carter found that necessary to do.

"If I had answered as I did for personal gain—for money or power or to gain high office—that would be another case. But my falsehood was in the interest of the nation—what I saw to be larger interests, more important considerations than strict adherence to the facts. I was required to make a judgment. Whether I was right or wrong is not the question. The issue is whether I acted in good faith. I know that I did.

"Even United States Senators occasionally find it necessary to lie. And I understand that, as I am sure you do. My most severe and partisan critic in the Senate, Senator Harley Oates, has apparently found it to be in the national interest to utter falsehoods, as I am sure he will readily admit. I do not criticize the Senator. I only cite his lies as an example. In public life one possessed of secret or privileged information simply cannot be expected always to speak the truth lest he endanger the nation.

"I do not intend to abandon my responsibilities or relinquish this office. What I have done was done in good faith and with only one motive: to serve the best interests of the United States. . . ."

David Hale nodded once. "No resignation," he said aloud to the empty room. "That's what I've been waiting to hear." He reached for a note pad and began to make a list.

". . . I am not unmindful of the reaction this admission of mine will stir up among my political and journalistic enemies. There will now be a great hue and cry, I am sure. In spite of my explanation to you, attacks will be made; others have been made in the past. And the purpose of these smears will be this: to silence me, to drive me from this office, to prevent me from acting in the interest of all of the people as I was elected to do.

"It seems clear to me at this moment that I could not expect to survive a run for reelection. I have no intention to run for President again at the end of this term, or any other time. Under ordinary circumstances a lame-duck President loses influence within the government. But, as you know, my influence with the Congress has been minimal from the time I took office. I have an idea that, in fact, my Congressional relations may improve now that I am not a candidate for reelection." Frankling tried to smile but only half grinned, lopsidedly. He felt the perspiration in the folds of his belly. He had lost all confidence in the speech. He realized he was reading and mouthing the words without the force of his mind behind them. He tried to refocus on the thought and meaning he had held when he wrote the words.

"If my attackers think that they can drive me off, they just don't know whom they are dealing with. I remember that in the dark days before President Carter's resignation some of the same columnists, the same television commentators and Senators who are attacking me now and misrepresenting my position, were violently opposing me when I was after Jimmy Carter.

"But I continued that fight because I knew I was right. And I intend to continue the fight, for two fundamental reasons: *First,* I know I acted in the country's interests, as best I saw them at the time. If you say I was wrong in my judgment, I can accept that. But if you say that to be wrong in the exercise of one of the thousands of judgments I am called upon to make in this office is to disqualify me from continuing in the office, I will resist.

"*Second,* I feel that I have an obligation to the institution of the Presidency. It is my duty to pass it on to my successor in good condition. The last four Presidents have each left the Presidency a measurably weaker institution, less effective than he received it. I will do everything I can to avoid that result.

"My resignation or impeachment would seriously weaken the ability of the next President to solve the nation's problems, I am sure.

"I don't believe I ought to quit; I'm not a quitter. And my wife, Gloria, is not a quitter. After all, her name was Gloria MacDonald, and, you know, the Scotch never quit. It was her advice that I explain the situation fully to the American people. She has confidence that you will understand, and so do I.

"The decision now is not entirely mine, my friends. I would do nothing that would harm the nation or this office. I believe you know that. I am going to ask you to help me decide what I should do. Please wire or write me whether you think I should hold firm here.

"Let me say this last word: Regardless of what happens, I'm going to continue the great work of public service which I began over thirty years ago. I'll not rest until the United States is safe and economically secure in this troubled world. America is a great country and I love her.

"Thank you, and good night."

The red light on the television camera blinked off. Gloria Frankling was the first person in the room to move. She went quickly to Frankling, stepping over the wires and cables which crisscrossed the canvas floor cover. The President was fumbling, trying to gather the pages of his manuscript. The bright lights went off with a metallic noise, relegating the room to its normal lighting. It seemed almost dark in contrast. A technician began to say something, but stopped talking in midsentence.

Frankling sat, drained, looking blindly at the manuscript. He half rose, pulled the rubber cushion off the chair and dropped it on the floor to his left.

"Sweetie," his wife said softly.

He looked at her.

She nodded. "It was good. Come on. Dinner is ready."

Sixty feet west of the Oval Office David Hale reached for the remote television control and suppressed the sound. He pressed a button to summon his young aide; while he waited for Turley to appear, he ran his finger down his notes.

"Yes sir," Turley announced his arrival.

Hale looked at him. "What do you think?"

"I liked it. It just might work."

"Not unless we help it, it won't. Here's what I want: by dawn there must be no fewer than one hundred twenty-five thousand telegrams in here, demanding that the President hold firm." He watched Turley make notes on his pad. "Senator Harley Oates must receive at least ten thousand wires condemning him and praising the President. No two alike. Let's have a big letter-writing effort this week, too. The biggest ever. A half-million letters supporting the President. No later than a week from Monday. And no screw-ups this time." He gave Turley a hard look which the young man looked up from his note-taking to dutifully receive. "Ask our friends in New York about a pro-Frankling rally in Madison Square Garden. Can they get the Garden and fill it next week?"

Turley nodded as he wrote.

"Letters to the papers," Hale continued. "All you can get. We need lots of favorable columns. And editorials. Tell Solomon to get off his ass over there and produce, for a change. I'll want a report on the phone calls every hour until two A.M. That's eleven P.M. Pacific time. Don't give them to Carew or anyone else. Be sure; just me."

Turley looked up from his note pad. "Right."

"One other thing," Hale said. "The polls. I want the Hill Poll to get rolling first thing in the morning. By Thursday they are to release a phone poll heavily in the President's favor. Tell Hughes Hill I instructed you to call, and that I want no slip-up in this. He's to call you Wednesday with the results. He'll deliver."

Turley nodded as he wrote.

"That's all, for now," Hale said.

"Right."

CHAPTER **36**   Jane Smythe sat erect, her clasped hands folded on her lap, looking out the window. A white wool blanket from the bed was shawled across her shoulders; she was always cold in this room. They kept the air conditioning too high.

Everything inside the room was dimensionless and white: walls, rug, furniture, linen. One's eyes slid over the planes and objects, since there was no color to hold them. So a person didn't look at the things in the room. One looked only out the window. The bright summer green outside the window was a magnet; Jane Smythe could not help but look out at the trees. She sat and looked at them constantly, day after day.

At first she had been a patient in this place; they gave her treatments and shots. Now she was merely a prisoner in her room, allowed an hour in the garden with a nurse every other day.

That was just fine. She no longer cared.

The sound of the doorknob turning startled her. It was too early for lunch. No one ever came to her room in the morning. She knew a tiny flicker of anticipation. She still harbored the vague, unstated hope that someone would get her out of here. But before the door opened she was once again certain it would never happen. Carley had consigned her to die here. It was hopeless.

"Well, Jane, how are you feeling today?"

"Fine, Doctor."

"The President made quite a speech yesterday."

"Oh? I didn't know that."

"He pardoned your husband."

"Carley? What do you mean? Pardoned?"

"The President said Mr. Smythe perjured himself for the President. Lied. Frankling admitted they both told lies. He pardoned your husband so he wouldn't be prosecuted."

"Po' Carley."

"He resigned."

"Carley or Hugh Franklin'?"

"Your husband."

"Oh dear. I should really be with him."

"He is coming to see you. He'll be here after lunch."

"Oh. Carley is coming? Will he get me out?"

"Do you think you're ready?"

"Ah surely am, Doctor. What more could you do to me? I won't drink anymore. Surely."

434

"We'll see, Jane. I'll talk to Mr. Smythe."

"Besides, the po' man needs me. You have got to think of that. Po' Carley."

"I understand."

"Did Hugh resign, too?"

"The President? No. He said he intends to stay and fight it out. Do you know him well? What is he really like?"

"Oh, my, yes, Doctor. We've known him for years. Why, he's a polished gentleman. He's always very thoughtful of the ladies. Has fine manners. A gentleman."

"Is he a smart man?"

"Oh, yes, a very smart man. Very smart."

"I guess most people are inclined to go along with him," the doctor said. Jane Smythe nodded without comprehending. "I guess, basically, he's done a pretty good job," the man said.

"A very smart man," Jane repeated. "And very successful, too. He's as rich as he can be. He even has money in Swiss banks."

"Indeed?" said the doctor. "Are you sure, Jane?"

"Oh, my, yes. He and Carley used to talk about things like that all the time. Why, a lot of people know about Hugh Franklin's money, you know. Carley knows, and that David Hale knows and Auguste Capron knows and . . ." Her voice faded as she tried to remember.

"And you know," the doctor said, seriously.

Jane Smythe brightened and smiled. "Yes, that's right," she said. "And I know. *I* know a lot of things."

Leonard Weil looked up from his reading and smiled broadly.

Sari Kahn led Bernard Sheffleman into Weil's office by the hand. "Here he is," she said, "the Prisoner of Zenda. The Naples One. Doesn't he look wonderful with prison pallor?"

Weil came around his desk to take Sheffleman's hand, solicitously. "Are you really well, young man? No mistreatment?"

"I'm fine, Mr. Weil. Fine. They just held me in a room—a bedroom, in a dormitory on that big Naples Navy base. They just wouldn't let me go free, that's all."

435

"What a mistake!" Sari Kahn said. "It was so dumb to arrest you. I hear the Secretary of the Navy will be fired, along with an admiral or two. No one over there at the Pentagon will admit who was responsible for your detention, but it's quite obvious the top people were involved."

"They have been trying to kill me with kindness ever since they let me go, of course," Sheffleman said. "Lieutenant Slinde and I really got VIP treatment on the Navy airplane coming back. Some admiral's aide was assigned to come with us, just to make sure we were happy."

Sari Kahn laughed. "While Carla and I were waiting for the plane at Andrews they offered us champagne. Some commander kept telling me what a regrettable mistake it all was. Such jerks. So heavy-handed!"

Weil's telephone rang.

Leonard Weil answered the telephone, raising his eyebrows at his two young associates across the desk.

"Good morning, Professor Anschults," Weil said.

"Good morning. I'm calling to tell you the chairman has once again recessed the hearings."

"We assumed he would. The papers said he would. Recessed them indefinitely, has he?"

"Yes. There is no continued date."

"Aha."

"I guess that's all. I just wanted to be sure you knew."

"Nothing else?"

"No. Such as?"

"Such as an apology to my client? You people beat him up for three days on national television and now you know he was telling the truth. You have no message for him?"

"I think any regrets and reparations ought to come from the White House, don't you?"

"No, I don't. That's too easy, Irving. Too easy for all of those Senators."

"Well, that's the best I can do. See you later, *Lenny*."

Weil shook his head slowly as he hung up.

436

"No more hearings? Or just another continuance?" Sari Kahn asked.

"They are indefinitely postponed. Without apology."

"Naturally," Bernie Sheffleman said. "Those people in the Senate are incapable of admitting they are wrong. At least you have to give Frankling credit for that—he stepped up to the line and confessed he lied."

"Because he was trapped," Sari Kahn said. "I'm not impressed at all. His lies harmed Robin Warren badly and his apology was pretty weak."

"Oh, I don't know. It took a lot of guts to do what he did," Sheffleman replied.

Leonard Weil smiled. "For a politician to admit he is wrong takes more than courage. Something like that defies the laws of physics. Bernie, do you really think Frankling confessed he did something wrong?"

"Sure," Sheffleman replied. "I didn't watch him on TV, but I read the news stories of what he said. He admitted wrongdoing, didn't he?"

"Not at all," Sari said. "He said he *lied*, but the whole speech was about how right it was to lie. He kept saying it was for the good of the country, and it wasn't immoral. All that stuff."

Weil nodded.

"The question is: Will he get away with it?" Sari continued. "What are the chances of the people forcing him out?"

"The White House said they had thousands of phone calls and a huge pile of telegrams supporting him," Sheffleman said.

"They probably did," Weil agreed. "But one wonders how many of those were spontaneous. Every administration has been able to generate hundreds of wires and letters almost by pushing a button. That doesn't prove much about public opinion. On the other hand, there will be polls out soon. And the Congress will return in September with a pretty good feel for popular sentiment. Then we'll know. My guess is that he'll survive."

"Don't people care?" Sari Kahn asked impatiently.

"Yes, I think so," Weil replied. "But I suspect most people also agree with Frankling about a President lying. They expect him to lie, in good faith, so to speak."

"Nixon lied in bad faith, right?" Sheffleman asked.

Weil laughed. "That's a bit metaphysical, isn't it? But that's about right. They thought he lied only to save his own neck. Frankling has made a pretty good case for lying in the national interest, I think. My guess is that the people will tell their Congressmen to forget it." Weil sipped from his coffee cup, set it down and stirred the coffee again.

"I think such apathy is frightening," Sari Kahn said.

"The President may have trouble with the Smythe pardon, however," Weil continued. "I'm not so sure this popular tolerance for Presidential dissembling extends to his cohorts. We shall see."

"What can anyone do about that? Smythe is pardoned for everything, isn't he?" Sheffleman asked.

Weil shrugged. "I'm not so sure the pardon covers contempt of Congress. I recall an old case that opened that question but never answered it."

"Robin Warren is the big loser in all of this. He deserves some reparations," Sari said. "Would Congress consider a private relief bill to pay his expenses, and maybe his back salary?"

"I doubt it," Sheffleman said. "He's got a pretty bad image now. All that Capron and Lani Romera stuff. No Congressman would want to stick his neck out for Robin."

"He'll get a good job. He'll come out of this all right," Leonard Weil said. "I'd hire him myself if he wanted to stay in Washington."

"So would I." Sari grinned.

"Where is Robin?" Sheffleman asked.

"In bed with Maggie Valle in New York, no doubt," Sari Kahn said ruefully.

"I had a call," Leonard Weil said, "from Clem Boucher at Smith, Wardwell in New York yesterday. Robin was interviewed there for an associate's job and gave me as a reference. They like his looks."

"So he and Maggie Valle will buy a Long Island ranch house on

438

a sixty-foot lot in Nassau County and raise little Warrens; and Hugh Frankling will live happily ever after," Sari said.

"And Auguste Capron will live happily, too," Bernie Sheffleman added. "Robin and Maggie will name the first boy Auguste."

"And the first girl Lani." Sari laughed.

Weil smiled. "A bit of irony: Clem Boucher was worried about one little thing. It seems that the firm does some work for United International; they do SEC registration and securities issues work for Capron's firm. The holding company."

"Capron will blackball him there," Sari Kahn said. "Won't he?"

"Who knows?" Weil replied. "Perhaps Auguste Capron feels he owes Robin something for all his trouble. The boy will find work somewhere. He has a good background. And he maintained a measure of integrity all through this mess down here."

"I'm not sure whether that's good for him or the kiss of death," Sari Kahn said. "All the Frankling supporters, all the Capron interests, everyone is going to make it tough for him."

"That's hardly a universe, my cynical maiden. I'd hire him and I'm sure many others would take him. He'll be all right."

"I hope," Sari Kahn said, unconvinced.

"Clem told me another little thing you might be interested in. Actually, I asked him about it. I've wondered who sends the telephone bills in Uruguay these days. After all this bloodshed and grief over that little telephone and telegraph company down there, what do you suppose has happened to it?"

"Nothing," Sheffleman said.

Weil nodded with amusement. "You are correct. Nothing. The Marxists evidently decided it was too hard to swallow. No expropriation."

"The final score is: Auguste Capron twenty-eight, the United States seven, in overtime," Sari Kahn said.

"Having won the cup three times in a row, he retires it," Sheffleman added.

"Of course, young friends. Of course. You knew he was immune right from the beginning, didn't you? He hires the gladiators. He seduces the White House youngsters. But he never does the dirty work. And he usually wins."

"He seduces oldsters too," Sari interjected. "He got Hugh Frankling to send in the CIA."

"But the Auguste Caprons and the Howard Hugheses and the others are seldom touched by the weapons which wound the Robin Warrens in the arena. You knew that, didn't you?"

"I knew that," Bernie Sheffleman said.

"I knew it, too," Sari Kahn said.

"Of course you did," Leonard Weil said with finality.

CHAPTER **37**   Maggie woke him when she opened and closed the front door. The hinges made an awful racket and it scraped the floor. He'd meant to fix the door; he had promised her he'd do something about it the week he moved in with her. But, at first, he'd spent most of his time writing a résumé and going out to law offices for job interviews. Three weeks had gone by, and he still hadn't gotten around to fixing the door. It was a noise of metal scraping over metal.

"Maggie? What time is it?"

"Nearly ten," she called from the kitchen. "Want some coffee?"

"Thanks. Yeah."

She brought him a mug, smiling.

"You look delicious, Bird. Nice and naked. Are you going to stay there all day?"

"Saturday, isn't it? A day of rest?"

"Not for us working folk."

"Ouch." He winced.

440

"Sorry, baby," she said. "I just meant that this is my day to get stuff done. I've got a hair appointment at ten-thirty."

"I understand. No offense. I'm learning to be one of the Gracious Unemployed, anyway."

"Oh, hey," she said, "there's mail for you. Something from that Massey firm." She went into the living room, returned with several envelopes and sat beside him on the bed. "Open it. Maybe it's a partnership offer."

"Ha. I don't have much hope about that bunch. They were distinctly cool. Hmmm. Look at this big one from Leonard Weil's office. A bunch of letters. He's sending me something from the Conway Agency. What's Conway?"

"Open and see. Hurry up! I've got to go in a minute." She took his coffee mug, drank a little and put it on the floor.

He opened the Conway envelope and laughed. "Listen: 'We represent such clients as Senator Lee Wong, whom I believe you know. We are confident you should command lecture fees in excess of $1,500, plus expenses. I believe it will be possible to organize a seven- or eight-appearance tour almost at once, if you are interested.' "

"Fifteen hundred." She laughed. "I guess you are just a little freak. The Big Freaks get four thousand."

The telephone on her night table rang shrilly as he read. She reached for it distractedly, her eyes on his face.

"Hello."

"Maggie, it's Mary."

"Hi, Sis."

"Is Robin with you?"

Maggie nodded. "Yes."

"Have you seen the article in the *Times?* It's about the whole Uruguay mess, but it mentions you."

"Oh?"

"That's right. It's written by somebody named Shurtleff."

"I don't know him. Is it nasty?"

"Well, it's not anything new about you; he just says you're

441

Robin's lover. But the whole thing is done with an ironic tone. It's sort of a wrap-up of what has become of everyone."

"Irony is very appropriate," Maggie said. She ran her index finger along the edge of the sheet, back and forth.

"I hadn't realized . . ." Maggie's sister began.

"Does he say how well everyone else is doing?" Maggie asked.

"He goes right down the list, yes. He tells about David Hale's big book deal and how much Lani Romera's picture is grossing and all that. Old Carleton Smythe is pardoned and getting big legal fees. Even awful Jane Smythe is getting offers, he says. And sanctimonious Oates is all over the tube."

"Well, Robin just got a letter from a lecture agent," Maggie said sarcastically. "Can't you just see him on a stage in his sincere suit lecturing on 'Truth Is Its Own Reward'?"

"No jobs?"

"None."

"Is he trying?"

"That's a matter of opinion." Maggie worked the sheet with her thumb and forefinger. "He thinks he is."

"Smythe has gone with a big Washington law firm."

"I think Robin could, too, but he won't go down there."

Robin shot her a glance, then worked lower under the covers and closed his eyes.

"That cornpone Senator is doing a book, too, this article says."

"I suggested that to Robin. I think that's what he should do. I could sell it, I'm sure," Maggie said.

"Why not?"

"He thinks it would queer his chances to go with a good law firm; it's not professional, whatever that means."

"That's crazy; he needs the money, doesn't he?"

"Well, I'm working," Maggie said. "Listen, I'll call you back. I have a hair appointment. OK?"

"Sure."

Robin was leaning back against the piled pillows, his eyes closed. "Has Robin found a job?" he mimicked as she hung up the telephone.

442

"Listen, you," Maggie said, "my sister is your friend. She's pulling for you."

"Sure," he said flatly. "Do you know how degrading it is to be talked about like that?"

"She says there's a piece on Uruguay and all of us in the *Times*. Not too good."

"It goes on and on." He shook his head.

"The point of the article apparently is that everyone has come out OK except you."

"Where's the news in that?"

"That's right, isn't it? Everyone but you."

"I guess."

"Have you thought about why that is, Robin?" She looked out the window, then back at him.

"Hell, Mags, you know very well what I'm up against. Between the White House and Capron, things are stacked so deep against me that I can't wiggle."

"Bullshit," she said. "You've been sitting here feeling sorry for yourself most of the time while the others have been fighting back. That's the main reason—"

"Maggie," he interrupted, shaking his head, "you know that's not true. I've been out there every day, beating the bushes. Damn, you're hard on me."

"What about Uncle Lenny?" she asked. "You haven't even called him."

"I don't want to be in Washington," he said. "You know that."

"Well, you're not exactly taking New York by storm, my boy. You've got to make up your mind what you're going to do and get started with it. All this self-pity is what is bogging you down. You know I love you, Bird. If you're fighting, I'll fight, too. But I won't sit here and wring my hands just because you're feeling sorry for yourself."

"I couldn't stand to be in Washington. New York is not much better. But, you know, I don't know where I belong, except I know I need to be with you. Stick by me, Mags; I'm trying. I'm really trying."

She stood. "OK, Bird. I know. I hear you. And you know that I love you. Listen, I've got to go or I'll lose my hair appointment. I'm going to get it cut short. I'll pick up the *Times* when I'm out. You can read all about it."

"Don't bother." He looked up at her. "Are we going out tonight?"

"I don't think we can afford to, Robin," she said. "We've got to make my check stretch, don't we?"

He shook his head in disbelief. She bent to kiss him, lingered and pulled away. "I've got to go."

"I like your hair short," he said.

From the living room she called to him, "When are you going to fix this damn door, Bird?"

"Maybe today."

He heard the door close, lay back on the pillows and closed his eyes. Something came clear to him. He needed a small victory of certain definition. Some measurable accomplishment.

He swung off the bed, pulled on a pair of shorts and went into the kitchen. Somewhere in the small drawer on the end there was supposed to be a screwdriver. If he could find it, he'd fix the door before Maggie returned, with her hair cut short.